Praise for *Wraith*

"*Wraith* is a highly original addition to urban fantasy. Fun and intense in turn, I thoroughly enjoyed this story. I look forward to reading more about Zoë Martinique and her world."

—Patricia Briggs, #1 *New York Times* bestselling author of *Iron Kissed*

"With a quick-witted heroine and truly frightening baddies, Weldon offers a fantastic kickoff to what promises to be a vibrant new series."

—*Booklist*

"Launching with a bang, this new detective series/urban fantasy cross-over plunges its astral-traveling heroine into the middle of the action. Martinique is strong, resourceful, self-deprecating, and fascinating."

—*Library Journal*

"Weldon's lively debut…keeps Zoë and her readers off balance with brisk pacing and brain-wrenching plot twists. [She draws] the story to a satisfying close while leaving enough loose ends to set up Zoë's next adventure."

—*Publishers Weekly*

"Interesting off-kilter characters…I can only hope that we will see more of Zoë Martinique and her family…Every~~~~~~ ~~~~matter-of-fact that you come to quickly a~~~~~~~ ~~~~~~~~ings—not because of *Buffy* and othe~~~~ ~~~~~~~~~~~~l, it seems so solidly real within the c~~~~~~~~~~~

—*SFRevu*

"This fresh urban fantasy s~~~~~ ~~~~~~~~~~~~~~ith its first-person point of view. Heavy~~~~ ~~~~~~~~references and quirky dialogue, it features original characters the reader will want to befriend. With a penchant for finding trouble, like Kim Harrison's protagonist [Rachel Morgan], and witty banter akin to that of *Buffy the Vampire Slayer*, Weldon's astral-traveling heroine, Zoë, makes this series a hit."

—*Romantic Times*

"[A] worthwhile debut that bodes well for disembodied adventures to come."

—*Kirkus Reviews*

Ace Books by Phaedra Weldon

WRAITH
SPECTRE

A ZOË MARTINIQUE INVESTIGATION

SPECTRE

Phaedra Weldon

ACE BOOKS, NEW YORK

THE BERKLEY PUBLISHING GROUP
Published by the Penguin Group
Penguin Group (USA) Inc.
375 Hudson Street, New York, New York 10014, USA
Penguin Group (Canada), 90 Eglinton Avenue East, Suite 700, Toronto, Ontario M4P 2Y3, Canada
(a division of Pearson Penguin Canada Inc.)
Penguin Books Ltd., 80 Strand, London WC2R 0RL, England
Penguin Group Ireland, 25 St. Stephen's Green, Dublin 2, Ireland (a division of Penguin Books Ltd.)
Penguin Group (Australia), 250 Camberwell Road, Camberwell, Victoria 3124, Australia
(a division of Pearson Australia Group Pty. Ltd.)
Penguin Books India Pvt. Ltd., 11 Community Centre, Panchsheel Park, New Delhi—110 017, India
Penguin Group (NZ), 67 Apollo Drive, Rosedale, North Shore 0632, New Zealand
(a division of Pearson New Zealand Ltd.)
Penguin Books (South Africa) (Pty.) Ltd., 24 Sturdee Avenue, Rosebank, Johannesburg 2196, South Africa

Penguin Books Ltd., Registered Offices: 80 Strand, London WC2R 0RL, England

This is an original publication of The Berkley Publishing Group.

This is a work of fiction. Names, characters, places, and incidents either are the product of the author's imagination or are used fictitiously, and any resemblance to actual persons, living or dead, business establishments, events, or locales is entirely coincidental. The publisher does not have any control over and does not assume any responsibility for author or third-party websites or their content.

First edition: June 2008

Library of Congress Cataloging-in-Publication Data

Weldon, Phaedra.
    Spectre : a Zoë Martinique investigation / Phaedra Weldon.—1st ed.
        p. cm.
    ISBN 978-0-441-01593-1
    1. Single   women—Fiction.   2. Astral   projection—Fiction.   3. Murder—Investigation—Fiction.
4. Atlanta (Ga.)—Fiction.   I. Title.
    PS3623.E4647S74 2008
    813'.6—dc22

                                                                                2008008223

PRINTED IN THE UNITED STATES OF AMERICA

10   9   8   7   6   5   4   3   2   1

IN APPRECIATION...

Once again I would love to thank my family, for their support, and my friends, who have been more than patient with my absence. To Dayle Dermatis, for volunteering to First Read for me, and to my daughter, whose big blue eyes always make the sun shine a little brighter. As always, to Kris and Dean, to the Oregon Writers Network, and to my incredible editor, Ginjer Buchanan.

But most of all, to my parents, my heroes. To my mom, who has shown strength in the face of more adversity than any human being should ever have to endure. She is the steady light in my harbor.

And to my father—I love you, Daddy.

1

January 25, 10:48 A.M.

CURLED brown dried leaves tumbled low along the ground, over brittle, warmth-starved grass in swirling patterns, carried by a cutting January breeze. Spindled bare branches stretched up among the evergreen pines to touch the canopy of gray clouds moving at a slow pace, casting the world in a monochromatic filter.

It was all such a maleficent backdrop to the sound of sobs, murmured whispers, and periodic coughs barked out by the mourners gathered in a tight knot around a coffin-shaped hole in the ground. The green funeral-home tent billowed in the wind, and the white-trimmed scalloped edges flapped with sharp popping noises. The white cords anchoring the tent in place strained and fought the increasing breeze as the silver posts creaked in their anchors in the hard ground.

I hate funerals.

Especially this kind of funeral, where the deceased was close and the loss weighed on everyone's shoulders. Everyone cried in unison. Even me—though I was still numb from shock.

The pallbearers approached, a row of dark, uniformed police, their heads bowed, carrying the dark oak casket with its brass handles. Oak was *his* favorite—that much I'd learned in the short time I'd known him. And he liked old black-and-white movies.

I stood to the right of the tent, amid a group of his friends or family—I didn't know which—and shook in the cold. I'd put on thick, wool socks, a black pantsuit with a high Mandarin collar, and my *X-Files* black trench coat. Rhonda, my best friend and cohort in all things metaphysical, stood beside me. She even looked like she belonged, with her flat black-dyed hair, black lipstick, and kohl-rimmed eyes. She'd recently had her hair cut even with her jawline, a little longer in front. On Rhonda it looked good.

My mother Nona was one of those sobbing women seated under the tent. Debbie Reynolds in fashionable black. She wasn't speaking to me this week. Fine by me. I couldn't talk back anyway. Not because I believed talking back to one's mother was bad (and it is, folks—don't do it) but because I'm mute.

I'd had a voice—deep and rough. Sort of a cross between Stevie Nicks and Nick Nolte. But it was stolen by a Symbiont, a parasitic creature of the Abysmal plane.

And when I thought of that moment, waking in a morgue to find myself with no voice and a toe tag—well—it was just one of those little alarm moments everyone has in life. Kinda like when your best friend steals your boyfriend—and your best friend is a guy.

I think I should clarify a few things. I'm a Wraith—and evidently the only one of my kind. What this means for those not schooled in the worlds of the Ethereal and Abysmal is that I travel out of my body, at will, and become something—*else*. Something more than a disembodied spirit or astral projection—which had been my life until a few months ago.

Mental note: *I need business cards. Wraith for Hire. We get 'em, dead or alive.*

Being a Wraith wasn't exactly what I'd dreamed of being as a child. I was more into the idea of being a pop star, adored by millions. Or even a Lara Croft type—kicking some serious butt. Hell—just having *some* idea of where my life was going would be a dream come true.

Wraith. Not a résumé blurb. I don't really know what a Wraith is yet, or understand any of it. I'm still learning. And so is Rhonda, who knows a great deal more about this stuff than me. Traveling out of my body had been the first step into the darker, larger world. A nifty talent I'd discovered during a rape.

Know that feeling of being in a bad situation and wishing you were *anywhere* else? Well, my wish came true that night in the park. And presto chango—I was standing a few feet away, *watching* my body get violated.

Not something to recover from quickly either.

Sort of like puberty.

The pallbearers moved under the tent and set the lieutenant's casket atop tight, flat green cords that would release later when the box was lowered into the ground. The priest stepped up, Father Maximillian Bishop (Father Bishop—wasn't that cool? Well—I *am* a Catholic—though nonpracticing; I thought it was cool) stepped forward, his black robes billowing out in the January wind. I knew he had to be cold and wondered only once whether or not he was wearing anything under his robes.

Nuns didn't wear underwear—or so I'd been told. But did priests? Were they nude, flapping in the wind under all those robes?

Gah—where is my mind these days?

"Friends, family, associates—" His voice was strong when he spoke. And clear. Not a single tremor or shake of his lips. If he was cold, he wasn't letting anyone else in on it. "We're gathered here today to express our grief at the loss of a strong, well-bodied member of the community. Today we pay our respects to Lieutenant Daniel—"

"Hey," said a familiar and sexy voice beside me. I smiled

to myself and leaned back into the welcome, warm arms of my boyfriend.

"—Charles Holmes, Charlie to his friends and family. A veteran of the Atlanta Police Department for twenty years. A solid man, a good father, and a widower."

Daniel Frasier kissed the top of my head, and I felt his cane next to my right calf. I knew Holmes's loss weighed hard on Daniel. Charlie Holmes had been Daniel's mentor and the one to get his depressed butt out of the hospital bed and into rehab a month ago. I'd been introduced to Lieutenant Holmes just before Christmas while Daniel was in the hospital. Then the seasoned cop started showing up at Mom's Botanica and Tea Shop in Little Five Points.

Of course, I'd been a little curious when the feisty old cop had formed a very friendly relationship with my mom—and then when I'd seen them kiss—

Ew.

"And now, Mrs. Nona Martinique has a few words to say in Charlie's memory."

Oh—by the way—Daniel doesn't know about me. About what I can do. It's not that I'm being untruthful. Well—yeah, I am. But I don't really know how to tell him.

Oh, hey there, babe. Guess what. I can watch you watch me while I'm sleeping. Isn't that a kick?

"You're cold." His breath was warm against my ear. I nodded and signed to him, *"Keep me warm."*

Since losing my voice, and since accepting it was going to be a permanent thing, I'd been taking sign-language lessons thanks to Mom's and Daniel's insistence. Daniel already had a half-working vocabulary in American Sign Language. And during those long days at the hospital, he and I had practiced. It wasn't a good version of ASL, but more of our own little language.

Aw...isn't that cute? Our own language. Too bad it hadn't

translated into some serious love language. I swear—if he grabs my ass and calls me SugarBuns one more time without taking me on the kitchen floor with hot moans and heavy breathing—I'm going to punch him.

I knew I should be patient. Daniel had only been out of the hospital a week, recovering from multiple fractures, a broken leg, internal bleeding, and a concussion, all thanks to Trench-Coat, or TC. That's what I call my Symbiont attacker, the one that now has my voice.

Daniel wasn't a hundred percent, and he walked with a cane, so his boss, Captain Kenneth Cooper, had him on light duty two or three days a week. Only half days and parked behind a desk.

He hadn't been happy about it at first, until this morning. Arriving at my house he'd told me Cooper had assigned him on that headless case I'd seen on TV that morning. Some VIP in Atlanta had been found in his home with his head neatly removed.

Geez, this city could oogy sometimes.

Up until his joy at investigating a headless body, I'd been suggesting some nice beast-with-two-backs therapy to alleviate his frustration. Nope. The response I usually got was a smile, a pat on the head, and a hug.

I half expected to get a cookie too. Silly girl! Thinking of sex! Have a chocolate chip.

Mom moved gracefully to stand beside the priest as the wind kicked up a notch. My own gaze moved out to the headstones surrounding us. One of the abilities I now had was being able to see ghosts when I'm *in* my body. Hospitals were the worst, 'cause ghosts, spirits, spectral entities—you name it—all hung out there. So did other bad things that I won't mention, things that haunt little children in their sleep. I could only assume they waited there for the weak and the dying. I'd sensed one or two of them hanging about Daniel's room. But once they'd sensed me, and I'd shown them my Wraith self, they quickly disappeared.

Graveyards weren't as busy as most people would think. And why would they be? There weren't any living people in them, except for days like today. I'd caught a few shades here and there, soft, gauzy movements that flitted in and out of sight.

There was one black-and-white image that lingered though.

I'd seen him a couple times since the funeral started. Joseph Maddox, my doctor's long-deceased son. He was the first ghost I'd seen since acquiring my newfound abilities. Well, that's not true. I'd seen other ghosts, like the two that live with my mom. Tim and Steve. They were the previous owners of her house in Little Five Points, and died quite a ghastly death in the basement.

But this was the first ghost that'd approached me—while I was in body—in Dr. Maddox's office. He'd been all monochromatic—and glaring at me in the shadows behind his dad's desk. Now he stood about twenty yards away, peaking out from behind a tombstone near one of the leafless, spindly oaks.

Dr. Melvin Maddox was here to comfort my mom. Which was unnerving. He'd gotten a bit chummy with Mom since diagnosing me with "diabetes." (Oh please—being a Wraith tended to make the blood sugar go wonky.) I liked my doctor—but he was my *doctor*—not my mother's next husband. And now that Lieutenant Holmes was gone—Maddox was put'n the moves on Mom.

Double ew.

I tried to listen to the priest, but Joseph was getting insistent. I frowned at him as hard as I could. Daniel had put his arms around me from behind, my hands clasped in his. I always thought it was his way of keeping me quiet, holding my hands.

By the time the eulogy was over, my toes were frozen in my boots, and the balls of my feet *hurt.* Youch. Why is it only the immediate family get chairs? Why not everyone?

Rhonda had one, a backpack sort of converting thing she'd gotten online. But Mom wouldn't let her use it. I think at times Mom wasn't sure what to make of her little part-time helper.

Daniel excused himself, muttering something about paying his respects to Lieutenant Holmes's mother, a thousand-year-old woman hunched over in a wheelchair near the casket. He kissed my forehead and limped off with his cane in her direction. I nodded and, with a glance at everyone else, moved quietly—though not quickly, as my heels were sinking into the grass—to the tree beside the headstone where Joseph was hiding.

Since November—and losing my voice—I'd discovered through trial and error with Tim and Steve, and unfortunately the ever-popping-up Joseph—that if I wanted them to, ghosts could hear my thoughts. So if I simply thought of myself as speaking, they'd hear me.

In some way I guess it was a form of telepathy. Too bad it didn't work on the living.

What's up, Joseph? I pulled the hair from my face. I'd let it hang long and unbraided today. That way my ears stayed warm, but with the wind it threatened to stick up in the air. I glanced back at the crowd gathered around the casket. Maddox had his arm around Nona. *Get your freak'n meat hooks off my mother!*

Mental note: *kill, kill, kill.*

Joseph's laughter was soft, mostly like bells in the January wind. "You're a strange one, Zoë. Dad likes your mom. And I do too."

I glared at him. *I am not going to be your stepsister.*

He nodded, and his expression instantly sobered.

I'd learned over the past several years that there was a difference between ghosts and shades. Ghosts were the tangible essence of a living being—the soul—so to speak. And shades were the lesser of the two. Not possessing any real vital corporeal energy. Once this had finally been explained to me, it made more sense as to why most of the spookies I'd seen since the Wraith transformation were black-and-white (shades) while Tim and Steve were in color (ghosts).

I have no idea why this was. Nobody gave me a game book in this wacky universe.

Shades never actually became corporeal, or solid, either. Whereas—with practice—ghosts could become solid.

I'd seen Steve, the eldest of the two home ghosts, become solid in the shop—to a point where a customer had asked him a question, turned to point out where the item was, and turned back to find him gone. Up until December, Mom had had this rule about no ghosts in the shop during business hours—but with Daniel in the hospital and me spending my time there—she'd bent those rules when Tim and Steve assured her they could keep an eye on things when Rhonda was busy.

Mom liked that—gave her shop a nice touristy feel. The haunted hoodoo shop. Come on by and spend your dime!

Joseph was a shade. He wasn't on this plane because he wanted to be but because he got caught in his father's grief at his eldest son's loss. His mom and younger brother escaped it. But I'd seen the fetters keeping him anchored to this plane. And I had no idea how to remove them. I didn't know if I could.

Two months ago I'd somehow released a dying old woman in the hospital while I was OOB—out of body. And I'd thought I'd released Daniel when I believed he was suffering. What I'd really done was inadvertently freed a Rogue—something they call a bodiless astral Traveler—but I still wasn't sure *how* I did it.

What I *was* sure of was the feeling it gave me. Complete and utter peace. Resounding. Satisfying.

And very alluring.

And that scared the shit out of me every time.

So much so that I realized when I'm in Wraith form, and too close to the living, I could tap their souls. I'd done it to Rhonda when my body was occupied by that same Rogue. I'd been tired and drained of juice—and she'd looked so tempting.

It was like being a psychic vampire—only without the cool

fangs. Ick. I didn't know what it meant, but I got the feeling it was bad. And for right now, I'd stopped myself on several occasions—but what happened if I ever got to the point where I couldn't? What would I do to them?

Kill them?

I'd tried the same thing on Tim, and Steve, and even Joseph.

Nada. Seemed my own oogy worked on the living only.

"Zoë." Joseph looked very serious. His brows furrowed over his eyes. "What's up is something that has to do with Sunday, when that cop was killed in that warehouse." He nodded at the gathered crowd behind me. "And the headless body they found yesterday. It's all related, but I'm not sure how. There's been a strange rumor amid the other walkers"—that's what they called themselves, the shades stuck here because they were fettered—"about some buildup of power."

I frowned. *And?*

"There are sides forming—factions—here on the physical plane. You stirred it up—they're aware of you now. One fears you, and the other desires your power." He shrugged. "I just wanted to let you know."

I narrowed my eyes at him and scratched my nose. Strands of hair continued to blow up and out around my head in the wind, and several moved in front of my face. I pulled them away. *Two factions? Desires my power?*

I wasn't liking the sound of this.

He nodded. "They're watching you." Joseph nodded past me at the crowd. "And your family and friends."

Who's watching me? Something from the Ethereal or Abysmal? Is it Trench-Coat? He been bothering you?

I liked the way I thought that last question—as if I were his sister, who could beat the Symbiont's ass for taking his lunch money.

"This isn't a joke, Zoë. I think you're in danger."

Oh, don't be silly. I shook my head and glanced at the funeral group. It was breaking up, and Daniel was talking to Mom and Rhonda. I looked back at Joseph. *You think it has something to do with the warehouse itself? Lieutenant Holmes was there on a drug bust. What has that got to do with factions and the headless body? Wasn't that like a senator or something?*

He looked skeptical. "Like I said, I don't know. But something's coming. Something—bad."

Okay, when a dead guy calls something bad, I usually take notice.

He turned away from me, then stopped. He did look sad. Really sad. "It might be that whatever it is—it's already here."

The wind picked up the dead, curled leaves at my feet and blew them through Joseph as he faded away.

2

I hate cryptic messages.

I think people, or ghosts, who ever give those sorts of not-making-perfect-sense responses to anything should have their speaking licenses revoked.

Sort of like mine was.

But I'd always made sense. At least to me I had.

The day didn't improve much, weather-wise either, once we got back to my condo on Virginia Avenue after the wake—which was held at the new Fadó's Pub down in Buckhead. The pub had moved one block north. That was Daniel's favorite hangout, and had been Lieutenant Holmes's as well. I was full of little pastries and one too many Guinnesses in a can—my favorite.

Once at my place, Daniel had to get back to work for a partial shift from two o'clock to five. Cooper stopped by to drive Daniel to the station. (Didn't need to be driving on meds.) He was eager to get busy on the headless case—and he mentioned the guy's name was Charles Randolph—a successful local businessman. He'd also left me a rose on my pillow, and a small box of Whitman's chocolates (my favorite!) beside my computer. He was such a good boyfriend!

Now if we could juuuuust get our clothes off.

And as we stood at the door, me still in my funeral rags and him still in his nice dark suit and cane, his shoulder-length sandy brown hair wisped back behind his ears, he looked at me with half-lidded eyes, touched my cheek with his left hand, and locked my lips with his on a very long and delectable kiss.

I heard some nice sexy Enigma music in my head and reached up to run my fingers through his hair—and then the record scratched as he pulled away and ended the kiss. And again I had to put the brakes on my libido.

Was I ever gonna get sex again?

He'd taken his doctor's advice to take things easy very literally. Meaning no monkey love on the kitchen table.

In fact—when I stopped and thought about meeting him in November—me and the beautiful police lieutenant had never even *had* monkey love, much less just plain old missionary position. Oh, we'd done some terrific petting; harsh kissing with bruised lips and swollen tongues (yum) but never had any deep, sensual, rhythmic, penetration—

—mmmm—

'Scuse me—vibrator's in the bedroom.

He waved at Mom and Rhonda, then left. Cooper lingered in the doorway for a second, gave me an intense look, and shut the door. I turned and leaned my back against the door and gave a long, huge sigh. Void sigh. No noise. Just air out of my nose. Mom came back from the coat closet, took me by the arm, and led me into my kitchen.

"He needs to cut that hair. It's getting too long."

Oh...so *now* she's talking to me.

Rhonda sat at the dining-room table and yanked her boots off. "I like it—and I like his sideburns too. Very retro."

Mom stopped both of us at the refrigerator. "I noticed you shaking, and it wasn't from the cold. You didn't eat breakfast. You have to keep your body healthy, Zoë. Otherwise, you can't use your powers to their full extent." She opened up the refrigerator and pulled out a carton of orange juice and handed it to me. "Use a glass."

Ah. Moms. Always the caregiver, no matter how wayward the children get.

"I'm going to fix dinner." She moved past me and started pulling out pots and pans.

I glanced at the clock—it was just before one. She was starting dinner now?

But I did as I was told and drank six glasses of orange juice (hey, I'm a growing Wraith), then went immediately to my room, flung off my dress duds, and changed into my house uniform: blue plaid flannel loungers, black bunny slippers, and my oversized Danny Phantom sweatshirt I'd gotten from Rhonda for Christmas.

Ha-ha.

At least this ghost hero could fly.

Not me. Which just sucked rocks.

Danny Phantom had white hair when he was a ghost.

And if the nasty white patch on the side of my head didn't stop growing, I was gonna look like Danny when I was *not* a Wraith.

Oy.

I stood in front of the huge mirror over the sink in my bathroom and made faces at myself, my emotions still on edge with what Joseph had said, as well as the continuing avoidance of sex by Daniel Frasier.

I'm not unattractive—having great Latino genes that gave me light brown eyes, olive skin, and mounds of dark hair—except for that glaring shock of white, which was starting to taunt me and grow exponentially. But I never saw myself as any great beauty either.

Besides the hair issue, there was that ever-present mark on my left arm, between my wrist and my elbow. I held up my hand in front of me, the back of the arm to the mirror. There it was—Trench-Coat's hand, looking all the world like a henna tattoo. No amount of washing could take it off, though. It was there, permanently burned into my skin.

Mom and Rhonda believed it happened when he first touched me, thinking I was a roaming spirit in the physical plane. Food, in other words. But he must've gotten the same shock I did when he tried to eat me and discovered I was rooted to a physical body.

I still remember the fear of running back to my body along my cord, the string that kept me attached to the physical. As well as the alluring touch of his hand on my skin.

Not to mention a few other memories of skin on skin that I'd somehow performed while out of body. Goose bumps popped up all over as I stood there, not realizing I'd wrapped my arms around my chest. I'd been thinking of that missing time—those twenty-four hours of my life spent with TC—

No, no, no, no!

La, la, la, la—dinosaur. Not gonna think about it.

I heard Rhonda coming into my room before I saw her. Her eyes were wide, and she motioned for me to follow her. "I just checked your e-mail—you need to come in here."

I followed her into my office, which was really my spare bedroom. Inside was a desk, my Macs, a PC, and a small single bed I used to store my body on when I was out being all Wraithy. There wasn't much on the wall. A single *Lord of the Rings* poster with Legolas the Elf. Mmmm…Orlando Bloom.

Rhonda had moved a six-foot shelf in and piled it with books she'd found on spirits, spooks, incubi, succubi, bogeymen, phantoms, etc.

Light reading for me.

Mental note: *you really should open one of those, you know.*

I sat down in my chair as Rhonda sat on the edge of the bed. I looked around and spotted my small dry erase board and pen on the little HP printer. I snatched them up and started to wipe away the scribbled FUCK YOU I'd put there yesterday.

"Zoë, look at the e-mail. I don't have time to play decipher Zoë's handwriting."

I stopped wiping and held up the UCK YOU, then wiped it all off. Scribble, scribble. JOSEPH AT FUNERAL.

She sighed. "Of course he was. Maddox was there. Joseph's always where his dad is. Zoë, read your eBay mail. Puuuleeease!"

After discovering my knack for slipping out of body, I had met Rhonda, and she helped me organize a small sleuth business. Not like a detective agency—not really—I wasn't open to the public though Daniel had promised to help me with a license.

I think that was his way of keeping better tabs on where I was. I did tend to do stupid things—but after reading his own record and seeing his own penchant for rushing in and shoving untreading angels out of the way, I could point my neener-nee finger back at him.

In truth, I used my ability to go incorporeal to gather information. And Rhonda and I'd discovered that if clients thought the gathering of this information was clandestine, as well as illegal, they had no qualms about paying extra.

And I had repeater clients who regularly deposited money into my accounts through PayPal. There were twelve of them—mostly insurance companies, plus a few internal services like Human Resources for big business (when they thought one of their employees was boinking the boss), and, of course, a couple of private eyes.

Those were the ones I tried to avoid because it meant divorce cases. Gratuitous sex. Lots of moaning. Springs squeaking. Hey, not that I mind, but I'd really rather be the one *doing* the moaning and making the squeaking.

Mental note: *check batteries in vibrator.*

Rhonda's impatience escalated, and she reached up with a black-nailed finger and pointed at a bold e-mail in my in-box.

Oh. Shit.

There was one client in particular that I'd had for almost the entire time I'd been doing this. And like all of them, I knew him or her or they only by the e-mail identity.

This one was called Maharba. This client usually requested odd bits of information. Their first job had been to listen in on a board meeting at some company downtown. It'd been mainly a bunch of talks about stocks, and money, and I saw charts.

Now, I technically don't have total recall—well, not with my conscious. But my subconscious works like a tape recorder—only I don't have control over the play button. I'd wait a half day or so, and bleargh. Up it comes.

Then I would dutifully type up what I could remember afterward and e-mail that information in, and the client would deposit nice sums of money in my accounts.

It was Maharba that had sent me on two of the more interesting jobs. One was to investigate a haunted house, only they hadn't told me it was already being investigated by some paranormal group called SPRITE. The Southeastern Paranormal Research Institute for Termination and Extermination. I learned that my astral self showed up on their instruments, but the real ghost—a nasty poltergeist that looked like a squid with an onion body—didn't.

Unfortunately, their proof of the mysterious female ghost vanished, and they were disbanded right afterward. And I couldn't help but wonder what had really happened.

Not that I wanted those idiots back in my face again.

Randall and Herb. Their last names I never knew.

There was another job that involved Shadow People. But the second interesting job from Maharba occurred a few weeks after that, and it was the one that changed me. It was how I first laid eyes on the most beautiful detective in the world, and the most frightening of succubus-ess-ess.

Suck-u-busses?

Succubi?

Though I never did find out if she was like the legendary succubus. As in did she tempt men? I would think so. Hell, she'd been gorgeous. Well, to me not so much. She hadn't had a face.

Of course, I gave the client what they asked for, but evidently it wasn't what they wanted. I sort of got—*involved* in that case—and was delinquent in reporting the whole episode. And while Daniel was in the hospital, Maharba had sent me a threatening e-mail.

They were disappointed. And they were watching me. And they would contact me for a job that would make up for my shoddy performance.

And my most popular client became my scariest. And I hadn't heard from them since.

Until now.

maharba@maharba.com.

3

"NONA!"

I blinked a few times before sticking my right pinky in my right ear and wiggling it. I wasn't deaf before Rhonda yelled for my mom—now I wasn't so sure.

Hello? Anyone there? Ow.

I stared at the e-mail address of the sender for several seconds. My right hand shook over the mouse, and I didn't want to double-click the damned thing open.

The last time I'd heard from Maharba—well—I'd been in the hospital sitting with Daniel. They hadn't exactly sent me a Good Luck! or Hope He Feels Better Soon! card. No. They'd definitely sent me a veiled threat. And I always knew I'd be hearing from them. Him. It. They.

Again.

I just wasn't prepared for it. Not for Joseph's more than cryptic message in the graveyard. And not for whatever this might be. For the past month, since Trench-Coat, Koba Hirokumi, and the Reverend, my life had been pretty bland. I was liking bland.

Mental note: *bland was good.*

I could smell Mom's perfume—a sick, sweet vanilla concoction she made up herself in her shop from essential oils—before I heard her shuffling in. She pressed both of her hands on my shoulders, and I caught a whiff of raw sausage. Sausage? What was she cooking in my kitchen? And when did I buy sausage?

"Who's Mar-har-ba?" Mom asked in a soft voice.

Rhonda and I both looked at her with faces of shock and surprise. Rhonda spoke. "Uh, Nona, remember them? They were the ones that sent Zoë out to spy on Daniel and Hirokumi? They sent that scary e-mail right before Christmas?"

I watched Mom's expression. It went from blank curiosity to abrupt recognition. She gave a slow nod. "Yes, yes. Now I remember. Had to find that piece in here." She tapped her head. "What does that header mean?" she asked in my ear, and leaned farther over me to point a greasy finger at my flat-screen monitor.

I waved her hand away and brushed at the spot, only managing to make a larger smudge of grease. Shit. Mothers. I shook my head and shrugged. And what was up with her disappearing memory lately? She'd completely forgotten Wednesday morning family time, when she delayed opening the shop and she, I, Rhonda, Tim, and Steve talked about things weird in the city.

Instead, we'd had day-old tea cakes and hot chocolate (Rhonda makes good hot chocolate), and talked about the headlines in the *Atlanta Journal-Constitution*.

In fact, Mom had been acting really strange since Monday when she'd had a doctor's appointment. Monday night, over spaghetti at the Atlanta Diner, Rhonda mentioned that Nona had been acting weird ever since she got home. We were both afraid she'd gotten bad news and it had really zonked her out. Only she hadn't mentioned it to me, or to Rhonda.

"Open it, Zoë. You've got to see what it says." Rhonda was still giving Mom the odd look.

Damn. Damn. Damn. I hated being frightened, which was weird, seeing as how I was part ghosty.

With a deep breath, I double-clicked the line. As a unit, all three of us leaned forward to read the message.

Miss Martinique,

We hope the New Year sees you well rested and your chosen partner healed. But in keeping with our promise at the end of business last year, it is time for you to fulfill your commitment to us—the one you were paid for.

We feel to maintain us as an employer, you must rebuild the bridge of trust between us, and we have need of a piece of information that we feel only you can retrieve. It has come to our attention that your "ability" to gather otherwise-unattainable knowledge has been…enhanced. Therefore, it is time for you to put that ability to the test.

Tonight, there is to be a gala event at the Westin Plaza Hotel, downtown. A benefit to raise money for the upcoming campaign of Congressman March Knowles, a well-liked, and well-respected member of the Republican Party. He will be running for senator to replace the retiring Senator Jerome Mason.

There is to be a meeting between Congressman Knowles and a high-ranking Atlanta businessman. Much like the last assignment you were given, is it not?

We would like a full report on what it is these two discuss. We would also like for you to bring us back proof that you were there. You will choose what it is to be, but it must be something unique, something that cannot be acquired by asking, to be delivered to us at a date and time we specify after you have completed the job.

If you do not succeed in retrieving the information, as

well as an item of proof, and/or you refuse this job, we can-
not be held responsible for the direction your life, or the lives
of your loved ones, will take.

Maharba

4

I didn't know I was starting to hyperventilate until Mom had her hands on my shoulders again and turned me around in the chair to face her. "Zoë, honey—take a deep breath."

I was shaking my head, staring at her, trying like hell to speak, and nothing was coming out but air. I tried to sign, but even that was getting sloppy.

Rhonda shoved the board and pen in my hands, and I started scribbling, very much aware of the pounding against my rib cage, the stuffiness of the room, and how nice it would be to go out of body and never come back.

THREAT HE THREAT YOU. THEEY THREAT!

Wow. That looked really bad.

But Mom wasn't having any of it. She took the board away from me and wiped it clean with a dishrag she'd tossed over her shoulder. (Don't all mothers do that? Keep dishrags over their shoulders?) "No, Zoë. You have to calm down. Your sugar—"

Fuck my sugar! Well, that would have been great if it'd had voice to it. *Nada*. Not even a squeak. Screw TC wherever he was. I hope he was enjoying my voice.

Rhonda had moved in beside me as Mom had somehow

wheeled my chair away from the desk. "Zoë—there's another e-mail here—sent about two hours later—but it doesn't say it's from Maharba. It's got an attachment." She double-clicked it. A simple text document opened. I moved in to read it.

Miss Martinique,

Due to recently received intel, you will need to arrive at the party physically. Please check your mail for your invitation.

Maharba

"Recently received intel?" Rhonda was shaking her head.

I stood up straight and looked at my mom.

Rhonda looked from the screen. "Evidently they left an invitation to tonight's event in your mailbox."

They did?

THEY DID?!

I snatched the board from Mom's hand. Scribble, scribble. KNOWS WHERE I LIVE.

Mom nodded. "It's okay, Zoë. Everything's going to be all right. It's just a job, right? I'll go check your mail." She turned and left my office.

I mean…she *calmly* turned and left my office. Miss Freaked-out-when-I-first-went-Wraith *calmly* went out.

What. The. Fuck?

I—me—she—were all just blatantly threatened by some madperson on eBay calling the shots. And she was going to check the mail?

I turned in my chair to look at Rhonda. She too looked a little perplexed. I smudged my board and wrote, YOU NOTICE THAT WAS WEIRD?

She pursed her blackish purple lips and nodded, her dark eyebrows creased into an almost straight line across her forehead, à la Bert from *Sesame Street*. "Yeah. It's kinda like she's been distracted." She sighed. "And she's had a hard time accepting everything that's happened to you in the last two months. I mean—you've put her through a lot."

Put *her* through a lot? Hello! What about *me*?

No, that was selfish. Rhonda was right.

I really had put her through a lot—starting with the rape nine years ago, then escalating to having me brought DOA to the hospital after my car was found wrapped around a tree and finding I couldn't speak anymore. I'd been in bad shape. And Mom had been there with me, all the way through to the wacky, and scary, end.

And she'd taken it all in stride, accepting me through everything. As had Rhonda. And Tim and Steve.

And the mysterious Joe, who had pulled me from the drawer in the morgue. His identity was still a mystery, a stranger who considered me being out of body too long more an inconvenience than a freakish thing.

"Zoë," Rhonda said, interrupting my nice, jolly thoughts. I looked at her. "Since Nona's not exactly forthcoming with whatever it was she learned at her doctor's appointment—maybe we should start thinking of gathering up more support. You know, having more people know what you are and teach them how to take care of your physical body." She looked sad. "Your mom's not always going to be here for you."

I did not want to talk about this right now. I was too upset. And I was hungry—because the smells of whatever it was Mom was whipping up in there had now moved into the office. I scribbled on the board, WHO YOU HAVE IN MIND?

She pursed her lips, and I could tell she was a little hesitant to name a name. "Daniel?"

I felt my eyes widen in surprise.

"He needs to know what he's gotten into with you." She held up her right hand, palm toward me. "Yeah, he's chalked up a lot of what happened on that roof to amnesia or dementia caused by the fall. But does he remember seeing you coming for him?"

I didn't honestly know. We hadn't talked about that night. Not even once. When I asked him about it in the hospital, his expression had been pleading, and I'd brushed the question away. He'd accepted my abrupt loss of voice as being attributed to being attacked by the succubus, Mitsuri. Not that Daniel knew that's what she'd been, of course. A rather nasty minion employed by the Symbiont inhabiting Reverend Theodore Rollins.

But in truth Daniel kept expecting me to talk, any day. My vocal cords were still there. And according to several specialists, they were working perfectly. Well, that was just great—but I couldn't talk. I had the faucets, just no pipes.

"Zoë"—Rhonda pointed to the screen and Maharba's letter and she was frowning again—"this new intel is bothering me. Why would you need an invitation? Why be physical?"

Uh.

Oh.

Hrm.

Good point.

And a very scary answer came to me. I grabbed up the board and erased it, scribbling again. WHAT IF THEY HAVE SNEAKY SNOOPER?

Rhonda's expression turned into a grimace of pain. "What?"

Oh, this was gonna be fun—my brain was thinking faster than I could scribble or sign. I wiped off the board again. Scribble. SPRITE SEE ME ON TAPE. WHAT IF PARTY HAS CAMERAS?

Rhonda pursed her lips as I wiped the board again. "Zoë— the SPRITE team were a couple of geeks looking for ghosts. Of course, they had all sorts of electronic equipment to find ghosts." She leaned her head forward at me and narrowed her eyes. "Why would they have those types of things at a political fund-raiser?"

Scribble. DON'T KNOW. WHY ELSE HAVE INVITE?

Screw it. I threw the board on the bed and gestured for her to get out of the way of the machine. I pulled up the simple text and typed. "Look—last time I did a job for Maharba, not only did they have some sort of shield up, but they had a succubus as well as a Soul Catcher dragon thing ready to eat me."

I finished and turned to give Rhonda a "Hurmph" look.

She read what I typed and seemed to think on it. "Ah—point taken. I'll do a bit of intel on the hotel and who's actually organizing the party—see if there is anything weird in the planning."

I moved back to the bed.

Rhonda flipped back to the e-mail on the computer. "I don't like this. I don't understand why they'd want you to snoop on Congressman Knowles—there's nothing dirty or underhanded in his past."

Huh. I frowned at Rhonda. It really wasn't like her to defend a mark like this. I grabbed my board, erased, and scribbled, GOOD MONEY.

She glanced at the ceiling. "This is serious. These people, or this person, are using you to do their dirty work. I mean—who are they? And how did they know about your new ability to go corporeal and grab solid objects? And let's say you're right—if this fundraiser does have ghost-seeing equipment, then I have to ask why. What kind of people are we dealing with? And if they do have this sneaky snooper like you guessed, then what would they do if they did detect you?"

I shrugged. I was feeling a bit light in the head too, and knew I should check my blood sugar. I'd gone out last night in Wraith form to do a bit of practice with my new strengths, going corporeal and noncorporeal, and that always screwed up my sugar.

Dr. Maddox was gung ho about my diabetes, and maybe that was what it looked like for him. But how do you tell your doctor your sugar level wasn't directly connected to low insulin—but something a bit more sinister?

"I just think you should tell Daniel—he's a cop, and it's obvious he's crazy about you. He might even be in love with you. He'd be the perfect backup." Rhonda was looking at me again with a very intense stare.

I erased and scribbled, CAN'T TELL DANIEL YET. MAYBE SOON. AFTER SEX.

Rhonda gave me an overexaggerated eye roll. "Zoë, sex doesn't solve problems. It sometimes complicates them."

I FEEL TRAPPED. I HAVE DO WHAT SAY.

I needed a bigger board too—or to learn to write smaller.

"You could go to the police?"

Erase. Scribble. YOU INSANE? WHO BELIEVE?

She nodded, and her shoulders lowered. "You're right. One look at what you could do, and you'd disappear. The government would lock you up and experiment on you—maybe even use you as a potential weapon. You'd make one hell of a spy, though. Wow...wonder what I could get for turning you in myself."

I arched an eyebrow at her.

"Just kidding. I'd be more afraid of what you'd do to me."

Oh. Make me feel real good here.

The door opened and Mom stepped back in. She had some junk mail in one hand and a small, five-by-five crisp envelope in the other. She handed it to me. It was addressed to Miss Zoetrope Adiran Martinique.

They knew my full name.

I NEVER used my full name on anything. It was too weird.

With a glance at Mom, then at Rhonda, I carefully opened the envelope with shaking hands. Inside was indeed a nicely printed invitation to the gala event at the Westin Plaza, eight o'clock, formal. The type was gold, embossed, on a creamy-colored stiff paper.

Okay—it was like Maharba had said. If they or it or them had this much power to pull me a formal invitation, then they had enough power to do their dirty work themselves.

It was chicken time.

I stood up really fast, nearly fell backward, then moved past Mom and out the door. I heard them follow me down the hall, through my living room, to the kitchen, where I immediately stomped on the open pedal of my garbage can and tossed the invite in.

Mom moved past me—pretty damned fast for a woman with her boobage—and scooped the invitation out of the garbage. "Zoë! I just dumped the grease in there." She patted at the now-grease-stained invite.

Seemed fitting to me.

I took a really good look at my kitchen then, and my eyes widened. The entire counter was covered in food preparations. Fresh-cut green beans, dough rising in a bowl, tea steeping in a steaming pot of water on the stove, along with two other pans bubbling with good smells.

And it looked like she'd been about to set the table.

For five.

She stuck the invite to the refrigerator with one of those carved plastic flowers she kept buying me for Christmas, and turned to face me.

I nailed her with a very well-executed sign-language yell of, "Who's coming to dinner?" Though I was sure I knew whom already.

"Honey, calm down. It's just Daniel and Melvin. We're going to eat early."

Daniel I already knew about. But Melvin?

Melvin? I mouthed to her with all the dislike I could muster in my face.

Mom wasn't going to be deterred. "Zoë, I like Melvin. He's been good to you, and to Daniel, ever since that whole"—she wiggled her fingers in the air in front of my face—"that whole thing with the Archer. And he's lonely…"

I signed back to her, *"It's not your job to make him unlonely. Mom...what about Joseph?"*

"Joseph?" Her face twisted up a bit, and I could have sworn I saw hamsters behind her eyes turning wheels.

I leaned toward her and signed his name again. *"Joseph? Maddox's son? The ghost that hangs around him? What about how he feels?"*

"Oh." A lightbulb came on behind Mom's eyes. She frowned. "Pesky ghosts. Pooh." She waved at me and turned back to the kitchen counter. "What is it with you, Zoë? Can't I enjoy life sometimes? Did it ever occur to you that I'm lonely too?"

Oh, this was not the conversation I wanted today. And the fact she was turned away from me did a great job of making any signs I threw her way null and void.

"Uh—I think this is my cue to leave."

I whirled on Rhonda and put up my hand with as fierce a look as I could muster. Which must've been a good one because goth chick actually looked frightened.

Taking a step toward Mom, I tapped her on the shoulder, and she turned. I signed at half speed, still not really good at this.

"I'm not kidding—Joseph doesn't like this new relationship any more than I do." Well, that wasn't all the truth. Joseph didn't seem to mind.

"Joseph is dead," Mom said, and put her hands on her hips. "Now, I'm sorry, if he's here and can hear me. But that's the truth. And he has to move on."

"He can't move on." My arms were going to wear thin. And the smells of food were making my stomach growl. *"I tell you that. You never listen."*

"I do listen. You don't listen, Zoetrope."

I cringed. I hated it when she used my full name.

"Now, you're going to that meeting. You owe this Meharbie

a job. You took their money. And besides"—she gave me a wide smile and wiggled her fingers in the air—"you might find out some really good gossip."

I shook my head and signed, *"Not going."*

Mom gave me a warning look. "Zoë…"

Damn, I wanted to yell at her. I wanted to ask her why she was so not-worried. Why she'd been acting all weird since Monday. Why she didn't seem as freaked-out as I was. And how could she forget Joseph like that?

But that was just too many words, to sign or write, and I'm lazy by nature. The only thing I could do was simply not go.

She couldn't make me go. I was over twenty-one—way past it. And this was my house.

And I didn't want Melvin Maddox in my house.

MELVIN sat across from me at my own table.

I was less than talkative—so he didn't bother to throw any conversation toward me. Mom had been really insistent about me going to this stupid gala.

And I had remained in my tee shirt, loungers, and put on a pair of pink Care Bear slippers in protest. Yes, I am the Imelda Marcos of slippers.

Hrmph.

Mom sat at the head of the table. Me on her left, Melvin on her right. Rhonda sat next to Melvin.

And Daniel—

—was knocking at the door.

I jumped up to answer it.

My darling cop smiled at me and held out a beautiful single white rose to go with my yellow one and my red one he'd already given me in two days. He looked tired, with dark circles under his eyes. But he still reached out and took me into his arms and gave me a nice, warm, wet, and juicy kiss.

Mmmmm...

"Detective!" Melvin called out. "Please—come and join us."

I pulled away from my baby long enough to glare at the jerk. This was my home, and my food (well—Mom bought it—but she'd used my pots and pans—that I'd stolen from her trash), and the quack was inviting him in.

Not that I didn't want him in.

I was in a foul mood.

"Hey, Doc," Daniel called out. He moved away from me and went to Mom to give her a sweet kiss on the cheek, then squeezed Rhonda's shoulder. He looked at me. "Cooper and Mastiff dropped me and my car off. Since I'm not supposed to drive yet, can I get you to take me home?"

I nodded. I kinda felt all warm and gushy at that moment—my boyfriend was liked by my immediate family. You know how odd that was? And he was soooo cute!

Daniel had the sort of face you wanted to paint. Strong chin with sculptured cheekbones. Nice lips, beautiful blue eyes framed with long, dark lashes, accented with little round wire glasses.

And he had a really nice butt.

All square and tight, like a man should have a butt.

Blink. What? You don't look at men's butts? I do.

"Oh, it smells wonderful, Nona," Daniel said, and looked at the food longingly. "But I'm afraid I can't stay."

He looked at me, standing by the table and his empty chair. I stuck out my bottom lip a sufficient distance to show my unhappiness.

I'm good at boo-boo lip.

"Well, why not, son?" Melvin said, while helping himself to a heaping pile of mashed potatoes. "They got you on a hot case?"

I caught the slight movement of Joseph then, just outside the sliding glass doors of my dining area. It was the first appearance he'd made since his father arrived. He looked...unhappy.

Well, to be honest, even when Joseph was alive, he'd looked unhappy.

"Actually, yes and no," Daniel said, and moved around the table back to me. He put his arm around my waist. Good thing I hadn't eaten much yet—kept my tummy flat.

And to be honest, Melvin's presence—no, let me rephrase that—*continued* presence—in my home had lost me my appetite.

And I usually had a really healthy appetite. Don't let my size fool you. I was terrified one day my metabolism was going to betray me. My "diabetes" had already lost me my favorite sweets. (Which, of course, I snuck into my diet regularly—à la chocolate. Daniel was my enabler.)

Daniel leaned in close to me. He smelled faintly of Halston. What I'd given his unconscious self on Christmas night. "There's an event I have to go to tonight. And the captain wants me there. So"—he shrugged—"I really need to get going and clean up."

I glared at him and pulled far enough away to sign, *"But you're exhausted. You need rest or you'll fall down."*

He smiled at me. I became goo.

Mom's face lit up. And I knew what was coming. "Oh? An event?" She stood. "It wouldn't happen to involve the Westin, would it?"

Daniel frowned. "Well...yeah. It's a fund-raising event."

If I had a voice, I'd have yelled at the woman to sit back down. But—of course—I didn't have one anymore.

Mental note: *Damn. It.*

I watched her take the invite off the refrigerator before she shuffled happily back to us. She never looked at me but beamed at Daniel as she handed it to him.

His eyes widened and he looked at me. "You got an invitation? How did *you* get an invitation?"

Hey...that was mean. And he must have realized what he'd said. Daniel took a step back and put out his hand as if I was going to deck him. And the thought had occurred.

"Zoë—I meant that in the sense of—you're not really politically active. Or at least, I didn't think you were." He frowned. It was a cute frown behind those glasses. "Are you?"

I shook my head.

He held up the card. "Are you going?"

I shook my head again. No.

Daniel glanced at Mom before saying in a soft voice, "It'd be sexy to see you all dolled up in a nice dress. And since I'm not supposed to be there in a formal capacity, it'd be nice to have you there on my arm."

He gave me one of his beautiful smiles.

I really didn't want to go—not because I didn't relish the idea of putting on a fancy dress and getting all dolled up—well, yeah, I didn't—but because I was terrified of why I shouldn't go.

I did not want to do what Maharba wanted. It was him/her/it/ they that sent me on that interview with Hirokumi—and, yeah, that's where I first saw Daniel too—and then I discovered I could become corporeal while out of body—and, of course, that led me to snooping on the Reverend, which cemented there was more happening—

Okay. So. Maybe I *should* go.

I signed, *"I don't have a fancy dress."*

Mom turned and went straight to her purse, which was perched like a small dog on the floor by her chair. She fumbled inside and came up with a credit card and handed it to me. "It's on me."

I looked at the card, then looked past it and Mom to Rhonda. She was frowning. So was Joseph, who was now inside the house and standing behind his dad. I did a double take when I saw him.

"Come on, Zoë," Mom was saying. "You need to get out. Mingle. And what a perfect date—a detective."

Joseph's headshake grew a little more urgent.

I spoke to him with a thought. *In my office. Now.*

He vanished.

I turned to Daniel and signed, *"Need to change. Wait?"*

He nodded and kissed me again. "This way we can spend some more time together, okay?"

I glared at Mom, kissed Daniel, glared at Rhonda, who stood up from the table and then followed me into the office. Joseph was there, his little black-and-white self pacing. The bad part of this was that I could see him, and Rhonda couldn't. Usually she and Mom saw ghosts. Most ghosts. But ones like Joseph—walkers—*nada*. So she was going to have to trust me on this.

What gives? I wasn't going to give him time to think.

He stopped and looked at me. When he spoke, his voice did that echoey thing in my head. "It's all wrong."

I know it's all wrong, because it's a setup for me to—

"No, no." Joseph shook his head and waved his hands in the air.

"What's he doing?" Rhonda said. Oh yeah, forgot. I started signing my questions, and his replies. I brought her up to speed before I continued.

No, no what? I prompted him to continue.

"No, no because something's wrong." He looked confused.

Yeah, I know it is because I'm being set up to go there.

Joseph looked directly at me. "Something's wrong with Dad. I don't know what—but its like a cloud that's following him. And it's not as easy for me to stay near him as usual."

I arched my eyebrows at him. *What has this got to do with the Westin tonight?*

"What's wrong with Dr. Maddox?" was Rhonda's response when I signed it. "Was it like this at the funeral today?" She started looking around the room.

Joseph was looking at Rhonda. "She's cute."

She's alive. You're dead. Point taken?

He nodded. "Zoë, I don't know what's wrong with Dad—and I'm not really sure if it's something wrong with me. I've never been a ghost before. But don't go to the Westin. And stay away from the Eidolon."

I started to sign that, then paused. *How do you spell that?*

He shook his head. "I—I don't know. Just stay away from it."

But I'm not going to be incorporeal. I should be fine. I paused. *What the hell is an Eidolon?*

"I don't—"

Is it a Phantasm?

He shook his head.

Incubus?

"No."

Symbiont?

"Zoë I can't say because I don't know. No one does. It's just a word I got from a ghost I met."

What ghost?

"Zoë," Rhonda said in a stern voice. She was looking at me just like you would an errant child. "What is he saying?"

I held up my finger—no time for flashbacks in American Sign Language. *Joseph, what ghost? And how am I supposed to avoid something if I don't know what it is? Or what it looks like? Is it a thing? A person?*

"I don't know, Zoë." The stern tone in his voice told me his frustration level had reached epic proportions. And I was aware I wasn't helping matters. "He wasn't really a ghost—more of a shade like me. And he was very insistent that you not go near them. He knew you by name."

WHO?

Joseph looked as if were about to cry. "I didn't get his name. I just know he was upset, and he wanted me to tell you that."

Look, I'll be with Daniel, and I'll make sure to stay away from this Eidolon, okay? Hrm. Maybe if I do this and look good and sexy enough I can finally lure him into some under-the-sheets bundling?

I looked at Rhonda, who'd settled into my chair in front of my computer and was still glaring at me under dark eyebrows. I could suddenly feel the January cold sieving through my office window and shivered.

Joseph sighed and faded away, but not before I caught his voice in my head. "It's your funeral..."

It always is, isn't it?

5

January 25, 4:25 P.M.

AFTER Joseph's second cryptic message for the day, I changed into a gray Old Navy zip-up fleece sweatshirt, jeans, thick wool socks (it was cold out there), and sneakers.

Rhonda came into my room then and handed me a—BlackBerry?

I looked at her, then looked at the phone, and signed, *"Can't use. No talk, remember?"* I handed it back to her.

After the loss of my voice, I'd canceled my previous PDA smartphone. What was the point?

"Text messaging?" Her dark black eyebrows rose high on her forehead. "Your fingers still work." And she shoved it back at me. "This is the first major job you've worked since the—" She pursed her lips. "Well, your change happened. Nona and I picked this up a week ago. It's got all of our numbers in it and all your previous numbers. I synced it with the Mac and your previous address book. Now take it."

I stared at her.

Rhonda looked worried. "Zoë—just humor me. Okay? I like you having a way to contact me if something goes—wrong."

I felt like I was gonna cry. Rhonda and I had grown close over the years—she being the only "normal" person I could talk to about my condition. And she'd always accepted me with no frills, and a matter-of-fact attitude.

Which just irritated the hell out of me sometimes.

She gave me a quick lesson on how to text message, and I found Jamael's number at Adore Hair Studio. I sent him a quick message, asking him if he had time for a quick hair fix. He answered almost immediately, and I agreed to meet him there by six. It was four thirty-nine by the clock on my nightstand.

I gave Rhonda a quick hug and pocketed the phone before grabbing my peacoat, and Daniel and I hit the road with me driving his Suburban.

Shopping for a last-minute dress proved to be a real bitch, especially at five in the evening. We had less than three hours, which meant I had a half hour to find something off the rack.

Ew.

I swear it wasn't me being picky. Honest. Well, maybe a little. It was five fifteen before Daniel and I got to Lenox Mall. I didn't find anything at Macy's—though I did sit through a twenty-minute makeover. (When else was I going to get my foundation on before eight?)

Didn't find anything in any store that I liked.

Not to mention the retail agents weren't really sure if Daniel was an overbearing oaf or one of the sweetest boyfriends in the world—because I never spoke. He did all the talking and negotiating for me.

I tried on a nice long black velvet and black sequin number. Very flattering, and with my hair up—could be doable. I was horribly worried I'd be either overdressed, or underdressed. But the salespeople had evidently sold dresses already for this event and reassured me, and Daniel, that this dress and a black tux on him, which he swore he had at home, would be perfect.

The saleslady leaned in close when I nodded okay, and said, "Don't worry—lots of the women going to this thing tried this dress on—but they couldn't carry it off like you. You're going to be the only dress like this in the whole place."

Well, that was reassuring. And I felt an inward glow too, knowing if this woman lied to me and there were seven other dresses like this at the Westin, I was going to come back as a Wraith and scare the shit out of her.

So I bought something—with shoes, gotta have matching shoes, don't ya know—at one of the boutiques. I hoped Mom's credit card could withstand the charge of all this. When it passed muster, I was surprised. Zinged right through.

Mom had A-1 credit.

Hrm...wonder if there was anything else at Lenox I could use. Maybe a PSP?

I signed that I could drop Daniel off at his place—I had to get over to Adore.

"I know where Adore is—I used to get my hair cut there. I'll go with you. You got a stylist ready?"

I nodded to him, a smile playing along my lips. This man never ceased to amaze me.

We dashed down North Highland, past Manuel's Tavern, and down to the newer condo-ridden areas. The things were popping up like mushrooms.

Adore was on the second floor of one of the newer buildings on the left, just next to a wine store. I turned left into the parking lot—which was nothing more than a vacant lot at the moment, with gravel and lots of dirt—and the two of us went up the steps—Daniel a little slower with his cane—and turned left.

Adore was a beautiful blend of earth tones and Ikea style—in my honest opinion. (Or as Rhonda would say IMHO.) Dark-tiled floor, glass-case front desk, paper lanterns hanging from the wall, and a really calming mixture of squared furniture with European flare.

Well—that's the way it was described to me.

"Danny!" the blonde behind the counter said with bright eyes as we stepped inside.

"Hey, Shelly." He beamed at her as she came around the front desk and gave him a huge bear hug. "How's the baby?"

Me? No jealously here. I'd known Shelly since she worked at Cortex in midtown. She'd been at the front counter there as well, and always knew my name when I came in. I'd been happy to hear she'd opened up her own salon, and once Jamael joined her legion of stylists—I was hooked.

She released Daniel and stepped back, giving him a look up and down. "You look better than I expected. Cooper's been in here once since your accident—he was really worried about you. It sounded exciting." She grabbed his hand and grinned at me. "Zoë—Jamael's in the back waiting for you. I'll keep Mr. Hot-Cop busy."

I understood Shelly and smiled. She wanted to know more about that night—about what had happened on the roof of that building (not that she was going to get any coherent answers from my sweetie), and she wanted to keep Daniel occupied while I had my hair done.

Daniel gave me a kiss on my cheek as he followed Shelly into the back, and Aly—a beautiful, slightly taller version of Veronica Mars—moved up to the counter to take her place.

"Girrrrl." Jamael came forward as I moved around the counter to the right. "That white stripe is look'n kick'n."

We hugged, and he pointed to his chair. Jamael is what I called a beautiful man. Cheery, golden, and covered in some of the most intricate tattoos I'd ever seen. What made them most unique was that they blended in so beautifully with his dark skin—it took some serious concentration to see them, but when you did—they were beautiful. He also had a stud through his lower lip—which was neat. Not something I'd do—but on him it looked right.

He also had a daughter named Zoë.

Good name.

He draped the black plastic cape over my shoulders and turned me to face the mirror. "Okay—black dress?" he said to my reflection.

I nodded.

"Strapless or jacket?"

I motioned a jacket.

"I've got the thing—and I know you want that stripe of white covered up. But I think I can make it look *good*."

And he did.

Before TC, Jamael and I carried on varied conversations about movies, celebrities, and even the local politics. But since my voice was stolen—Jamael did most of the talking.

"—busy when I noticed an article on this big party tonight," he said as he worked his magic. "You're going to be rubbing shoulders with most of the elite Republicans of Atlanta, aren't you? I didn't know you were a Republican."

I shook my head and stuck my tongue out. I was nondenominational.

Wait…that wasn't the right word…I meant I was nonpartisan. Though in today's political climate, nondenominational seemed appropriate at times.

He gave that adorable belly laugh of his and abruptly lowered his voice. "Your bartender friend was in here yesterday."

That got my attention.

My bartender friend was a man named Dags McKinty—part-time magician, bartender, and medium. He'd been the bartender at Fadó's that afternoon I followed Daniel from Hirokumi's to the pub. I suspected while sitting there that the ponytailed little cutie could see me—but I really hadn't been paying attention.

It wasn't until I caught him naked, poking it to the daughter of the chief of surgery of Northside Hospital in a bathroom stall that I knew he had seen me that afternoon.

And we became fast friends. In truth, he was my backup when Rhonda wasn't available. Seemed Mr. Dags was quite the snoop himself.

I looked up at Jamael and arched my eyebrows as if to say, "And?"

With a good conspiratorial look around, the broad man leaned forward. "He gave me something to give you—said he was going out of town for a few days. Savannah."

Hrm. I nodded. What did he need to do in Savannah? The most I knew about Dags was he led a simple life—rented a house in Roswell, just north of Atlanta, worked as a bartender around town, and tinkered with cars. Now he had a sah-weet '69 Fastback. Even if he had replaced the steering wheel with one out of a Bonneville.

Strange bird.

When Jamael turned me back around, I beamed at him in the mirror. He'd managed to curl, poke, tease, cajole, and spray my unruly mass into an elegant upsweep. The white hair was blended into the fabric of his design and, well—it looked good.

Just like he said it would.

"You look beautiful," came a soft voice from behind me. I looked above my head in the mirror and saw Daniel standing there.

Jamael handed me a mirror and turned my chair so I could see the back. Oh! I had tendrils of curls hanging down my back just like a real girl!

I nodded up at him, and he gave me a perfect, white smile. "Now, don't go getting into trouble."

Getting up, I hugged him and thanked him. He nodded. "Peace out, girlfriend." He grabbed my hand—and pressed something into it. I didn't look at it immediately and instead tucked it into my coat pocket.

Daniel had already settled the bill and ignored my look of ire as we made our way back to his car. The sun was setting—not that it made much of an impact on the already-overcast day.

I told him we could drop by his house and pick up his tux— and go get ready at Mom's.

"No time," he said, and glanced at me with a very snarky smile on his face as he slid behind the wheel and handed me his cane.

I waved at him—*You should not be driving under medication!*

"It'd be faster if we get ready at my place and go directly there."

Gulp.

We were going to *his* place.

When I didn't get in, he gave me a sweet smile. "I'm fine, Zoë. I'm not loopy, and I'm fit enough to drive just to my house. Now get in, or you'll be hailing a taxi."

I got in.

Since I'd met him in November, I'd never seen Daniel's home. I was going into the man's domain. Ever since we met, we'd always been on my turf, with my mom and my friends. But we were entering man's land.

His place. His abode. The King's castle.

I suddenly had stage fright.

DANIEL lived not very far from my mom's place in Little Five Points. His house sat on Boulevard, just a mile or so south from Interstate 20 and two blocks from the Atlanta Zoo and Cyclorama. I wasn't sure which one it was as he turned left beside the CVS and took an immediate right into a graveled alley.

I counted the rear of one house to the right, then a small patch of trees to the right, and he turned his car right into a paved driveway.

The sun had nearly set, so it was hard to see the whole house, its shape or color. But I got the impression it was a good size.

And he lived here by himself? On a cop's salary?

He pulled the car up to the back door and got out, grabbing his cane from my paralyzed hand. A light came on, illuminating a nicely bricked back deck with a tiled barbecue area along a privacy fence. It was still damned cold outside, and damp, and I moved around the front of the Suburban and followed him through the door.

And stopped dead in my tracks, my mouth wide open.

How does one describe actually walking into a house decorated by *Southern Living*? I just couldn't.

The first room was a kitchen—and it was the size of my entire living room. The ceiling had to have been fourteen feet high, with a beautiful stainless brushed-steel lamp that hung all the way down over a marble-topped island that housed two deep, sparkling sinks. The cabinets were all dark-stained wood, with glass doors that revealed neatly stacked dishes, matching coffee cups and saucers. A double-sided stainless-steel refrigerator stood to the right of the room, beside a homemade wine rack.

The room smelled of air freshener. Rose?

"Zoë?" He gently prodded me in the butt with his cane.

I blinked, looked at Daniel. He was half-turned, looking back at me, my bags in his hand. I held out my hands and gestured to the entire room.

My cute cop smiled. "Don't be too impressed. It isn't mine. Come on." He gestured for me to follow, and I did, noticing the floors were well-polished wood.

I caught a glimpse of deep, wine red walls and dark trim, Tiffany lamps, and a center fireplace before Daniel took my hand and pulled me to my right.

Into the bedroom.

No mistaking this room. And the bed. Four-poster. Elevated. Mounds of pillows in cream and forest green. The room itself was a monument to trey ceilings. High and decorated with a mosaic pattern—I know my mouth was open as I looked up.

"Hey, just be glad she took the mirrors off the ceiling." Hefting his cane in his left hand, Daniel took my hand with his right one and led me past the bed to a living-room-sized bathroom. Free-standing sinks, his and hers. A separate shower and a deep, sunken tub. The floor was covered in several different soft, deep pile rugs in burgundy and gold. The window behind the tub was stained glass, but without the sunlight behind it, I couldn't see the pattern. But I guessed it to be of the same color scheme.

Daniel went to a door by the shower, leaned his cane against the wall just outside of the frame, and disappeared inside. When he limped back out he held up a garment bag and hung it up on the outside of the same door. He looked at me and smiled before he pointed to the sink behind me. "In the closet over there you'll find a complete, unopened overnight kit."

I nodded, then something he said dawned on me. I waved at him to catch his attention. *"She took the mirrors down?"* I signed to him. And I put in a lot of surprise in my expression.

Uh...that expression wasn't difficult. I was shocked.

Who was *she*?

His look sobered. "Long story. Not a lot of time. But I'll tell you. I promise. Right now I need you to get ready. You need a shower?"

I shook my head. A shower would just remove the makeup and hair, and I didn't have time to do it over. I'd just change and brush my teeth and freshen up.

"I'll shower while you get dressed. We've got about an hour, and that's it."

I signed, *"Fashionably late?"*

He smiled. "I wish. But it would be better if we were there for the congressman's entrance and speech."

"Why?" I loved that sign. Real easy gesture. Could do it one-handed.

He came to me then and gathered my cold fingers into his warm callused ones. I loved it when he looked at me with those intense blue eyes. "All I know is I'm supposed to keep an eye out. Be part of the eyes and the ears of the security—but invisible." He tapped my upturned nose with his finger. "But with you on my arm, I'm sure I'm going to get noticed. Hopefully, Cooper won't be too upset with me."

And then he kissed me. It was deeper this time than any that came before it. And he held me closer, moving his lips from mine and kissing my earlobe, then touching his mouth to my neck.

He shivered and pulled back but didn't let go. "I want you, Zoë Martinique. And if we didn't have to go..."

He didn't need to finish the statement. I saw it in his eyes.

Mental note: *Damn! Want monkey sex now!*

Daniel cleared his throat, kissed my nose, and turned away. As I stood there, stunned, he reached inside the shower and turned it on. I moved, blinking, and gathered up my dress, hose, and shoes so that I could undress and change when he was in the shower.

While I was turned he'd stripped, and when I heard the clank of the shower, all I saw was a beautiful, distorted outline of his naked body.

I must have stood there for a good five minutes watching him move, watching the nice curve of his hips as well as his butt before the steam threatened to uncurl my hair. I shook myself and undressed.

Good thing I wasn't wearing underwear—I'd have had to peel them off.

Yummy naked man!

Hairspray, deodorant, lotion. It was all here in this bag he'd had me pull from the closet. I used it all, or at least sampled it. Brushed my teeth, flossed. Mouthwash too.

After I wiggled into my dress, stockings, and shoes, I went back to the bathroom mirror and checked my face. The clerk at Macy's really hadn't applied much makeup to my face—I'd been given one of those faces that didn't need much. Slight olive skin, smooth too. Which was nice. Mom's skin had been acne pitted as a teenager, though she said my dad's was as smooth as a baby's butt.

Another testament to good Latino genes.

I was finishing up my lipstick—a nice coral shade I'd found in the bag—when I heard a low swearing.

I turned to see the most magnificent man I'd ever laid eyes on leaning against the closet door.

Daniel looked hawt, let me tell you. I dropped an egg looking at him, my eyes bulging out of my head.

I hadn't heard him get out of the shower, nor had I noticed a naked man behind me as I dressed and primped as well. (Uh, the mirrors were fogged?)

His hair was still wet—or moussed—I didn't know which—and was combed back behind his ears to brush his shoulders. He was beautifully decorated in a very nice-cut lowbrow tuxedo. Not wedding or meeting royalty formal, but—DAMN.

No glasses. His eyes shone bright blue, and his teeth were straight and white when he smiled at me. He turned and grabbed his cane by the door before turning to look at me.

"Don't move. Even holding that lipstick you're beautiful, Zoë Martinique."

Awwwww. I blushed. I hate blushing.

I replaced the lipstick into the tube and set it on the sink. With a quick straightening of my dress I pointed to him and, without thinking, made the sign of copulation and grabbing his butt.

Okay. Not American Sign Language. But ouch—he was hurting my womanly places in that tux.

Daniel's grin broadened even if I felt more than a little embarrassed at my own brazenness. I was Nona's daughter—I shouldn't be surprised at myself. But I was.

God, I was so horny.

He moved to me and stood in front. There was no space between us. My breasts, uplifted inside the gown's sewn-in bra, pressed against his chest. I felt my nipples harden.

His hands found my bare shoulders and caressed them. He leaned down and pressed his lips to mine, teasing at first, and then firmer. More confident. So much like a first date. Unsure.

In an instant I felt his tongue against my lips, and I parted them, taking him in and wrapping my arms around his neck. My Kegel muscles contracted as he pulled me in and up closer.

The kiss became my world—I was so lost in him. And I wanted him sooooo badly. *Oh please, can't we be late? Just fifteen minutes? That's all?*

Pleeeeease!

His hands trailed over the curve of my back, dipped into the space over my butt, and cupped my cheeks. He squeezed once and pulled back.

I gasped. No sound, just air. And I tried to get him back. Hell, I was ready to yank him back and hog-tie him to me.

He had his hands on my face and was looking at me. I know I must've looked drunk to him, my eyes half-lidded with desire. Pleasure. "Oh God, you're beautiful," he said in a breathless voice. "I'm so lucky to have found you, Zoë. I want you—I really want you."

Then take me damnit!

"But we have to go. We *need* to get going." He lifted my face up to his and kissed my lips. Soft. Teasing. A soft bite.

A promise?

"You're going to have to put your lipstick back on."

I could have smacked him.

Ah, but no. This was my future husband. I needed to be a good future cop's wife.

When he turned, I reached out and pinched his tight, firm butt. He laughed and motioned me to follow. I checked myself in the mirror. Yep, had that sex glow going. Without actually having sex. Damn.

Once I had my lipstick back in place, my hair nicely sprayed, and my shoes fastened, Daniel had produced a full-length black velvet coat. I'd never seen anything like it.

"It's a loan. We have to get this back."

It was then I noticed a front room with two white sofas, lots of mint green pillows, and a fluffy white rug. There was a black baby grand and a bar built into the wall.

And books. Lots of books in glass-fronted shelves on the other walls.

Whose house was this?

But we were out the back door and into the Suburban in minutes—well, as fast as a sexy man with a cane could move. I made sure I had the invitation in the little black purse I'd borrowed from the closet.

And it was cold. Damned cold. The wind hit my face on the way to the car, and I sucked in air. My teeth chattered in my head, and I was glad the shoulderless dress had a cute little velvet bolero jacket to go with it. I hoped the Westin was warm.

Traffic was a bit congested, with lots of Atlanta Police Department in uniform, present and directing traffic. With my invite and Daniel's badge, we got through the mess a little faster than most.

The Westin Peachtree Plaza sits in the center of downtown Atlanta—a cylindrical monument to the architect's ingenuity. For me, when I thought of the city's skyline, I always thought of the Westin. I'd eaten once in the Sun Dial, which sat atop the building—a rotating restaurant boasting one hell of a view of the city—as well as Stone Mountain.

Mom had taken me there—as a kid—and I'd been terrified of eating in a restaurant that spun around. Thought I'd get sick. When in truth, I was mesmerized by the grandeur of the city—a view we so seldom see. If there is one thing Atlanta has over most other cities I've been to—it's the color green.

Our pipes are clogged with it.

Namely pines.

I'd never stayed in any of the luxury suites, but I had heard they'd added workout areas, where guests can exercise in the privacy of their own rooms.

Which always sounded cool to me since I'd rather not sweat and stink around men. Or other women. Especially not those prissy blondes that never perspire and keep their hair perfectly coiffed. Not me—I sweat like any normal Latino, with dark patches under my arms and oil slicks of sweat down my face, back, and the crack of my ass.

And as for my hair when I'm done? Oh, let's not go there.

Daniel pulled the Suburban up to the front behind a long line of cars. A uniformed man came to the side and opened the door, blasting me again with cold air. He smiled with white teeth and beautiful dreadlocks. I took his hand and stepped out. Daniel approached and palmed him cash (slick there, milk shake), and the Suburban was driven away to be parked while we moved the few feet to the red carpet leading into the Westin's lobby.

Lights flashed everywhere. It was like the Golden Globes of Atlanta or something. Paparazzi jammed the sidewalks. And I did notice a lot of cameras. Of course, there were cameras held by the local station crews—and I could identify them by their call letters. But there were also cameras near the entrance—men dressed in tuxedos with those weird, curly wires going into their ears, all holding little box cameras at arm's length, scanning the crowd.

I'd seen that sort of camera before—infrared. SPRITE had used those cameras, and my image had shown up big as shit on them. Damn—was that why Maharba had wanted me here in physical form as well? Was this the intel they'd gotten? SPRITE couldn't detect me while I was in my body.

And to top it off—I recognized the guy on the left. Medium height, lanky, dark hair, and a serious expression, dressed in an oversized tuxedo.

Randall whatsis bucket. The leader of SPRITE.

And here he was in what looked like a VIP position, behind the barricade of the Atlanta Police Department and red velvet ropes.

Shit! I needed to text Rhonda! SPRITE was here. And what begged a deeper question was—why? Were they expecting an influx of ghosts?

Or just me?

With his cane in his left hand, Daniel had a tight hold on me with his right hand and arm as we made our way to the steps behind other men and women, all dressed as we were. Which made me feel a little bit better. At least the salesperson had been honest in that I wasn't going to be under- or overdressed.

"Well, well, well—Detective Daniel Frasier. How we've moved up in the world."

I didn't know the voice, but I was surprised it cut through the shouts of reporters and guests alike to find us.

Daniel paused, and his grip on my waist and hand increased. He was looking at the crowd to the left, and I followed his gaze.

I sort of recognized the face. Thin, gaunt, with glowing white skin the color of a bleached bone. Thin shiny black hair. Her lips were pink, and she was dressed in a dark red shimmering dress. She wore a fur coat that looked like it'd been made out of cats. She was standing on the press side of the ropes with a microphone in her hand and a tall cameraman hovering over her right shoulder, the lens pointed directly at us.

And she looked very familiar.

Synapses fired—lazy due to lack of sex.

Ah! Of course! Channel 5 Action News. This was Heather Noir.

I blinked. *But she knows Daniel?*

I could feel my cute cop tensing up as we paused, and he looked at Heather. His jaw tightened, and I was sure his backbone had transformed into a board.

"Heather." Daniel gave a tight smile. "Wow. You've put on weight."

I narrowed my eyes at the dark-haired waif. Put on weight? Where? I was sure this woman would have to dance around in the shower to get wet.

She returned Daniel's unpleasant smile, and I felt her dark, beady eyes concentrating on him, looking for some sort of weakness. Her eyes rested on the cane he clutched with white knuckles in his hand but then looked back up at him. "I wouldn't know, Danny. You have my house, with my bathroom, and my scales."

Gulp.

Oh. Then—was this her coat and purse?

Mental note: *be careful with the coat.*

And if it was—then how the hell was I wearing it? Unless, say, she used to weigh more?

"And you look a lot better than previously reported." She pursed her lips, and I wondered if the camera was still rolling tape. Heather didn't have the microphone up to her face. "I thought you were on death's bed—after all that bullshit about saving that little girl at Thanksgiving."

Daniel held me closer. I felt a little like a support system, and I knew I was staring. Mainly because I was amazed that someone that thin could stand upright and not snap like a twig. She looked like a toothpick with an olive for a head. I could see her bones in her bare shoulders. Wasn't this woman cold?

"I'm fine, Heather."

"Quite a career maker."

"Yes. Now if you'll excuse me."

I looked down at her shoes. Sandals? In January?

"Oh—and is this my replacement?"

I looked up from her bony bare feet and into her face.

There are times I'm glad I don't have a voice 'cause at that moment I'd have shouted out *marymotherofgodholyshit*. And pretty loud too.

I'd already seen Heather's face. Glanced at it. Recognized it. But she hadn't been looking *at* me. Now that she was (and rather nastily I might add), I could *see* it.

The skull.

A full, icky, eyeless skull imposed over her face.

This was another little trick I'd discovered I had—part of being a Wraith I supposed—seeing a death mask.

And there was no mistaking what I was looking at. Heather Noir was going to die. And soon. I just didn't know how—and as nasty as she appeared to be on the outside, I really hoped I wasn't the harbinger to bring that death to her.

I reschooled my face though I knew Daniel had seen me flinch, and felt me take a step back. I forced a smile to my face—though I'm sure it looked like I was gritting my teeth.

"Heather, this is Zoë Martinique. Zoë, Heather Noir."

Heather handed me a limp hand, and I shook it. Bitch had ice fingers. I also bet she slept in a coffin too. The woman was too pale.

I nodded and dropped that dead hand as fast as I could.

"What is it, honey?" Heather gave me a raised eyebrow. "You can't speak? Cat got your tongue? Or is Daniel here only hiring you by the hour and told you to keep your mouth shut?"

I felt him tense even harder beside me. That's it. This bitch just called me a ho.

Mental note: *throw coat on ground—jump up and down on it.*

I pulled my right hand from his and politely signed exactly

what I thought of her. And I used every bit of ASL slang I could think of as I made up even more colorful metaphors.

It was obvious the woman had no idea what it was I said. But a few of the reporters behind her on the other side of the rope did, and started howling with laughter. Some even gave me a thumbs-up and fired off a few shots.

I smiled sweetly.

And to my surprise, Heather looked almost apologetic.

Almost.

"So...you're a deaf mute." She shifted her face away from me so that I didn't see her lips. But I did hear her words. "Cheap, bitchy wetback."

I reached out, grabbed her bony wrist, and touched her—and I mean *touched* her—with what now lived inside of me. Those same reporters had heard her speak under her breath as well, and when my hand grabbed her wrist, a wall of flashing lights went off around us.

But I knew Heather had noticed. She felt my hand on her skin. I knew it was like having the hand of death touch her, my hand colder than her own, and her heart clenched as I felt the stirring of her long-abandoned warmth.

The warmth of her soul.

She stared at me with wide eyes, and I removed my hand after I gave her wrist a painful squeeze and pointed to my ears.

"She hears just fine, Heather." Daniel glared at her and pulled me closer. "And so do I. If you'll excuse us."

And we started walking to the stairs. I risked a glance back, and the dark-haired woman was still looking at us.

Or rather me. And I felt something dark overshadow me as well. I wasn't sure if I'd made a friend at that moment, or a mortal enemy.

I touched Daniel's shoulder and willed him to look at me. He did when we reached the top step, then looked back down at the red carpet. He knew what I was asking without so much as a gesture. *Who was she? What connection did she have? Was that her house we were in?*

Daniel reached up and put a warm hand to my cheek. "I'm sorry, Zoë. Heather is my ex-wife."

6

EX-WIFE? Daniel had been married? I didn't remember there being a marriage on record, and she sure as hell didn't come see him while he was hospitalized.

I glanced back at the woman. She was still looking at me.

If they were married, and he had the house—how did that happen? Didn't the wife usually get the house in the state of Georgia? And—I glanced at her again—what in the hell had he seen in *that*?

Mental note: *Interrogate boyfriend at length after mission. If needed, use genital pressure.*

;)

For the record, let me say that I'm not one of those big party girls. I usually don't hobnob, nor do I have any business in a fancy dress. So in keeping with the theme of things, let me say, I was as nervous as a long-tailed cat in a room full of rocking chairs (I always loved that saying).

I also got the feeling Daniel *wasn't* as uncomfortable in this atmosphere or in his tux—which he looked fine in. When we got to the door, I handed them my invite. There was one of those split-second thoughts that what if it was a fake? What if there was some sort of electronic device in them that let the security guards posted at the doors know if you were some sort of crazy assassin come to shoot someone?

Tense moment all around. Even Daniel seemed to go all quiet when the invitation was passed through a machine. What? Did he think I'd faked it? A wand was run over our bodies. (I must say the really big burly brute was using his wand on me with a wee bit more relish than I thought he should.)

I was also very aware of the men walking around with infrared cameras. Randall was close by—and he'd actually looked at me a few times. But I didn't see any recognition in his eyes either.

Whew.

But then we were through the checkpoint and herded along with all the other guests inside the Westin Peachtree Plaza.

Shiny, dark floors, huge columns with green leather seats surrounding the base greeted us near the front desk. We were directed to the main lobby, to what I could only call a meet and greet. My shoes sank into dark, navy blue carpet. The furniture was shaped in boxes—beige, white, brown—even the coffee tables were squares and rectangles. All resting on dark, wood bases.

Kinda reminded me of the sixties in an urban, retro way.

Men and women with happy faces dressed in black-and-white pants and jackets moved around the guests, holding platters of fluted champagne glasses, filled with bubbly, gold liquid.

I was vaguely aware of Daniel on my arm and his hand pushing something hard and cold into my fingers.

I looked back at him and closed my mouth as I looked down. He'd snatched me a glass of that sparkling, bubbly goodness.

"It's Asti Spumanti," he said in my ear. "The silver trays are for guests who don't like champagne. Asti is a good substitute." He smiled at me. "And your favorite."

Oh…I think I'm in love. He remembered from New Year's that

I loved Asti. Of course, he hadn't been able to enjoy any spirits in his hospital bed, but he seemed happy enough to let me enjoy them.

With cane and me in tow—my mouth still wide open in pure Southern gawking at the dresses and sparkles—Daniel led us through the tuxed and begowned people to a set of elevators.

"The main reception is in the Overlook," Daniel said as he pressed the button. "Which is on the sixth floor."

And up we went.

Man, the mouth-dropping kept right on coming as we stepped into the Overlook ballroom. Knee-to-ceiling windows made up two of the room's walls, giving a surprisingly nice view of the surrounding buildings. A baby grand sat in one corner, a man in a black suit playing softly.

Round tables covered in bright white linens dotted the floor. On each sat a foot-high arrangement of bright flowers, and in each center was a bird-of-paradise. The silverware gleamed in the more subdued light of the ballroom.

At the far end I could see a podium. There were tables and chairs there too. That was where I assumed the fun would begin and hoped we could get a seat up that far. I wondered if there was assigned seating. And it looked like there was a buffet on the far end of the room.

Yeah!

To our right was a familiar couple—only I didn't know why they were familiar, until the man waved at Daniel and as we strolled closer Daniel shook his hand. "Detective Frasier—nice to see you."

"Representative Stephens, it's been a long time."

The man shook his head. "Two months. I'm glad to see you looking much better."

"Zoë"—Daniel put his hand on my back—"this is State Representative Robert Stephens. He's March Knowles's successor in Congress."

Robert Stephens was young—young in comparison to the people gathered in this room. His hair was blond and cut fairly close to his head. Thin. His face was long, and he had more chin than cheek. He wore a simple tux like Daniel and had an odd familiarity about him that I couldn't put a finger on.

"Ah, Zoë—Martinique? Are you Nona's daughter?" Stephens put his hand out.

I blinked at him with surprise and nodded as I slipped my hand in his. His grip was warm, but not clammy. And I was sure I'd met this man before—but where? He apparently knew my mom.

Stephens's smile deepened as he read my expression. "Ah—I've known your mother a long time, Zoë. Old friends. Allow me to introduce my wife, Vanessa."

Old friends? Mom never mentioned knowing people in government.

He stepped to the side and a woman several inches shorter than me moved forward. She had black hair, cut in a harsh line along her jaw, and wore thick glasses. She was dressed in a long, midnight blue gown, with a low-scooped neck.

What caught my attention was her necklace. A silver chain hung down just above her breasts, weighted by a white, oval stone. Silver filigree woven patterns over the stone fastened it tightly to the silver backing.

It wasn't a particularly fascinating piece of jewelry. My mom had one very much like it, only with a green stone in it. On Mom it looked like the biggest, gaudiest piece of jewelry I'd ever seen. And now here was some hoity-toity uppity prune with one around her neck.

I held out my hand, but Vanessa only stared down her nose at it as if I'd put my fingers in dog poop before offering them to her. She looked over at her husband. "Robert, I want a drink."

I caught a slight shift in Robert's expression—it went blank for a second—before he nodded, and said, "Yes, dear." He looked at us. "Good to see you again, Daniel. Nice to see you, Zoë. Tell your mother hi for me." And he moved away.

Daniel shifted his feet, and I narrowed my eyes at Vanessa. She just stood there, expecting something. I smiled.

She arched her eyebrows. "Don't you speak?"

Daniel spoke up. "She's a mute, ma'am. Result of an assault."

Vanessa's expression didn't change. "Well, begone, please."

Daniel and I turned and immediately walked away.

Wow. How did Vivian put it in *Pretty Woman*? You could freeze ice on her ass? What a bitch.

Mental note: *if Daniel ever runs for office—be nice and not pruney.*

Daniel moved us closer to the window on our right far away from Vanessa Stephens. I wasn't sure why I almost hung back. It was like a part of me was abruptly afraid of everything, but I didn't know why.

I didn't see much outside—only my own reflection. And Daniel's.

That's when I noticed cameras set up about the room—which made sense if the campaign managers wanted to tape it for future use in sound bites and bits of visual inspiration.

But why was one of the men in black holding an infrared?

Damnit. This wasn't making sense. Who were these people that they would know about ghosts. Or me? And how had Maharba known? I pulled out the BlackBerry and sent Rhonda a quick text about seeing Randall.

But even as I put the phone back in my purse, my thoughts skipped back to Heather and the death mask I'd seen. I hadn't seen any death masks other than the one on her face. Which I wasn't that concerned about. Not really. She was mean. I don't like mean people.

And her death could be attributed to starvation. Or vampirism. Which reminded me—I needed Rhonda to look that up. If creatures like me existed, and like Trench-Coat, then maybe vampires did too.

With that thought came the feeling I was being watched. I turned to my right and caught Vanessa Stephens looking away. She had a martini in her hand, and Robert was close by, talking to another couple.

But why was she looking at me?

Zoinks.

I pulled Daniel away from the window, careful not to bump into people or any tables. He took my hand in his, and we moved to the center of the room before he stopped and looked down at me. "You're scared of heights? If this gets to you—don't go up to the Sun Dial."

I cast a glance back at Vanessa. She was looking at me again—only this time she didn't turn away quickly. I looked back to Daniel and signed, *"She doesn't like me."*

He smiled. "How could anyone not like you?"

"Well, now," came a male, if not somehow vaguely familiar voice, from behind me. "That's a good question, Detective Frasier."

The look on Daniel's face was less than happy as he looked past me. In fact, he looked darker than I'd ever seen him. And angry. "Hello, Sergeant Halloran. Odd seeing Vice here."

Vice? Halloran? I didn't know the second name. Not sure Daniel had ever mentioned a Halloran. Vice I knew was what the police called the drug squads. My cute cop worked in Homicide, which was murder, and this guy worked with druggies, dopeheads, and pushers.

"And who is this charming lady?"

I didn't know the name—but I did know that voice!

Daniel looked down at me and winked. I smiled and turned around, ready to charm the pants off of whoever this might be.

What I hadn't counted on was dropping my glass the moment we made eye contact. Daniel immediately bent down, leaning on his cane, and retrieved it.

I knew the eyes, the spiky black hair, the long face, and the smarmy expression.

Joe!

It was *him*! Here! The guy that'd helped me out of the morgue, gotten my body up and walking because he knew I wasn't really dead!

He was…*here*?

Rhonda and I had tried desperately to find him after that because he seemed to know what I was. And he'd disappeared. Much like I do.

Joe's expression shifted slightly, from smarmy to wary, then back to smarmy. He smiled down at me, and it was the same haughty, cocky, charming smile he'd had in the morgue. "Well, hello there. Let me say you're looking a bit better than the last time I saw you. Though I must say you look different with your clothes on."

I glared at him. He stood nearly a half foot taller than Daniel. His body was longer, wiry, though when I'd seen him last he'd been wearing a flannel shirt and jeans. His face was longer than Daniel's, his chin pointed, and his features much less masculine. His hair was dark and spike-cut just as it'd been that night I woke up dead.

I noticed his tux wasn't as nice as Daniel's, and his pants were just a tad too short. Ha! Flaw!

Never bothered at that moment to wonder *why* I was looking for flaws to begin with.

Joe looked at Daniel, then back to me. "Cat still got your tongue?"

"Zoë…" Daniel put his hand on my shoulder, but my gaze was still locked on Joe. Joe Halloran. "You know Halloran?"

I opened my mouth, then closed it. I turned and glanced at Daniel, then looked back at Joe. What—what was I going to say?

Yeah. Me speechless. It does happen on occasion. Just—more frequently lately.

"I see it has." Joe smiled. It was the same charming smile that had grated my nerves in the morgue. Jerk. "Though I admit, I liked you with no clothes." He gestured with a wave of his champagne glass. "Though this little number is very nice."

"Halloran." Daniel's voice had a certain warning edge to it. "How do you know Zoë?"

"Well, first, I met Zoë the night they thought she was dead. I was there checking on an overdose, though I see she didn't tell you." He frowned. "But if I recall the situation correctly, she wasn't really in any shape to tell anyone anything. Nasty things, drugs, aren't they?"

I started toward him with my hand ready to slap him. I did *not* take drugs and resented the insinuation. He *knew* how horrible I'd felt when I woke up. What a nightmare that was. He'd said so himself. He even said he'd given me something to make sure I'd come back to my body!

Daniel grabbed me and pulled me back to him before I *did* deck Joe—which was a nice feat seeing as how Daniel was balancing his cane, a drink, and me. "I'm sorry, but you must have Zoë confused with someone else. If you're talking about her carjacking and subsequent coma, I saw her tox screen. There were no drugs involved."

Huh? I turned and glared at Daniel. *You looked at my tox screen? You were checking up on me?* I hadn't signed my surprise and anger—I was too—well—angry.

Joe seemed a little surprised, and his expression changed when he glanced from Daniel back to me. He shoved his free hand into his pants pocket. "Really? You hadn't taken any drugs that night?"

I was happy that I'd just proven him wrong, and I had a cop to back me up. Then again, I was pissed off at Daniel because he'd felt the need to look at my blood work because he suspected I'd been on drugs.

I met Joe's gaze and shook my head. I signed, *"No drugs."*

"And you never got your voice back?"

I shook my head.

I saw his gaze flicker over me, and at that moment I was happy my velvet bolero jacket covered my arm where TC's handprint was. I wasn't really sure he hadn't seen it that night—I mean—I *was* naked. And if he did, I didn't remember.

"Halloran," Daniel said in a brisk voice. "Why are you here?"

Joe's gaze pulled away from me to Daniel, and I'd noticed the almost masked incredulousness in Joe's expression beforehand. "I'm not here officially. You?"

Daniel pursed his lips. "Me neither."

Joe smiled. Smug. "So a couple of schmoes like us are here just to schmooze?"

Daniel nodded. "You could say that."

"And our being here has nothing to do with any certain guests?"

My cop narrowed his eyes at Joe. I narrowed mine too like an echo. "Spit it out."

The Vice detective shrugged. "I'm just saying that tonight is a perfect opportunity, isn't it?"

"Opportunity for what, Halloran? It's a fund-raiser."

"Yeah, but look at this guest list. I mean, Congressman Knowles just over there, making his rounds of thanks to his constituents. Senators from several states. Even Senator Wong is here."

Daniel pursed his lips and sighed. "Halloran, you aren't here working a case are you? What? The bust at the warehouse out on forty-one?"

Joe smirked and brought his own glass up to his lips. "Heard about Holmes. Tough break, eh? I mean, him being your sponsor and all."

"Back off, Halloran."

I watched the interplay between these two and felt a little left out. I wondered what was going on and why there seemed to be this contentiousness between the two of them. And I liked even less the inquisitive looks Joe kept giving me.

I sort of hated the fact that I would now be on Joe's radar too. Wasn't sure if that was a good thing either. I mean I was happy to finally know who Joe was—but I wasn't happy to find out he was as smarmy as I remembered.

"Sorry, Frasier. I really am upset to hear about his death. Tough break—what was the haul? Maybe three boxes? Cocaine and coffee? Not really enough for a cop to lose his life. And no leads either." He shook his head. "Damn shame."

I felt Daniel tense behind me. Whatever these two were playing out was about to get violent, and I wasn't sure Joe had noticed Daniel was carrying a cane, with a steel-reinforced center.

A handsome man in an expensive tuxedo appeared at Joe's left. "Well, hello, everyone." His voice boomed out. "Thank you for coming—thank you." He patted Joe's back and shook his hand. And he shook Daniel's hand and paused. "Wait...I *know* your face. You were that brave young man that rescued that little girl several months ago—Susan Hirokumi? Your face was in all the papers, sir. I'm glad to see you survived your fight with the kidnapper."

I smiled beside him. I knew the real story. Not even Daniel did, since his memory of that had been tweaked a bit by a rogue walker named Rai. The last spirit I'd released and sent on his way.

Or perhaps I'd eaten. I really don't know which.

"And who might this lovely vision be?"

Congressman Knowles was my height, at five-foot-nine. He

had a trim frame, with dark hair just graying at the temples, giving him that Dr. Strange look. His eyes were darker than my own, and I could see just a slight olive complexion. And his teeth were Day-Glo white. Yow.

He took both of my hands in his.

The handprint on my arm immediately burned. Seared was more like it. I just knew my flesh was peeling away from my bone and would ooze out of the confines of my jacket and onto the plush carpet. The ballroom faded away as I focused on his eyes.

Dark eyes.

Empty sockets with filed, sharp teeth. Large, leather bat's wings extended from his back and curled around to point at me. I smelled something awful like rotting chicken, the kind you leave in the garbage overnight. He was talking to me, saying something, and I could hear Daniel's voice as well, but they were far away.

So far away as I drowned standing on my feet.

"—such a pleasure to meet you, Congressman Knowles, and I must say this is really some kind of shindig your people have pulled off."

Mental note: *shindig?*

I blinked. The beating of wings was gone, the texture of leather and musty scent of decay vanishing to disappear into the smell of flowers at a nearby table. I was also falling backward, figuratively and literally, into Daniel's arms. I shook my head to clear the cobwebs and saw Joe pumping the Congressman's hand and watching me, his gaze furrowed.

"Zoë?" Daniel's voice was in my ears, and I turned in his embrace to hold him. I wanted to block out whatever it was that I'd just seen. And felt. And smelled.

"Is the young woman okay?" Knowles said. "Did she faint?"

Daniel said, "Diabetic. I think her sugar's acting up."

I could have beaten him with a stick. My sugar *wasn't* the problem, and I was getting irritated with him using that as an excuse for everything. It was like men blaming everything on PMS. Did it ever occur to the weaker sex that we women sometimes were just sick of testosterone poisoning?

That—that—whatever he was—*he* was the problem. That thing masquerading as a United States congressman!

"Diabetic?" Knowles took a step closer, and I moved as far into Daniel as I could. My gut reaction was to run screaming from the room—but I figured that would be embarrassing later.

"Should I call a doctor?"

I shook my head and glared at Knowles. Joe was watching me and had a hand on Knowles's shoulder. Two very large, burly men in black suits appeared. Each wore black shades and had a little black curly wire trailing out of his ear.

One of them had an infrared camera, though they weren't looking through it at that moment.

"Is there a problem, sir?" one of them said in a voice that would have made Michael Dorn proud.

"No, not with me." He pointed at me. "But I think this lady needs a doctor. Would you find a place for her to rest?"

No, no, no, no. I felt that that was a bad idea. Knowles hadn't given any indication that he'd had the same experience when touching my hand as I'd had. Something inside of me screamed for me to get far away.

Which sucked, since this was the man Maharba wanted me to spy on—but when he was having a conversation with a prominent businessman. And if this man could gather that kind of reaction from just touching me, what was I going to see when I went Wraith?

Joe spoke up quickly. Daniel seemed torn between me and whatever it was he was supposed to be doing here. "I don't think that's necessary. Here." He reached into his pocket and took out a wrapped peppermint and handed it to me. "She just needs a little boost. No harm done."

Knowles looked skeptical, and he watched as I opened the wrapper with shaking hands and popped it into my mouth. Knowles smiled. I smiled.

I felt oily.

I wanted to be away from this man. And I wanted to spit the peppermint into Joe's face. P'tooey.

"Sir," Joe said, and Knowles tore his gaze from me. "May I have a word with you? Your boys here can come too."

Knowles nodded, then reached out to touch my arm. Daniel actually grabbed the congressman's hand and shook it, preventing him from touching me. "It's been a pleasure, sir."

Joe smiled too. "Yes, and it's nice to see you with your clothes on." He glanced back at me, still frowning, as he moved away with the congressman.

I opened my mouth. You...oh...he...argh!

Daniel moved me to a chair and pulled it out. I sat down hard and he knelt in front of me, which was an accomplishment for a man with a cane. His expression was a miasma of concern and frustration and what looked like a little bit of anger.

"Clothes on?" He looked back at Joe and then at me. "Zoë—is that the Joe you asked me to look for? The one you said was in the morgue with you? He pulled you out of the drawer?"

I took a deep breath and considered telling Daniel the truth about Joe's role in getting me out of the morgue drawer. Other than the tox admonishment, Daniel had been so good to me. And tonight I planned on spending it with him. Alone. He said he wanted me. I think he was falling in love with me.

And maybe—maybe I should tell him now, before I got myself into trouble. If he knew what I was going through, he could watch out for me.

I wouldn't be alone in this.

I signed to him, "Yes, that's the same man. Didn't know he was a cop."

I watched his face, marveled at his eyes and how deep a blue they were. He really deserved to know the truth.

A few seconds passed, but Daniel seemed to accept what I'd said—for now. There appeared to be some sort of rift between the two cops, and I didn't know the history. Obviously, Joe and Daniel knew one another.

He took my hands in his. "Listen—stay away from Joe Halloran, okay? That's the best advice I can give. The man's a nutcase. Believes in ghosts. Goes on ghost hunts and professes that he's talked to dead people." He made a very unpleasant face. "Ghosts—it's all fucking bullshit if you ask me."

7

GHOSTS were bullshit.

I hadn't expected that sort of reaction from Daniel. Especially not after everything he'd been through with me and my family. I mean—he'd obviously seen Mom and Rhonda at work that evening, after walking in on that bizarre ritual they were doing to interrogate the incubus Mitsuri. Hell—I'd been the one to save his butt when it went for him.

I moved my hands slowly. *"You don't believe in ghosts?"*

My cute cop looked at me, and a lightbulb went off in his head. He smiled, and his entire expression softened. "Babe, I believe in a lot of things. And I believe that you and your family believe in some wacky things—just look at Nona's shop." He reached out and pushed an errant hair away from my forehead. I flinched at the contact, but he didn't appear to notice. "I believe in you, and in me."

But you don't believe in ghosts.

I looked down at my left forearm and considered the mark hidden there beneath the jacket. He didn't believe in ghosts—how could he believe in me? Or what I am? If he didn't believe in spirits, then why spend so much time at my mom's store? Or with me for that matter?

I knew that wasn't a fair assessment—Daniel didn't know about me. I'd never confided in him. But still—it hurt. It was like finding a flaw in something you'd dreamed about all your life. Only to discover it wasn't—perfect.

I felt as if someone had hit me in the stomach. I needed air. I wanted to cry.

I stood, and Daniel pressed down on his cane and stood with me. I signed to him that I needed air, and he nodded. But I could see in his eyes that he understood on some level that I was upset.

But I could almost guarantee he didn't know why.

I weaved through the throng of people to the hallway outside, where there were even more people—all of them milling up from the lobby downstairs. Congressman Knowles was there, talking with a man in an Armani suit. He wasn't thin, but he wasn't fat. He sported a full black beard and from what I could see, a short black ponytail, sort of like an afterthought. His cheeks looked round beneath the facial hair, and his gaze circled the room even as Knowles spoke.

Abruptly the man's gaze rested on me as I stood near the elevator doors. Knowles looked at me as well. Both men smiled.

Shit!

I started away from the door, then stopped. I wanted to go to the bathroom—but where was it? The room was so crowded with people I was getting lost.

A little Q-tip (white-haired) lady approached me. White hair that looked like meringue on top of her head, wearing a Smurf-blue dress of sequins that might have looked okay on a prom queen. Wow. My eyes were in sparkle overload.

"Dear, do you need some help?"

Uh-oh. I don't talk. And I didn't have a pad with me. I smiled at her and signed, *"Need to lie down—feeling ill."*

To my amazement she smiled, nodded, and signed back, *"Follow me."*

Whoa! What were the odds? I found another person who knew sign language, or at least could interpret my use of it.

Lady Smurf led me through the crowds of people to the end of the hall before turning right. More doors lined the hallway, with one at the very end. A card reader glowed red in the dim light. She pulled a card from her tiny sequined purse and slid it through. The door buzzed, and a green light came on.

She opened the door and motioned for me to follow her in. A flick of the light, and we were in a small parlor. Dark burgundy carpet created a staging ground for rich, beige-gold walls, a plush white sofa, and deep wine chairs. A flat-screen television hung on the wall to the left, and the bathroom stalls and sinks were visible through an opening on the right. Everything was the same boxy style as the lobby downstairs—but with a feminine bent.

The room smelled like expensive perfume. I thought I was going to sneeze.

"This is a staff bathroom," the lady said as well as signed to me, and motioned for me to sit on the couch. "You should be comfortable here."

I smiled at her as I went to the sofa. I pulled the tiny purse from my shoulder and pulled out my testing kit and set it on a rectangular coffee table of blue marble. I'd hoped the action would sort of hint to Lady Smurf to go away.

She didn't.

I went through the motions of loading the test strip, swabbing, pricking (ow, I hate that part), and touching the strip to the blood. Five seconds.

One hundred and ninety-two.

Whoa. And I hadn't even gone Wraith yet. That wasn't a good sign—not for my physical body. Why was it so high? I was a bit woozy—but I figured that was some weird residual effect from touching Congressman Creepy.

What was most irritating about this whole facet of my condition was that I didn't really know what was going on half the time. Heh—story of my life.

She read the look on my face and signed, *"You should rest, dear. I'll check on you later."*

I watched her leave. Wow. That was friendly. Was it normal for strangers—well, hotel employees, as was evident from her keycard—to just let guests rest in staff bathrooms?

Who was I to argue? This place was secure enough to leave my body while I went after Knowles and the bearded guy—who I was assuming was the businessman mentioned in the e-mail.

After the kit was tucked away, I lay back on the sofa and tried to relax. Stepping out of body was usually pretty easy lately— whereas before I'd have to really concentrate.

I closed my eyes, took a deep breath, and pretty much shucked my mortal coil.

A whisper and a chill later and I was standing beside myself. And you know—I didn't look too bad. The dress was definitely a keeper. Even my boobs looked nice and moundy in the tight bodice. I was pale though—paler than I ever had been—especially for someone with my ethnic background.

There are two interesting things about being incorporeal. One is I seem to have control over my appearance. The first couple of times I'd gone out of body on purpose, I'd been naked, corresponding with what I'd been sleeping in—which is the buff for me.

Well, even though the general populace can't see me, there are those strange odd bits that do see naked dead people.

Subconsciously I clothed myself in whatever it was I was wearing. So here I stood in my gown, my coifed hair, and my heels. Okay, I'm losing the heels. Even being in a spiritual form does not mean I can teleport or fly. I still have to walk, run, and take the bus.

And presto chango, no more pumps. Another thought and poof—I was back in my black tights and bunny slippers, hair braided down my back.

The second interesting thing about being like this is how I *see* things. My mom used to say learning Spanish for her was hard because she didn't *think* in Spanish, she thought in English. Which, of course, at the time never made sense to me.

Until I tried to learn Spanish myself, and then it all fell together. When someone spoke in a different language, my English-speaking subconscious took the step to translate it into English before I could process it.

Does that make sense? It did to me. Still does.

But I never learned Spanish. Shame on me.

It's got to do with being in a mind-set, or seeing from that angle. I was, in a sense, a ghost, and now I saw things the way *they* saw them. Only I learned I had a sharper focus. The world was much more shadowy like this. Corners seemed to be deeper, the world taking on a more burned appearance. Sinister. And I was always sure there was something looking out at me from those dark places. Faces sometimes showed up and floated by like a hazy mist. And I heard hushed voices, whispers sometimes. The best way to describe this was the thin black smoke that drifted off a snuffed candle.

It permeated everything.

I was used to it—didn't mean I liked it. Before my brush with TC, this hadn't been how I'd seen things. No—everything changed when he changed me.

I moved out of the room and through the door. And noticed at first the absence of voices. Nothing. Not even living voices. Odd. There was also a distant pressure—like the air was changing in the building as I moved down the hallway.

People still lingered in the hallway outside of the Overlook.

I didn't see Lady Smurf as I passed by, and I stopped to think—where would I go if I needed to talk? In private?

A room. Had to be a room. And if I were a very important person and a successful businessman, what room would I take?

Even though I was invisible to everyone, I made sure not to walk through them. Doing so usually meant they felt a chill, and I got a sneak peak at what was on their mind at that moment.

No—thanks. Been there. Done that. I did not want to know if any of these hoity-toity people had skeletons in their closets—literally.

I was also very aware of where the men with the infrared cameras were. I didn't see any in the hallway, but I was sure they were in the Overlook ballroom.

I checked the directory. Hrm...there were several suites, but I figured the presidential was the best bet.

I also checked my watch. It was glowing a dull blue and counting down. I'd been incorporeal for six minutes. Whoohoo. I rode the elevator up—becoming corporeal to push the buttons—and then moved into the small foyer. Marble floor and three room doors.

Bingo! To the left, at the end of the hall, were the guards I'd seen before with Knowles, standing all brutish with their arms over their chests, glaring at each other. Well, glaring at the elevator door that just opened though nobody got off.

They weren't looking through their infrareds either. I moved past them and through the door, my gaze lingering on them for a few seconds.

Niiiiice. In a male masculine type of way.

Mental note: *testosterone—the only way to fly.*

Once upstairs there was a second of hesitation on my part. Would I encounter one of those wacko barriers like I had at Hirokumi's? I mean, they did have people with cameras downstairs.

I tested the waters to the door.

Not even a change in smell.

I sieved on through the double doors.

And the suite?

It was like walking into the living room for the Forbes Five Hundred winner.

Atlanta gleamed and sparkled through the floor-to-ceiling windows covering the farthest wall. To the left was a small, round, dark wood table with navy blue chairs. On the table sat a tray of cheeses and a bottle of wine. To the right was a sitting area, complete with wall-mounted flat-screen television. A blue sofa sat with its back against the panoramic view. To the right was a brown recliner, and to the left was a beige one. In the center sat a low, polished block of wood.

Displayed in a fan arrangement on that table were the latest issues of *Time*, *BusinessWeek*, *Forbes*, and *Atlanta Magazine*. To the right beneath the television was a half-sphere chest that reached waist high.

Beside the door was a fully stocked bar. And between the bar and the sitting area was a door into the bedroom. Wow... wonder if I could get the boyfriend up here for a night of cosplay. I could be the wealthy female entrepreneur, and he could be my chauffeur.

Heh. Hehe.

Knowles sat in the beige recliner, facing the view, a tumbler of amber liquid in his hands. The ponytail man stood at the bar. He dropped cubes into a tumbler, then poured himself a nice helping from one of the crystal decanters.

"Where is it, Francisco?" Knowles said as he stared at the windows. "It was supposed to be in that shipment. All of our operatives said they were shipping it in from Peru via Cuba. And who tipped off the police?"

"We did."

Knowles half turned in his seat. "We did? Why?"

"Because we received intel too late that L-6 was planning that raid—there was no way to reschedule or reassign. You didn't let us know."

Knowles looked irritated. "Well, they didn't tell me. I'm not always in the loop for their soldier activities. But if you knew, then why didn't we just send in our own soldiers to counterattack?"

"Because we don't work that way, March. You know that." Francisco looked harder at the ice cubes in the tumbler, as if he were looking for a bug. "We couldn't let them get ahold of it—if the information was true. They don't have any operatives with the APD. We do."

"Oh—then those officers were a part of—"

When Knowles stopped I nearly fell over from leaning toward him, waiting for the rest of the sentence. I'd been here two minutes and was already confused. L-6? What the hell was that? Operatives in the Atlanta Police Department (or APD)? Oh—wow. Daniel was gonna love this—not to mention Captain Cooper.

"*One* of them was a member." Francisco nodded, capped the decanter, and took up his tumbler. He took a heavy swig and made a face.

Ah. The face was always a sign of good scotch.

I moved closer to them and perched my invisible ass on top of the shelf below the television. Front-row seat. *Neener-nee on you, Maharba.*

"Did he find anything?" Knowles sighed and held his drink in his hand.

"She. And no, we haven't heard a word, but we know it's locked up in evidence. Which means at least one of them is safe—for the moment. There are still so many missing."

"Maybe we should go to the police—tell them what these fools are doing."

"No, certainly not," Francisco moved from the bar and strode with purpose to where Knowles lounged. "The police can't do anything about it—not to mention they'd never believe us."

"I just don't understand why they act this way—so reckless. So stupid. Someone's bound to notice their activities like this."

Standing in front of the floor-to-ceiling view, Francisco faced the Atlanta skyline. "We do know why they act this way, March—because they're insane with righteous indignation, that's why." He took another swig from his glass. Another face. Why do people drink that stuff if it tastes so bad? "They're crazy."

Knowles sat forward, his drink locked in both hands. "What exactly *are* they doing?"

"They're experimenting. Seeing what works and what doesn't. But because we don't know how they're using them, we can't stop them."

Knowles looked less than appeased. "Can't, or won't? Those rogues have been at this for over twenty years, and we've never done a damned thing about them."

"Because we didn't think they'd ever mass themselves." Francisco sighed. "Even I never believed they would. And I should be panicking more at this point. They watch us, March. They have eyes everywhere. And I suspect they have their sights on *her*."

Knowles's eyes widened. "No—they can't. They don't know about her, do they?"

Okay—I was feeling a little creeped out. Personal ego thought for a split second that *her* meant *me*. But that was stupid. These people didn't know me—well, that Robert Stephens guy sort of did, the one with the bitchy wife—but he wasn't up here in this strange little boys club meeting.

So who was *her*?

Francisco shook his glass, the ice rattling. He looked at the amber liquid. "You saw the infrareds downstairs? I'd say they know. And they've enlisted help in locating her and possibly catching her. Mrs. Stephens is a shrewd woman, and shouldn't be underestimated, March."

Mrs. Stephens? The bitchy woman? What the hell were they talking about? Was she in charge of Randall and the cameras? Arrrgh! I just wanted to wring their necks and demand they stop speaking in code!

Knowles shakily set his glass on the side table. He sat forward, clasping his hands together, but kept his gaze focused on the ground at Francisco's feet. "I noticed them. I also know the name of the young man they've indoctrinated. Very brilliant—was on television a few months back."

He put his hand to his face. He looked—frightened. "If they know about *her*—and what she's capable of—is it possible they know about me?" He looked at the dark-haired man. "It's like I'm being eaten alive, slowly, dealing with them. Smiling for the camera. Being a puppet. I'm not sure I can keep doing this anymore."

Okay—what?

Francisco finally moved and sat on the sofa table directly in front of Knowles, his back to Atlanta. "You'll be free of them tonight. I've made arrangements for that. And you can keep doing this." He smiled. "You're perfectly positioned where you're sitting as well. You'll be elected senator—of that we're sure. And I don't mean we have a crystal ball or we're buying the seat. It's just a feeling I have." He gave Knowles a weak smile—hidden beneath his beard. "We'll find out what they're up to, and we'll stop them. We have to." He shook his head as his own gaze shifted and became unfocused, as if he were looking at the future. "It's what we do."

Uh-huh. Right. Wackos.

"Oh." Francisco turned and set his tumbler on the coffee table before reaching inside his tux jacket and pulling out a small gold box. He handed it to Knowles. "A little gift from us. They might be premature, but they show you we're behind you."

Oh...looked like something kinda interesting, and I was too far away to see. I jumped down from my perch and moved to my left around the two recliners. It was easy enough to move to the left of Knowles's chair and lean over his shoulder to see what the goodie was.

The case was flat and had the initials MLK on the front.

MLK? Were they kidding me? Martin Luther King? And then I remembered this guy's name from the television ads I'd seen— March Lowell Knowles. Oh, very weird.

I watched him pop the top of the case back. Inside were very nice-looking business cards. White, with a small Georgia seal embossed on the right side. In nice black letters the title read MARCH L. KNOWLES, SENATOR, GEORGIA.

Oh, how sweet—if a bit premature. Wasn't there supposed to be another candidate for the position? Like, the *other* party?

I froze as an idea came to me. There it was—that unique thing I could get for Maharba. Francisco had already said they were a gift, and Knowles certainly wouldn't give them out before he won the election. That would make them one-of-a-kind for right now. I'd have to hide it though—not let Daniel see it.

Daniel...I briefly wondered what he was up to. Was he still schmoozing at the party, or what if he'd gone looking for me. Yikes...what if he'd started asking around and little Lady Smurf had told him where I was.

Jinkies!

If he went in there and found me now—I'd be nonresponsive. Oh, and that would just be great. He'd start giving me mouth-to-mouth—

Wait. Not a bad image there. Getting mouth-to-mouth from Detective Frasier would be nice.

Okay—get this done and get out.

So what did I learn? Exactly nothing.

These two were being vague as hell, almost as if they suspected they were, or might be, under surveillance. It all sounded like code to me. L-6? Her? Even if I didn't know what this was about, maybe Maharba would. I was over the whole cloak-'n'-dagger thing.

Now about the card—

Oooh-kay. How to do this? Knowles was looking at the cards, talking to Francisco. I'd wondered if it were possible to just make a piece of myself corporeal. Like, just my arm? So I could snitch a card.

But then what? Once I snitched it and went invisible again, the card would stay solid, and I'd drop it.

Nuts. Shit. Now what?

Knowles shook his head and snapped the case shut. "That's very flattering, Francisco." He set the case on the side table between the two recliners and took up his tumbler. "But it's too premature. We don't know anything is certain, and I'm more worried about them."

Them. *Them.* Why are *they* always called *them*? And why, even in a private conversation, do the marks (oh, I always wanted to be able to use that word) talk in code? Were they afraid someone was listening?

Mental note: *have Rhonda look up* Them.

Well, someone *was* listening. But it was *me.* But they weren't supposed to know that. It was time to motor—and the card holder was on the table in an easily accessible spot.

I knelt behind the chair and side table and positioned myself so that I could see the holder. Two deep breaths—and I thought of sex.

And nothing happened.

Mother guppy.

Sex always worked. Or at least the fantasy of it with Daniel. But I was still too irritated at Daniel to think of sex with him. But I had to think of sex with someone!

And, oddly enough, Joe Halloran came to mind. And why not? I wasn't interested in him, and I was mad at Daniel, and if I had sex with Joe in my head, Daniel might get a little jealous.

Served him right.

So I used my imagination. I could see Joe's chest in my mind and imagine myself running my fingers over it, toying with his nipples, sliding my hands down to his belly button and on to the love trail of soft brown hairs that lead to—

Foosh.

It worked, which always amazed me. Sex made me solid. Isn't that swell? Unfortunately, I was all solid, not *just* my hand. Christ.

I reached up carefully and slid the holder toward me and snatched it off the table. I listened to their talking for a second to make sure they hadn't noticed either.

"—ready for tonight?"

Knowles paused as he answered, and I assumed he'd taken a gulp out of his tumbler. I heard ice clink. I glanced at my watch. A half hour OOB.

I noticed something else on the outside of the case from my vantage point on my knees, in my fancy dress, behind the chair. Behind the MLK was a soft etching of something else. I turned it right and left under the lamplight. I couldn't really tell what it was, but I thought I could remember it if I needed to redraw it.

I opened the case and slid out a card, then closed the case carefully and had just closed it when—

"...time to start, isn't it? I'm hungry too."

I heard the two of them stand—they both made a sort of grunting noise—and I freaked for a second. I still had the case in my hand.

"March, do you have the business card case?"

Shit. I shoved the card I'd removed under the sofa, then thought of sad puppies crying.

Fwoomp (there really isn't any noise), I was invisible. I knew that because the case bounced onto the carpet from where I'd been clasping it in my hand.

There wasn't any time to move either as Knowles must've leaned over the recliner and said, "There it is, on the floor."

"I'll get that," Francisco said, and I stayed as still as I could, hoping no errant thought of sex with Daniel popped into my mind.

Things could get awkward then, couldn't they?

I closed my hand as I saw Francisco's expensive leather shoe—was that Versace?—at my right shoulder and felt him reach through my head to retrieve the—

Howling winds.

Screams.

Smoke that stung my eyes, and I blinked harder and harder.

Fire.

Heat so intense it would burn the skin from bone in seconds.

Sulfur—the aroma of rotten eggs.

Laughter.

Oh-so-familiar laughter.

The Phantasm.

And it was gone. As if someone had shut the door.

I realized I was lying on my stomach behind the recliners. Had I fainted? In Wraith form? Was that possible? I blinked several times and pushed myself up on my elbows to my knees.

Yow... and I was sore. That wasn't possible. Not when I wasn't physical.

Wait. I reached down and patted my dress. Felt the sequins. I looked down. I *was* visible!

The door to this suite was shut and the lights were turned off, the only illumination coming from the Atlanta skyline beyond the glass. I checked under the recliner. The card was still there. What the hell had just happened? And had they seen me?

Obviously not, because they left. I checked my watch.

!!! It said forty minutes out of body. Forty minutes!

It was ten minutes later than it was. Ten minutes? I lost *ten minutes?* Oh shit. The only other time I'd done that was when Trench-Coat had taken me and removed my voice.

But that'd been a wee bit more than ten minutes. Try twenty-four hours.

And there was something else too—a very familiar pain along my left arm.

I yanked up the sleeve of the jacket to expose the mark, the imprint of the Symbiont's hand. It throbbed like a raw burn, and it was darker than before, no longer a deep henna. More like fresh blood.

It had only been like this when TC was near.

Fuck, fuck, fuck.

I snatched up the card and wobbled to my feet. Whoa…solid and not very stable. With a deep breath to prevent myself from fainting, or crying, I pulled my sleeve back down and went to the door. I hoped there wasn't an alarm, but to be on the safe side, I slid the card beneath the door, went invisible, then sieved through.

Nope. Nobody there. No guards.

I punched the down button. The elevator slid open and I picked up the card and dashed in. Staying visible on the way down, I started taking in some deep breaths. The back of my mind was ordering me to calm down about the flippant way those two assholes had talked about the warehouse. About the whatever-it-was.

That whatever-it-was had cost a dear, sweet man his life.

Jerks.

Once on the sixth floor I could hear the sound of someone's voice through the doors. Amplified. Was the dinner starting? Then I heard laughter and applause.

Yep. Late to dinner again.

I nearly jumped out of the elevator and turned right toward the hallway where Lady Smurf had taken me. Luckily, there weren't any brutey men stationed along the way. They were probably all near the ballroom and down in the lobby, keeping a lookout for terrorists.

I ran up to the door, knelt, and shoved the card underneath, then went incorporeal and sieved through.

Out of habit I went solid again, lazily thinking of Joe in a less-than-compromising position—and nearly stumbled and fell onto the body of Lady Smurf lying prone on the floor just inside the room. She was on her back, her arms and legs splayed out at her sides—she kinda looked like a big, blue starfish.

And then I saw a man in a dark suit—leaning over my body—his back to me. He had something in his hand.

And there was blood on the floor. Lots of it. I didn't know where it was coming from. Until I saw the darkened part of Lady Smurf's chest.

I went incorporeal—whether from shock or self-preservation, thinking he couldn't hurt me if I were invisible—and I was only vaguely aware of the business card soaking up blood from the carpet where I had stepped on it while solid.

I took in a deep breath, ready to charge whoever it was leaning over me with one hell of a banshee wail until he turned abruptly.

Joe.

It was Joe! His entire front was covered in blood—and clutched in his left hand was a knife.

A bloody knife.

And he was staring at me. *At me!* I was invisible, I was the Wraith, and he was looking *at* me, his eyes as wide and brilliant as golf balls. He staggered where he stood, then glanced back at my body and back up at me.

Up.

He was looking *up* at me.

"You…" he said as he took a step back from my body, toward me. The knife flashed silver, a reflection from a single lamp in the back of the room.

Anger shot through me like an electric charge. I felt myself actually expand as I sneered at him. A *knife*? He killed this helpless old blue lady, and now he'd planned on stabbing me? While my body lay helpless?

What the hell *was* he?

Joe Halloran gaped openly, blinked slowly, and closed his mouth. Though he continued to look up at me in something like horrified wonder, he managed to say, "What the hell *are* you?"

8

January 25, 9:30 P.M.

ME? What the hell am *I*?

I moved around the body (did not want to step in that!) to where he stood, intent on—what? What exactly did I intend on doing to this asshole? Well—I was going to bitch-slap him for one—and luckily I could actually go solid enough to do that.

He took several steps back and was halted by the sofa to the back of his calves. I felt the charge ignite inside of me again and remembered feeling this angry only once, when I believed Trench-Coat had killed Daniel.

And I wanted to kill *him*.

Joe turned back from his glance at the sofa and looked up at me.

Why was he looking *up* at me?

Hrm...I narrowed my eyes and looked—down.

Wow...I was hovering! Ooh...and I wasn't sure I recognized my feet. My bunny slippers had red, glowing eyes. What was up with that?

"Christ, Zoë," Joe said softly, and I could see sweat bead on his forehead. "What the hell happened to you?" He looked over at the hand wielding the knife, and his expression changed from fascinated horror to that of a child who'd been caught with his hand in the cookie jar. "Oh. No, no, no—Zoë—this is not what you think." He dropped the knife and it bounced on the carpet. "Oh God, please—I was not doing what you think I was doing."

You were going to stab my body! I reached out for him.

But he ducked, moved to my left, then pointed at something behind me. "I was going after *that*!"

Oh. Yeah. Right. The old "Ooh! Look at that baby wolf!" routine. I was supposed to look away, and he'd turn tail and run. Uh-uh. I wasn't stupid. I was pissed off—and still maybe a little unsettled by what'd happened upstairs in that room—and I hate dead bodies. I mean I really don't like dead bodies.

But then there was this really, creepy, eerie, not-so-normal noise behind me. And I watched Joe's expression switch to horror.

I turned and looked at the body—and saw something... moving... *out* of it.

It wasn't the nice lady's spirit, which I was all ready to help along its way if I needed to, but something else that looked more like a thick, slippery piece of skinned chicken neck. I always remember Mom cooking those things. "They add flavor," she always said. Ew.

My sense of oogy shot into the red of doom at that instant. I didn't know what this thing was—but it wasn't normal.

Oh well, yeah, duh. And when was the last time I bumped into normal?

It wasn't breaking skin, either. It looked more like it was sieving out of her body, and I knew on one level that it wasn't something any normal living person could see. No—this was something on a different plane—and I somehow didn't think it was the astral.

No, this was from a much darker area.

It pulled itself out then and shook its body, much like a cat or dog would shake water off after a bath. It shape-shifted, and the long chicken neck morphed into a small baby with dragon-fly wings. Correction—a small *ugly* baby with charred skin and wings. Then it squared on me, and it shape-shifted again. I found myself staring at something that looked like a cross between a tadpole and an eel. It hovered, the back of its spindly tail flickering quickly, like a tadpole's tail did in the water.

What. The. Fuck.

Then it hissed at me.

I took a step back and it slid forward, over what I could only assume was its former host. I didn't think it was a Symbiont, because they didn't really look like this. They looked more like big scary cats.

Whatever it was, this had to be from the Abysmal plane. It wasn't from around Atlanta, that was for sure, unless it was the southside.

I took another step to the side, realizing too late that I'd given it an open view of my body lying motionless on the sofa.

Shit!

The thing looked at me, then at my body, and I could have sworn it smiled. The motherfucker thought it was going to dive into my body?

Oh, I don't *think* so.

But what exactly was I supposed to do to stop it? I knew I had one heck of a scream, but I hadn't been able to pull that one off since I attacked TC. Oh yeah, I was gonna try it a moment ago—I was mad enough.

Now I was just freaked-out.

The thing slithered right toward my body, gaining a quick burst of speed. Shit! If I didn't stop it, it was going leap right *into* me!

Unsure what else to do, I dove along my cord and slammed into something very hard. My teeth rattled inside my incorporeal head. I felt as if I were being wrapped up very tight with wet, thick ropes, around and around my body, pinning my arms to my sides and my legs together.

I struggled, realizing then that I had actually made it *inside* my body but not before the evil tadpole had first. I felt my physical body convulsing as the tadpole and I fought. I bit down on the coils as they neared my neck, feeling thoroughly panicked as well as relieved I really didn't taste anything in this form.

I could hear it howl in pain—not physically—but inside my head. And it tightened its hold on my body, I opened my mouth—with every intention of screaming this thing out of existence (without really giving any thought to what might happen to my physical body surrounding us)—but something slimy and as thick as a tongue wrapped around my neck and snaked its way between my lips. I gagged over and over as it inched its way into my throat, and then turned upward, into the roof of the back of my mouth.

Jesusmotherfuckingmary!

What the hell was this thing that I couldn't fight it? It was like being consumed by Trench-Coat all over again, only there weren't any pleasant parts. And I knew somehow this thing had every intention of sticking its tail (it had to be its tail, right?) upward into my brain and draining my soul, my—

No…my soul wasn't housed in my brain. It was in my solar plexus. That much I knew. It was all interconnected to my heart. It was the base of where my cord attached itself to my body.

At this thought I could feel my cord even as I gagged and tried to spit the thing out of my mouth. And I could see the cord if I opened my eyes in the black void where I was held. Glowing, silver cord, looping up and up like a lasso, spinning in the darkness until it launched itself at my mental command, lashing out with precise strokes like the lash of punishment against a mutineer.

Get. Off. Of. ME!

I could actually smell searing flesh and felt the thing tremble around me. Its hold loosened, and I pushed more and more power into my cord. I cut at the thing, sliced at it, and my cord wrapped around and around the lead piece of it like a garrote, then pinched it off.

Snip.

The thing's hold vanished and the slimy tentacle around me dissolved. I soared upward inside of my self, realizing I was near my solar plexus, an incandescent thing inside my body, but the enemy was nearer to my brain, and the brain is where control was.

I saw the end of it—saw the truncated tail move just ahead of me. I smiled to myself as I powered my ascent from my cord and gained speed on it. And in the distance, shining in the darkness, was the central nervous system of my body.

A vast, blue white miasma of spirals and circles.

I reached out, feeling my nails turn to long, dark claws as I swiped at the wounded end of the thing. I caught it, snagging its leathery skin with my claws and pulling it back to me. It screamed and fought, but I'd wounded it. Badly.

But badly enough to kill it?

The only thing I could think of doing was to get it out of my body. NOW.

I grabbed it with my other hand and pulled it down and down. We spun together and I envisioned an exit, a way out of my body, just as I did when I stepped out of it normally—like this was anything in the norm.

Abruptly something else was there with me—warm, strong, and panicked. It latched on to my left arm, and I looked down to see a human hand.

A male human hand.

What the hell? I tried to wrench it off of me, and the tadpole from hell noticed my abrupt loss of concentration. It nearly got away from me as I spun to dislodge this—hand!

But the hand tightened as well and I felt myself being yanked away. I lost my grip on the tadpole, and it disappeared.

Pissed off, I turned on this hand and grabbed *it*. I hissed and removed it from my arm, then pulled it farther inside of me.

I heard words—words that made no sense but echoed inside the darkness and rolled liked waves of the ocean on a shore. They were peaceful words. Soothing. And I felt myself relax.

No! I can't relax! There's a freak'n monster tadpole running loose in my body!

And then I was tumbling over and over. The world brightened, and I physically slammed into something very hard and went down on my butt. Ow. I lay on my side for a few seconds before opening my eyes.

Me—as in my astral body—was on the floor—staring at—me—my physical body. I blinked a few times right before my physical eyes opened. Only what stared out of my eyes wasn't me.

It wasn't even human. A red glow shone out of my pupils, and I scrambled into a sitting position. I was corporeal, and out of body. And that thing was still in there!

I watched my body move jerkily to its feet (and was impressed that my hair still looked pretty good), heard my own ankle crack as it tried to walk on the high heels and allowed my left foot to bend sideways.

Hey! That was my body it was damaging. And damage was right. It continued to move on that ankle. I jumped up with all intentions of diving back in and forcing it out—but then fell immediately back to the ground. This time it wasn't a solid thunk, but more of a float. I was shaking…time…time…

What is the time?

I looked at my watch. It'd only been an hour—but I felt as if I were closing in on those last minutes of body-soul separation anxiety that usually yanked me back along my cord.

I watched in weak frustration as my body moved around dead Lady Smurf, then out of the door.

I managed to stand, with the full intention of going after it.

I'd had my body possessed once before by a rogue Traveler—and the experience hadn't been pleasant. My astral form had grown weak, and Mom had had this wonderful idea of shoving me into an ancient stone dragon statue to "recharge my astral battery."

Fuck that. Last thing I needed was for Nona Martinique to think she could just store her daughter in inanimate objects, then put her on the shelf to dust!

But even as I started off to the door a voice called out.

"Wait—it won't work."

Who—

I turned and saw Joe Halloran. He was picking himself up off of the floor. He looked a little shaky and his tuxedo was disheveled. There was a dark mark on the left side of his head.

Had he fainted?

"Look," he said as he stood and dusted himself off. "No thanks are needed—I was just doing my civic duty—helping out a fellow—whatever it is you are. But that's two you owe me." He put a hand to the odd mark on his head, and that's when I noticed it was bloody.

I stared at him. What the hell was he talking about?

And then I saw he was cradling his hand, and I recognized it.

Him. It had been *his* hand I'd seen on my arm.

I pointed at him, and my index finger crackled with arcs of electricity.

Wow—that was new.

Joe took a step back. "Whoa—wait. It looked like whatever you were doing in there was painful, and I needed to get one of you out." He frowned. "Of course, I'd wanted to get the Daimon out, but somehow I got you instead."

I took a wobbly step toward him. Then it was my turn to frown. Day-mon? He thought that was a Day-mon?

Blink. What the hell was a Day-mon?

The door to the lounge abruptly cracked open, and several uniformed policemen barged in, guns drawn.

"Freeze!"

"Hold it right there!"

"Don't move!"

I took a step back as well, unsure if I was actually visible or not.

Joe put up his hands. "Wait—I'm a cop. Can I get my badge out?"

"Don't move!" one of them shouted again and gingerly stepped over the body to Joe. He moved right past me and grabbed Joe's shoulder and began a pat-down. He found a gun in a shoulder holster and removed it, then reached inside Joe's jacket and pulled out his badge.

He nodded to the others just as Daniel appeared in the doorway, along with his boss, Captain Kenneth Cooper. The other two uniforms stepped aside as Daniel and Cooper stepped in, both careful not to disturb the scene.

Me? I just stood there. I wasn't sure what the hell was going on. How had Captain Cooper gotten there so fast? Or was he already here to begin with? And how had they known there was trouble in the staff lounge on the sixth floor?

Cameras?

Mental note: *oh good God, I hope not.*

Cooper pulled a latex glove from his pocket, as did Daniel. What—did these guys just keep spares on them at all times? Geez. Cooper moved to the right side of the body before kneeling.

After making a grunt, he reached into his pocket again, pulled out a pair of tweezers, and picked up the card I'd dropped.

Oops.

With a frown he handed it to Daniel, who took it by taking the tweezers, never touching the card itself. "Well—that's awfully confident of him—to have cards printed ahead of schedule."

"And stupid for him to leave one at the scene of a murder." Cooper stood. "I guess this is his new calling card."

Whoa. Wait! That card wasn't supposed to be here! I dropped

it. Damn. Oh no—they were going to think Knowles had something to do with this.

Daniel continued to stare at the business card. He raised his
head and looked at Cooper through his glasses. *Damn, he looked
really good in that tuxedo even if I was irritated at him.*

"We need to get her identified." Captain Cooper motioned to
one of the uniformed officers. "Has the bus arrived yet?"

*I figured by bus he meant either the hearse or the ambulance
for the dead body.*

"They're just pulling up now, sir."

"What do we do with him?" asked the officer standing guard
beside Joe. "He's Vice."

"Well, Detective Halloran," Captain Cooper said slowly.
"Care to tell me what the hell happened here?" He pointed to Joe's
head. "Did someone strike you?"

Daniel moved suddenly at that moment, nearly diving to the
side sofa as he reached down into the shadow. He came up with my
little sequined purse in his hand. Well, not really my little purse. But
Heather's. "This is Zoë's." His eyes widened. "She came in here?"

Uh-oh. This was getting worse. My body was out there somewhere on what had to be a busted ankle with a—a—a something
piloting it, the guest of honor's business card just turned up next to
a dead body, and now Daniel was probably going to try and interrogate Joe instead of looking for me!

I wanted to hit something. I checked my watch instead.
Hrm…five hours out was pushing it for me, but I'd been out
seventy-three minutes. Just *under* four hours left. That is—if I
hadn't already sucked it up fighting that—thing. But I was going to
need my solid form just to get a cab.

Uh—and then go where? I had no idea where my body had run
off to. I didn't even know what had ahold of it.

Joe was looking at me, his face twisted in what I hoped was a
plan. "She was why I was in here."

Oh? I couldn't wait to hear this. *As I recall you were holding a knife over my body.*

"You saw her in here?" Daniel was looking a bit frayed.

But Joe appeared to be puzzling something out in his head. He could see me, so that marked him as someone to stick by at the moment—even if he had been attempting to kill me.

The Vice detective pointed to the dead blue starfish. "She—she came in here, and I was watching. So I stepped in and—" He actually looked at me. "And there was this guy in here standing over Zoë, so I fought him, he hit me, stabbed the old lady, and took off with Zoë."

I held up my right hand and made it talk like a hand puppet. I mouthed the words "lame, lame, lame." I then pointed at him, made the psycho-stabbing-in-the-shower motion, then pointed at me.

To my surprise, his eyes widened and he looked really defensive—and a little hurt. He shook his head, his dark eyebrows making a unibrow over his eyes.

"Joe, you saw him take off with her? Was she hurt?"

Aw. I smiled at my cop. He really cared, didn't he? Too bad he didn't believe in ghosts.

'Cause his girlfriend was STANDING RIGHT IN FRONT OF HIM!

A uniformed officer stepped inside the room. "Captain Cooper, the bag's here, and there are several witnesses outside that say they saw a tall, Spanish-looking woman in a dark dress stumbling out of the front doors just a little while ago."

Spanish?

"She was stumbling?" Daniel moved closer to the body. "Did anyone see a man?" He turned to Joe. "What did he look like?"

"Tall and dark." Joe was still looking at me. He pursed his lips and turned to Captain Cooper. "Sir—might I suggest we let the boys in here to investigate the scene?"

"You're right, Halloran." Cooper ushered everyone out.

I waited until the only one left was the dead body. I had to think. Think. Think. I also needed to get the business card back as it was my only proof to Maharba that I'd been here, besides the weirdo conversation the two had had.

But my first priority had to be my body. If I lost it, or something severed my cord, what happened then?

Standing in the middle of the ladies' lounge with a body, I looked down to see my cord. I had to concentrate sometimes to see it, and I figured that was because seeing it all the time might actually be a little annoying—kinda like being an underwater deep-sea diver and being constantly reminded about that lifeline to air.

It looked exactly as it did in the stories I'd always heard. A silver cord. Only it had a faint silverfish glow to it, incandescent in the semidarkness of the lounge.

It wouldn't hurt to try to get back to my body.

I felt the tug and the room blurred as I was yanked back—and then abruptly bounced right back out on my ass. Oddly enough I'd learned when that happened I ended back at the starting point, and not somewhere in the vicinity of my body. Which would seem to make more sense to me—but I wasn't the creator of this whacked-out universe.

After getting back to my incorporeal feet, I moved past the new guys in the room, all dressed in blue jackets with APD in white vinyl across their backs, and into the hallway.

More people milling about. Yellow tape with the black words POLICE LINE DO NOT CROSS stenciled over and over again. I moved through it and looked about the hallway. I could just see Daniel, Joe, Cooper, and several old men in suits.

Moving carefully through the plainclothes detectives as they interviewed party-dressed guests, I managed to get closer. Close enough for me to see Joe, and for him to see me. He had a white cloth to his head, and I saw blood on it and felt a little guilty. I did wonder where he'd gotten the bump and hoped I didn't have anything to do with it.

I spotted Randall and two of the other infrared men in suits nearby. I kept myself hidden behind other people—which defeated the whole freak'n fun of being OOB. Unless those little cameras could see through people, I should keep invisible.

Joe narrowed his eyes at me and made a quick gesture with his head like a nod in the general direction of the elevators. I nodded and followed him through the police barricade that was keeping all the guests in one area, then onto the elevator.

The trip down wasn't long, and Joe kept his attention on the floor. He looked bad. Dark circles hung beneath his eyes. Had him pulling me out of my body done that to him?

Joe made a straight line through the lobby to the front doors, flashing his badge to the officers standing guard. I followed him like glue and out the door to the concrete beyond.

Lots of traffic. Flashing lights too. Red, white, and blue. An ambulance was here as well—and I assumed they'd taken the gurney upstairs to Lady Smurf.

Joe moved away from me to a group of uniformed officers. Cooper came out of the door then and yelled at him. Joe nodded to him and listened intently while Cooper berated him about something. I was very glad he wasn't my boss. No sense of humor.

Daniel hobbled out of the doors then, walking a little slower than he had been. He looked really pale—and I was afraid he was going to collapse. This was too much for him. And I felt really bad for having been irritated with him. He saw Joe and Cooper and walked to them, moving his fingers through his beautiful hair with his free hand as he moved.

I moved away from it all, my thoughts a jumbled mess. Officers walked in and out of the Westin as news trucks and their little newspeople gathered around. I didn't see Heather Noir. Didn't care to either.

Joe moved away from the little cluster to the right and back toward me. He'd actually hung his badge around his neck and his tux bow tie lay flat and unfastened over his shoulders. The top button was open, and I could just see wisps of hair peeking over the starched white collar.

Ew. Hairy chest. In my honest opinion, hairy chests were not sexy. Grass shouldn't grow on a playground.

He moved past me, and muttered, "Come on," before stepping outside the line of officers toward several of the parked and blinking marked cars.

Once we were out of sight he looked at me and held up his hands. I noticed the cut on his temple had stopped bleeding, but it looked like it hurt. His spiky black hair was a bit mussed with blood in that area too. He looked from his left to his right, and in a lower voice said, "I did not try and stab you."

I opened my mouth to say, "Oh yes, you did," and then closed it. I signed it instead.

To my utter surprise he signed back as well as spoke, "No, I didn't."

Wow. I was impressed. A little.

I signed, *"I can hear you."*

"Look, I'm telling the truth about not trying to stab you. I was watching the hallway when I saw the old lady direct you in there—and then I watched your—whatever it is you are—come back out through the door into the elevator. I figured you were doing a bit of sneaking about, and I was about to head up there myself"—he paused—"but I got pulled into a conversation about ghosts with some guy named Harcourt. A while later I saw the blue lady come back out of the ballroom and go back into the room, only I thought I saw something else—kinda overshadowing her."

Overshadowing? I shook my head and arched my eyebrows high.

He put his right hand behind his neck and pulled forward in

a stretch. "Look—I can see things—okay? Spirits, ghosts, astral walkers—like I thought you were that night we first met. And I thought I saw something around her that just felt—oh—for lack of a better word—oogy."

Hey...that's *my* word.

"So I waited a beat and followed her in. I saw her standing over you with a knife and jumped in when I thought she was going to stab you. We fought—and that's when I knew there was something else there because that old broad was strong—and then I stabbed her. I really didn't know I'd hit her heart."

I nodded slowly. I could sense he at least believed he was telling the truth. And a small part of me that liked him (ugh!) was beginning to believe him.

"I'd just stepped over to see if you were still breathing when you walked in." He frowned. "Which is still bugging the hell out of me, because you looked as living standing there as you did lying there. And right now"—he stopped and sighed before moving his hand from his neck and shrugging—"you look like a ghost."

I nodded and signed, *"Right now I am a ghost. Spectral entity. Astral projection. Pick one. But something more important is getting my body back."*

He pursed his lips. "So—is this like an occupational hazard? Getting your body hijacked like this?"

I wanted to whack his face. But that wouldn't do because I needed him. And it did seem like this was becoming more of a problem. Twice now something had climbed inside of my body and run off with it, and left me out in the cold to—

And an awkward, really wacko idea came to my head.

Could *I* climb inside of someone *else's* body?

I looked up to see Randall and those men step outside the hotel, focusing their cameras on the street. Shit!

Well, it was time to put my question to the test.

I narrowed my eyes at Joe. He wasn't my first choice—not really even my type. Too rugged-looking. I mean, he was cute and all, but my heart was set on my beautiful cop. He was purdy.

I took a step toward him.

Mr. Halloran appeared also to possess the ability to read minds. His eyes widened, and I noticed they were green. He put up both hands. "Now wait just a minute…I don't think—"

That's right. Don't think.

Do!

I took two running steps and jumped in, pretty much the same way I jumped into my own body.

I hit another solid wall, and the lights went out for me, as well as for Joe Halloran.

9

January 25, 9:48 P.M.

I woke suffocating, pushing my way through something solid, but it turned to caramel when I touched it. And it smelled like—

Old Spice?

Abruptly the struggle ended, and I tumbled end over end into a dark room. I lay on my back. I was barefoot again. Yay. And very tired.

I felt someone smack me on the side of the cheek, but the voice that answered out to stop the roughness wasn't mine. It was deep, and it rumbled inside of my head.

"Hey, Halloran—you okay?"

That was Captain Cooper's voice. And I was a little taken by the almost-kind tone to it—Cooper never spoke to me with nice things to say. Might be because he thinks I'm a whack job.

Who could blame him?

But I think I even heard Officer Mastiff somewhere in mix. There was laughter too.

"Did you see that? He was just standing there, then boom—went down like a house of cards."

Uh-oh. What was going on? I was in darkness, but I could *hear* people. It was like listening with my eyes closed inside of a theater. I could smell too—which was odd because until then when I was incorporeal, smell wasn't an issue. Neither was temperature, yet whatever I was lying on was like a slab of ice beneath me.

Light flooded my dark room, and I could suddenly see faces, all hovering in a circle around me. Captain Cooper, Mastiff, two guys I'd never seen in my life, and just past them was Daniel's concerned expression.

Oh, baby...you look pale.

"Oh God," came the deep voice from my throat again. "Would you all just get out of my face?"

That was Joe's voice!

Wait—I did it! I was *inside* of him. I'd actually made it *inside* another living being.

Hold the phone.

Was this a good thing? And could I actually get back out?

"I sure as hell hope you can," came Joe's voice from the outside. "'Cause you're loud as hell in there."

"What?" Captain Cooper said. "What'd you say?"

"Nothing." Joe sat up, and I could actually feel him moving, almost like I was doing it myself. It was like I was experiencing his body, just not in control of it. It was more like a ride at Disney. One of those weird kinda simulators. I was in a dark room with a screen in front of me and invisible speakers in the darkness. I sensed motion, smells, sounds, and feelings. I was inside of Joe, but I was still myself.

Sah—WEET.

"Halloran, maybe you should let the doctor take a better look at that bump," Daniel was saying nearby. "You just went down really hard."

Joe put a hand to my—his—right temple, and I could feel his finger gingerly touching a tender spot there. Ouch. "No, no. I'm fine."

But I was looking at Daniel. If anyone looked bad, he did. His face looked drawn, and I wondered if he'd taken his medication.

Keep holding the phone. At the salon he'd insisted on driving, and then he'd driven here. If he'd been taking his meds, there was no way he could have done that.

Ah! That rat! He hadn't been taking his pills! No wonder he looked like hell. What was it with men and their macho-stupid need to prove they were strong?

Stupid, stupid, stupid.

I didn't know if Joe was just tired, or unprepared, but apparently I could exert will over my host's body if I wanted to. Without really thinking about it, I reached out—or rather Joe reached out—and put my hand gently on Daniel's cheek.

Daniel's eyes widened at about the same time Joe did a huge mental "Ew." He seized control and snatched his hand away. DON'T DO THAT came the echoing thought of Joe Halloran.

Whups.

"Uh," Joe said.

"Right." Daniel moved away. In fact, he moved a great distance away from Joe.

Daniel!

"Would you just get over it," Joe mumbled. "You act like you've never poked a guy before."

I—I really wasn't sure how to answer that.

Joe was talking out loud. "Maybe I just need to get home."

"I'll have someone drive you," Cooper said.

"I'm fine, Captain. Really." He waved at them and finally pushed himself into a straight, if wobbly standing position. I tried to right him, looking for the pedals and joysticks to keep this ride in balance.

"Let *me* have control, damnit," Joe muttered under his breath.

And I realized he was talking to me.

Can you hear me when I'm just thinking?

He didn't answer, but I got the overwhelming feeling he did and that he was *not* happy.

Whups.

"I'll just move down here and make sure I'm okay." I could feel Joe smiling, and I could almost imagine his smugness from the other side.

The captain looked skeptical until another uniformed man came up and handed him a cell phone. Cooper put it his ear, and said, "Go ahead."

I didn't like the look of his face, and he frowned harder at me. Uh, Joe—he frowned at Joe. He moved the phone away from his chin. "Are you sure there was an assailant with her? She wasn't by herself?"

"Oh, I'm sure she wasn't alone." And that wasn't a lie. He put both hands to his bruised head.

"Walters in zone three just got a report of a crazy hot Puerto Rican woman in a black dress hobbling into his store spitting gibberish at him."

Spitting gibberish? Wait…did that mean that thing had a voice while it was in my body, and I didn't? Damn. I was beginning to think maybe Dr. Maddox was right, and it was all in my mind.

And who's he calling crazy? Do I look Puerto Rican? I didn't think I looked Puerto Rican. Somebody else thought I looked Spanish. Hrm. But he did call me hot.

Captain Cooper turned away and continued his phone conversation. The others did too, and Joe moved slowly and evenly in the other direction. The wind whipped up a little as he moved, and I was abruptly very—cold. Geez…weren't manly men supposed to have a built-in heater to keep damsels in distress warm? This guy was freak'n freezing.

And for crying out loud! The rumbling from his stomach was causing my own Ethereal one to knot up. When was the last time he'd eaten? And what is with this itch in my—

"Would you please either shut up"—he stopped in his tracks and shouted out to people as they huddled by in their winter coats and gave the crazy, bleeding man in a tuxedo a wide berth on the sidewalk—"or get the hell out?"

You can hear me even when I'm just thinking?

"Of course I can hear you. You're like a little scratchy-sounding conscious thought that never shuts up! Now get—*out*!"

The darkness rumbled around me, and I could see through his eyes. He was standing several feet from the area of action, away from the black-and-white cars.

No! I need my body back, and you have to take me to it.

"I'm not sure that was you he was talking about."

Do you know of any other Puerto Rican hottie in a black dress right now?

He swore under his breath and stopped in front of a pickup truck.

How did I just *know* he'd have a truck? Aw geez... and it had a cowcatcher bolted onto the front.

Redneck.

"I am not a redneck. This is a practical vehicle."

A country boy can survive!

He pulled his keys from his pants pocket. "Stop it! You're so damned loud. I kinda like you mute at this point."

I pouted.

He paused, the key inserted into the lock. "Is that your voice? That sort of sexy, scratchy noise?"

It was all good, till he called me a noise.

The door thunked like a tin can. The seat was one of those bench kind—went from driver's door to passenger's door. Wasn't much inside. No empty crushed beer cans. No bags of leftover fast food. And no gun rack. He started the engine, and I was amazed at the vibration that reached some of Joe's more private parts.

Hrm... I wonder if I could feel that if I tried to—

"Stop that—you know that might be considered rape."

As we moved slowly out of the parking lot, Joe flashing his badge to the barricade of APD at the entrance, I felt a yank on my cord.

"Whoa...what was that?"

You feel that?

"Yeah...like someone just pulled at my belly button."

I wondered if he had an innie or an outtie.

"I have an innie."

Mental note: *careful—he can hear everything!*

Follow the tug. It should lead us to my body.

"And what happens once we get there? You gonna try and kick out the Daimon again?"

Why do you call it that?

"Because that's what it is."

You don't know that.

"Yes, I do. I've been at this longer than you have."

Been at what?

Another tug, and this one was much more urgent. The streets were slick and reflected back the streetlights. I could just see the drizzle of rain in the lamplights, see it bounce off the windshield as Joe made a left, then a right. There wasn't much traffic for a Friday night, and that was nice. Everyone was probably already in their clubs, enjoying their blinky lights, tasty beverages, and loud music.

Me? I was stuck inside a cop. *Maybe you could heebee-jeebee it out the way you did me.*

"That was an accident. I told you." He made a quick right as we both felt the tug and passed by the store where the report had come from. I had completely lost track of where we were—but it couldn't be far from the Westin. "I thought I had ahold of it, not you."

Care to tell me how you did that?

"Care to tell me what the hell you are?"

Actually, I wasn't in the mood for anything at the moment but getting my body back.

The tug grew stronger as we approached one of the less-populated areas. It looked like a deserted apartment building, only a few dimmed lights from inside told me that people actually still lived there.

The tug became more physical, and Joe stopped the truck. He got out, and we moved to the front beside the cowcatcher and waited. The tug came from the right, under a blinking and buzzing streetlamp. The smell from a stack of cans nearby was overwhelming.

Tug.

Ahhhh!

That last tug actually smarted, and I didn't understand what was happening. Why was it tugging like this? And why was it now starting to—hurt.

"Zoë?" Joe started running in the right direction of the pull, straight into a half-lit alley.

Something moved toward the back. It looked like it was struggling as it popped up, then fell down again, crashing into cans and kicking up more garbage.

"I think that's your body."

I knew it was, and the closer we got, the harder the tug. I felt myself lifted out of my little theater home inside of Joe, and with a blur of lights and sound, I was outside of him, rolling on the ground in a half-corporeal and half-noncorporeal fashion.

And I noticed my ankle was on fire. As was my stomach. I hunched over double.

Joe was beside me, and his hands didn't pass through me. "Zoë? What's happening? Why are you solid over here? Your body's over there!"

I had no idea. This whole Wraith thing was new to me, and I hadn't found the PDF manual yet. Life through trapdoors.

I heard a low moan and a small curse. Male voice. Not mine. There was someone else in that alley where my body was tripping up and down. I managed to stand, and the two of us ran into the alley, to its end.

My body was there, standing on two perfectly good ankles (*WTF?*) and had some poor wino pinned into a corner, his back against a brick wall, his eyes wide. My body was spitting and hissing at him as a fire crackled inside a metal drum to the right, illuminating the scene.

When Joe and I approached, my body turned and did the same rude noises at us.

Oh no...this was not the way it was going to be. That was my body—and look at my dress! Where were my shoes?

I got mad.

I liked those shoes!

Really mad.

And when it turned its back on me to face the prey in the corner, I started running at it and did a nosedive back inside.

Whether it was sheer force of will or just plan old velocity, I knocked into that thing inside of me, and we both sailed right through and out the other side. My body collapsed behind us.

I rolled and came up on my feet.

The wormlike creature rolled like a ball of yarn against the wall beside the wino, who took one look at it and fainted dead away.

Well, I couldn't really blame him. I mean...it looked like a huge slug at this point. It wasn't the same color or shape it'd been in that lounge. In fact—it looked a little aged.

The color was black now, and it was withered much like an apple head. It straightened up and turned to face me. I stood my ground and straightened, ready and hoping to scream it into a million pieces, waiting for it to charge at me.

But it didn't. It turned and dove into the wino.

I cursed as I ran to the wino, but stopped as his eyes popped open, and he scrambled up on his feet. He squinted at me and cackled, the light from the fire exposing his ragged teeth. "Wraith! I was right... you're the Wraith!"

I became corporeal and moved to stand in front of him and pointed. *Demon! I was right... you're a demon.* I then put both hands in the air and shrugged. *Oh, this isn't really a fun game, is it?*

He snarled at me. "I will not let this body go. You will not stop us."

Stop us? Are there more of you in there?

He launched at me for his answer. I wasn't really paying attention, and he managed to clip my left side, shoving me to the right and into the metal barrel. The metal was hot, and I gave a mental howl as my right hand made contact with it, as did my right shoulder and then my back. It tipped over, spilling burning refuse into the alley. Several pieces of garbage caught fire, and the flames spread along the back wall.

In the direction of my limp body.

Gah!

I rolled up on my knees as the wino/demon came at me again, charging like a mad bull. I moved out of his way, but then went incorporeal as he passed, and I reached inside of him. My fingers grabbed hold of the demon's form. It was a lot like grabbing hold of a thrashing alligator in the water. It yanked me in, and I pulled part of it out—an Ethereal tug-of-war with the wino caught in the middle. I tried to dig my noncorporeal feet into the slick, refuse-strewn concrete, but the demon seemed to be latched on to something inside the wino.

"Zoë," Joe called out behind me. "Your body!"

I glanced to my left and saw the fire getting a bit too close.

I also heard the distant whine of sirens. Someone had probably called the fire department.

The thing tried to pull itself back into the body of the wino, who was now on his knees, facing the fire and the wall, his hands in the air as I pulled the worm out of his body.

Only that wasn't the only thing I yanked out. When the tension gave and I landed back on my butt I saw that the demon had a new set of front pincers like a scarab, and he'd latched those beauties into the soft, glowing image of the wino. The body had fallen forward on its face, unmoving, its soul separated.

No!

I stood and grabbed at the wino's soul with the intention of putting it back in its body. But whether the spirit had already released from his cord, or whether the demon had done it for him, the man's soul was free.

And the moment my hand touched the gossamer spirit, it dissolved in my grasp, and I felt its energy sieve through my gathered fist and travel along my arm and into my body. My back arched as that same euphoria I'd experienced in the hospital traveled along my arms and legs, whirled and bubbled inside my chest and heart.

I was on my knees, half-corporeal, half-spirit.

And completely Wraith.

I tilted my head back and let out a scream. It wasn't a physical scream, nothing that could have been heard by the human ear. But the sound traveled through each of the planes, to the Ethereal and the Abysmal, and I knew on some level that what had just happened wasn't bad. But it wasn't—moral.

I was somehow strengthened again.

And I was powerful.

And I felt...invincible.

Slowly the initial high dissipated, and I took in a deep, astral breath. It was more symbolic than needed, and I lowered my head and opened my eyes.

I stood up in the center of the fire. It'd moved around the back of the alley and was now consuming everything in its path. I looked for my body but couldn't see it. I moved through the flames, back toward the alley's opening, and saw Joe placing something on the ground.

Relief washed over me and I glided to him on waves of power.

His eyes were the size of golf balls and I could see their whites as he looked *up* at me. His skin had changed to the color of pale bones baked on a desert plain. He stood and took a step back as I blinked at him.

I could see a faint glow around him. Something I'd not noticed before. It was there, a nice haze of yellow surrounding the edges of his physical body, then it was gone.

I felt myself lower, based on the way Joe's own eyes tracked my movement. He looked—delicious.

"What…?" he said, and his voice was rough. He looked like a man about to bolt into a run for his life but too rooted to the ground in fear to move. "What the fuck *are* you?"

I *felt* the earth beneath my feet, and I *heard* the sky above me. I could see the shadows of the astral realm bend and move, and sensed the small entities bound by the Abysmal and Ethereal planes. All of them—all of them watched me. And they bowed down.

The wind blew through the alley and moved the man's hair and jacket. I reached out, my hand little more than a sooty shadow against the night's satin, and touched his cheek.

He lurched, his eyes rolling back into his head, and I caught him as he crumpled forward into my arms. I could feel his energy, taste the life of his soul. It was strong—and flavored with the power of my home.

Joe Halloran had touched the Abysmal.

And in a voice I barely recognized I spoke to the darkness. "I am Wraith."

10

I don't know how long I stood in the alley, beside my limp body, as well as Joe's unmoving form, listening to the sounds of life around me. A small part of what I was becoming listened. Watched. And leeched.

It fed slowly from the man's body. Though I knew on some level that I was going to make him sick.

But when the euphoria died away, and I'm sure my Day-Glo presence dimmed as well, I started to shake. And with some effort on my part, I slowly became simply me.

Zoë.

Ex–retail salesperson.

I saw Joe stir, pushing himself up on his palms. I watched him and listened to him grunt. Joe said in a very small voice, "Are you done with the theatrics?"

I nodded. Spoke to him in my thoughts. *Yes.*

The wind that had kicked up seconds earlier vanished entirely, leaving an eerie silence in its wake. He managed to stand again and face me. Joe's fear was palpable in the air. I could almost taste it.

And what scared me most was that I liked it.

Panic set in for me then, and I shrank back. I felt like Dr. Bruce Banner—the Hulk had just taken over my spirit—and it was powerful and primordial. Base. Elemental.

But now it was gone, and I was back. And I wasn't powerful, or primordial. I was just me. And me was getting very scared. I moved to my body and looked it over. As a Wraith I could see in the dark. In fact, I could see a lot of things in the dark. And most of them were hovering nearby, insubstantial things like wispy smoke that skittered back and forth. And there were always the small, tiny voices.

I wondered if wacko serial killers who claimed they heard voices were hearing the same thing. No wonder they were nuts.

My body lay on my right side, the dress wet and caked with mud along the hem. The soles of my feet were dark as were the tops.

I was wet, and covered in dirt along my arms, neck, and face.

I felt Joe kneel on the opposite side of my body before I looked up to see him. He looked bad. Pale. Large dark half-moons hung beneath his eyes, and I could see the hollows of his cheeks on his thin face. He was watching me the spooky spook even as he reached out and started carefully feeling along my body.

Is anything broken? I asked in my thoughts. I didn't sign the question—I was too tired to sign. Too muddled in my head. But I was vaguely aware I'd actually spoken minutes earlier. Which definitely brought to mind a big whopping question: why? And why couldn't I now? And did it have something to do with the dead bum's soul?

Okay, so that was several questions.

I don't know why I'd asked him about my body as if I were talking to another ghost. He couldn't hear me, not unless I stepped back into his body.

Joe looked a little frazzled and lowered his gaze to look at me.

He gently turned my head and I caught sight of a sweet knock to the left side of my face. There was blood. My blood.

And even as a Wraith I was still me. And me felt very, very ill in her stomach at the sight of my own blood.

"I can't tell if bones are broken. Looks like a nasty hit to the head, though I have no idea how you—it—got it. Might have fallen and hit it." He moved his hands away from me and looked at me the Wraith with wide eyes. "The cops are going to need a description of your kidnapper."

Oh…hell. That was right. They thought of it as a physical being, not as the wormy, nasty Abysmal thing it really had been. I shook my head and shrugged, thinking, *I'll just make it up.*

"Yeah…or be really vague."

That's when I noticed he'd actually answered me. I narrowed my eyes at him. To my surprise he scooted a bit back from me, my body between us, his expression fearful. *You can hear me?*

He nodded quickly. "Noticed that. Sort of like you're still inside my head—speaking of which"—the Vice detective abruptly developed a little bravado and held up his right index finger at me—"I want a promise you'll *never* do that again without express permission."

I think it was at that moment I realized I'd totally freaked Joe Halloran out. Which in itself was cool. He wasn't so cocky right now, not like he'd been that night in the morgue, or earlier at the Westin. I liked this. Not so tough, was he?

I promise. I frowned as I cocked my head to my left shoulder and heard the sounds of sirens. *They're nearly here.*

"Yeah—so—you'd better do what it is you do to get back in there." He nodded at my body, then looked at it. Again his expression changed on his long face and winced. "Man—it looks like it might be painful. I called in for an ambulance. You have to make it look good—play the victim."

I was the victim.

"So was that little blue lady." He put a hand to his head and ran fingers through his thick spiky hair. "I don't have a fucking clue what just happened here—but I intend on you telling me later. Like what happened to the Daimon?"

I shook my head. I didn't sense it. Hadn't sensed it since the instant I took the wino's soul. *I have no idea.*

"Well, I think we'd better find out."

For someone who'd just had a woman's disembodied spirit jump inside of his head and then, in essence, kill a strange wino in a back alley as well as devour its soul, then had that same thing give him the equivalent of an Ethereal shock, Detective Halloran was taking all of this in good form.

The sirens were right around the corner. I could see the reflections of their lights against the walls at the alley's entrance.

I needed to get back into my body, though I was also a little afraid to. I mean—this nasty wormy creature had just been in there. Had he left it a mess?

I sieved back in with a sigh, which quickly became a moan as I sucked in air. I was conscious inside my body, barely, and a million little hurts all assailed my senses at the same time, making it one big OW!

My head was the worst, and I didn't want to open my eyes. I could hear a car door through the darkness, and voices. I could make out moving lights through my closed lids and assumed those were flashlights.

I shivered in the cold, though the heat from the fire was nice, even if the smell wasn't.

"Zoë!"

Daniel!

I wanted to call out to him and reach up, open my eyes and smile. But those parts weren't working real well. In fact, the whole process of trying to wake up was sluggish. I did manage to open my eyes. But I was blinking constantly trying to clear my head.

Hands touched me all over as I was told to relax and lie back. Someone opened up my eyelids and shined a really bright fucking light in them. Yow! I tried to move my head away, but the mean people weren't going to let me.

I was touched and prodded. And there was a melodic male voice over me, telling me to take deep breaths and try to relax. Relax? Are you freak'n kidding me? My body was banged to hell and all because of some worm creature.

Oh God. My life. What a shit.

"How is she?" I knew that voice. It was Captain Cooper.

The melodic voice answered even as I felt a sting along my left wrist. "Banged up pretty bad. Cuts and bruises like the perp slapped her around, which would be consistent with her fighting him. I think it's the blow to her head that's slowed her reflexes."

No, it's the aftermath of a demon possession. *Gah—don't you people know anything?*

"Ma'am." Daniel knelt close beside me as my vision focused, and I could see him. Damn, he looked terrible. His bow tie was gone, and his white shirt was open. I reached up and saw the IV taped to the back of my wrist. (When did that get there? Geez, but these people were quick with the needles.) But he wasn't talking to me—though he might be looking at me, he had said it to the EMT, then reached out for her badge. "Chris. This lady's diabetic."

"Thanks for the warning, Detective. Though she should be wearing a bracelet or something to tell us that. Bill, check glucose levels," Chris said. "We need to get her back and have the hospital check that head injury. I don't think anything's broken."

I shook my head. I did not want to go back to a hospital.

Ow...that hurt.

"Zoë, you can't be stubborn about this." He reached out and touched my head. "It looks like he hit you pretty hard. You need to at least go and make sure you're all right. For me? Please?"

I signed sloppily, *"You come too?"*

He nodded.

"She deaf too?" asked Chris the EMT.

"No, just mute." Daniel smiled at me, and I knew somewhere in his head he was missing my rough, scratchy voice. The one I used to have. I was too.

"Halloran," Cooper barked. "Did you see the perp?"

I blinked several times and looked straight up at the night sky as the stretcher was brought over and the two professionals hoisted me on it. Within seconds I was buckled in securely, IV bag on top of my chest, blankets preventing any and all movements.

I couldn't see the stars or even the clouds. The night sky in the city always stayed a bright pinkish hue because of all the lights. I was achy and felt a little helpless in my body. It was hard not to just leave it again to become a Wraith, but I couldn't. The havoc my jumping out would cause at that moment wasn't worth it, or the headache after.

Ever had someone try to restart your heart when you're standing right there beside your body?

Not pleasant.

And a mite painful too.

I heard Joe giving a somewhat vague description of my assailant. "He was tall, pale skin. White guy. Was wearing a tuxedo, so I'm assuming he was at the party."

Smooth, Halloran. Ouch. My head.

"Chris, she's ready."

I'm always ready. Hehehehe.

"His face?"

"Hidden, sir. I'm hoping the victim here can identify him."

"That'll sure be fun," Cooper said sarcastically. *Oh, screw you, Captain.* "She's a mute. Why didn't you go after him?"

As I was rolled past him, I moved my head and looked at him.

Joe looked back at me, his expression unreadable. "I couldn't leave the victim, sir."

"And the dead bum? Did you see him kill him?"

"No, sir. He was dead when I arrived."

The stretcher paused outside the ambulance as they kicked it in, and the lower legs collapsed. "Well—I'll be calling your captain tonight and asking for a full disclosure of your report. This should be interesting—especially with you so easily finding Miss Martinique."

They pushed the stretcher inside, and Daniel moved onto one of the side bench seats with me. I was surprised Cooper hadn't wanted him to stay, but in truth Daniel had been with him, not with us. He didn't know what had happened. Joe was the one in the hot seat.

Daniel touched my face then and smiled down at me. "You give me so much grief, Zoë Martinique."

I stuck out my lower lip. My head felt as if there were tiny little gnomes inside blasting away with jackhammers. I felt—odd. And though my conscious mind kept going back to the dead bum, I didn't want to. I didn't know if the Daimon had killed the wino's physical body or if I had.

I was afraid I had done it. I suspected I'd devoured his soul instead of releasing it. And that was something I did not want my mom knowing.

Oh yes, this is my daughter, she can't talk, but she eats dead people.

FIVE hours later, at three thirty in the morning, early Saturday, given a clean bill of health with only a Band-Aid on my cheek to show where I'd hit my head, and after answering a thousand questions by the police with Daniel as my translator, I was back at my mom's. I'd hoped Daniel would take me back to his crib, and had felt a little bummed when he'd turned on down Ponce de Leon toward Moreland and Little Five Points.

Mom was up, having been called earlier by Daniel and given the light version of the story. She'd called Rhonda, who was on her way. Tim and Steve were awake—though I'm not really sure ghosts ever sleep—and were puttering about, corporeal, and helping with some light cooking.

At three thirty in the morning?

Daniel could see them sometimes, like now, but had no real idea they were dead. Which was kinda cool. He just assumed they were this little gay couple that helped Mom out in the shop sometimes, and I guess he thought they lived in the basement.

The shop on Euclid was a historic Victorian with a wraparound porch and a divided interior. On the left was what I called her Gitchee-goomie side, the Botanica, where she sold everything from Shakti Gawain books to seven-day candles to homemade incense.

On the right was the tea shop, where Mom made her own blends and sold commercial as well as specialty teas. She'd expanded a bit at Christmas and put in a small glass cabinet to showcase her cakes and pies, which she sold by the slice with her tea. There were several different shapes of tables in varying styles and wood colors on this side, all with wicker chairs and pillows. She was in the process of installing free Wi-Fi, which would appeal to the younger coffee-drinking crowd.

Though here they could get a really good Chai instead of a latte.

The back of the shop was a full kitchen and pantry, and upstairs was where she lived, complete with den/living room, three bedrooms, and a full bathroom. I sometimes stayed in one of the rooms, as did Rhonda.

Okay—so lately I'd stayed there a *lot*. But a girl with my problems just sometimes had to stay with her mom. Especially when her mom knew all of her secrets.

Snort.

Mom pulled steaming cinnamon rolls out of the oven, and

Steve managed to tangibly spread the white sugar icing over the tops in zigzag patterns. I sat on the papasan by the fireplace in the Botanica side, watching the fire flicker and listening to the pine snap and pop. Daniel had started it for me and now came in with a steaming cup of something oddly orange-smelling.

"It's one of your mom's blends," he said as he handed it to me. He held the cup (which I was sure was burning his fingers), and I took hold of the handle. "She thinks you should drink it."

Which in Mom-speak meant she'd probably laced it with some sort of natural calming agent and I'd be asleep in ten minutes. Tucked into bed. Safe. And under her nose.

I smiled at him and set it on the side table the second he turned around. No drugs. Not tonight. My mind was too awake, and I desperately needed to talk to Rhonda.

I had to tell her and Mom about SPRITE being there, and the cameras. And about Joe! Tell them that I'd found him—or he'd found me. And he was as much an ass as I remembered—and how I'd jumped inside of him and how he now knew about me.

Crash course.

I reached out for Daniel and grabbed his hand. I still wasn't all that happy with him—with the ghost comments from the Westin. But he was here, and he was limping badly. And I was getting very worried about him. He smiled at me and pulled one of the spare wicker chairs from the side to sit beside me, propping his cane against the papasan. "You look incredible for someone who just went through what you did."

I smiled. *Uhm. Yeah, don't I? It really helps when you suck a soul now and then.*

Watch it, Zoë. You're in danger of becoming cynical.

Too late.

My dry erase board had been brought into the room, and I had it tucked in the chair with me. I pulled it out and scribbled, YOU LOOK LIKE HELL. LEG HURT?

He nodded, his expression finally betraying the fatigue he was feeling. "Yes, it does. I'm past my meds, and I know I'm going to pay for it tomorrow. But—" He looked at me with a very serious expression before removing his glasses. His eyes, though framed in dark circles, were intense. And I knew he was looking and thinking only of me. "I'm sorry I left you alone, Zoë. If I hadn't of, you wouldn't have gone through that."

NO. SUGAR WONKY, I lied on the board. Once he'd read it I wiped it away and then wrote, YOU LEARN ANYTHING WHILE I GONE?

Pfft. The grammar was heading over the cliff I noticed.

Daniel shook his head. "No—not really sure what Cooper expected anyone to find out. Joe was with Knowles for a while." He sighed. "I'm still trying to figure out Halloran's angle on this. These kinda cases aren't really his thing, you know? He says he was there because of the warehouse sting—but Knowles didn't have anything to do with it."

I pursed my lips. YOU DON'T LIKE HIM.

"I don't really know Congressman Knowles, Zoë."

Och. The cop needed sleep. Not keeping up here. I erased and scribbled, NO. JOE. YOU DON'T LIKE JOE.

"Oh. Well, I don't hate him. He just has a very unprofessional way of doing things." He snorted. "The man looks for the most unlikely answers in the most ridiculous places. You know he's been close to being bumped off the force twice." Daniel gave me a matter-of-fact nod, as if it were important for me to know just how crazy Joe Halloran was. "He even accused the captain of being possessed once. By a demon of all things."

Ah. Ha-ha. Right. But I wondered if he meant Captain Cooper or a different captain.

Events of the night jumbled about, and I needed to get as many answers as possible. I couldn't ask Daniel about the body-possessing worm that made off with my body, then practically threatened me. I could ask him about the more mundane things. WHY YOU NEEDED TO GO?

"To the event?" He tried to skirt that question. "Police business, Zoë."

I pointed to my bandage. *Oh yeah? Badge right here. Talk, bub.* So he was open to saying he didn't know why Cooper wanted him there, and now it was police business. That was a one-eighty in sixty flat.

Youch.

Time to shake up the not truthful one. I narrowed my eyes at him and then wrote, I SAW KNOWLES TALKING TO MAN NAME FRANCISCO.

Ooh! Score! His eyes widened, then it was his turn to narrow them at me. "How did you know about Rodriguez? Did you see him there?"

Ah. Last name. So it was Francisco *Rodriguez.* Wait—someone else had mentioned the name Rodriguez during the night. Who was that?

"You *saw* him talking to Congressman Knowles?"

I paused, then nodded. As long as he didn't really ask me *where* I'd seen them.

"Where did you see them together?"

Oof. Shit. Truth? Why not? Maharba was going to be upset that I didn't get the card anyway and that the police had it. IN HALLWAY, ON WAY TO BATHROOM.

"You saw them when you went to the lounge? Did they see you?"

I shook my head.

"Are you sure, Zoë?"

I cocked an eyebrow at him. *So...was this why you wanted to go?* I didn't need to write my question out, or use my sloppy sign language. He knew what I meant.

Shaking his head, Daniel said in a soft voice, "Yes, keeping an eye on Rodriguez was my original goal tonight—I needed to see him and Knowles together. And if you saw them paired up, and they saw you with me—if they knew who I was—then it might give an answer why you were attacked and dragged off. We've known those two were affiliated somehow—I just wish I could have been a fly on the wall to their conversation."

I nodded. *Yeah, and you'd have found it as boring and confusing as I did.*

Hrm. So Daniel wanted to see if they met, and Maharba had known they would meet—both wanted to know what was said. This was getting interesting.

"When was this?"

I looked at Daniel, blinking. I'd been deep in my own thoughts. I held up the board again and pointed to the words, IN HALL-WAY, ON WAY TO BATHROOM. I pointed to my Harry Potter watch (it had been a Powerpuff watch, plastic with a pink band—one of Rhonda's specials—but after TC burned up the band with his touch, Rhonda had made a more "mature" one) and shrugged, meaning I didn't know what time.

"That explains why I couldn't find them for a while. Neither him nor Knowles."

I wiped at my board. RODRIGUEZ BAD MAN?

"Francisco Almiez Rodriguez." Daniel said the name with a roll of his tongue. I wondered if he spoke Spanish. "He's pretty important in business circles in Atlanta, Miami, and Washington. Rumor has it he wanted the land the Georgia Aquarium was built on, but the city outbid him for the project."

Daniel shook his head. "No one knows if he's good or bad. He's got to be the single-most-elusive businessman in Atlanta. All his holdings appear legitimate, and he has ties to several people in Washington. He's been on the cover of almost every business publication, and he's always painted as a hero—but he just smells dirty to me."

I didn't understand cop sense. But Daniel had been right before, about a reverend being responsible for a man's death, when no one else believed him.

I wasn't sure about Rodriguez being dirty, but I knew Knowles was having issues, as I remembered the feeling I'd gotten when I'd come near him, and then when he stuck his physical hand into my OOB self. The beating of wings. That smell.

Eww. And I wasn't supposed to smell anything while OOB.

Daniel gave a long sigh. I leaned over to him and took his chin in my hand. It didn't take much for him to lean closer to me and our lips to press firmly together. I felt his tongue flicker against mine, and my nipples turned to raisins. Mmmm...

The front door banged open with the tinkling of the irritating but informative bell. Rhonda shuffled through, her black backpack with its white skulls and anarchy symbols dragging the ground. She wore a knit hat with little anime cat ears on it, perched precariously on her head, which meant her hair wasn't combed. In her hand she clutched her car keys, a toothbrush, and toothpaste.

Mom brought the tray of steaming, cinnamonly goodness into the room with us and nodded to Rhonda. "Upstairs. Room's ready." She shook her head as she placed the tray on the low coffee table, directly on top of the *Aquarius* and *Psychic Detective* magazines. "I really should just have her move in here. But she insists on having her own space." Then Mom looked at me. "You're looking better. Some rest, and you'll be as good as new."

It dawned on me then, as I watched my caftan-cloaked mother drift back into the tea shop, that she seemed to be taking the events of the night quite calmly and hadn't once asked me what'd happened. Now—it could be she was just waiting to pounce on me once Daniel left—but I would think she'd be a little interested in me and not baking.

Baking wasn't really Nona Martinique's strong point. Now deep frying? Adding a lot of butter—enough to make Paula Dean swoon?

That was Nona.

And as I recalled from a few months ago, the woman was ready to chain me to my bed to keep me safe.

I got a whiff of the tea on the table and remembered it was one of Mom's brews. That would explain it, if she thought I was drinking her potion and would be on my ass in a half hour. Asleep.

Daniel took a few of the zodiac-printed napkins and set two large rolls on top, leaving them on the table to cool. Then, to my surprise, he limped behind the papasan, leaned over, and reached down to begin massaging my neck.

The memory of the power I'd felt earlier with the bum and the demon returned to me, and I shivered. I was beginning to think that kind of euphoria was better than sex.

No!

Mistaking my shivers as something akin to actually being cold, Daniel pulled away and pulled the mauve blanket up around me. Sitting in the papasan chair, I felt like Thumbelina sprouting from a big pink flower.

But I knew he had to be exhausted, and he needed rest more than me. I signed to him to get some sleep.

"Only if you promise me you'll get some rest too." He limped from behind the chair and looked down at me. "I'll be back here tomorrow to check on you. And hopefully we'll have a lead on who killed that woman and attacked you and Halloran." He touched my cheek, and I smiled. "And please—remember what I said about him." Daniel took his index finger and made a spiral around his left ear.

Crazy. Nuts. Wacko.

I leaned forward and grabbed his cane, lifting it up for him.

Yeah, ghosts are bullshit, Daniel. Too bad a huge pile of bullshit just handed you your cane.

I forced a smile again, and Daniel said good-bye to Nona, waved to Steve by the tea counter, and stepped outside the door, the bell announcing his departure.

11

January 26, 4:15 A.M.

THE next few seconds looked like the California gold rush on fast forward. Steve and Tim were abruptly by the fireplace (poof!), as was Nona, taking up her usual seat in the high-backed wicker chair to the right of the fire, directly across from me. Even Rhonda seemed to materialize downstairs, her hair pulled back in a ponytail—or like one, as her hair was shoulder length and the end of the ponytail looked more like the end stalk of gathered black wire—dressed in her black-and-white Jolly Roger pajamas.

The little goth chick settled in the seat where Daniel had been and opened her iBook to a blank page and handed it to me.

I knew the routine. They wanted details of the night. What had happened. The truth. Not the police story.

With a sigh I started to type. Ten minutes later I had it pretty much down and set the laptop on the coffee table. Everyone moved to it to read.

I ignored my tea and settled down into my blankets. I hadn't been out of body (OOB) an overly long time—an hour and a half at most—but I was tired. And it was after 4:00 A.M.

I yawned. My mom looked up. "Joe Halloran? Who's that?"

"He's the guy that pulled her out of the morgue drawer," Rhonda said as she read.

I nodded.

"And he's the same man?" Mom asked. "He recognized you?"

I did a mental eye roll at the memory of the man's smugness and nodded.

"Whoa! Zoë." Rhonda looked up at me with wide, happy eyes. "You can shadow people? Actually *possess* them?"

I grabbed up my board, erased, and scribbled, DON'T KNOW ABOUT POSSESS, BUT I SLIPPED INSIDE.

"That is *so* cool." She went back to reading.

"Did you hurt this man?" Mom asked.

I shook my head. At least, Joe didn't seem to be hurt. A little upset, yeah. And embarrassed when I accidentally caressed Daniel's cheek, but then again, he'd had a woman inside of him.

Hehehe. Served the smarmy sergeant right. Jerk.

There was another long silence, and I'd nearly slipped into a nice nap when Rhonda sat back and pursed her lips. "I know who Francisco Rodriguez is. And I've been reading up on March Knowles." She glanced at me. "Always know the enemy." I got the feeling she was a Democrat.

"But the truth is I haven't read anything widely negative about either of them, which is what intrigued me about Knowles. So— what was the purpose of spying on them? Why would Maharba want you to do that?"

"Actually," Tim began as he sat on the floor on the opposite side of the coffee table. Tim was thinner than Steve, his build much more petite, and where Steve's hair was a soft reddish color, Tim's was as dark as chocolate. Tim had large brown eyes and high cheekbones. "Well, given Joseph's warnings to Zoë about the warehouse and the headless body being related, and that he believed they were after her, and the fact that someone had alerted the security to the presence of ghosts"—he looked around—"I'd say Maharba was curious to know what they know."

"So they're all linked in some way, just like Joseph said." Rhonda sighed. "But who? Who's got righteous indignation? Who's been at what for over twenty years?" She paused. "Rogue what?"

I shrugged. My head was hurting. Was it from whatever that demon had slammed my head into? Or was it because life had abruptly jumped back on that roller coaster of fun.

Whoopee.

Too bad I can't get real excited about it right now.

Nona crossed her arms over her ample chest. "And who are *them*? Why are they always called *them*? And if they're having a private conversation, why speak in code?"

I blinked, thinking back over my own train of thought while listening to these two. Hrm. I guess apples *don't* fall too far from the tree, huh?

"Rhonda," Steve said softly. "You still have the electronic *Harper's Guide to the Planes*?"

She nodded and knew why Steve was asking. Grabbing her iBook, the magical genius began typing, then scrolling down, her eyes narrowing at the screen, which illuminated her face. "Ah— *Daimon*. Spelled d.a.i.m.o.n. Not much here. A blurb really."

"It says they're basically tricksters, right?" Steve said as he moved around to the couch and sat beside Rhonda.

"Yeah, sort of. It says they're flotsam. They are known for their brief possession of human bodies, foul language, and smell." Rhonda looked up from the iBook at me. "Sound familiar?"

"It's missing something else." Steve had their attention. He definitely had mine. Steve was the more serious of the couple, having been an international banker and the breadwinner in his and Tim's living life. If he weren't limited to the house itself, I was sure the ghost would be out in the world putting together his own spiritual firm for spook networking. "Daimons are used mostly by Symbionts. They're castoffs of themselves. When Symbionts gain enough power, they can control their Abysmal essence—or parts of it—and they use it to spy on the living. The bits can rejoin to the Symbionts, and the information is transferred."

Uh-oh. Symbiont. I grabbed up my board and erased it before scribbling again. YOU THINK TC IS INVOLVED?

Steve shook his head. "No—there are a lot of Symbionts out there, Zoë, and I think he's now just as unique as you are. I don't think he'd use a Daimon. They have a very short shelf life once out of a body."

Rhonda raised her dark eyebrows as she leaned back in the couch. "Oh?"

"Wait." Nona spoke up. "I know about these. They sort of ride around in bodies mostly, and some do the possession thing if caught. But doing so burns up their energy."

Steve nodded. "You've been reading those books I recommended. Good. I think when this thing jumped from the woman's body, it was desperately trying to protect itself, and saw Zoë's empty body. Trying to power a body all by itself, without a soul to ride on"—he shrugged—"burned it out. Which is why it tried to jump again to the bum, and you took it."

All eyes were on me. I blinked. *What?*

"Is that what you did, Zoë?" Mom asked. "Did you absorb it, and the old man just like you did that old lady?"

How to answer that? I didn't know. I was still so new at this, and I'd just learned I could slip inside a body and, in a sense, shadow it. (I liked that term—kinda cool.) Old argument with Mom, since she'd seen me release that elderly lady. How could I actually explain to her what had happened that day when I didn't even know myself?

Wraiths throughout legend were usually described as harbingers of life and death. Which was in essence a power greater than that of a Phantasm—which seemed to be the high-grand-muckety-muck of the Abysmal plane. Or at least as far as I knew, since I didn't know of anything scarier. I'd met a Phantasm. I didn't know if that was *the* Phantasm.

I mean, was there only one? If so—then that would mean there was only one Big Bad, and I had already managed to snag his radar.

Mental note: *there's always a Big Bad, isn't there?*

"Did anyone mention who that elderly lady was?" Rhonda said, looking at each of them. "The one that died?"

I shook my head. I wasn't even sure that if they had discovered her identity, Daniel would be very forthcoming. I thought again of the scene in the lounge when I'd come through the door, and again I saw Joe standing there, looking a bit frazzled. Did he know who that lady was?

"Why is that important?" Mom asked. She took up a cinnamon roll in a napkin and nibbled on the end.

I stared at Mom. Who was this woman? She'd been so nonchalant since Maharba's e-mail, and now she didn't think the identity of the old lady who tried to kill her daughter was important?

Och. Parents.

Rhonda tapped a black-nailed finger to her lips. "We have to ask the question why it was even in the old lady. Why did it go into the lounge to stab Zoë? It led her in there in the beginning, all friendly-like. And once she'd left her body, it had the opportunity to stab her right then, but it didn't. It waited until after she'd spied on the two men."

Steve scratched his own chin and nodded. Do ghosts really get itches, and if so, do they feel it when they scratch? "That's a good point. Zoë said she'd gotten the impression of something dark when Knowles had passed his hand through her—what if the Daimon was already riding the Congressman and sensed her when she sensed it? What if it sensed her and jumped out of Knowles's body to escape? In essence, she scared it out of him?"

Now this idea really creeped me out on several levels. First off, this guy was a congressman. Meaning he represented his Georgia district in the United States Congress. What the hell would a piece of flotsam from the Abysmal plane want with living politics? Hell, it was boring to me, and it affected me directly. Wouldn't it be boring to them?

Rhonda caught on to the oh-this-is-a-good-plot-thread idea. "So it skipped out of the congressman—and maybe in that brief instant the two touched, it'd seen the old lady show her where the lounge was?"

Tim whistled. "And it went there with the idea to kill Zoë's body, releasing her Ethereal presence."

Mom set the roll down on the coffee table and took up her steaming cup of tea. "Well—that's all well and good—but it would be a really dumb Daimon to think that cutting the fetter of a Wraith would just make it go away. Zoë would just become even more powerful than she is."

!!!

I don't think in my twenty-seven years of life I'd ever realized that silence could be a tangible thing. When I could talk, I did it all the time. And when I wasn't talking, I had the TV on for noise.

But I could hear the rats moving about in the attic during the silence that completely blanketed the room. All gazes snapped to my mom. Rhonda's mouth was open, Tim had his dark eyebrows narrowed, and Steve—well, Steve was looking a bit curious. Me? I was gaping at Mom. Jaw hitting floor and all.

But I do that a lot. Had been doing it since she'd shown up at my fifth-grade Christmas dance dressed as a snowflake. Too bad when I met up with old high school friends *that* was what they remembered most about me. My big snowflake mom.

"Nona," Steve said. "How do you know this?"

Mom was looking completely cool. She had no idea she'd said anything profound. "What? About Wraiths?" Now she frowned at Steve. "It's in those books you suggested I read. There's a whole chapter on Wraiths—or really—on their legend. They really don't exist as far as that writer was concerned. But the general belief has it that when a Wraith is made of a living soul, just like with Zoë, it grows stronger while still connected to its living counterpart. But if that connection is severed, then its power only grows stronger. It also talks about Wraiths losing their souls."

Steve pursed his lips, but his gaze at Nona didn't look any friendlier. "I seem to remember that. If a Wraith loses connection to its soul—say the soul is ripped from it or lost in the planes—then it can become a force for pure evil."

Mom picked up her roll again and nibbled. I frowned at her again. Since when did Mom actually nibble at anything? Mom continued to nibble. "And then we'd have to kill Zoë."

"Well, we wouldn't really be killing Zoë because her soul would already have been taken or destroyed. So we'd just be killing what—the part that makes her a Wraith?"

Tim piped up. "Or maybe we'd be killing the dark part of her. We all have the capacity for evil, and maybe it's the soul that keeps things in check. If she lost her soul, like with a vampire, maybe the evil takes over."

"Might be," Steve said. "But either way we'd have to destroy her. Either by exorcism or banishment."

"I'd go for exorcism," Rhonda said, with a little too much relish at the thought. "It would pretty much melt away all trace of her to jibbering bits of shadow."

"True," Steve said. "But banishment might peel away the outer flesh to reveal what's really inside."

Huh? I wiped at my board, scribbled, then held it up. HELLO? STILL IN THE ROOM!

Rhonda looked apologetic. "Sorry, Zoë. It's just that we're all on the outside of this, me and your mom more so." She glanced at Steve and Tim to emphasize that, as ghosts, they were a little closer to the situation. "We're really on this roller-coaster ride same as you. We don't know what's happening inside of you, and your voice being gone"—she shrugged—"makes it harder."

No, not harder. It sucked. It so sucked.

"Let's get back to what we know," Steve said, corralling everyone's attention.

I looked at Mom who was really enjoying her roll. Ew. Never knew Mom could make love to food. It was her job usually to conduct these spontaneous what-the-hell-has-Zoë-stepped-into-this-time meetings. Why wasn't she doing so now?

Okay...feeling a little abandoned here by Mom.

The redheaded ghost sat forward in his chair. I noticed the cushion beneath him never moved. Creepy. "First, Maharba knew Knowles and Francisco were going to talk, and we can assume he or she didn't know what it was about—which is why they asked Zoë.

"Yet someone within their security for the Westin believed there might be a ghost or something there and has hired SPRITE to keep tabs on the event. Very interesting. The two men did have a more-than-veiled conversation that essentially generated more questions than answers.

"We believe Knowles was being shadowed by a Daimon, and we suspect that same Daimon is the one she sensed in the congressman earlier. Then it tried to possess Zoë's body. We know she absorbed it, which is probably why her injuries are healing quickly." He stood and moved through the coffee table to me. Then in one movement he was corporeal in front of me and yanked the bandage off of my temple.

Ow! What the—

I put a hand up defensively, but it passed through Steve's arm.

I watched his face. *Uh-oh.* "In fact, it's gone. Cut and all."

"Is that normal?" Rhonda said.

Steve shrugged, and the bandage floated into my lap as he went intangible again and returned to his seat. I reached up and touched my forehead. I couldn't find the cut. Only a slight bruised spot where it might have been.

Well, I wasn't surprised at my miraculous healing ability. I was apparently in a coma and dying in the hospital at one point in November, then fifteen hours later I was being released all okey-dokey. That was after I'd touched the old lady's spirit.

What the hell am I? Definitely not a superhero. But not a villain either.

Or was I? I guess it depended on one's point of view.

"We also know," Rhonda chimed in, "that this Joe Halloran, the same mystery dude that helped Zoë in the morgue, claims he saw the old lady about to stab Zoë."

"What do we know about this guy?" Mom asked as she set the roll down again. I narrowed my eyes at it. She'd barely eaten half. "What if he was lying, and he really had tried to kill my daughter? I mean, she saw him that night in the morgue, where he wasn't supposed to be." She looked at me. "And you did mention that it looked as if he'd appeared and disappeared."

Ah. Good memory. That was true. But I'd also chalked a lot of what happened that night up to my waking up dead. I didn't really trust me on that one, but Mom had remembered it. I actually thought I'd imagined Joe because none of the doctors, or Mom, remembered seeing him when they stepped into the morgue to identify my body.

It was my turn, and I erased and scribbled, NEED TO TALK TO JOE.

Everyone nodded.

I erased and scribbled in smaller letters, BIG QUESTION IS

WHO CREATED THE DAYMON TO SHADOW KNOWLES?
WHY FOR?

"That's the other unknown," Steve said.

"I think you spell *Daimon* with an *i*," Rhonda said, but didn't look up from her iBook. I realized then she'd been dictating everything Steve said.

"And if you hadn't of eaten it"—Tim half smiled—"we could have sicced Nona and her Wicca hoodoo on it and interrogated it."

He was referring to my mom and Rhonda's little séancelike thing they'd done on the succubus named Mitsuri. That interrogation had proven quiet informative, and it had shown me my scream, which had destroyed her.

I signed, *"I didn't eat it."* Which was the truth. I'd eaten the wino—but I didn't have the strength to get into that right now.

Conversation dulled after that. Mom continued to eat the same cinnamon roll. My stomach couldn't take it. I was tired too, really tired. And oddly enough, not the least bit hungry *or* thirsty.

Weird.

Tim and Steve faded away, going to wherever it was ghosts go when they're not visible, and Rhonda continued to tap on her iBook.

I needed to report what I found out to Maharba. If only to keep them off my back and away from my bank account. They'd given me a nice sum of money a few months back, and they hadn't withdrawn it. That pile had kept the mortgage paid, as well as the utilities on, since. And it'd made for a nice family Christmas.

I waved at Rhonda and signed that I needed to use her computer to make a report. She smiled and handed it over, then went into the kitchen to make some more tea.

Mom watched me as I logged onto my Yahoo! account and typed in Maharba's address. I copied the text file I'd typed out on the computer earlier and pasted it in, then edited it here and there. They'd only asked for the report on the meeting, not all the stuff on Joe and on the subsequent stab, possess, and chase scenes afterward.

Once done, I reread it, added in about not being able to lift a card as there wasn't an opportunity, and hit SEND. There. I'd fulfilled that little bit they'd asked me to do. I only hoped they weren't mad about the card I'd tried to get.

Maharba thought it was necessary to see what the two men were going to talk about. Maybe all their nonsense was important in some way. I googled Rodriguez's name and got a few hits. Magazine articles, photos, but not much beyond those. Seems there wasn't much dirt on Rodriguez in the broad world.

I hit several more google search pages and came across a teaser header link that said *Francisco Rodriguez, local business entrepreneur cryptographer.*

Now that was weird.

I clicked on the link and was taken to an article in the *Atlanta Journal-Constitution* dated May 12, 1996. The Olympics were coming and apparently Mr. Rodriguez had given generously to the funds needed to build Centennial Park.

I read a bit more and it seemed Francisco Rodriguez had been, early on in his career, a cryptographer for the Air Force. He'd finished his tour and retired to Washington, where he'd made a living at the Smithsonian deciphering texts, and had worked with several big names in the field.

Impressive.

Then he'd abruptly quit that job, moved to Atlanta, started buying up real estate, turning it, and making a profit. The reporter mentioned that Rodriguez owned several properties locally, as well as in Savannah, Michigan, and Oregon, that he refused to part with. He'd also recently lent out his skills at ciphers to a local archeological team he'd brought in to do a bit of digging on one of his Georgia properties.

After that the article sort of spiraled back into the Olympics, and how great Mr. Rodriguez was.

I did notice it said he'd never married. Had no children. But it didn't say how old he was. He looked like he was in his midfifties.

Well, I wasn't sure exactly how helpful the information was going to be, but I bookmarked the site in her browser, then copied it into an e-mail to myself. I could check it later at my place.

I felt the hairs on the back of my neck rise and looked across the coffee table at my mom.

She was finished with her cinnamon roll and was now watching me. There was a peculiar expression on her face. It wasn't irritation, or anger, and not even that stern-mother look she usually shot me. It looked more like—fascination—with a little curiosity.

I signed, *"What?"*

She kept watching me, and then her gaze trailed down to the mug on the table. "You didn't drink your tea."

I shook my head. *"Not thirsty."* I yawned. Not planned, but really good odd-moment breaker. *"Think I'll get some sleep."*

Mom sighed and stood. She took up my now-cold tea and moved into the kitchen as Rhonda stepped out with a steaming cup herself. "I made some chamomile." She set her tea on the table, then with a glance at Mom's disappearing back, whispered, "Nona's latest concoction smells awful."

Well, yeah. But it usually did. Mom tended to like to dabble in herbal remedies. Unfortunately, they tended to give the drinker more stomachache than cure.

I waved at Rhonda to catch her attention after she sat down, then with my own furtive look to the kitchen, signed, *"She's still acting strange."*

I'd expected Rhonda's reaction. She snorted. "Nona? Strange?

That's the same thing as asking me if I thought black was a great color. Leave her be, Zoë. She's confused over what's happening to you, and you won't listen to most of her advice. She's just being a mom."

I frowned, felt my fairly dark but carefully tweezed eyebrows knit over my nose. *"Mom never nibbled on anything in her life."*

At least Rhonda had to agree with me on that with a nod. "Yeah—I've only known her a few years, but nibbling isn't her way. But like I said before—she seems distracted."

I pursed my lips. *"She still didn't say if Maddox found something wrong? Is that what's got her acting all kooky?"* My anger was immediately extinguished in a puff of steam. Uh-oh. What if he had found something wrong? And that something was life-threatening? And Mom was simply reacting to that news by being overly cautious?

Maybe it was stomach-related, which is why she'd nibbled?

"She's been very tight-lipped." Rhonda shrugged and took up her tea. She held it close to her lips and blew over the top of the ginger-colored liquid. "I figured she'd tell me and you when she was ready."

I closed the iBook and set it on the coffee table. Rhonda set her tea down and put the computer back in her backpack. Nona returned to the room with another steaming cup of tea and set it in front of me.

"Drink this one."

I frowned at it. It was oddly dark, and I was afraid she'd mixed some of her coffee beans in it again like she'd did when she thought creating a hybrid of Starbucks House and Ginseng tea would be a good pick-me-up blend with a hint of calming effect. As I recalled, it killed the plant whose pot I poured it in.

I didn't want to drink it. For one thing, it smelled awful. But Mom had always tried to make me healthy, and she was always there for me. And now there was some sort of distracting medical news she was obviously too afraid or embarrassed to tell me.

Guilt forced me to pick up the cup and bring it to my lips. I looked over the steaming surface at Mom and Rhonda. Mom looked eager.

Rhonda looked scared.

She too had been a victim of Mom's herbal remedies.

So—what could happen? At the worst a simple upset stomach, right?

Wrong.

12

AT first I attributed my aches and pains to my body's possession the night before.

But then my stomach started to argue with me, and unless the Daimon ate a mouse while in my body, I was going to throw up in my bed. I sat up and slapped a hand to my mouth as my gut seized and a dry heave propelled me out of the bed.

Blue sheets tossed into the air as I stumbled into the bathroom connecting my room to the other spare bedroom upstairs in Mom's house. I shut the door and heaved over the toilet.

It was probably the quietest puke anyone ever didn't hear.

Except for the contents of my stomach splashing into the bowl. After a few seconds of pure embarrassment, I finally gained control of myself but waited a few more minutes before staggering off of my knees and to the sink. I turned the cold water on full and doused my face several times with handfuls of it. I was shaking from my head to my feet.

I didn't hear the door open through the splash of the water and nearly jumped right out of my body the instant I felt a hand on my shoulder.

"Zoë?"

It was Rhonda, and I straightened, looking at her reflection in the bathroom mirror. Not really knowing what the ASL sign for puke was, I gestured to the toilet and stuck my tongue out.

She nodded. "I'll say. The toilet flush woke me. Sort of reminded me that I needed to pee. Nona really needs to get the plumbing in this house fixed. Or muffled."

When Rhonda spent the night at Mom's, she usually stayed in the adjoining room. And she was right. The house's plumbing sort of announced itself. If Mom turned on the faucet in the sink downstairs, it would sound like it was in the bathroom adjoining the room.

My stomach seized again, and I grabbed it, doubling over. Rhonda grabbed my shoulders and led me to the toilet, where another round of dry heaves robbed me of my strength as well as my dignity.

After that I rinsed my mouth and nearly fell on my ass when my legs gave beneath me. Rhonda helped me back to my room and back in my bed.

The sun was barely up, and a quick glance at the clock beside my bed said it was six thirty. I leaned back into the sheets, very much aware of their soft, linen texture on my skin.

I felt a very cold hand on my forehead. "Zoë—you have a fever. I'll go wake up Nona."

I reached out and grabbed her arm and shook my head. I motioned for my board, but it was downstairs. Instead, Rhonda went to her room and retrieved a notepad and pencil.

Propping up against my pillows I started writing as Rhonda turned on my headless Mary-Had-a-Little-Lamb lamp. Spooky thing.

SOMETHING IN TEA. SHE DID THIS TO ME A WEEK AGO. SAME THING. I'LL BE FINE.

Rhonda read the message and scowled. "Zoë—I don't think it's the tea this time. But it might be residual from the Daimon." She set the pad on the bed beside me. "They're not exactly the healthiest creatures in the Abysmal plane. Sort of like rats—and you had one running around inside of you."

Oh. Ew. And I bit it! ACK! I signed, *"Need disinfectant."*

"No, I think you need a doctor. Even if it's not Daimon mess, it might be food poisoning."

I frowned at her and started signing—poorly. *"Poison from what? When I eat?"*

She pursed her lips and nodded. "You have a point. You didn't even eat any of Nona's sweets. But you're sick. And just out of the hospital again. You know Maddox would be more than happy to make a house call this early in the morning." She started to get up.

I grabbed her arm and shoved all of the fear I could into my expression. I did *not* want to see Dr. Maddox. And I did *not* want him in my mom's house.

Reading my mind—or my face—Rhonda sat back down and sighed. I made a pleading face. She nodded. "Okay. You sleep. It's still early. And I don't think we had plans for the day, right?"

I shook my head. Maybe I did, but not now. I was too damned tired, and my stomach was *not* well.

Dreams came in weird little scenes, vignettes of things I'd never done, nor would do. Or I hoped so. One was of me sitting naked on top of the state capitol building—bare-assed on the gold dome. Another one had me kissing Rhonda (!!!). And then there was one where I was holding on to a rocket for dear life as it soared up out of the earth's atmosphere and into space.

Yow.

But the one that shot me out of sleep was by far the worst. I was in that damned corridor again, the one I'd dreamed about months ago, with bits and pieces of dead bodies flailing at me. And I could hear laughter ringing out of the floors and the walls. I'd had this one before, only this time I recognized the laughter.

I'd lived with it all of my life, and heard it even now from somewhere in the house.

I rounded a corner in my dream and nearly fell over the side of a precipice, a gap that led into a dark, vast nowhere. Wind whipped my hair and my shredded clothing about my body as I balanced on the edge, then moved backward to land on my butt on the sand floor.

And above me I saw a face in the darkness. It was made of light shadows that moved and wriggled, and as it neared, I realized the moving shadows were in fact small ghosts of people, and their wriggling was actually writhing in agony.

The face laughed as it grew closer to me, filled the tunnel's opening as I tried to move back in time.

I knew this face. A face I was intimately familiar with.

It was my own.

Gah!

I jumped awake, my eyes instantly opened. A cool hand touched my forehead and cheek, and I nearly leapt off the bed at that moment as I stared up at blue eyes.

"Sshhhhh," said Daniel as he leaned in close to me and put a reassuring hand on my shoulder. He was sitting on the left edge of my bed. "It's okay. You were having one hell of a nightmare."

I frowned at him. Daniel. How was Daniel in my house? He didn't have a key yet—we hadn't made it that far in the relationship.

A quick glance around at the sheers over the windows, at the wicker furniture, and the garish toddler-sized stuffed bear in the corner told me I wasn't in my home.

I was in Mom's home.

I'd stayed there last night. And I woke up earlier and threw up.

I instantly was glad I didn't have to speak since I hadn't brushed my teeth afterward.

Ick.

"Rhonda said you woke earlier and weren't feeling good. I came up here to check on you—you're sweating, by the way. Did you just break a fever? When I touched you, you woke up."

I propped myself up on my elbows and took stock. I was fine and in one piece. I saw my bare feet peaking out from beneath the blue sheets and wiggled my toes. Hrm. Time for a pedicure and more pink polish.

Daniel reached behind me and plumped my pillows. I pushed myself backward and leaned up on them in a near-sitting position. That's when I smelled something sweet and chocolaty.

Mmmm. I looked over at the nightstand. A single pink rose sat inside of a green glass vase. Beside it sat a steaming cup of goodness with whipped cream on top, waiting for me. I pointed at it, then pointed at Daniel.

He smiled and shook his head before handing it to me. "Rhonda made it and had me carry it upstairs. I watched her. She used real milk and chocolate. Rhonda's downstairs making love to her own mug."

I laughed. Mouth open. No sound. And then remembered the puke earlier and closed it. I licked at the whipped cream and smiled. Mmmm. I wanted so much to take a sip, but remembered my last encounter with Rhonda's hot chocolate, emphasis on the hot part. McDonald's coffee ain't got nothing on that woman's beverage temperature.

I wanted my tongue intact so I just kept licking at the whipped cream.

"I also wanted to sort of bring you up to speed," Daniel said, and retrieved another cup I'd not seen from the nightstand. It didn't have any whipped cream on it and from the smell I knew he had his plain black coffee. "Rodriguez and Knowles are coming in later today for questioning about last night. They've identified the lady in the blue dress."

My eyebrows arched in a show of, "And?"

He sipped his coffee. He looked so good in his weekend attire of gray sweatshirt with its red Georgia State University logo and the faded jeans I knew cupped his butt in all the right places. He wasn't wearing his glasses either, which meant he had contacts in. I learned he had them but only put them in when he wasn't in a hurry, since he still had problems getting his finger that close to his eyeball. I could soooo understand. Wasn't putting anything in my eye.

Uh-uh.

And his hair…mmm-mmm good. And sideburns. Daniel Frasier had some really nice sideburns. I never thought I'd think sideburns were sexy.

Mental note: *You're still mad at him. Grrrr.*

"…available for questioning, but what we can't figure out was why this mystery person tried to stab you while you were in the staff lounge." He sighed and shook his head before lowering his cup to his lap, where he supported it with both hands. "That is if Halloran is to be believed."

Wait. What? Damn. I'd been watching him and not listening. Shit. I set my chocolate down and looked about for my pad. It was still on the bed where Rhonda had left it and I pulled it out. Pen?

Daniel reached over with his left hand and grabbed the pen.

Scribble. SORRY. DAYDREAMING. WHO WAS WOMAN?

He smiled that smile he usually gave me. That one that I imagined meant "Oh, what a cute little dumb girl." "Sara Nell Pearson. One of the Westin's employees. Coordinates events like last night. She was milling about, helping guests at one point. They said she went backstage to make sure Congressman Knowles was fine, then she left after he went onstage. The next thing they knew she was dead."

I erased and scribbled, thinking about the theories we'd worked out last night. WASN'T ACTING WEIRD?

He shook his head before he sipped his coffee again. "Apparently she was the sweetest of Southern belles."

This was interesting, though I wasn't sure how yet. I needed to talk to Rhonda again and confirm what we'd been talking about last night. Eh. I also needed to brush my teeth.

"What are you thinking about so hard?"

I blinked and looked at Daniel. He'd set his coffee on the nightstand.

I erased my board and wrote, ASK JOE OPINION.

Daniel snorted.

I erased and scribbled, YOU NEED TO GET OVER THIS.

My cute cop snorted again and added in an eye roll. "He's a nut job, I told you that. And his story." Daniel did a strange movement with his shoulders, sort of something between a shrug and a breast thrust. "I just don't know. If you weren't backing up his story about this mystery intruder, I'd almost swear he was lying. That he stabbed that poor old lady himself because he thought she was possessed by some demon."

Ouch. Wow. Must—control—face. Daniel had no idea how close he'd just nailed the truth. I was getting a little irritated, but he had brought me a rose.

Mental note: *still mad...grrrr?*

I frowned at him and signed, *"Why?"* I mean really—why think a perfectly normal person like Joe would stab a defenseless old lady?

Daniel's expression was the epitome of sarcastic. If you looked up that word in the book, you'd see this face. His left eyebrow arched high. "Well, knowing Joe, he probably thought the old bird really was possessed. He does that, you know?"

DOES WHAT?

There was that odd shrug again. It was almost as if he was

embarrassed—not for himself, but for Joe. "Because the idiot believes in all that crap, Zoë."

CRAP. YOU MEAN GHOSTS.

Daniel looked a little put out. Well, actually, he looked a lot put out. "Babe, I know your family sort of goes along with this shit." He waved around at the floor, but I knew he meant the Botanica and tea shop downstairs. "But even Nona explained about the theatrics she uses to bilk her customers—"

I knew what he meant. I mean, I knew what incident he was referring to—back when Daniel had walked in on us and the séance to interrogate Mitsuri. He'd seen the succubus (well, it had practically attacked him when he walked in the door) and the pentagram painted on the floor beneath the rugs downstairs.

But still—my mom never bilked her customers. She honestly tried to help them find what it was they needed. The truth was the pentagram had nothing to do with the customers.

But the very idea that Daniel thought my mom was a fraud just grated against my backbone. Honestly—I was hearing the sound of fingernails on chalkboard.

I erased my board. SO YOU THINK MY MOM IS SHISTER.

He frowned at the board. "No—well, I don't know. Sometimes maybe. She mixes those god-awful teas, and I know I've gotten sick on occasion. Look." He put up his hands. "What has this got to do with Joe Halloran?"

Erase. Scribble. I BELIEVE IN GHOSTS.

His expression didn't change. He just looked at me. "I know you do. But Joe's a little—different. For crying out loud, Zoë. He wears a pentagram."

I didn't know that, but I did find the information pretty interesting. I erased and scribbled, SO DOES RHONDA.

"Yeah, but that sort of goes with Rhonda's look. She's into that whole goth thing."

I wished at that moment that I had a pentagram and I could whip it out. Not that I even really understood the significance of one. Other than shock value.

SO YOU DISLIKE JOE BECAUSE HE LIKE GHOST JEWELRY.

Daniel frowned at the board, then I looked at it again. Shit—I hadn't meant to write ghost. I meant goth.

To his credit, he shook his head. "Zoë, there's so much you don't know about me. About my past."

Well, yeah, bub, that goes two ways. I smirked at him, thinking of Joe's usual smug expression, and hoped I'd mimicked it just to irritate him.

I erased with my hand and wrote, SO TELL ME.

He frowned when he read it, and his shoulders dropped. I hadn't realized he was so tense. "It's not a good time, Zoë. I just—" He stood abruptly and moved to the two outset windows that from the outside always reminded me of eyes. Then he put his hands in his pockets and faced me. "How well do you know a Mr. R. R. Kemp?"

I blinked and signed, *"Who?"*

"Richard Randall Kemp. I got a call from him this morning while I was finishing up the paperwork on last night. Said he belonged to a paranormal organization that investigated strange and unexplained happenings in the Southeast. They call themselves SPRITE."

!!!

Oh. Fuck.

The Southeastern Paranormal Research Institute for Termination and Extermination.

SPRITE.

And Randall was calling Daniel now.

"He wanted to interview me about Koba Hirokumi, about his

death, and about his sometime affiliation with some wacko organization called the Society of Ishmael. Says he saw me at the event
last night—because his team was working security for Representative Robert Stephens—the one behind the fund-raiser.”

Oh, this could not be a coincidence. I thought it might be better
if Daniel didn’t know I knew who they were. Or at least, personally. Because as far as I knew, they didn’t know whom the mysterious ghost had been. Though I’d always thought it odd I’d ended up
on their camera and the poltergeist hadn’t.

I scribbled, THEY’RE GHOST HUNTERS.

“Yeah, I know. I heard of them. But not since Halloween of last year.” He took several steps closer to my bed. “I just
found it odd that he dropped *your* name when he asked to interview me.”

My *name? WTF?*

Daniel read my expression. “Yeah, I was a bit surprised too. I
told him no, I didn’t have time, and I’ve alerted some of the officers that you might have a stalker. But I’d like to know why he felt
knowing you was important.”

Uh.

Hrm.

No idea. Panic. Not big panic. But panic. Because if Randall
was still as determined now as he had been back in October to
prove the existence of this female spook, how had he gotten my
name? And why was he interested in Hirokumi?

And how had he gotten my name? Wait—I asked that already,
didn’t I?

“I see you’re a little confused.”

No. Duh. I frowned at him and just shrugged. I scribbled,
WHAT IS SOCIETY OF ISHMUSH?

He laughed at me. Ah!

“Ishmael. Not Ishmush. Don’t know. I asked Rhonda to check

it out for me—sounds like a secret society sort of thing. And I wouldn't be surprised if Joe knows about it either."

Oh? Really? You asked the pentagram-wearing goth chick to help you? Of course, I didn't write any of that down. I was too irritated.

He sighed when I didn't answer. "I'm not going to give Mr. Kemp much attention at the moment. Last night's events are still heavy on everyone's mind. Miss Pearson is dead, and we don't have a suspect in custody, or even an ID. Oh, and I took your dress and purse to the GBI. Maybe they can find some sort of trace material or something the murderer left behind."

I thought about the dress and purse. *"What about my phone?"* I signed to him. I kinda liked the BlackBerry, even though I'd only used it once or twice.

"Rhonda's got it downstairs. I didn't think they needed that."

Well, I knew it was going to be a fruitless search with the dress and purse. I didn't personally know anybody at the Georgia Bureau of Investigation, but I could feel for the man-hours someone was going to put in on finding nothing. The only thing that might turn up was Daniel's and Joe's hair and some classy Atlanta alley garbage.

I couldn't shake the SPRITE issue though. Daniel might dismiss them. But with my luck, it might be better to keep an eye on things.

I licked my lips at this while the ole hamsters cranked up the way-back machine. How would Randall have gotten my name—he looked right at me last night with no recognition. Yeah, I'm pretty sure my name came up in connection with the whole Hirokumi debacle—since the police have it on file that the Reverend kidnapped me from Triangle Park.

But that was as far as it went, or so Captain Cooper and Daniel had assured me. I was a simple blip on the radar, a brunette that got caught in the cross fire when she saw something.

This week's guest star on *Law & Order*.

"Zoë?"

I looked at Daniel. He was looking intently at me. YOU THINK JOE KNOW ABOUT ISHMAEL?

Daniel's sigh was long and full of irritation. "You want Joe's number? I'm sure I could get it for you—then the two of you could chat about ghosts and demons and secret societies all you wanted."

Ah!

Hey, now my question wasn't bad enough to receive that kind of a response. I drew out a sad face on my board and showed it to him.

A smile pulled at the corners of his mouth, and he took in a deep breath. "Sorry—I'm just out of my element here. Because I was there, Cooper's assigned me on the Pearson murder and we still haven't found evidence of the butcher on the Randolph decapitation." He checked his watch. "Look, how about tonight I pick you up at about seven and we go back to my place and eat pizza and watch old movies? I've got *Casablanca* on DVD."

Casablanca? Okay. Never seen it. And it was obvious he was trying to make an effort to smooth over the spikiness of our conversation.

"Well, that is if you're feeling better. If you have a cold, I can come here and spend time with you."

Yeah, in the "ghost house." But I didn't say that out loud.

I nodded. I was feeling a bit confused with him. I really liked Daniel—I'd poured out a lot of time for him during his recovery, and I'd always made sure he knew I was there. And Daniel had to be the most romantic man I knew. If I went to his house tonight, I was sure he'd have roses and maybe even a box of chocolates.

And he was so damned good-looking.

I nodded. Smiled.

He looked like he felt better and leaned forward to kiss me.

Yikes! Puke lips!

But just as he was near enough to touch his mouth to mine, a voice broke from downstairs.

"Zoë!" came Rhonda's voice from the bottom of the stairs. "There's a hot guy here to see you. He says his name is Joe."

13

DANIEL followed me down the stairs after I threw on some jeans and a sweater. I also hurriedly brushed my teeth and scowled at my wild hair—giving that damned white streak the hairy eyeball. I needed a shower, but that could wait. Daniel looked about ready to explode, and I didn't want him going splat over any of Mom's imported statues.

The shop was chilly on the tea side. Steve was behind the counter slicing up a lemon-spice cake. I didn't see Tim anywhere.

I signed for Daniel's benefit, but I knew Steve could hear me. *"Hey, where's Mom?"*

Steve glanced up at me. "Don't know. She left early this morning. I think she was with Mrs. Shultz, but I'm not sure." He glanced at the beaded curtain that separated the two shops. "He's in there. He's kinda cute."

Ew.

Joe was in the Botanica shop, sipping tea in a white cup and saucer with Rhonda, whose expression was marked with concentrated determination. In fact, if Joe wasn't careful, he might burst into flames from Rhonda's glare.

I studied his long face, sharp chin, and high cheekbones. His hair was choppier than usual, and he wore a long-sleeved black tee shirt with the Sci Fi Channel logo on it and jeans.

I stepped into the room through the beads that separated the two shops. He smiled at me—a beaming white smile that oozed charm.

Well, okay, maybe he was a little cute. But totally not my type. Too outdoorsy.

Wait, I've said that already, right?

Joe set his tea on the coffee table and stood, but his smile disappeared when Daniel came through the beads to my left. "Ah, Detective Frasier."

I glanced at Daniel on my left side. He gave Joe a tight smile. "Ah, Sergeant Halloran. What the hell are you doing here?"

I glanced back at Daniel. Down boy!

Joe looked nonplussed. "Why, I've come for tea, Daniel." He grinned as he looked all about the room. "And you have to admit, this is more *my* kind of place than yours."

"Do you come here often?" Daniel asked.

We all knew the answer to that one. Hell no.

And Joe shook his head. "Once. I really didn't know this place was here. I usually visit the Phoenix and Dragon bookstore up off of Roswell Road." His gaze lit on me, and it was an intense one. My antics from the night before hadn't frightened this one off. Nope. "I'm here to see Zoë."

"Why?"

Sit boy.

Joe frowned. "Because I'm investigating the bust at the warehouse, Detective Frasier. She and her mom were friends with Lieutenant Holmes—I'm doing my job."

Zing.

"Well, that'll be a change." Daniel turned to me and yanked me closer to him. Then he pressed his lips into mine—but I knew his heart wasn't in it. This was more show—marking his territory.

Woman, mine. You stay away. Ugh.

At least he didn't pee on me.

When he let go, he looked at Rhonda. "You watch him."

She gave him a conspiratorial look and nodded.

We moved as a unit back through the beads to the front door. A customer came in as Daniel left, bringing with her a cold, biting breeze.

I shivered and wrapped my arms around my chest.

"We're supposed to get a wintry mix today," Steve said from behind the counter. He was helping a customer. He physically rang up the register, then packaged the teas. The middle-aged man flirted a bit with the handsome redhead, oblivious that he was a ghost, and left. I approached Steve, who faded visibly for a bit and smiled.

You're a flirt.

"And so are you. Two men vying for your attention?" He glanced at the curtain. I could hear Rhonda and Joe talking.

Joe is not here for my attention. He's here because he's curious. He saw me Wraith out last night.

"He's sensitive, you know. He can see Tim and me, even when we're invisible. He has a glow about him very similar to yours."

Oh? I pursed my lips and stared again at the curtain.

"Zoë," Steve said, and I looked back at him because of the odd tone of his voice. "Be careful, okay? Something's...off."

Off? With Joe?

"With everything. Something's up." He rubbed his neck and shrugged. "It's just something we can all feel. Ghosts, shades, spirits. A few of the fettered ones that have been in here have all mentioned something happening."

You mean like a disturbance in the force? I had to give a silent laugh on that one. *Relax, Steve. I know something's up and it has to do with the congressman and Representative Stephens, and somehow with my client Maharba. I don't know how or what, but I'm keeping my eyes out.*

"And so am I," Joe said as he made an appearance through the beads. "Hey, did you know you've got Mexican jumping beans in that dragon statue over the fireplace?"

I started to mentally yell at him, then stopped. *Mexican jumping beans?*

"Yeah—you've got that cool Soul Catcher over the mantel. It's sort of rocking now and then." He smiled. "Did you catch something in it?"

Rhonda burst through the beads at that moment and put both hands to her hips as she marched up to me and glared. Which was sort of odd for her since I'm a good foot taller. "Why didn't you tell us? I really think it was a very important piece of info, Zoë."

Uhm. Okay. Charades. I give up. I shrugged, not having a clue what Rhonda was on about.

She pointed at Joe. "He can *hear* you!"

I looked at him. *You told her?*

Joe nodded. "Why, is it a secret? Apparently it's an effect of having her inside of me." He frowned. "I *think*. Dunno, really. I'm still adjusting to the fact that she doesn't take drugs to go out of body."

My stomach growled. Loudly.

I shook my head. *No, no drugs. Natural.* I pushed my sleeves up and put my hands on my hips. I was getting hungrier by the second. I thought of noodles with lemon sauce, and fat shrimp with pine nuts.

Ah! Macaroni Grill!

Joe moved quickly from across the room and took my left arm and turned it over. TC's little calling card was as visible as ever. What made it mostly resemble a tattoo was the soft striations of flesh, fingerprints, and scars that dotted the palm.

Joe's touch sizzled, almost burned, and I snatched my arm away rubbing it. *Hey!*

He was looking at his hands, then rubbed them together. "Did you feel that? It was like heat when I touched that mark. I saw that on your arm that night in the morgue, but I figured it was a tattoo. It's not, is it? Not a real one."

I shook my head. *No—it's a long story.*

"I'd really love to hear it." And he did look as if he'd love to hear it. All of it. In fact, Joe Halloran was buzzing from the inside and looked like a kid in a comic shop who'd just found *Superman* one in mint condition.

Wow... I'm such a geek. What a bad analogy.

"Stop, stop, stop," Rhonda said. "This isn't going to work. I can't hear Zoë. It's a two-way and she has to scribble down things to tell me. Or sign, and her signing is so atrocious I have to fill in the blanks."

Atrocious? I glared at her and signed, *"My signing is not—"* I stopped. I didn't know if there was a gesture for *atrocious* or even how to spell it.

Well, maybe it was bad. But, hey, I'd only started a month ago when I got hand cramps from writing all the time. And I couldn't carry a laptop around all day—not like Rhonda.

I had no idea how to solve this problem, and I really wanted to talk to her about what had happened upstairs and being so upset about Daniel and his callous attitude about ghosts. About SPRITE and how they got my name and why the hell they were working for a state representative. And about this Ishmael group. I thought of Joe standing beside me and immediately thought of a wall of iron. No, make that lead.

Joe frowned at me. "Oh, I could have told you Frasier hates ghosts," he said softly. "Oh, come on, Zoë. Don't shut me out."

You're rude. My thoughts. MY thoughts.

Rhonda looked at me and Joe. "Shut you out? You mean like

out of her thoughts? Can you read her thoughts when she's in there?" She looked at me. "And can you read his?"

I shook my head.

Joe shrugged. "The only reason I can read parts of Zoë's is because she runs her head like she runs her mouth. All the time. It's like her mind's open twenty-four seven."

I stuck my tongue out at him. I looked at Rhonda and noticed a not-so-pleasant expression on her face. It looked like she was afraid of trying. Was she afraid of me?

"Why don't you just slip inside of Rhonda and see if it works?" Steve piped up.

"He's right," Rhonda said, as the door opened and a customer stepped in.

"He's just a ghost," Joe said, and thumbed Steve.

Well, I guess Joe really was a sensitive like Rhonda and Mom if he already knew Steve was a ghost. And it didn't send him running from the house.

"I can hear you, tall boy," the ghost said.

"Sorry."

Rhonda gestured for me to follow her through the beads. I glanced at Steve, who became a little more visible. "I'll watch the counter," he said, and smiled to the customer.

It was kinda cool having a working ghost. Creepy. But cool.

Standing by the fireplace, she pointed to the couch. "Lie down and Wraith on me."

I blinked. *What?*

Joe said, "What?"

Rhonda leaned toward me. "Go OOB and become the Wraith, and possess me. Just for a few minutes and see if it works."

This is crazy. I shook my head. Uh-uh.

"Well, she didn't actually possess me..." Joe said.

Rhonda pointed at me. "Come on—take me." And then she

did this really weird thing where she stood with her arms out, her head thrust back, and her chest out.

She looked like a plant warming up to the sun.

Joe held up a finger. "Wraith? You said that last night. You call yourself a Wraith?"

I nodded to him as I moved to one of the chairs in the corner, beside the shelves where Mom kept the books on Egyptian mythology and astrology. *You'll see.*

I made sure I was propped up good and wouldn't slide out of the chair before I took a deep breath and stepped out of my body. So easy—once again worrying me that the spiritual Velcro holding me in might wear out.

Joe stepped back, his calves banging into the coffee table and shoving it forcefully toward the fireplace. "Whoa...what the..." He pointed at me. "You didn't look like that before."

Look like what? I hadn't actually seen myself in Wraith form—not really wanting to for fear of *what* I'd see. Rhonda and Mom had been adamant enough about the subtle changes my astral form had taken on since TC.

Since his touch.

I looked down. Sweatshirt, jeans, and sneakers. Huh. I looked like me to me. What was he on about?

I moved to Rhonda and decided just stepping into her was probably the best way to handle this. Shadows like misty, sooty smoke moved around in the room, though not nearly as many as there were in other parts of Atlanta. Mom and Rhonda periodically "cleansed" the Botanica to keep out all the nasty spirits. Which I liked. Less creepies around me.

With a glance at a very wide-eyed Vice detective, I sieved right into Rhonda—

—and bounced right back out.

It wasn't the same as being physically thrown against a wall or anything, but it had the same mental feel. I was abruptly facing the beaded curtain to the tea shop. I turned and looked at Joe. *Did you see what just happened?*

He looked at me, then Rhonda, and then back to me. "Yeah...you walked into her, then you were...where you are now."

Damn.

Rhonda opened her eyes and looked at me. There was that slight pinching of her eyebrows together over the bridge of her nose—the one she was regularly giving my Wraith form—before she said, "Well?"

"No, it's not her fault," Joe said, and hesitantly moved closer to Rhonda. "You"—he pointed at her—"kicked her out. Somehow."

"No way." Rhonda stepped away from us. "I did not. I'm wanting you to step inside my body."

Joe shook his head. "Then there's something about you that's not letting her. You got a charm on? Or maybe an amulet?"

Rhonda's face brightened. She snapped her fingers. "Of course—when we were worried about Mitsuri I cast a protection on this." She reached down her shirt and pulled out a silver triskelion pendant on a leather thong around her neck.

I nodded at her and then motioned for her to take it off. If I was going to see if this worked, then we needed to step it up. All we needed was for a customer to step through those beads and see my body slumped over on the chair and these two just standing there. Wouldn't be good for business. And Mom's business is what kept me stocked in biscuits.

And as if on cue, my stomach growled from inside my body on the chair.

Okay—that was weird.

She took the charm off and tossed it on the couch. I moved into her and felt the same resistance I had before. It wasn't as harsh, or as strong, but it was there. Like moving through a wall of caramel. (Wow...I was so hungry even my analogies were foodcentric.) It wasn't much different than my experience with Joe—almost seeming as if I shrunk in on myself. I was in a dark room again, and there was a big screen up in front of me. I could see Joe looking at me.

He narrowed his eyes. "You in there?"

My, he's taking this calmer than most people would.

"Is she in here?" Rhonda put her hand to her head.

"Can you hear her?"

I yelled at her, jumped up and down, and screamed her name from my little theater behind her eyes.

Rhonda shook her head. "Nope."

Joe had his hands over his ears. "Ow...I did."

Nuts.

I stepped out, and Rhonda wobbled a few seconds. I was sure my new Wraith nature gobbled up a tiny bit of her on its way out. I moved to my body and sat down inside of it, then opened my own physical eyes and looked at Rhonda. I made an over-the-top shrug.

I could see my little buddy's disappointment then, and I stood. *"I'm sorry,"* I signed.

"Hey, it's not your fault." She looked sideways at Joe. "But how come you can hear her?"

He didn't have the answer, but he did have a whole bunch of questions.

"Okay"—he pointed at me—"when I knew you weren't dead in that drawer, you were like this? Normally? This Wraith thing?"

Rhonda put up her hands. "Look—you two talk in silence. I'm going to go get my backpack and laptop. Zoë owes me lunch, and I want good food." She left through the beads.

I looked back at Joe. *As in normally you mean I was a Wraith?* I pursed my lips. *I think it was starting to happen then.*

He looked as if he were thinking about something really hard. Too bad I couldn't hear his thoughts.

Look, would you care to explain to me who you are that you

*know about out of body? And how did you know I wasn't dead?
How did you know that thing was a Daimon? And what was it
you gave me when I was in that box?*

"Drawer."

Screw you.

Joe shook his head. "Uh-uh. You got a lot of talking to do
yourself. And I'll modify the question I asked you last night—why
do you call yourself a Wraith?"

And I answered it, explaining to him about Mitsuri, and how
she'd called me a Wraith that first time in Hirokumi's office.

He made a face that looked as if he smelled something bad.
"So I'm thinking this isn't the normal definition of Wraith. What
kind of a Wraith are you?"

*Uh-uh. Your turn. What kind of cop are you that you hang in
morgues?*

"I'm the good kind of cop that saves confused kids and teens
from an early death. Sometimes the drugs don't just kill, they—"
He looked just past my left shoulder, then said, "What?"

I turned to see Rhonda step back in, her backpack over her
shoulder and her iBook in her hand. "You two...you realize it's
a one-sided conversation." She pointed at Joe. "And you look like
you're crazy. Silence, then you just start talking."

I smirked. Rhonda was my hero.

"Let's go. Steve's going to look after the place, and he's trying
to wrangle Tim out of invisibility land. Nona prolly won't be back
for another hour or two."

"I'm going with you," Joe said.

Rhonda shook her head. "No, you're not. You're in this too
deep, and you don't know what you're dealing with."

I smiled as Joe crossed his arms over his chest and said,
"Enlighten me. What are we dealing with on what?"

"We're dealing with—" And that's where Rhonda wasn't sure
where to go. Frankly, neither was I. I was losing track of things

again, which meant I needed a notebook, food, a soda, and sleep. Sex would be nice, but I was sort of losing my craving for it.

Mental note: *gasp!*

I looked at Joe. He was listening. He was interested in what we did. And with Mom acting all weirded out, it might be nice to have him along. Kinda like the muscle. I signed to Rhonda, *"Take him to lunch. Talk."*

She looked less than happy and gave me an exasperated look. I heard an odd knocking from somewhere. Joe turned and ducked back behind the beads a few seconds before reemerging. "The dragon's dancing again."

Rhonda waved at him. "Forget that. Nona said she lit it the other night 'cause a customer was complaining of being cold. Evidently it caught something. Let's go."

I peeked inside the beads before we left and looked at the dragon. It didn't move. I stuck my tongue out at it and turned around.

It knocked a few times before we left out the back door. I wonder if I could find an Ethereal pest control in the paranormal yellow pages.

Wait! Jacket. I needed my peacoat. I went to the closet for it, but it wasn't there. Where was my coat? And then I remembered I'd had it on when I went shopping with Daniel yesterday.

When we went to Adore—

And Jamael gave me that thing from Dags!

Oh hell! It was still in the pocket of my peacoat.

I looked at Rhonda, then at Joe. *We have a little detour to make—you got anything against breaking and entering?*

14

January 26, 11:35 A.M.

THE weather wasn't all that great on the way to Daniel's house. A gray roof of clouds covered the sky, giving everything that old-time-movie feel. And it was bitter cold. I couldn't remember it ever being this cold in Atlanta.

My nipples were in a permanent state of freezing.

Following my directions, Rhonda pulled her Beetle into the alley behind the house and parked in the empty driveway. All three of us—with Joe folded up into the nonexistent backseat—sat there in awe as we looked at the monstrosity in the daylight.

Joe's reaction to Daniel's house was about the same as mine.

"You gotta be kidd'n me." But—he did fill in a few blanks as he pulled out a small black zippered case. "I'm pretty sure Heather makes a good bundle"—he pulled out a small black stick—"to compensate for a cop's pay."

Wait, wait, wait.

I touched Joe's arm—and he jumped back so suddenly he conked his head on the low car ceiling.

Stupid.

What?

Rhonda twisted in her seat. "That was smooth."

Joe seemed to recompose himself. "Sorry—you just—after last night I'm a little jumpy when you touch me. I mean—it's really a cool thing that you do—and I can act all suave and calm about this—"

But on the inside you're freaking out?

"You could say that."

Greeeat. What is it with this Heather woman? Are she and Daniel still married?

"Who's Heather?" Rhonda looked at Joe, then me.

Ooops. I sort of let that part out of my wee bit of writing last night. I looked over at Joe. *Can you fill her in? That way I can learn too?*

Joe glanced at me with a knowing smile—one I wanted to punch mind you—as he rubbed at his pointy chin. "He didn't tell you about Heather?" The question was directed at me.

I glared at him. *Watch it, or I'll go Wraithy on your ass.*

Joe ducked his head and looked again at the back of the house in front of us through the mist-sprinkled windshield. "Daniel and Heather Noir—"

"The TV anchor?" Rhonda's eyes bugged out.

I did a mental eye roll. Whoopee. So she was famous. Didn't give her permission to be a complete Be-OTCH.

Joe nodded. "They met about two years ago while Daniel was working a case, and Heather was covering it. Two months later they got married. And trust me—it wasn't a vacation. I was working Homicide back then and saw Daniel on a regular basis."

Knowledge dawned hot and fast on me at that moment. Sometimes I even surprised myself when I showed how smart I could be. I signed so Rhonda could hear it too. *You and Daniel were partners.*

Joe nodded. "Yep."

"Oh shite," Rhonda said.

"Even then I could see—things—and I usually had feelings when something was wrong. Well, I knew Heather was a wrong choice, and Danny-boy was working his ass off. I warned him he needed to keep an eye on her, but he ignored me. Started getting mad."

"You catch her cheating?" I signed.

I wasn't surprised when Joe nodded. "She even tried to come on to me. He'd told me to butt out, so I did. And he learned the hard way what a real piece of work that bitch was."

I felt terrible for Daniel then. He'd been betrayed by his own wife, someone he'd trusted. No wonder I didn't suspect any residual feelings left in him for Heather. She'd burned them all out.

"And he blamed you?" Rhonda said.

"He'd have blamed me even if I told him. So after it all came down, I put in a transfer to Vice. Worked out pretty good." He looked at the house again. "I knew he was trying to get the house in the settlement—but I don't see how he can afford this."

He couldn't. That much I knew. But it was a nice house. I pointed to his zippered case. *What's that?*

"My breaking-and-entering kit."

Pssshhh. *Put that away and let the pro do this.* I leaned back in the seat and closed my eyes. My head thunked against the passenger window as I went OOB and sat forward. I'm sure I looked a bit weird, with half of me sitting out of my waist.

"That looks—wrong."

I looked back at Joe. *And your point is?* With a wink I moved out of the car (ew, ew, ew—I hate sieving through metal and glass—it's a lot like chewing on tinfoil) and stood just outside the car. I checked myself. Though I wasn't wearing my normal OOB uniform physically—lately my astral form was compensating.

And changing it a bit. Yeah, I was all in black down to the bunny slippers, but the black was starting to look shiny like vinyl, and my bunnies were getting a bit more of an—I don't know—an evil bunny look to them. Did they have red eyes before?

Running to the front door, I sieved through the wood (I sieve better when I take a running start at it) and into the kitchen. Everything looked just as it had the night before. Clean. Unused.

I wondered if Daniel ever even cooked in here. Well, I'd find out tonight since we were doing pizza and movies. Yum! A night with the hottie cop.

Moving to the bedroom, I spotted my coat on the bed. Thinking of Daniel writhing naked on that bed, I felt my body become corporeal and started rifling through my pockets. With Daniel being a cop, he probably already knew the coat was still here. So if I took it, he'd notice it was gone and know someone had been in his house.

Ah, there it was. I pulled out the little bugger. A small silver jump drive. Or flash drive. Whichever was easier.

Now as to what was on the thing—beats me. But knowing Dags, it was something weird. Yeah, it might be easier to e-mail me, but I'd learned over the past month that Dags was more of a conspiracy theorist person. Not so bug-nuts over it that he was creepy, but he didn't trust e-mail. He'd been burned once with his e-mail being read while working at a company, and he didn't trust anybody.

He preferred handing me information via gadgets.

Honestly—I think he was just a gadget freak.

Okay, time to get this out the door and get back in the Beetle and get some food—

Something moved out of the corner of my eye—over by the door into the front room. The one with the piano.

I froze, cocking my head to my right shoulder as I listened. I caught a faint shushing noise from somewhere. I wasn't sure where. It was just—there.

Quenching the desire to go incorporeal and therefore a bit

impervious to physical attack, I moved back through the side door toward the kitchen. But even as I moved through the door something slid by to my right in the shadows of the dining room.

Just a bit curious—and not happy about there being something in my boyfriend's house—I reached out and flipped on the light. It illuminated a glass-and-iron table, complete with some sort of black-and-red table center and a brick fireplace separating the dining room from another front room.

The walls were red—which was okay if it just didn't remind me of blood. Real Amityville here.

But as my eyes tracked along the furnishings they moved back to a shadow between the farthest bookcase and a reading chair. It was darkest there, the light from the overhead barely reaching that side of the room. I gripped the drive in my left hand and stepped into the room.

Come out little bugger—or whatever you are. You know you're not supposed to be in here...

I really didn't expect anything to come out.

Ha. Imagine my surprise when a tiny little—something—peeked its flattened little face out of that corner. It was about the size of a soccer ball, black with dark lines to distinguish features like a nose and two red eyes and—

Lots of teeth!

I screamed.

It screamed.

I turned and ran toward the back door—but it was in front of me. No taller than my knees. A worm with a soccer ball and flat face for a head. It reared up like a snake and looked at me.

I didn't know how I knew, but I was certain this was a Daimon. Not the same one from last night, but definitely of the same variety. But what was it doing in this house?

What was it doing in Daniel's house?

Booodddyyyyyy... came a soft, whispered voice in my ears.

I narrowed my eyes at it—forget the fact I was about to faint from fright—and smiled. *You want my body?*

It nodded, and a long, snakelike tongue protruded from the mouth slit.

Wow. What a stupid little bugger.

Okay. I held out my arms. *Come and take it.*

I had no idea why I said that—but it seemed like the right thing to do.

The thing looked like it was going to cream its jeans. Wait—that was gross.

It dove at me. I immediately went OOB, the drive bouncing on the kitchen floor. It sailed into me—

And vanished.

Heat abruptly flooded my body. I threw my head back and screamed—a silent wail that announced my very being to the invisible world. I could feel the energy of the creature dissipating, merging with me, and I knew on a core level that it wasn't shadowing me as that one Daimon had done to the poor Blue Lady, Miss Pearson.

No—it wasn't consuming me.

But I had consumed it.

Stupid little insect. Mistook my manifestation for a real body. A body it thought it could take. I felt myself lift in the air just as another noise filled in the background of the maelstrom inside of me. I picked at the little creature, tearing it apart, wanting to know who had sent it. Why was it lurking in the shadows of this house?

And to whom had it been sent!

But it didn't know. It was feeble. New and poorly made. And it died quickly, becoming a part of me.

Just like a piece of pizza when I ate it.

Gone.

Burp.

"Zoë!"

I knew that voice. Distant. Troubled. And I opened my eyes and looked down at a little woman with dark lips and an odd hat. And a man—a tall man with dark hair. I noticed his aura, a faint glow about his body. And there was something else about him—something—wrong.

"Zoë, get down here." The little woman pointed to the floor.

The warmth left me then, and I was on the ground, my incorporeal feet just touching the hardwood. My knees buckled as the last of the power disappeared, and I went down on all fours, gasping for air I didn't need.

"What's wrong?" the woman was asking me. She was beside me, and I knew her.

I remembered her name.

Rhonda. She was—she was my best friend.

Th-there was a—

"There was a Daimon here," the man said, and I felt the vibration of his shoes along the floor as he went from room to room. "Where is it, Zoë?"

I knew him too. His name was Joe. Joe the asshole.

I swallowed and sat back on my haunches. I actually felt fine. Really. I felt great! The initial shock was more like the euphoria of surviving a dangerous fall. And then knowing it was all right.

And I was alive.

But—for an instant—I'd felt different. As if I were something else. It'd happened before. Only—I didn't want to think about it.

"Zoë." Joe was beside me, kneeling on one leg. He reached out to touch me, and his hand passed through. He jerked it back and looked at me with wide eyes.

I looked at him and gave him a weak smile as the power I'd felt a few seconds ago dribbled away.

"Zoë," he said in a very soft voice. "Where is the Daimon?"

I blinked once and sniffed. *I ate it.*

15

HE broke down the door.

The dickweed broke down the 'effing door!

I stood on the outside of the house, snugly back in my body, getting softly sprinkled on with tiny pieces of ice. The wintry mix promised earlier had begun.

Joe was on the phone with Daniel—and it didn't sound like a very good conversation.

He'd explained that I'd needed my coat, and didn't want to disturb Daniel so they were going to quietly—

Break in.

"—not exactly a burglar. Or not something you could classify as a burglar. But, yeah, when she got up to the door—Zoë saw a thing—well, a sort of thing. Looked like a person. She said it was a person... Well, of course, I can use sign language..."

I looked over at Joe. Rhonda was busy in the Beetle copying Dags's drive to her laptop.

Joe was drowning in a sea of lies. And I did take note that the git couldn't lie his way out of jury duty. Which was an admirable quality. In the right situation.

Finally, Joe hung up and shoved the phone back into his pocket. He moved to stand beside me. We both faced the door, now propped up in place but at a slightly skewed angle. "He's pissed."

I'd assume so.

"I offered to pay for his door."

Uh-huh.

"He threatened to sue."

I'm not surprised.

"I have people."

Sure you do.

Pause. "You hungry? I'm starving. I mean, after porking down a Daimon, you might be full—"

I knuckle-punched his left arm. Hard.

"Ow."

We decided on the Macaroni Grill past Perimeter Mall. (Yay!)

It was cold. The sky was a metallic gray, and the rain that drizzled down meandered from sleet to flurry during our drive from Interstate 20 to 85 North, then to 285.

While in the car I kept quiet. Not sure I really wanted to talk yet. Or at least think out loud. If Joe could hear my thoughts over Rhonda's *Reader's Digest* version of our little setup, he wasn't letting on about it.

She filled Mr. Halloran in on the basics of what it was that we do—starting with the eBay account and a few of my less exciting jobs.

He didn't say much, but I attributed that to either his dread of the door bill for Daniel, fright at Rhonda's driving, or the lack of oxygen in the cramped back. I listened to the radio as the weatherman confirmed there were winter storms over Alabama and heading our way. Not to mention another drop in temperature overnight.

Great. Cold ground, plus rain and freezing temperatures.

Another damned ice storm. Well, I didn't have a fireplace, or a backup generator like Mom. So it looked like it was another night at the old Botanica again.

Well, maybe not tonight. Unless Daniel canceled our date on account of broken door stupid-itis.

Mental note: *if Joe's testosterone screws up our date, I vote we beat him.*

Since it was closer to one o'clock, we got a booth near the open kitchen. Rhonda claimed she needed a side to herself for her laptop, so I scooted in, and Joe sat on the outside. Our waitress's name was Jackie. And Jackie evidently thought Joe was the main course. Me and Rhonda. The sides.

Actually, Rhonda was pretty much unique-looking enough to be a side. I was more garnish. Call me parsley.

But even if the service was a bit offsides, the wine was nice, the place was warm, and the food was incredible. I ordered my favorite, Shrimp Portofino. Mmmm...buttery, lemony goodness with pine nuts, spinach, plump shrimp, and al dente pasta. The rosemary bread was just perfect and the cracked pepper accoutrements...I was in heaven.

I drank everybody's water while the two of them talked. And I also ordered and drank two Cokes. I knew the sugar wasn't a good idea—but I was craving it. More so than usual.

We all ate with gusto, Joe asking his questions. I let Rhonda do the answering since we could both hear her, and if I answered, then she got put out at being the third in a one-sided conversation. I'd actually started to figure out how to have him not hear me. Droning inward conversation didn't seem to register on his radar. It was when I emphasized a thought that he could hear it.

But if I kept my thoughts low—that's when he was as deaf to me as Rhonda was.

Which definitely brought up that question again as to why Joe could hear me and ghosts in general could hear me. Trench-Coat heard me, as did the Phantasm. Oh, wait—I'd had my voice back at that point. But I was sure that even if I hadn't, he still could have heard me.

Once everyone was finished forking off of each other's meal and the plates were clean, I sat back and patted my tummy. So did Rhonda. Joe smiled and wiped his mouth with his napkin.

"You up to speed, now?" Rhonda said, and finished off her soda with a final sucking noise on her straw.

Joe thinned out his lips and looked at me to his right. "I think so. You were a Traveler—astral Traveler—and a Symbiont changed you. Now you're a Wraith. You can do things while out of body now that you couldn't before. The same Symbiont—TC?—that touched you also took your voice. As well as your health."

"Well, the health is only speculation," Rhonda said, burped, and grinned. "We haven't really had the opportunity to sit down with him or any other expert on the workings of the Abysmal and figure exactly what it is that he did. Or why he's affected Zoë like this. The fact she was a Traveler, still connected to a body, is *my* theory. Sort of like making a cake in the dark, only you grab a few wrong ingredients, and the cake isn't what you intended it to be."

I think what she meant was Trench-Coat had intended to eat my soul, and instead latched on to a living ghost. Gave both of us a shock at the time. I got a freakish tattoo.

I wondered what he got on that first meeting where I gained the ability for corporeal agility.

"Are you okay?"

I looked across the table at Rhonda. She was staring at me with that Mom look again. I arched my eyebrows and nodded.

"You're awfully quiet. And even for you with no voice, that's saying a lot."

She was right. Something very odd had just happened to me. And it really wasn't the first time. I needed to tell her, and I needed to tell Mom. But Mom was off with her geriatric Scooby partner and I had—Joe.

Uh-huh? And your problem is? He knows all about you, Zoë. More than Daniel does.

Not wanting to deal with Rhonda's laptop, I motioned for paper and pen. This was too much to sign, and I wanted Rhonda to hear it. When I was done I pushed it out on the table.

Rhonda was done first and looked up at me. "What do you mean you felt like you lost yourself?"

Joe was first on the mark. "You mean, when you consumed the Daimon, you felt overwhelmed with power? You lost yourself?"

I nodded. *It happened before. In the alley. I looked at you and thought "bug."*

Joe made a face.

"Okay, stop that. Can't hear."

I looked at Rhonda but Joe repeated what I said to her.

"So you didn't know us at first? At Daniel's house?"

I shook my head. I tried to sign what I needed to say. *"I felt trapped inside—looking out. Powerful. I felt like…"*

And words failed me.

"You felt like someone else." Joe looked down at me.

I looked at him. *I felt like something else. And nothing else mattered. Not you. Not Rhonda. And not Daniel. Because I was all there was.*

Joe relayed what I said to Rhonda, and everybody got quiet.

"Well, this is a new development on the path to Wraith," Rhonda said. "You happen to think of me or Joe as a bug again, you let us know, okay?"

I nodded. I felt a little uncomfortable talking about me. I used to like talking about me. But now—now me was scaring the hell out of—*me.*

I waved at Rhonda and signed to her, *"His turn."*

With a sigh of what I knew had to be bloated content, Joe rested both elbows on the table, pushing his plate away, and cupping his elbows in his palms. "I've been able to see things—like Zoë and the guys in your store—for about a year and a half. At first I wasn't sure if it was just work-related stress. Too much time on the job. My recovery." He shrugged. "I don't do drugs, but I did notice that sometimes when we checked out a scene of an overdose, I saw a thread—like a tiny silver string—coming from right here." He unfolded his arms and leaned back in the booth and pointed to his belly button. "And it sort of floated like one of those tubes you see connected to astronaut suits—just sort of there and coiled around, then usually disappearing into the wall or the floor."

I knew exactly what he was talking about. The silver cord—the tether that connected us all to our bodies—kept us rooted in the physical world. I knew my silver cord was my lifeline to my humanity. I don't know how I knew it, but I did.

Rhonda was intrigued. Her eyes were round, kohl-lined marbles, and her smile would have split her face in two if it weren't for her cheeks. She was leaning closer to Joe. "You just started seeing the cord one day? Just like that?"

He shook his head and shrugged. "It was after I was shot. Me and my partner walked in on some kids holding up a QT. The clerks were shot and down behind the counter, and the kids were already looting the registers. I got hit before I could pull out my gun. My partner took them down." He smiled at me. "I died."

Yikes.

Wait. I rounded on him. *Daniel told me he got this partner killed in a shooting. Was that you?*

"Yep."

But he made it seem like you really died. As in you're still dead.

"That was about the time he found out about Heather. And he knew I was right. That's a whole different story, so I'll leave it for later.

"It was after I was out of the hospital I started seeing them. The first one I remember clearest was my third day back to work. We were in a playground where some kids had been shot in a drive-by. I was kneeling over one kid, couldn't have been more than ten, and I saw the cord. It flashed in the sun, and I was sure if I could touch it, it'd feel like warm wire." His expression darkened, and he leaned forward again, put his arms on the table. "Then I saw the same kid standing on the opposite side of me—just inches away—watching. I saw the cord went from the middle of the kid in my arms to the kid standing there."

You saw his ghost.

Joe looked at me, and his gaze locked onto mine. I got the impression that if I looked away, he'd fall as he spoke. "I didn't know what was happening. What I did know was that the boy standing was crying, and he kept saying 'Mama's gonna be so mad,' over and over again. And the cord just broke"—he snapped his fingers—"and he was gone."

The waitress came by and offered to refill Joe's wine. He declined, and I had to practically shove my glass up her nose to get the same service. Be-otch.

When she was gone—with Rhonda's order for tiramisu and mine a coffee—Joe continued. "I went to the doctor then—and he put me on drugs. But those didn't work. I started calling off work—I worried I was actually crazy and might hurt someone. Daniel was in the middle of hell with Heather, and I was no help. My doctor suggested I go see a different kind of help. A shrink."

"And?" Rhonda said.

Joe looked at her and smiled. "I saw *three* shrinks. All of them said I needed an extended stay in a hospital. No—not my way. Well, it was a friend's birthday, and I went over to this shop that sells all that New Age crap. You know, the Crystal Christians."

Oh! Rich! I had to remember that one.

We nodded. He shook his head at the memory. "There was a

reader—you know for cards—in one of the back rooms. I moved past the door, and she came out after me. Demanded to see my palm. So I showed it to her."

And? I sort of knew where this was going. She told him he had a gift and blah, blah, blah. The usual. I burped. Ooooh. Garlic. And . . . something I didn't remember eating.

Oh gross. Daimon tasted like boiled eggs?

"She immediately gave me a card with a ghost on it and a guy's name—said I should look into ghost hunting."

Okay. I didn't see that one coming.

"Ghost hunting?" Rhonda looked as perplexed as I felt. "Are you kidding?"

"No." He shook his head. "And then we sat down, and she told me I wasn't crazy. That she could see the ghost in the right corner of the room—which, of course, I thought was a real person sitting there waiting for her to finish—and she'd accepted her abilities, and I should accept mine. She explained the cord, and what I was seeing."

So you decided to put your ability to use—by watching the morgue to make sure the kids that were pronounced dead really were?

He nodded at me. "Precisely."

Rhonda put her hands up. "You two have got to stop doing that."

But he wasn't going leave her out. "Basically—I decided to try and help those kids that had strayed from their bodies but could and needed to find their way back. Like I did with Zoë."

That brought my attention up short. My coffee arrived, and I ignored it. *You did what?*

He looked embarrassed. "Sorry—I didn't know what to tell you at the time. I saw you wandering the halls of the hospital. It's like you'd gotten most of the way there—but you were totally out of it. Dazed. And you looked a little—" He stopped.

I leaned forward and prodded him with an arched eyebrow.

"What?" Rhonda said.

Joe really looked uncomfortable. He shrugged. "Ah hell. You looked like you'd just had the best fuck of your life. You were so real to me. You even cast a shadow. And when I was trying to get you to see me, you vanished. I thought I was losing my ability."

I looked like WHAT?

He explained he'd caught sight of me, ghostlike, drifting from room to room. My cord had been practically nonexistent.

And the rest was history.

But even after the dessert came, and Joe joined Rhonda in several rich spoonfuls, I was still chewing over the whole event. I had no memory of wandering the halls of the hospital. I had had flashes of something—pleasurable. Alluring. Satisfying.

Later on I'd remembered a lot more of those missing hours, and I'd done a damned good job of pushing those memories away.

But I didn't remember anything else other than the sex. And I'd started to wonder—did I really want to?

Rhonda put her laptop on the table and opened it. "Okay, down to Dags's message." She turned the computer to face me.

It was a text document addressed to me. Very short. And very…

Oh hell.

Hi Zoë,

Look, don't be mad at me, but I think I might have let your name slip to someone you wouldn't want to get involved in. See, I was bartending up at the Livery in Roswell, and this guy came upstairs for a drink and dessert. He looked familiar, but I wasn't sure from where. Said he had some pictures of a ghost and wanted to know if I wanted to see them. Well, you know me, I said yeah, and when I looked at them, I was very impressed.

*I told him it looked like the profile of a friend of mine.
I told him your name and that you were dating an Atlanta
detective. Uh—it wasn't until later that I realized he was
part of that ghost-hunting fiasco back in October out at Web
Ginn House Road.*

*Don't eat me, okay? I did find out some interesting stuff
though off my ghost watch Web site. Seems there's been a lot
of interest in finding a couple of necklaces—they call them
Eidolons—and there are reportedly five of them. Don't know
what they're for yet, but I'll keep digging. I'll be working
down at Fadó's this weekend—all weekend—if you need me.*

And again, I'm so sorry!
Dags

So *that* was how Randall Kemp got my name. All he had to
do was look it up and find out I was mentioned in the story about
Susan Hirokumi. And about Daniel Frasier.

I'm going to kill him.

Joe nodded as he read the letter over my shoulder. "I'd kill
him too."

Rhonda was nodding. "Randall could present a problem. He
sort of struck me as the type of person that gets a bug up his butt
and doesn't let it go."

Yeah, well. That bug was me. And if I was up his butt, I was
gonna sting the hell out of him if he caused trouble.

That's when I noticed a strange feeling—something that didn't
have anything to do with any supernatural ability. I felt eyes on me.
I was being watched. While the other two talked, I started looking
around the restaurant. But I didn't see anyone situated where they
could actually watch me.

So—where was the feeling coming from? I needed to take a
walk. And normally I wouldn't have bothered with it—I mean

being with Rhonda with some of her looks, I always got stared at. Of course, it was usually with the condescending look of those who knew they chose better friends.

Jerks.

But this—

"What's up?" Rhonda said.

I signed, *"Watched,"* to her, then looked up at Joe. *Need to borrow your shoulder.*

Before he could protest I leaned against him and slipped out of my body, moving through him and the seat to stand beside the table.

Joe shivered but put a protective arm around my shoulder. He glanced up at me. "You promised not to do that."

I did not. I promised not to overshadow you. I'll be right back.

I slipped out and sieved through the door, then through the second one and into the lobby, careful not to step through anyone or to allow them to move through me. Luckily, it was off-hours—practically no customers.

I scanned the parking lot as I stepped out into the gloomy day.

As I suspected, there was a guy sitting in the front seat of a huge white kidnap van (meaning it had no windows on the sides or back), and he had some sort of camera lens mounted to the dashboard. I had a sinking feeling as I moved to the side of the van and saw the nasty green fairy with its ghoulish face.

Damn. SPRITE. And the guy in the front seat, when I looked even closer, was none other than Randall Kemp. I recognized him now. He was still thin, and still very much as intent-looking as he had been months ago.

From the look on his face—the way he looked down at his lap, then up through his windshield—I figured he was seeing something through his thermal imager again. Nice equipment. And the van looked new. After seeing the cameras at the Westin, I assumed that Randall had found a very nice backer.

The way he was looking at the infrared in his lap he'd just seen something.

Greeeat. *You just gave him ammo again, Martinique, by standing directly in his line of sight.* Yay for my side. I moved to the side of the van and looked in. I'd gotten used to the no-reflection angle of being incorporeal. I knew most people couldn't see me like this—and notice I said most. There were always those few that screamed out, "Hey, nice bunny slippers."

Whups.

I could see the imager in his hands again, and he was looking very perplexed. And, well, I was a little pissed off. I liked my privacy, thank you. And I'd already been ticked that he'd tried to worm his way in with my boyfriend via the bartender.

A ghost's electromagnetic makeup usually shot electrical appliances and tools all to hell. This I'd learned from Rhonda, though she had a knack for making things work through this little handicap—like my watch, for instance, which counted down my time out of body and actually worked on me in the astral.

Well, this little fucker had picked on the wrong astral entity. Ghost. Wraith. Whatever I wanted to call myself. The ideal situation would be to overshadow him and find out who's backing him and who hired him to work at the Westin.

But I didn't have time for the aftermath of that. Not yet.

But I was going to fuck up his stuff.

With a deep breath, I moved to the back of the van and proceeded to walk through the walls, through the equipment back there, through anything that remotely looked like it could record me.

Everything I touched sparked or bounced with its internal cry of death as I charged wires and fried circuitry.

And then I did the ultimate—and I braced myself for this one since I had no idea what a man like Randall Kemp thought about— and walked through him and the electronic device in his lap.

The images I got weren't what I'd thought they'd be. You know, seeing images of porn tapes, and maybe even some *Star Trek* posters and shelves of fantasy and science-fiction books in his room in his mom's basement.

No—that wasn't what I saw.

I saw me—or his version of me—inside of a glass cage. I was shady, like a movie or television ghost, and I was weak and helpless. And he was standing in front of a podium with the presidential seal.

The images blinked by fast, and even as I stumbled out of the van's driver's side, and Randall started swearing because he got a chill and his machine went dead all at once, I understood something that might be a problem later.

Randall Kemp was working on something that could capture and hold a ghost. And if not hold them, weaken them enough for capture. And he had backing. Lots of backing.

Money.

And the drive to prove he was right.

16

ONCE back in my body, I gave Joe and Rhonda a quick version of what I'd learned by typing it into a blank page of her word-processing program. The two of them huddled up to read it.

Rhonda was the first one to look up at me. "You saw this weapon in his head?"

I nodded.

Joe didn't comment. He'd paid for lunch—oh wow!—and was folding the receipt up into his wallet.

"This is bad." She pulled the computer closer and reread it. "I have to know how this thing works. If it really exists I have to have one of them so I can reverse-engineer it. See how to create something that will offset such an ability."

"I doubt it," Joe said, and we both looked at him. He clasped his hands together on the table and looked at both of us. "What? You said it yourself—when you pass through a person, you see what's on their mind. Or rather what's sitting around in their sub-conscious. Who's to say this weapon just wasn't a part of that? A wish or a dream?"

Then if it's his dream, we'd better keep an eye on him.

Rhonda was shaking her head. "I still need to meet this guy and pick his brain. See what he's coming up with that'll do what he wants it to do." She tapped her chin. "Might work off the same principle as the Soul Catcher."

"Yeah, yeah—but what about this backing?" Joe looked from Rhonda to me. "What kind of organization is going to shell out that kind of money for research on a weapon to capture a ghost?"

I nodded. *And what about Stephens? He hired the security for the fund-raiser.*

Joe relayed my thoughts to Rhonda, who nodded. "Most definitely," she said. "Why else would SPRITE be at the Westin? It's like Joseph said—it's all tied together. We just have to figure out how."

I continued to digest the images I'd just seen as we left the restaurant. The wind had picked up and was even colder. The wintry mix had descended. Kinda cool really. Atlanta didn't get much in the way of snow. We usually saw ice.

And ice was dangerous. Dangerous because us Southern folks don't know how to drive in weather. Period. Oughta see it when it rains.

Ack! Rain! Everybody put on the brakes.

Add snow in the mix? We're talking parking lot.

The van was gone when we left. At least he'd been able to start it.

"I need to stop by Phoenix and Dragon before we head back to Little Five," Rhonda said as she unlocked the car.

I nodded.

Once inside and in Roswell Road traffic, I half turned in the passenger's seat. *Joe...*

He leaned in to rest his face between the headrests.

Joe, I need to know more about this warehouse, the one where Holmes was killed.

He shrugged. "Not much. Kinda a scary place if you ask me. Went out there Friday after the funeral—"

You were at the funeral? I bent my brain backward trying to remember if I'd seen him there or not. Joe doesn't have a face anyone can soon forget.

"No, I wasn't there. I was digging around into the warehouse's history. Old owners. Present owners."

Who owns it?

"It used to belong to Visitar Incorporated. Guy named Koba Hirokumi—but when he died a few months back, ownership was transferred over to a guy named Francisco Rodriguez."

I heard the screech of brakes somewhere in my head. Or was that the scratching of a needle across a vinyl record?

Koba Hirokumi? Francisco Rodriguez?

Wow...it really was a small world.

Rhonda was listening. "Whazzat? Hello. Alone over here. Did you say Hirokumi and Francisco Rodriguez?"

Joe filled her in on our tiny conversation. I was sure anything that dealt with Hirokumi dealt with Symbionts and the Abysmal plane. And if ownership was transferred to Francisco—well—we could bet his interest rested along similar lines.

And though I didn't have any evidence, I had a hunch the warehouse tied in with the missing whatever-it-was that was locked safely away in evidence. The very thing Knowles seemed worried about.

And I'd bet my left Kegel muscle there was an Eidolon in that box.

But how did this tie in with the headless body Daniel was investigating? Or did it?

Joe, what was taken from that warehouse? Do you know?

He shook his head. "I think it was a bunch of boxes."

I'd appreciate it if you found out for sure.

I needed to take a look at the warehouse. And I wasn't sure I wanted Joe with me while I was there.

Not yet.

Rhonda glanced over at me, and I furrowed my brows at her. She obviously caught my train of thought and looked at Joe in the rearview mirror. She was thinking of the conversation between Francisco and Knowles, same as me.

Time to let Rhonda proceed with her bad self. "Joe, ever heard of a group called Society of Ishmael?"

I watched his expression. Didn't reveal much. His eyebrows arched up into his forehead. "Not much. From what little I know they're kinda like your Rosicrucian, or maybe Shiners. One of those old secret societies—old white men that sit around in big chairs, read up on old tomes, and smoke cigars." He frowned. "Come to think of it, Rodriguez is a member."

Which is as much as Daniel had mentioned.

"What is their philosophy? Their doctrine?"

"Quacks mostly." He shrugged. "I know enough to know to stay the hell away from them. It's rumored they deal in electronic espionage. Nothing ever proven, but you really don't want to show up on their radar."

I looked at Rhonda. Her expression had returned to that unibrow scowl. "Quacks? From what I know of them, the Society works to protect the innocent from the wicked."

"Yeah?" Joe leaned to his right against my seat and pinned our driver with a stare. "The wicked what? Why did you ask me that when you already seem to know something about them?"

The car came to an abrupt stop. I looked through the front windshield. *Oh, look. We're here!*

The Phoenix and Dragon sat nestled back in a wooded area off of Roswell Road, up and across from the shopping center called the Prado. The store wasn't much more than a converted house, and it catered to the strange and unusual. Unlike the shops in Little Five Points, P&D had a more varied crowd, from the upwardly mobile entrepreneur looking for a good self-promotion book, to the local high school kid interested in the latest Wicca fad.

The sounds of a dulcimer CD filtered through hidden speakers as we entered and followed Rhonda to the left, past the fireplace decorated with handmade pixies and fairies, selling for prices close to that of an iPod.

Books were in the back room to the left, and Rhonda appeared to know what she needed. Joe moved into the main room where beads, jewelry, boxes, glass, wind chimes, and glass cabinets filled with handmade pendants and earrings sat. He went to the essential oils, and I moved to the right, where a door led out onto a porch and meditation area. Behind me and to the left were three doors. The first door led into a private room, while the second two doors opened up to a larger room. Different groups held meetings here, and the schedule even talked about an open house for a local Wiccan group once a month.

Shiny.

Wondered if Rhonda or Mom ever came out here. Sort of cool, really.

I returned to where Rhonda was talking to a small, compact woman with short red hair and chandelier earrings. She looked pale and withered.

"...been a frightful week," the woman was saying to Rhonda. I noticed Joe a few feet away, bent down at the jewelry counter with his nose pressed against the glass. What was so engaging? He looked kinda cute, all pushed up against the glass like that.

Kinda.

"Did they report it to the police?" Rhonda said, her hands folded over her chest.

"Yes—both stores were hit and ransacked. Nothing was missing—both had a full inventory. And just over a week ago there had been a man in asking about an Eidolon amulet."

!!!

I stepped forward and mouthed, "A what?"

Rhonda frowned at me and put a hand on my shoulder. I'd

forgotten she'd been in the room with me when Joseph gave his warning on an Eidolon.

"A what?" Rhonda said.

"Eidolon. I had no idea what he was talking about, but it intrigued me enough to go look it up. It's a stone pendant. Plain, really. They were made by a famous ceremonial magician about thirty years ago. I think there were five in all. He was also said to have created the Dioscuri, but that was never proven."

Dis-what?

The woman noticed my confused look. "The Dioscuri is the name of a rumored archive of supposed experiments in the outer planes—the mental, the astral, and the Ethereal. But just like the Akashic Records, it's a myth. Allegedly this ceremonial magician discovered a bridge between this plane and the astral."

Oh. Interesting. But I had no idea what an Akashic Record was either. Wasn't that a kind of breakfast-cereal maker?

I nudged closer, my gaze targeting a rather creepy-looking handmade tree-guy. Someone had to have way too much talent and way too much time, and be way too into *The Lord of the Rings* to make such a detailed tree Ent. The entire thing was made of natural items, from a real tree branch, moss, black peas for eyes, and real flowers. Huh.

Here was this masterpiece created by human hands, with no instructions, only imagination.

And I always managed to screw up a box of brownies.

"What did these amulets do?" Rhonda said.

"Don't know really. They were reported missing after the magician was murdered. Somewhere in Savannah. There was a rumor of one here in Georgia—owned by a local man named Charles Randolph. Each one's made with a different stone."

Charles Randolph—that rings a bell. But where had I heard it?

Rhonda was about a half mile ahead of me. "Wait—Charles

Randolph was the name of that man they found murdered—last week?"

Gulp.

Yep. That was it. That was the name of the headless body.

I suddenly felt flushed. It was warm in the store, and I looked through the window at the moving trees. The wintry mix had stopped (pooh), but it still looked as if the entire world had been drained of color.

The sky was still looking a little spooky, and I pushed my sleeves up to my elbows. I thought about heading outside and taking a breather by the car when something to the left of the doors caught my eyes.

Ooh...sparkly wind chimes. I loved wind chimes. And there were several. One was made of amethyst crystal with thin fish wire suspending long silver tubes of metal. I stepped backward a few paces to get a better look at it in the light.

The door to the tarot room opened again as I backed into it, and into somebody. I turned to apologize and looked directly into the dark and handsome face of Francisco Rodriguez.

"Oh, terribly sorry, Miss Martinique. Forgive me." He gave me a smile, a nod, and moved past me in a pleasant breeze of cologne.

I stood there with wide eyes and watched him move away, my mouth open, my right hand up.

How...

Wha—

Does he...

How does he know my name?

Rhonda rounded the corner then, a bag in her hands, her cell in her other hand. It was ringing—a downloaded mp3 of "Tubular Bells." She stopped in front of me and answered it.

Rhonda frowned at my openmouthed expression.

Joe showed up then, a bag in his hand too, and we were all standing by the wind chimes. "Zoë?"

I put my other hand to my head. *Rodriguez…he was just here. Francisco Rodriguez was here. And he knew my name! And the guy with the Eidolon was the guy who had his head chopped off!*

Joe blinked, then he looked back the way he came. "Wait— you really saw Francisco Rodriguez? Here? He was in here?" He pointed to the floor with a long index finger.

Rhonda was still talking in a low voice and had turned away. I was hoping it was one of her many informants. She always did seem to know the right people for the right bit of information.

"Did he say anything?" Joe said.

He said excuse me before he called me by name. And he was incredibly polite!

Abruptly Joe put his hand to his hip and pulled his shirt out of the way, exposing a very hairy midsection.

Ew.

He had a pager on his left hip, attached to his belt. Grabbing it off, he checked the number and hit a side button and looked at the LCD. "Uh—I'm gonna need to get back to my car."

Rhonda disconnected. I pointed to the phone. She smiled. "One of my sources."

I pointed to Joe. *You tell her I just saw Francisco!*

He did. Her eyes widened, and her mouth dropped. "Here? He was in there getting a tarot reading?"

I nodded.

Joe replaced his pager to his hip and handed me the bag in his hand. "This is for you."

I opened up the bag and pulled out a silver necklace. On the end was a small, unpolished blue stone wrapped in silver wire. It was beautiful.

"That's azurite," Rhonda said as she put her phone back in her backpack.

Joe nodded. "It helps enhance the mental plane. Helps connect mind to spirit."

I looked up at him. *You think my mind and spirit aren't connected?*

The look he gave me wasn't a reassuring one. "Let's just say I think with what it is you can do—and given your recent experiences with it—keeping your mind locked to your spirit is a good idea."

Uh. Thanks.

I unhooked the clasp and put it on. The stone fell just above my cleavage line. Well, that was convenient.

Joe smiled at it and looked at Rhonda. "We ready to go?"

Sometimes I can pick up signals, subtle hints that tell me there is something a bit weird happening. The problem is that I rarely understand what that is until after the fact. My hindsight is indeed twenty-twenty—I just wish it were my foresight.

Having someone come here looking for an Eidolon was oogy, then to find Rodriguez here of all places just added to the oogy.

Über-oogy.

The whole Eidolon warning from Joseph was taking on a much bigger part here—especially now that I knew the headless guy actually had an Eidolon—and I'd bet the police had found no sign of it in his house.

Add that into the warehouse and the boxes, SPRITE at the Westin and Knowles and Francisco's weirdo conversation, compounded by two Daimons—and Joe was more worried about his page call?

I followed them out, clutching the bag Joe had given me in my hand. We piled into the car and headed back to Nona's. In relative silence. Rhonda was on the phone two more times and talking in code. Lot's of "Uh-huh," "No way," and "Can't say," as she drove. Joe stayed in the back and didn't say a word.

Once back at the shop, he jumped out and waved before jogging to his car. When he was gone, Rhonda turned to me, and said, "We're going to the warehouse."

I'd planned on doing just that—but not at that very moment. She put the car in reverse and backed out of the drive onto Euclid.

I signed, *"Now?"*

"Now."

Apparently one of Rhonda's sources had called back with information on the warehouse. It wasn't owned by Francisco Rodriguez as Joe had discovered, but had been purchased less than six weeks ago by an anonymous party. There were also rumors that the warehouse had at one time been a meeting place for a group of ghost hunters.

Oh, this is just getting confusing again. Bring on the stupid.

Rhonda pulled up at my condo. I got out and headed upstairs. And after setting the little warding bubble, I left my body on the bed in my office and met her downstairs, sieving through the car and into the passenger's seat.

The warehouse in question was near Interstate 20, south on Gresham Road. It wasn't the happiest part of town. In fact, it was downright scary here. Sort of reminded me of the row houses over near Grant Park and some of the less-populated areas on Hollowell.

I sort of discussed in a bad sign-language way ('cause you know, she was driving) that maybe the headless part was part of the ritual for this Society of Ishmael. Didn't societies—especially secret ones—have weirdo rituals like that?

Rhonda put a firm no stamp on that one. A little intense at that.

Due to Atlanta weekend traffic, it was nearly six thirty and the sun was disappearing. But when I thought about the day and the gray clouds, it was doubtful it'd ever really been there. Temperature drop was incredible. So while I'd been upstairs going all OOB, Rhonda had done a quick change in the car.

I'd always wondered what made up the contents of her backpack, other than her laptop. She'd switched to gloves, black sweats with tights beneath, Doc Martens, and two shirts. As well as the funky hat with ears.

She kinda looked like a warm Ninja Mickey Mouse.

Me? Same as usual. Black with bunny slippers, now with that odd shiny look. I just wish I could have a Batman utility belt sometimes. You know, grappling hook, guns, smoke bombs. It'd be so cool.

Rhonda stopped the Beetle at the entrance to a very dark, very spooky driveway. The warehouse loomed several feet in the background behind a very high, barbwire-topped fence.

I signed, *"Why here again?"* Yeah, I'd decided I needed to investigate this place myself, but I was abruptly getting cold feet.

I had an oogy feeling.

Might be that glaring, yellow-and-black police tape plastered all over the front telling us to go away.

"Because everything leads back to this warehouse. Holmes's death, Joseph's warning, and Francisco Rodriguez. I mean, this thing was even owned by Hirokumi. My informant said there'd been more odd activity here even after the police left."

I frowned at her. Uh-huh. Her informant. I grabbed my board and scribbled, YOUR INFORMANT BEEN HERE?

She shrugged. "Dunno. They didn't say." She glanced at me. "Let's go."

I held up my hand. Whoa, whoa, whoa…grabbed up pad again. WHERE YOU GOING?

"In there with you. And don't say it's too dangerous." She smiled. "I've got a Wraith protecting me."

Swell.

With a glance at me, Rhonda parked the bug, and we walked to the fence. It wasn't locked. In fact, the padlock hung on the right-hand door. She shrugged and pushed the gate aside, ignoring the plastic tape that gave and popped apart. I walked through it and followed her onto the property, to a side door.

Rhonda pulled a flashlight out of her pocket and clicked it on, then pushed the door. It was open as well.

Not liking the ease of this. This was a crime scene—why wasn't it all locked up?

"Hello?"

I nearly jumped out of my skin when she did that. I shushed her with a wave of my hand. I could see without the light. And though I didn't see anything odd—except maybe the occasional wisp of something Ethereal move by—I still didn't want anyone to know we were here.

"Hello?" a voice answered back.

Too late.

"Did you hear that?" Rhonda said.

I nodded. The interior of the warehouse was like any other—cavernous. Because it was apparently empty. Devoid of whatever it once played house to. Debris that looked like rags, bricks, and some thick rope littered the floor. Along with a lot of bugs.

I hate bugs.

Almost as much as clowns.

I caught a soft glow to the right in the darkness.

The glow grew closer and started to take on form. Rhonda drew in a breath about the same time I nearly fell backward from shock.

"Lieutenant Holmes?" Rhonda said.

His ghostly form grew brighter. He wasn't black-and-white like Joseph, but he was definitely a spirit. His colors weren't Technicolor, but golden. He was still wearing his uniform and hat, his gun drawn and in his right hand. "Rhonda? Is that you?" Ah. Languid vowels and extended consonants.

Lieutenant Charlie Holmes all right.

She took a step forward. "What—why are you here?"

Then he saw me, and his eyes widened. His expression grew sad. "Zoë—oh, honey. They killed you too?"

I put up my hand. *No, Charlie. I'm out of body right now. I'm spirit. But I'm not dead.*

Charlie Holmes took a step back. "Well, I'll be damned, Zoë— I can *hear* you. Something wrong with your throat? Your voice is all scratchy." He leaned his head forward. "You sure they didn't strangle you?" A frown. He pointed at me. "This new?"

Uh—not so much. But why are you still here?

"Because they shot me," he said with the tone of a disapproving father. "And I have no idea why."

We were three people alone in a sea of black, with only the light of a ghost to illuminate us. And Rhonda's flashlight.

"Charlie, what happened? Who shot you?"

"You don't know? The thugs in fatigues and black masks— that's who shot me. I got here and was doing my rounds of the place. Was a few calls about cars driving in and out of here. So I got out here and lo and behold, there were a whole bunch of them."

"Them what?"

"Them thugs. About six or so. And they were in a circle, facing out, kinda like guarding this stack of boxes."

Boxes?

Charlie was still talking. He seemed very happy to be telling someone his story. "And there was this man with the boxes, with a crowbar, and he was hacking away at them."

Hacking at what?

"The boxes." Charlie demonstrated, his gun vanishing and a crowbar appearing in his hand. He waved it about as if hammering something large into the ground. "And he seemed very upset. Kept saying, 'Where's the eye-dee-lon? Where's the eye-dee-lon?' "

Eye-dee-lon. Eidolon.

Rhonda looked at me and smiled. "Bingo. From what I read in the paper, the police found drugs and reported that Holmes was killed because he interrupted a drug sale."

But Charlie was shaking his head. "No, no. There weren't no

sale going on. That guy was looking for something, and he wasn't finding it. And he was really mad too."

"Well, well, well…" boomed a voice from the darkness.

I crouched low, making myself as invisible as possible.

A light came on behind us, and we turned. I could make out a woman in a coat and a man holding a camera over his shoulder. In the silhouette cast by the light I recognized the skinny figure poised there.

"What *do* we have here?"

Heather Noir.

17

OHHELLMOTHERFUCKER. Not now!

She walked briskly over the concrete floor and stood beside Rhonda. The cameraman followed her. "I don't know you."

Rhonda had her hand up to deflect the light. "Thank God. So can you get that fucking light out of my face before I bust it?"

My little goth buddy wasn't a big girl, possessing a metabolism to rival my own. Nor was she very tall, standing a good foot or two shorter than me. But she had one good advantage over me. She was tough, and people tended to believe her when she threatened to do something.

He didn't turn the light out, but he did turn it to the floor, where the illumination bounced up.

"Who are you?"

Rhonda crossed her arms over her chest. She looked sort of frumpy standing next to Heather's willowy figure. "I was here first. Who are you?"

I got the feeling Rhonda knew exactly who this was, given that the woman's face was plastered all over the local stations and bill-boards. But she'd ticked my wee buddy off.

"I am Heather Noir. I was given a tip to be here and catch the men who murdered Lieutenant Charlie Holmes." She looked around at the dark. "Where are they?"

"Who? There's no one else here."

Heather whirled on Rhonda and stuck out a very well-lacquered nail. "I heard you talking to someone."

"She doesn't see us, does she?" Charlie asked me.

I shook my head and moved out of the camera light's illumination. I didn't know if he had that thing on, but since my little incident with SPRITE, I didn't want to take a chance.

Rhonda spread her arms wide. "You see anybody else?" She looked back at Heather. "Who called in the tip? Did you talk to them?"

It was a good question—and I could understand the cautious tone in Rhonda's voice. The only reason we were here was because of a tip from *her* informant. And now Heather was told by someone to be here. I really hoped they weren't the same person.

Heather had her hands on her hips. "I would never reveal my sources."

A small clack resonated inside the dark warehouse. The outside metal of the building creaked and moaned as the wind picked up. A low whistling sounded high above our heads as it threaded the holes and ruts rotted away by rust and time.

Charlie—do you sense something?

The ghost nodded. "Yeah—you girls best be going. Run if you can."

Why—what is it?

"Do you hear that?" Heather said, a little too loudly. She and her cameraman turned in circles as he brought the light up and shined it in all directions.

"Zoë," Charlie hissed.

I looked at him.

"Remember how I said I was shot by some thugs in black masks?"

I nodded.

"Well, they sort of looked like that." He nodded past my shoulder.

That's when I saw them, crouching low. Five of them, dressed in dark colors. Even their faces were masked. They flanked left and right to surround the five of us standing near the center of the room.

I turned just as the entire room lit up like a football field. Evidently the boys in black had had portable floodlights set up in advance. My hands went up defensively, blocking my eyes from the glare. Rhonda, Heather, and the cameraman were a bit more vocal. And more creative with their metaphors.

Wow...Heather. Potty mouth.

She was also the first one to regain her composure. "My name is Heather Noir—I'm here for an exclusive interview."

Movement on all sides brought our attention back down to ground level. The five men wore dark fatigues, their faces hidden by ski masks. And they had guns. Most of them were long, riflelike weapons, and I recognized them as tranquilizer guns.

But one of the men, the taller one who came closest—he was holding a real gun.

One of the men nearby spoke in a distorted voice. "Heather Noir—we have no quarrel with you. Please leave."

Uh-uh. Heather had a story, and she wasn't about to let it go. Lowering her arms to her sides, she looked around the circle of men surrounding us. "I don't think so. Not when I've found the men who killed Charlie Holmes. You rolling tape, Brian?"

And he was.

Until the closest man fired a single shot into the camera. It exploded outward, and Brian dropped the very expensive piece of equipment and moved a step back.

"Please, Miss Noir," came the voice again. "I will only ask you one more time to leave."

You know—I really didn't like Heather from the moment I saw her in that line. She was nasty. Bitchy. And completely self-absorbed. Not to mention she was Daniel's ex-wife.

And Joe said she made his life hell.

But—if nothing else—she was also ready for this kind of shit.

She and Brian.

And the boys in masks *weren't* ready for her.

Before I could blink Heather had a gun in each hand. So did Brian, who looked a bit more beefy without the camera half-hiding him. They stood back to back, holding up the handguns, in the four directions of the winds.

"Whoa," Rhonda said in a perfect Keanu Reeves impersonation.

Heather glanced at her. "You didn't think I'd come to a deserted warehouse unprepared, did you?" She pursed her lips. "I wasn't married to a cop for two years for nothing."

Okay, that was my cue to look impressed, because I knew she was speaking of Daniel. And, yeah, he'd taught her well.

"Now," Heather said in a strong voice. "I think we all need to have a little conversation."

"Miss Noir," said the voice again. I noticed the masked men hadn't lowered their guns, but they had taken a step back. "Please understand, the living are free to go. This is a matter between us and our prey."

Well, that little statement caused several mixed emotions. For Heather and Brian it was an exchange of WTF looks. For me, well, I got just a little unnerved. I didn't have a clue who these guys were.

But I was beginning to suspect we were set up. (Duh!) All of us. Though I didn't know why they'd bring Heather into this.

"The living?" Heather removed the safety from both guns. "I'm afraid if you don't call off your goons, there won't be any living. I didn't come here without making a call to a friend either."

I really hoped it was Daniel she called. And I hoped he would answer the phone—

Shit!

I realized right there that I'd completely forgotten our date! Oh my God—he was going to hate me. I'd stood him up. Our first chance to be alone, and if I didn't get out of this, I was a no-show. Oh, I was still wary of him, but I guess in the back of my mind I'd been thinking maybe if I got him alone, we could readdress this little ghost problem he had.

One of the armed men lowered his gun and pulled a small monitor from inside his jacket. He held it up and out like someone would a digital camera. "Sir, I don't see the Wraith."

"She's there, between the traitor and the witch."

Rhonda and I glanced at one another. Between the what and the who? I was standing between her and Heather.

"Sir, how can we capture something we can't see?"

Oh. Wait. Capture? *Moi?*

Heather cleared her throat. "Excuse me? I think all four of you should put your guns on the ground and your hands in the air."

Three of the men with guns held them up higher and focused them on Heather and Brian.

Heather licked her lips. "Or not."

"Disarm them," the one on the left said. He appeared to be the leader and the one with the dramatic voice box. "Wraith, show yourself, or we shoot one of them."

I'd grown a bit cynical over the past few months. I didn't trust men with masks. And I certainly didn't trust masked men with guns. I did not believe for one minute that if I showed myself, they wouldn't hurt or even take Heather, Brian, or Rhonda with them, wherever that might be.

I didn't know who they were, but they knew what I was. And they wanted me. I always liked to be wanted, but not like this. I checked my watch. I had three hours left on the old chronometer.

While attention was focused on the others, I moved into a quick run and dove into the leader—the one with the bullet-throwing gun—but instead of falling into the familiar little black room behind his eyes like I had for Joe and Rhonda, I found myself on my back with this guy's hands around my neck.

I looked up at him, but his face was still masked even inside his head. "Get out of me!" He was shouting this over and over and over.

Wow...I hadn't encountered a real fight before. Then again, I'd only shadowed two people. I reached up with my own hands and grabbed him around the neck as I got my feet beneath his stomach and pushed up, slamming my heels into his pelvis and flipping him over my head.

I rolled back over then, and while he was getting up I saw a bunch of those twist-tie holders I saw used on *Cops* strewn all over the "floor" and grabbed them. Only these things unfurled like a whip, and when I snapped them at him, they wrapped around him, binding him up in a neat little ball.

Sah-weet.

Didn't bother to wonder where they'd come from. I could only assume Mr. Mighty-Man here had conjured them up in his head to use on me.

Ha-ha.

Abruptly I was in the dark room looking out of the leader's eyes. I put a hand up to my head to experiment, and the physical body did the same. I was in control! I'd really done it! So by incapacitating the host's spirit—soul—whatever—I'd become the boss.

Kewel.

The one with the camera was looking all around. "I—I can't see her anymore. Where is she?"

One of the other masks was looking at me. "Sir—are you okay?"

I turned the gun from Heather and pointed it at the person closest to me. "Everyone drop your weapons," I made him say. I had a voice again! Yay! Okay, so I sounded like Darth Vader, but it worked!

They all looked a bit skeptical then.

"Sir?" the closest one said. The one that had asked how I was, Mr. Polite. That's when I realized his voice was a bit familiar.

I took enough information from my host to know he was the only one with a real gun. The other two had Tasers as well as tranq guns, which could debilitate but not kill. Normally. So the first order of business was to put the most dangerous one out of commission. Which happened to be the one I was standing in.

And what was the quickest way to do this?

You got it. I squeezed his nuts. It was only a mental thing, but I managed to think his balls shrinking. Somehow he believed his precious jewels were caught in a vise grip. He made a noise like a choking duck and doubled over. I made sure his hands pressed the clip release on the gun before he dropped it to the concrete with a clatter that echoed throughout the warehouse and went to his knees.

The sudden movement of the bad guy made the one closest get a little trigger-happy. He shot the Taser at us, the two electrodes sticking into my man's chest. The resulting blast of volts scrambled my control of him, and I was vaguely aware of him wetting himself before I was thrown out and on my ass behind the whole group.

Ow.

That *sucked*.

My entire body was hurting, which was normally something I never noticed before. Feeling, that is. I was still incorporeal, though. But it was a little harder to move, my reaction time slowed. But I did hear Heather make a girlie "Hi-yah!" noise. The others were fighting the masked men as well. I could hear the scuffling all around me.

I blinked several times, shaking my head to clear the cobwebs. Rhonda had used the opportunity to put a little of her defense training to use. I can only assume one of the idiots tried to grab her from behind, she feinted, braced herself, and managed to flip him over her head and deliver a well-aimed chop to the neck.

Hrm. I don't remember learning the chop to the neck part. Which lesson was that? We took them together, every week. The move worked, and the thug went down with a thud, gun on the concrete.

That left three.

The sound of grunting brought my attention around to the far right. Brian was in a fistfight with one of them—and from the looks of things Brian was the more experienced fighter. I could see their breath clearly in the light as Brian feinted backward when the attacker swung a hard right, then moved under the outstretched arm and dove into the man's torso, the two of them hitting the ground with a good loud "ommph."

I had every intention of helping cameraman Brian, and I even stepped toward the two of them. I'd use my new shadowing power and—

That's as far as I got.

Something slammed into me from behind, pretty much like a speeding truck, and knocked the astral wind out of me. I stumbled and fell forward, catching myself with my elbows. There wasn't any pain, per se, but there was an odd echoing sensation along my arms and knees, as if the impact of my astral body had a significant influence on my physical one.

That didn't bode well.

I didn't have stars dancing in front of my eyes. As an astral presence, I'd never really run into weakness, except when I'd been out of body too long. And I knew I still had nearly three hours left.

I remained on my hands and knees for a few seconds before turning my head to the left. The attacker who had had the camera managed a quick clip to the back of Heather's head. She went down fast, her gun clattering to the floor.

He moved closer to me. The camera was still in his left hand and he was watching me through it (or so I assumed 'cause he never took his eyes from it but seemed to know right where I was), but in his right hand—well, there really wasn't anything I could compare it to. It looked like a gun, if not a pretty large one. It was rounder than a normal gun and matte black. The fluorescent lights didn't even leave a glint on it.

If I didn't know any better, I'd have said it was made of shadows.

He was pointing it at me. Had he actually shot me with it? Was that what knocked me down?

Was that possible?

"I command you to become tangible, ghost."

Well, the authority was there, but was buried in a quiver of a voice. There was a kid behind that mask, and I was beginning to wonder if these guys were SPRITE gone hood on us. I mean, I did sort of wreck Randall's van earlier.

I also had a few rebuttals I wish I could have spit at him—but, well—there was that lack of voice thing again. Damnit. The overwhelming need to puke disappeared about as quickly as it came. I didn't feel better, but I did feel stronger. Maybe the effects of his little ghost gun were temporary?

"If you don't become tangible, I'll shoot you again."

And if you don't point that thing somewhere else...

I gathered my returning strength into my thighs, hips, and calves and feinted downward, as if I were going to collapse on the floor.

Yep. He fell for it. Young and stupid.

I launched upward as he came down toward me, and I slipped into his body. Not much of a fight in this one. In fact, his internal image sort of screamed and fainted. He was easy to control. I shivered—and damn, it was cold. This kid wasn't wearing much. And I realized at that moment as I checked out the body this wasn't a kid, but a guy of about thirty. Oh—who really needed to use the bathroom. Youch.

I checked out the gun in my hand. It felt as odd in this hand as it looked from the other side of the barrel.

Might be something for my magical MacGyver to—

The sound of a gun going off nearly deafened me. I ducked my head into my shoulders and put up my hands, camera, and gun, to ward off any potential threats.

"What the—" I heard myself say inside this body.

God, I loved having a voice again, even if it wasn't mine.

I turned to where Brian and attacker three were scuffling. Neither one of them was moving. I froze. *I thought—I thought I rendered the one with the gun defenseless.*

I turned around and looked at the pitiful man rolling on the ground several feet away. Yeah—he was still there. Moaning.

Abruptly Brian moved. He'd been on top of the attacker when the sound of the gun went off. He pulled the gun out of the unmoving kid's hand as he straightened up. I realized then it was Brian's gun that had gone off. Brian then looked at me standing there and pointed it at me. "You, on the ground, hands behind your head."

I held up the fun gun. Shit—he didn't know I was in here. He thought I was one of the attackers. Of the five, the one that'd attacked Rhonda was facedown, the one I'd taken care of was still moaning, I was in the weird-gun shooter and the camera holder, and Brian had just knocked out number four.

Number five stood next to me—the one who'd asked the leader if he was okay. Mr. Polite.

His eyes were wide, visible through the holes in the mask. And he was looking past me to my right.

I turned as well and nearly cried out.

When fired, a bullet, compelled by force, shoots out with tremendous power and will continue to travel until it either loses speed or is intercepted.

This bullet had been intercepted.

"Zoë—" Rhonda said, her voice holding a slight quiver.

I stepped to the side and looked at Rhonda, standing where Charlie Holmes had stood earlier. She had both her hands over her middle. Something was pooling between her fingers, moving in small waterfalls to the wood at her feet.

Rhonda had intercepted the bullet.

She went down on her knees, her kohl-rimmed eyes wide as she looked from her torso to me. I jumped out of the guy so fast he actually collapsed beneath me. I was moving fast across the small space, but not as fast as Mr. Polite. He got to her first and caught her. I was ready to jump into him and destroy his nuts as well if he didn't let my best friend go!

Why wasn't Brian shooting him? Decking him? Taking him out?

I was on the ground beside Rhonda and the masked man as he lowered her to the ground. I was all ready to overshadow his ass when he wrenched off his mask and bent low over my best friend.

I sat back—my eyes wide—as I stared into the face of Joe Halloran.

He checked her vitals as Brian knelt beside him. "Where did it impact?" the cameraman said to Joe in an almost familiar way.

Joe started ripping Rhonda's tee shirts away as he started to examine her. "It's bad. Right in the center. Might have nicked the stomach as well as a lung."

As if on cue Rhonda started to cough as blood came out of her mouth.

"Joe, we gotta call it in."

I looked at Brian. And then at Joe.

Joe looked directly at me. "You've got to get in there."

I blinked at him. He was—he was one of the masked men?

And Brian the cameraman knew him?

"No time for explanations right now, Zoë. You have got to get into Rhonda right now and slow down her heart. If not, she's going to bleed out."

Brian had his cell phone out and was waiting for the call to pick up. "Who you talk'n to?"

"Casper," Joe snarked, and then glared at me again. "Get. In. Now!"

"You better do it, honey," came Holmes's voice from the dark. "She's gonna die."

I did as they said.

There was no resistance as I went in, but I couldn't feel anything. I screamed at her from inside the darkness of her mind. But Rhonda hadn't been able to hear me before, why would I think she could now?

I could hear Joe though, on the outside, yelling at us both.

"Zoë? Are you in there? Rhonda? Oh shit, oh shit, oh shit."

Joe. Joe?

18

January . . . Saturday . . . Unknown . . .

THERE was only a slight resistance when I tried to take full control of her body. I extended my arms out into hers, my feet down into her feet, then lifted my head up—

Sonfoabitchmotherofallthingsholy!

I wasn't a stranger to pain—not at all. I'd suffered my own share in my life, from being raped to being banged up inside the trunk of my Mustang (my car!), and I'd been hit. Several times. By a few bad spirits.

But this—this was insufferable. This—no wonder Rhonda had let go and put me in charge. I could almost hear her voice echoing around me as I settled into her body. "Oh. It's you. Good. You deal with it."

My eyes sprang open, and I saw Joe looking down at me. He had his hand up. It was slick. A glove of blood.

"Oh . . ." I croaked, then my stomach seized up. And I tasted blood. I had a mouthful of it. I spit and choked as I tried to talk. Oh, this was worse than anything my mother put in her teas. "Fuck—"

"Rhonda?" Joe said.

I shook my head. "Me…" I managed to gasp out. The pain was blinding. The only thing I could compare this sort of agony to was the time I'd had my appendix out. I'd told Mom there were tiny little gumballs inside of my skin (the burred seed balls that dropped from sweet gum trees), sticking and ripping out muscles from the inside.

I really hate those things.

"Zoë—you're really in control of her body?" He looked really surprised even though it'd been *his* idea to get back in here. "Can you control Rhonda's heartbeat?"

"Wha—" I blinked several times. I was crying—and my eyes were stinging from the kohl I knew was running into them. I probably looked like Dracula's ho. "Control…her heart…?"

"Yeah." He nodded quickly. "She's been hit directly in the stomach area—I don't know if it's *in* the stomach, or the spleen, or even her liver. But she's losing a lot of blood, and if it's in her bowels, then she's depositing waste into her bloodstream. I need you to slow her heartbeat down."

Well, that was an idea where I didn't have any. I nodded and closed Rhonda's eyes, and sort of dove back inside the body. I was blind (I had my own eyes closed) and I listened carefully to where her heartbeat was. Just down, a little to the left.

I centered on the sound first, and then moved my hands out of hers and down to where her heart was furiously pumping in almost blind panic. I reached out, a hand on either side, and with sheer thought, set both hands on the organ. I sent calm thoughts, about slow lazy walks, about sunny afternoons on the porch at Mom's, with lemonade and fudge brownies. I thought about pillow fights in the bedroom of my place, and sitting on the sofa watching a good movie. I pulled out memories of eating huge chocolate sundaes at Brewster's Ice Cream in Brookhaven.

As I held her heart, willing it to slow, I dredged up every fun, calming memory the two of us had ever shared together. And believe me—there were a lot of them.

I had no idea if what I was doing was working, but I felt myself pulled along the same theme. I felt my own heart slow, I felt my breathing grow even, deep. And somewhere in the miasma of memories I felt a long, lingering sigh.

I'm not sure when it ended either. I saw the images as I thought of them. I could smell the fresh-cut grass in the backyard of Mom's house, the aroma of wild onions in the air, and the musty scent of a summer thunderstorm on the horizon.

I had my feet propped up on the banister. We were facing the old house behind ours—a brick ranch style with a string of hung laundry flapping in the wind beneath darkening clouds. Mom's car, respectfully named Elizabeth, a scary old powder blue Volvo, circa 1985, sat by the basket of overturned daisies.

"Storm's coming."

I nodded. A breeze moved my hair, and I sipped at my tea. Mint. Rhonda made it. Mom wasn't there. She was out with her friend Mrs. Shultz.

"I should probably leave now." Rhonda sipped her own tea.

I turned my head to look at her. I could hear the cars move by on the road, passing north and south on Euclid. "No—I want you to stay."

She looked away from me. "You won't."

"Yes, I will." I sighed. Deep. Relaxing. Slow. One beat when necessary. Stop the flow of blood. Engage the blood, fill the capillaries, pull it back to the lungs, fill with oxygen. "Why would you think I wouldn't want you here?"

"Because things will change soon." She looked at me. She was squinting. It was Sunday afternoon. No kohl rimming those eyes. They were brilliant blue. Weren't Rhonda's eyes brown like mine? "You won't want me here."

"Tish." I liked the sound of my voice. It irritated a lot of people. Scratchy. It was unique. I really missed it. "I can't do this without you."

"Nona's going to need you more than you need me." Rhonda coughed. She looked pained.

Slow. Deep breath. One beat, bring the blood of life around, pull it back in. Easy on the heart. Keep it steady. "You okay?"

She nodded. "You're making me okay. I'll live—because of you."

I smiled.

Her expression darkened. "The storm's closer now."

I nodded. I could see the clouds. They reminded me of clown faces. Angry clown faces. With fangs and feral eyes.

I disliked clowns.

I heard voices in the house. Soft at first. But urgent. I felt like I needed to go back inside. Mom might be home. She and I needed to talk.

"You're going to have to let go now."

I turned back to Rhonda. I was sitting forward in my chair. I didn't remember doing that. "I know. Promise me you won't go?"

"I promise. You'll send me away when the time comes."

I stood up. The voices were louder now. Very urgent. The back of my left hand stung. I pulled it up and looked at it. There was a needle sticking out of a large vein that ran between my fingers. But I wasn't sure that was my hand, or Rhonda's. Was I still there? Inside of her? I looked back at my friend. She looked better now. Not so pale or washed-out. "Why would I do that?"

"Joe."

"Joe? I'll send you away because of Joe Halloran?"

But Rhonda didn't answer me, and I really wanted to go into the house to see what was happening. Something tugged at my belly button, and I looked down at the cord.

"Never lose that, Zoë," Rhonda said as I started in the back door. "Never cut that cord. It's what keeps you human."

I promised myself I'd remember that as I walked inside the house.

THE house was filled with voices. Hundreds of them crying out for attention. Release. Oblivion. They all wanted me. They demanded I release them all.

I wasn't in my mom's house now, and I knew I wasn't in Rhonda's body anymore either. I'd done my work there, and I had to believe that that little interchange on the porch was something private between her and me. We'd been in some "other" place—maybe on the mental plane.

I only hoped I remembered it at a good time later.

I was standing in the middle of a hallway. Dingy, foot-traveled tile made up the floor. The walls were medium blue. There were doors every few feet on either side, in either direction. There weren't any smells though. Just the sounds of voices.

And a hush-whoof noise. Rhythmic. Peaceful. Very dependable. It was coming from one of the doors. Light came from above me and below me, and I moved on my bunny slippers with silent footfalls to the door on my right. Inside was a machine, and in the machine was a man, and in the man there lived a soul, and in that soul there lived a strong will to survive. I could sense it as I stood there. Watching him.

Men. Women. All in hospital scrubs, moved around the room. Checking dials. Adjusting IVs. Shaking their heads. They wanted him to die. It was pointless to linger like this. The body had shut down. But the mind...

Ah...the mind was alive! And it wanted to scream.

I neared the machine and looked down at the wilted face. *It's hard to scream with a tube in your mouth, isn't it?*

His eyes opened. He looked at me. And I saw defiance in that gaze. I sensed he wanted to run. He wanted to escape me. He hated me. He feared me. And yet he longed for me.

But there was no escape, was there? Death was nearby. And I was in a sense her servant.

"Yes, my child. You are."

The voice came from behind me. I knew it. I'd heard it. And I'd never forget it.

It was my voice.

I wasn't panicked like I thought I should be. I carried the calm I'd given Rhonda with me. And I was thankful for it. Especially when I turned and saw a clown standing in the doorway behind me. His skin was bone white, and his eyes were painted on much like a cartoon. His nose was a red ball, and his mouth was an overstated upturned weenie.

He wore a vertical rainbow-striped jumpsuit with large red pom-poms for buttons. And his feet were the size of skis.

In one hand he held four chains ending in four shackles. In the other he held a thick, metal collar on a thick chain. The chains weren't attached to anything I could see, but I knew they connected to something in a very dark place.

And I knew this creature. We had spoken once before.

Phantasm.

He smiled. But then clowns always smile, don't they? "Oh posh. Titles only. You can call me Friendly. Friendly the Clown."

I took a step back with a sting of shock. That was where I'd seen this image before! A childhood memory. A clown at a friend's birthday. He'd tried to hug me, and I'd been afraid of him. And then he'd cornered me in the bathroom. He'd locked the door.

And then he'd shown me—

STOP!

The memory dissolved. No, that wasn't *my* memory. That never happened to me. So whose memory was it? I took a deep astral breath and knew at that moment I was really standing in a hospital. I was really standing in the ICU. I was standing beside a man who would not die.

"Are you, Zoë?" Friendly the Phantasm cocked his head to one side. "Or is this *your* dream? And is that poor soul over there your feast?"

I do not consume souls. I release them.

He nodded. "For now. But you see—the Wraith and the Angel of Death do not see eye to eye. He is of the Ethereal, and you—" He smiled, and his large round red nose twitched. "You are of the Abysmal. You are opposites in every way."

That isn't true. I felt that calm I'd been enjoying slip away. I balled my hands into fists.

"You willingly took in the power of a Symbiont. It is now a part of you, and you a part of it. One of you will fall." The weenie elongated and turned up in each corner. "But where he is naturally born of the Ether, you are an abomination."

Riddles. He'd done this before, when I'd made my decision to remain a Wraith and save Susan Hirokumi. I looked at the chains, at the shackles. *You think to bind me with those?*

He shrugged. "No—these are not for you. These were once mine. I was once bound, and I broke free. I am all things in my realm, Zoë Martinique." His eyes flashed a glowing red. "And you will be a part of that realm. Nothing moves without my permission. Without my will."

I straightened up. *Except for me.*

I expected him to get all mad and pissy. But he only smiled brighter. Pretty soon that weenie was going to touch ends. "Yes. Except for you. For now. You must release life to live, my child. But you don't exist in order—you release souls to wander aimlessly. You do not send them on as Death does, nor do you give them a purpose. You damn them for eternity, little Wraith. You are, as you said, Death's servant. The Spectre of Death."

And he was gone.

I lowered my shoulders, aware of an incessant tug on my stomach. I looked down. My cord was faint. How long had I been gone from my body? There were windows in this room, and the sun was rising.

"Please take him," came a small voice to my right. I looked over, then down, into the eyes of a small brown-eyed little boy. He was dressed in a pair of wet cutoff brown jeans, and had a haircut right out of *The Andy Griffith Show.*

Why?

He gave me a half grin. "Because he's afraid to come and face me, that's why. It's been seventy-one years since I drowned. He was too chicken to come into the water to get me out, and now he's too chicken to die and face me on this side."

I blinked. Oh. Well, I didn't need a diagram to get that story retold. I looked back at the old man. I really didn't think he was going to pull out of this mess. I checked his chart. I couldn't read doc speak, but I could understand enough to know kidney failure and liver failure weren't easily recovered from. Not for a man over seventy-one.

Who is he?

The kid snorted. "He's my little brother."

Wow. I was really glad at that moment I didn't have siblings.

I neared the old man's bed. A nurse moved nearby, doing her thing with dials. I was a little miffed at old Friendly for coming into my life and just stirring things up. I was not anybody's servant. And I wasn't after the AOD's job either. I was a harbinger of death, right?

Right?

What did he mean by *spectre?*

I warned people they were going to die. Only—I seemed to be the one who saw the death masks. No one else. But—was he telling the truth? Was I just releasing them into the realms, with no home? No direction? And Death feared me?

"Oh, go on. He'll be okay. He's going to Heaven, after he settles with me."

I looked at the old man's eyes. I didn't see comfort there. I saw fear. Terror.

I also felt the tug of my cord. I knew my physical body was nearby. Which either meant I was here visiting Rhonda, or I was checked in somewhere. I was thinking it was the latter, which meant I was going to catch hell from Mom.

Again.

Ooh. And Daniel. Whom I'd stood up.

"Go ahead. Take him. End his suffering. Send him on his way."

I reached out and touched the old man's shoulder.

That same overwhelming light filled the room. Blinded me. Followed by the indulgent feeling of euphoria. Every time that happened, I felt lifted, as if I were no longer on the ground but in the air.

I closed my eyes and lifted my arms up as I felt the release of the old man's spirit. I heard his cry. I heard him call out in fear.

And an echo of terror imprinted on my soul.

19

Saturday . . . Or was it Sunday?

"ZOË?"

"I think she's coming around."

Who was talking? Was that Tim?

"Oh—I'd say she's back."

Okay, that last voice was unmistakably Joe Halloran's.

I pried my eyes open, just in time to feel the overwhelming owies of being out of body too long. It wasn't a full slam back in place—that happens sometimes, and it's not a pretty picture. It was still an electrifying experience. Every muscle from the tips of my fingers to the ends of my toes contracted all at once as my blood turned to molten lava inside my veins. Sort of like having a charley horse in every muscle of my body.

This particular reentry—not so bad. Maybe only ten muscle spasms. But still painful. I felt my back arch, my hands balled into fists, and my toes curled under.

Breathe, breathe, breathe . . . come on . . . you've done this before!

Didn't mean I liked it.

I heard the beep-beep of a heart monitor (oh goodie), as well as more voices in the room, and Joe in the background calmly saying, "She's okay. She'll be all right."

My muscles relaxed—a little—or at least stopped fussing at me the way a pissed-off cat would, and I was able to take in long gulps of air. There was a mask over my face, and the air was pure. Cool. And tasted like—metal.

Yick.

I opened my eyes and saw the familiar scrubs and jackets of hospital attendants. I saw Dr. Maddox to the right—he was the one holding the mask over my face—and I saw Daniel just beyond him. He had his glasses on, and he hadn't shaved.

Ooh, he looked good enough to pounce.

I rethought the way I felt physically—okay—pouncing later.

"Okay, she's good—she's good," Maddox said in a commanding voice, and removed the mask. I blinked a few times and raised my arms as if to fend off the crowd. Wow—I had a plastic bracelet on. That meant I'd been admitted.

My heart leapt into my throat. Hold the phone. I'd left my body in my condo, in the office, safe and sound, right? So—how did I get here?

I tried to sit up, but Dr. Maddox put a hand on my shoulder and collarbone and gently pressed me back down again. "Relax, Zoë. Back again, I see?"

He didn't look mad—but somehow I got the impression he wasn't happy either. And I'm sure I was a less-than-ideal patient. Always in and out of the hospital. I gave a mental eye roll. There had to be a better way to do this. And I couldn't wait for my insurance company to finally dump me out on my keister.

I signed Rhonda's name to him. He was clueless, not knowing any ASL. But Daniel did and edged Maddox out of the way. That's when I noticed all the other people had left the room. It was just me, Daniel, Joe, and Maddox.

And Tim! He was behind Daniel, a shade of himself, but there. How did he get here? Had Mom brought him?

Mom? Where was Mom?

I looked at Joe. He waved. And then I remembered the warehouse, and the shooting. I held up my hand and pointed at him, mouthing, "killer!" and, "traitor," in a soundless bluster. But Daniel and Maddox had their hands on my shoulders, and Daniel was speaking in a soothing voice.

"Zoë, please, relax. Please," he was saying, and I looked over at him. Didn't he know? Didn't any of them know? Joe was one of them—them—those—uh, those men!

Daniel took my hand and kissed it as he sat on the edge of the bed. Those damned bars were up, the metal ones that I supposed were to stop the patient from falling out of the bed. "Listen to me, baby," he said. I looked at him again and swallowed hard. "I had to break into your condo to find you. When you didn't show up for our date, I thought you'd stood me up."

Well, I did.

"And then I got a call from Heather—that Rhonda had been brought in with a gunshot wound, and they were taking her to surgery. I started asking about you, but she and Brian—her cameraman—they hadn't seen you. So that's when I went to your place and found you. You weren't moving, barely breathing and unresponsive. I figured it was a diabetic coma. So I brought you here." He glanced up and over at Maddox. "The doc said your sugar slipped again. I was right."

Well—that wasn't the real truth. But it seemed to be a really good excuse. I also had the impression that a lot of time had passed. More than just a Saturday night.

I signed Rhonda's name again.

"She's fine, Zoë. She took a bullet to her midsection." His frown deepened. "They got it out—and she'll recover. Heather told

me she and Rhonda were at the warehouse because of an anonymous tip."

I glanced over his shoulder at Joe. His expression was unreadable.

Daniel followed my gaze. "Detective Halloran was apparently
already here at the hospital. Seems to hang out in morgues."

I noticed that Joe was no longer dressed in his black fatigues
and ski mask either. Instead, he wore jeans, a flannel shirt, and a
jean jacket. I wanted to throttle him. I wanted to scream to Daniel
that Joe wasn't to be trusted—I didn't care if he'd shown concern
for Rhonda. He was an attacker, and possibly one of the sons of
bitches that killed Charlie Holmes.

I remembered Brian the cameraman on the phone, and he had
to have seen Joe hovering over Rhonda. Seen the uniform. Known
Joe was one of them.

So—why wasn't he under arrest? In handcuffs? Carted off to
jail?

Joe was glaring at Daniel but was surprisingly quiet. Daniel
pulled out his notepad and pen, and I made a gesture as if to ask to
use them. I flipped over to a clean page and wrote, HOW LONG
IN HERE?

Of course, I was thinking a couple of hours. Sunday morning
maybe?

Daniel sighed and put his hand to my cheek. That's when I
noticed the scent of roses and saw several vases full of them about
the room. "It's Tuesday midmorning, Zoë."

Tuesday morning.

I blinked.

TUESDAY MIDMORNING? WHAT HAPPEN TO SUN-
DAY? MONDAY?

He put up his hands as I scribbled on the paper. He didn't need
to see the note to know how I felt. "You've got to calm down,
baby."

Baby. He called me baby. *Screw* baby—two days?

Maddox stepped forward and touched Daniel's shoulder. Daniel stood and let Maddox in closer. "Okay, Zoë. You're going to have to calm down for me. We've been through this before—"

But I was scribbling on a new piece of paper. WHERE IS MY MOTHER?

The doctor glanced at it and shook his head. "Nona's not here. She's a little busy this morning. She was here earlier, though. Both of the detectives can vouch for her, okay? I'm going to check your blood pressure again."

I nodded to him but continued to glance at Joe, then at Daniel. Two days. I'd missed something—and somehow Mr. Ski-Mask over there had gotten away with whatever had happened in that warehouse.

Just behind Joe, blending into the shadows of the corner of the room, was Joseph Maddox. He looked pale. Paler than usual. And he wasn't as sharp as he had been. I knew he needed to talk to me. *Now.*

But...if Tim was here too, then how? If Mom wasn't here, who else would know to bring the piece of brick from the house so Tim could travel?

Dr. Maddox did his thing with the pressure collar on my upper arm, then he checked his chart. Joe and Daniel stood opposite one another, Daniel with his arms crossed in front of him, Joe with his hands shoved into his pockets.

Joseph was in the shadows on the left, Tim to the right. A room of living and dead.

As Maddox moved away I caught sight of something long and wispy trailing out of the center of his back. I thought it was a string at first, something caught on his doctor's white coat. But then it sort of moved and looked as if it had the consistency of a spiderweb.

I realized I was seeing Joseph's fetter. Maddox had been my

doctor before and after his son's death. But I'd never seen the fetter—not since Joseph had appeared in Maddox's office that day back in November. Why was I seeing it now? What was the difference? I glanced over at Joe. He was looking back behind himself and frowning at me. He was following my gaze to Joseph.

Ack...he didn't see Joseph! Why didn't he see Joseph? That was just like Rhonda—she couldn't see Joseph either. Ah—it was that shade vs. ghost thing again. Damnit.

"Zoë." Daniel moved close to me again and sat on the edge of the bed. He took my hand. His skin was warm. Soft. Comforting. "You can't keep doing this to your body, you realize this, don't you? This is two comas in less than three months."

Well, yes and no.

"Odd," Maddox said as he turned back to us, my chart in his hand. "Everything checks out normal. This morning you were unconscious with a low heart rate, off-the-scale blood sugar, and little to no brain activity. And now—" He narrowed his eyes at me. "Now you appear to be fine."

I smiled. I wanted to go home.

I wanted my mommy.

But obviously she didn't particularly want me.

I put my hands to my face. I wanted to sleep in my own bed. Eat out of my own refrigerator. And use my own bathtub.

Oooh...a bath sounded really nice on my sore muscles.

I tried to sit up, and this time both Daniel and Maddox put their hands out. I lay back and signed, *"I go home."*

Daniel shook his head. "Oh no—I think you need to stay here."

Maddox nodded. "I agree. Another day or two of observation would be good."

Observation? Hell no. I couldn't stay here. If I went out of body again, all these tubes and wires on me would alert the media outside that something was up. No—I needed to be back home, and get some questions answered. I also felt like giving Mom a piece of my mind. I didn't care what it was she'd found out in that doctor's appointment—when the daughter was in the hospital, her place was right here beside her.

Humph.

I grabbed up the pad and pencil again, which had fallen off my lap in my bid to get up. YOU CAN'T KEEP ME HERE. I WANT TO GO.

Maddox gave a long, fatherly sigh. "Actually, Zoë, we can. You were diagnosed with diabetes, type II. And in two months you've failed to monitor your blood sugar, eat properly, and have lapsed into a coma twice. Now, yes, while your recoveries have been nothing less than astonishing, you've proven you can't take care of yourself. All it would take is one word from me about you being noncompliant and I could hold you here indefinitely."

Was he serious? Could he really do that? I didn't know. I honestly didn't know how insurance worked. I mean, I was sure there were diabetics out there who screwed up all the time, and did their doctors threaten them? Was that legal? And then again—maybe ordinary doctors didn't do such things. Maybe he was using the threat to make me do what he wanted.

At that moment I hated Melvin Maddox. More so than clowns. I didn't know if he was right, but I knew he was serious. And I also knew he was hatching an insidious plan to steal my mother and be her next husband. And I was obviously in the way.

I looked at Daniel. He looked upset.

Joe looked—well—like Joe. Unreadable.

I flipped the paper over. I STAY ONE NIGHT?

Maddox pursed his lips and appeared to agree reluctantly. "One night. I want to run some more tests later this afternoon. I'm going to go check on a few things, then have a nurse come in to give you a small sedative, okay?" He smiled at the detectives and left the room.

Joseph remained in the corner. He paced and gestured at the two living men.

Daniel kissed my hand. "Thanks, Zoë. I'd rather you stay here and be safe, please? I can't—" He closed his eyes and took a deep breath. "I can't bear the thought of losing you right now. You mean a lot to me, and I'm sorry if I've upset you—with all the talk about ghosts and how I feel. I just want you well, and I want you to talk again." He gave me a slow smile. He had dark half-moons beneath his eyes.

He really looked bad, as if he'd not slept in over twenty-four hours. He took my chin in his right hand and tilted my face up to look directly at him. "I love you."

Somewhere in the world cathedral bells went off. I know they did in my head. All this time I'd debated on how I felt about Daniel. Yeah, it's one thing to want to get into a man's jeans. And it's entirely another thing to have true, life-giving emotions for him.

Daniel had stuck with me through everything, and, yeah, I'd been there for him. And maybe it was out of guilt. I'd wanted him to love me. I had. And I wanted to love him.

And I think I did.

I held up the paper in my hands and moved it to a blank sheet. I could write it here, and convince myself I'd never actually said it. Right? In case I changed my mind?

Or in case he completely freaked out when he learned what I was.

That is—whenever I figured out exactly what I was.

I LOVE YOU.

There. I closed the pad and handed it back to him.

He leaned down and kissed my forehead. "I have to go back to the station—Cooper's waiting for me—but I'll be back later. Okay? Stay safe for me."

I knew something else was wrong and grabbed his hand. I narrowed my eyes at him, demanding that he tell me. But Daniel only gave me a half smile, a nod to Joe, then left the room.

"He really does love you, Zoë," Tim said as he came closer, his color such a contrast to Joseph's shadowy monochromatic look.

Joe immediately gave three slow claps. "Very touching."

You! I pushed myself up in the bed. *You stay away from me. It's your fault Rhonda was shot!*

But Joe seemed nonplussed. His phone rang, and he pulled it out and answered it.

How rude!

"…no, no sugar." He looked at me. "You like mochas, right?"

I blinked. Nodded.

"Yeah, you got it. Oh, and make them venti." With that he disconnected and replaced the phone back in its hip holster.

I leaned forward. *Who—?*

"You'll see." Joe took the chair out of the corner of the room, very close to where Joseph was, and pulled it next to the bed. "First off, little missy, before you drifted back in here"—he narrowed his eyes at me—"were you anywhere near the ICU?"

"Joe don't," Tim said. I looked at my little buddy—having always felt a little closer to Tim than Steve (Steve was Mom's pet)—and noticed he seemed a little stronger. Larger than before, somehow. And he was giving Joe the hairy eyeball.

I blinked. *Yes. Why?*

"Oh, no reason." But his expression said something different. "As for your earlier barrage of questions—I had no idea you were going to be at that warehouse. Or Rhonda. Second—never go into a darkened warehouse with no backup. Very dumb. At least Heather had had the right idea with her little gun display." He sighed. "Too bad it didn't help much."

I was still sort of up on my hands in the bed and leaned away from him. I looked at Tim. *How did you get here?*

He nodded at Joe. "He came by the shop looking for Nona

yesterday—to let her know they moved you out of ICU. I asked him to bring me here."

Joe pursed his lips. "Nice trick with the rock. Kinda weird." He looked at me. "But I'm thinking weird is just another day for you, isn't it?"

I ignored him and looked back at Tim. *Where's Mom?*

Tim shook his head. "I wish I knew. She came by here this morning." He sighed. "For about a second or two. Saw you were still in a coma and left. Said she was going to be out. Daniel left her several messages when your condition improved."

But she hasn't called back? My mom hadn't been here the whole time? After my altercation with TC back in November, my mother had barely left the hospital. And now she'd simply dropped by?

I looked at the flowers. *Who bought all these?*

"Daniel." Joe tilted his head to the right. "He's smitten, Zoë. Don't you think you should let him in on your little condition before things get too serious?"

I narrowed my eyes at him. *You back off, asswipe.*

Joseph moved forward a step or two, his image fading as he came into the light.

Why didn't Heather and Brian tell on you? Why aren't you in jail? I glared at Joe.

"First, because Brian's an undercover cop, same as me. He's Heather's replacement cameraman—her regular one was out with the flu. And second—" Joe paused. "Because Heather Noir is dead, Zoë."

Dead? No—she was alive in the warehouse. She wasn't hit hard enough to be killed. Yeah, I'd seen the death mask on her, but she hadn't died that night.

"Death mask?" Joe started, then held up his right hand. "No, never mind. She didn't die there. She was murdered in Daniel's house." Joe winced. "Her house. But it's worse. That's why Daniel looks so rough, and why he's so gung ho that you stay safe. After the attack in the warehouse, he let her stay in the house. They were married for two years, and he did care for her. He was here with you when it happened, though he's been through the wringer with the police himself since he found her body night before last. If it hadn't been for me being here, vouching for his whereabouts, he might have been suspect number two."

Number two?

"Yeah—seems a few pictures of you and Heather at the Westin function made it into the local tabloid rags. Only you've been in a coma all this time. And don't think a few of those officers suspected you'd killed her and put yourself in this condition, since you're a repeat hospital offender."

Me? But I—I would never—I can't—

"Relax." He held up a hand. "The manner in which Daniel found Heather's body is what sort of cleared up you and Daniel."

I got the feeling I wasn't going to like this.

"But it didn't do us any favors—especially when you review what you, me, and Rhonda were talking about the other day. Whoever killed Heather cut off her hands and her feet." He shook his head. "Seems like Charles Randolph's missing head now has hands and feet."

I stared at him, gaping.

Heather was dead. No, I hadn't liked her much. But she had gone up on the old impressed meter back at the warehouse. She'd been a tough cookie.

And she'd been killed—in that house? The house where I'd found the Daimon snurking about?

Something big was happening here. Something that involved pendants, secret societies, government officials, and body parts.

Yep. Welcome to my life. Full of sweet oogyness.

I heard a page to ICU. *Joe—why did you ask me that question? Earlier? About where I was when I was out of body?*

His expression darkened. "Because as of ten twenty-three this morning—right before you woke up—ten patients in ICU had died. All at once. All at the same time." Joe's eyebrows arched onto his forehead. "Anything you care to tell me?"

20

January 29 . . . Is it really Tuesday?

SOMEONE knocked at the door, and Joe moved to open it.

Dags the bartender walked in, a tray of Starbucks coffees in his hand, his backpack slung over one shoulder. If it weren't for his endearing smile, I'd say he was a male version of Rhonda, sans goth.

And he had a longer ponytail.

And a nicer butt. Too bad he was shorter than me. By about the same height as Rhonda.

With a nod to Joe, Dags dropped his bag by the door and set the tray on the bedside table. He came closer to me, and I was assailed by the wonderful smell of soap and shaving cream.

I also noticed he was dressed in scrubs.

He kissed my forehead and leaned his head to the side. "What'd I miss?"

"Miss Soul Sucker here was about to tell me how she took out an entire ward in ICU."

Ah! I glared at the bastard. *I did not! I only took one spirit—and he needed to be released. I did* not *bogart an entire ward.*

"Oh wow," Dags said, and shook his head. He looked over at Tim. "Hey, good to see you here."

Tim smiled. And—I think he blushed.

Dags McKinty wasn't the most handsome of men. Though he did possess a subtle beauty that radiated out with the sweetest personality. I'd noticed him back in November, sitting at that bar at Fadó's while watching and listening to Detective Daniel Frasier. He was wiry in a healthy way, with a slight build, slightly crooked nose, dark eyes, and beautiful long black hair, which he usually kept in a neat ponytail.

What Dags had was boyish charm.

So opposite of Mr. Joe-the-Schmoe.

I looked at the coffee. *He call you?*

Oh, and Dags can hear me. Not like Joe or Tim or Steve. Dags hears me in a different way—through pictures in his head. It's got to be the wackiest way to talk, but it seems to work. Usually if something was confusing, Rhonda was there to interpret.

But not now.

Dags frowned at me. "He call me? Yes. Well, I called Nona's, and Tim told him I called. I have some information, and I'm working here tonight."

A bartender and orderly. Wow. What a life. *He just met you, and he had you drive to Starbucks?*

"No." Dags smiled. "There's one downstairs."

Where am I?

"Northside."

Oh.

"Now." He reached over and grabbed up a venti and handed it to me. "Sugar substitute, nonfat milk, but whipped cream."

I nodded and took a sip. Aahhhhhh. Heaven.

"Now what was this about you taking out an entire ward?"

"We'll talk about that later." Joe grabbed a coffee and rubbed his spiky hair with his left hand. "Moving back to the missing body parts—to add a bit more—as you put it most times, oogy, to your rejoining the living—this morning they found Robert Stephens dead. Or rather, they found his head, arms and legs. No torso."

Dags grabbed the last venti. "Seems I'm here in time."

That made me sit up even farther. *What the hell is going on?*

Joe shook his head slowly. "Don't know—but it's why I've been working two lives for the past two months."

Two lives? I reached out and took his hairy forearm. *Who were those men in the warehouse? And why were you with them? I think you owe me and Rhonda an explanation.*

Tim crossed his arms over his chest. "This oughta be pretty good."

Joe pulled his arm back and rubbed it, as if I'd somehow hurt him, or tainted him. "First off, I can't tell you anything yet because even I'm not sure. When I know more, I'll let you know. Just realize that I'm getting closer to who killed Charlie Holmes and why."

Charlie said he was killed because some guy couldn't find an Eidolon.

Joe's eyes widened. "You—you talked to his spirit? You saw Charlie Holmes?"

I nodded. *Yeah, before Heather showed up, then you and your goons did. He was answering a call that night—someone reported lights in the building, and it was supposed to be empty. He heard a guy looking for the Eidolon and when Charlie interrupted, he was shot.*

Dags looked in Joseph's direction. He turned his head to me but kept his eyes on the ghost. "You know there's a shade in the corner of this room?"

I nodded. *That's Joseph.*

Dags nodded. "Crowded room. Well, I have some news I think you'll enjoy." He stopped and looked at me. "You're not mad at me about this Randall Kemp guy are you?"

I shook my head. *Get on with it.*

"Okay, I did a little digging after I got off work last night and again this morning—made a few inquiries. On Eidolons. I found an obscure reference to the name in an old newspaper article from a Savannah paper where a similar string of bizarre murders took place. Missing body parts. The killer was found with the parts sewn together in his home, and he claimed he was using them to gain power over his enemies."

I stuck out my tongue.

Joe blanched. "Yuck. Sewn together. Like Frankenstein?"

Dags shook his head. "I was thinking more like the old myth of the scarecrow."

I frowned at him, but it was Joe who relayed my exact thoughts. "Why do I get the feeling you're not talking about a stand in the fields, made of straw, frighten the crows scarecrow, are you?"

He shook his head.

You mean like the golem?

"Similar. But the golem was made of clay," Dags answered. "This old urban legend sort of follows the golem myth. But instead of clay, it's body parts. Usually of the creator's enemies. A golem was used to defend and seek justice." He looked grim. "A scarecrow is made to seek revenge."

I shook my head. *Never heard of it. And what's the point of sewing body parts together? I mean, if you made anything out of parts, whether it's clay or pieces, and sent it out to do your bidding, wouldn't it sort of be—well—conspicuous?* I ran my tongue over my lips.

I was thirsty. There was a water canister on the table next to my bed. I reached over the metal railing and grabbed it, then tipped the spout to my lips and drank. Ow—ice! Brain freeze!

"Zoë, you've got a straw right here." Dags picked up the white plastic and shoved it into the open canister. "Look, don't pooh-pooh it yet, Zoë. Believe it or not that article is only twenty years old, and the man in question worked on several articles about voodoo with a Mr. Francisco Rodriguez."

I set the canister back on the nightstand, empty, and pressed my fingers into the spot between my eyebrows.

Him. AGAIN!

Joe gave a long, exasperated sigh. "Not him again."

Eidolons, Daimon-possessing spies, missing body parts, men in fatigues with ski masks trying to capture me—it was beginning to look like a supernatural B movie. And none of it connected or made sense.

It was like trying to put together a puzzle with half the pieces and no picture of the final product. Och, haven't we been here before?

"Did the article give any leads on suspects back then? Did the police have any ideas? What was stolen exactly?" Joe said as he took up his chair again.

Dags sipped his coffee. "No suspects. Cops never figured it out— and no real ideas. If you mean stolen body parts, the list was similar to what we're seeing on the news. Same gruesome MO."

"A head, torso, hands, and feet. Why stop there?" Joe sighed.

"What more could they need?" Tim said.

"How about arms and legs? How's it going to go out and seek revenge?"

Dags shook his head. "You're thinking two-dimensionally here. I think the purpose of a scarecrow is much more insidious."

I waved my hand, wincing at the headache now coalescing between my eyebrows. *We don't have any answers yet.*

Joe looked back at me. "No we don't. And that's what's so damned scary." He gave a long sigh and reached out to pat my hand. "Oh, by the way, great work on Rhonda. She's recuperating at lightning speed."

Yeah?

"She looks great," Dags said. "I saw her yesterday."

"The bullet was lodged in her large intestine. But the blood flow had almost stopped, and her systems had all sort of slowed to minimal output. The doctors were all freaked-out because when they got to the bullet it somehow had years of scar tissue covering it, which, of course, protected the organs nearby. You do good work, Zoë."

I didn't know I did that. Look, Joe, most of what I do like that is a blur. I just go on instinct.

"Well, good instinct means she'll live. Now we have to figure out who's putting together a scarecrow."

I pursed my lips. *Rodriguez?*

"Maybe." He held up a hand. "His name keeps popping up, doesn't it? And it is a little suspicious that he knew your name in the P&D."

I narrowed my eyes at him. *What do you mean by that?*

Now he looked cocky again. "I'm a detective, Zoë. I'm just putting the pieces together."

Well, Mr. Put-It-Together, did you research Mr. Rodriguez further for more secret society stuff? I glanced at Joseph, who was really starting to get impatient.

Put-It-Together nodded. "Not much more than what you and MacGyver upstairs came up with—he's powerful already. He has money—so why build a scarecrow?"

Blanching, I stifled a yawn with my hand. Money doesn't solve everything. And it certainly doesn't make you happy. *If he is doing it, then there has to be some other reason. Something else to gain that money can't provide.* I did yawn this time. I was still very tired. Bone tired, as my mom would say.

Where was my mom?

Where do we go now, Mr. Detective-Man?

Joseph moved in the corner, winked out of sight, then back

again. Why was he hiding? And what was with the off-and-on show?

"Well, I'd say we need to start looking at Rodriguez's contacts, in case it's not him that needs the power, but an associate, and Rodriguez is only footing the expense."

Why not look into Knowles?

He looked at me as if I had a bug on my nose. The look was so startling that I actually crossed my eyes to look down at it. He reached out and took my arms. "Zoë, that's it. The conversation you said the two had in the Westin. The conversation this Maharba wanted you to report on—what again was it that was said?"

Knowles was worried about a shipment—and their people called the police. It wasn't found—but it was safely locked up in evidence.

Joe snapped his fingers. "That's it! We need to sneak into evidence and get whatever it was they were looking for out. My guess it was an Eidolon, which we know is some sort of amulet or pendant. And I'll bet you it was part of the stuff hauled in from the warehouse bust."

I nodded to him and glanced at Joseph. He had moved closer. *Well, yeah. Good luck with that.*

"Oh no, I need you to go with me. I need your Wraith ability to get me into evidence and sneak the thing out."

Can't you do that by yourself and let me sleep?

With a frown Joe fixed his green gaze on me. "Can we do something about the thing I can't see over there, but you keep looking at?"

I was right. He couldn't see Joseph. Interesting.

"You mean the shade?" Dags nodded. "He has a very strong presence."

With a little help from Joe in finding the control button for the bed, I moved myself up into a sitting position and motioned for

Joseph to come closer. He sort of floated over, and I had to look over the bed railing to make sure I wasn't seeing his feet.

I wasn't. They weren't there. And for the first time I noticed he was more or less a half apparition. Something was wrong. I asked him as much. He was looking at Joe with a wary expression but came closer to me.

Tim looked at Joe, then at me. "Zoë, I can sense him, but I can't see him either."

What? Since when can't a ghost see a ghost?

Joe pursed his lips. "When they're on different planes. Which might explain why I can't see him. And you can, given your Wraith abilities."

"Well, he's a shade—which means he has a different corporeal makeup than you do. You being a full spirit. He's more of a"— Dags snapped his fingers—"a memory. Think of a whisper."

Joseph moved closer. He was as monochromatic as ever—but even more so. "Zoë, I don't have much time, but I needed to warn you."

Much time? I tried to push myself up in the bed but was caught by the sheets. *Joseph, what's happening to you?* I looked down over the side of the bed again. *You don't have any feet.*

"I don't know, Zoë, but I think it's got something to do with my dad. He's not himself—and I mean he's literally not himself. I don't know what to do."

Your dad's not himself? Like he's being shadowed by a Daimon?

He shrugged. "I—no. Not like that. It's like he's not in there—all the way. He's—he's stopped talking to me. Or even thinking of me."

I put a hand to my mouth, the IV pulling at the sheet. *Oh God—is it those things that keep you fettered?*

He nodded. "I think I'm finally moving on. But I'm not sure to where. But that's not why I'm here." He licked his lips and gestured with his hands. "You have to leave here. As soon as you can. Don't let my dad's threats stop you. Just get out of the hospital."

Tonight? But your dad wanted me to—

"Don't listen to *him*! It's dangerous for you to stay here. Whatever it is that's being planned—what I sensed before—it's got something to do with what you were just talking about. And it has a hell of a lot to do with you."

The widening of my eyes alerted Joe. He was beside the bed with his hand on my shoulder. I looked up at him. He had very long eyelashes, the lower ones just brushing the upper part of his cheeks. "Hey—what's this Joseph doing?"

"Zoë," Joseph said, and I looked back at him. "I'm sorry—you have to leave."

Why? Jesus, Joseph—you're scaring me. And I talk to ghosts. (No irony intended here.)

"Because *they* want you. But they're afraid of you. You have to leave the hospital. Tonight. Now if possible. Don't let Dad inject you with anything. He couldn't do anything before—not with the cops hanging out. But if he"—Joseph nodded at Joe—"leaves, then something terrible will happen."

Wait, wait, wait. I put up my hands, and Joe moved back. *They? They who? The same they that had a congressman and an Atlanta businessman nervous?*

The same they or them that thought it was big fun to chop up bodies in people's living rooms?

The same they or them responsible for green ketchup?

Ew.

"Zoë, I shouldn't tell you—but I think the Phan—"

A teeth-chattering cold swept into the room at that moment, with a force that actually moved the hair around my face. I knew it wasn't a real wind per se—it wasn't something generated by the planet's nature—but by something supernatural.

Whatever it was swept Joseph's image away in midsentence.

And then it was gone. That quick.

I tried to call out to him, but there wasn't an answer. And somehow I didn't think there would be one in the future—not until I figured out what was happening to the ghosts.

Joseph?

There was a void there. An empty space.

What the hell just happened?

"That sucked," Dags shivered.

"Damn," Joe said. I noticed he'd stood up and now rubbed his hands up and down his arms. He turned once, looked around, then turned again before looking back at me. "It's not this Joseph, is it? He's not—inside of me now, is he?"

Tim was gone as well. I gripped the metal railing. *Tim?*

"Here." The dark-haired young man reappeared beside Joe. "Something really bad just happened."

What was it? Come on, please. If anyone should know, it'd be a ghost, right?

But he was shaking his head. "No. Joseph was on a different plane, a different level of existence. I could only feel an echo." He looked at me with his large, dark eyes. "Of a scream."

I'd just seen a ghost vanish in front of my eyes—not that I hadn't seen that before—but this time it wasn't Joseph's choice. Whatever had just happened, I was certain it was caused by something external.

And very large.

Joseph's gone, Joe.

"Gone?" He frowned. "Gone as in that was him that left the room like that?"

I shook my head. *Something else was here, Joe.* I pushed myself up into a sitting position and started working on getting the white tape off of the needle inserted into my right wrist. When that didn't work, I grabbed at the wires taped to my chest.

Dags grabbed my hand. "Wait—I don't think you're supposed to be doing that."

I glared at him and started on the IV again. I managed to pull up a side of the tape, then, holding my breath (I really hate needles), yanked the needle out of the vein.

Owsonofabitchshit!

My fingers worked into a fist, then out. Seemed okay to me. I looked again at the spaghetti extruding from the neck of my gown. Hrm...this probably wouldn't be a good idea, removing the monitors without warning. Or I'd have someone in here. Stat.

"Zoë—what are you doing? Dr. Maddox said you needed to stay here overnight."

And you just said you wanted me to help you sneak this Eidolon out of evidence. Make up your mind!

Joe wasn't hindering me, but he wasn't helping me either. Mom would. And she'd understand, and she'd get me out of here with no fuss. Well—there would be Nona fuss. And Nona fuss had always embarrassed me. But now, I wanted that fuss. I wanted my mommy.

Instead, I had Joe, Dags, and a Tim.

Wow—all these men and no sex in sight.

I felt myself sigh, my shoulders rising high, then sinking pretty low. I told him what Joseph had said, right up until the creepy feeling came in and took him away.

"Then what was that? How do you know you can trust him? What if he's actually leading you into something?"

You mean like you? Leading a double life you won't tell me about? Nearly getting Rhonda killed? Not warning us the moment you saw us there?

"Ah. Point well-taken."

Dags put his coffee back in the tray. "You two wait here."

He was gone for several minutes, then came back in with a handful of scrubs and a white lab coat. He set it all on the bed and handed Joe a stethoscope. "Okay." He checked his watch. "You've got about ten minutes in about five."

"Ten minutes for what?"

"To make your escape." He smiled. "I'm going to be keeping the front nurse busy. I asked her to silence the alarms for this room 'cause you wanted some time with your fiancé." Dags smiled at Joe. "She'll be able to reset the monitor and cut it off at that point. You two need to get into these scrubs and take the elevator out. Got it?" He held out his hands in triumph.

Fiancé? I was filled with righteous indignation.

"I got to put the booties on?" Joe said.

"God, you two," Tim said in frustration. "Get dressed!"

Dags signaled us to start by looking at his watch. I yanked the wires loose (*greatgoogleymoogley!*), then pulled a pair of the pants up while still in the bed, careful not to expose my exposed womanness.

Joe pulled on the coat but refused the booties before stepping outside with Dags to let me change. I was putting on every piece Dags said to—except when it came time to put on the top, and it wasn't going to go over the gown.

Oh, screw it. I unfastened the backless gown.

My nipples instantly hardened to the size of English peas. Wow. This was a cold room.

The gown had slipped to the floor when the door opened and I turned, baring my breasts once again for Joe Halloran.

He stopped, smiled, and a naughty glint twinkled in his eye. "My, my, my, Zoë, seems I'm always seeing you naked."

Bite me.

And then I wished I wouldn't have thought that. Joe seemed the kind of personality that just might take the suggestion literally.

It was at that moment I decided Joe Halloran was born in the wrong year—hell, the wrong century. He was every bit the chivalrous rogue of legend.

And just as cocky.

I finished getting dressed and pulled on my bunny slippers. They were all I had, and I wasn't leaving them here. Then I pulled the booties on over them. There. All professional.

"Dags has gone on ahead to make sure the coast is clear. No Maddox about." Joe pulled something out of his pocket. It was Tim's rock. "Got this."

Tim vanished.

And then he handed me what was on his arm. "This is Rhonda's coat. No blood, but you're going to be cold out there in just scrubs."

Oh, I've been cold before.

"I'm on a motorcycle."

Oh.

"And it's snowing."

!!!

21

Freak'n cold Tuesday . . . What time is it?

I held on tight to Joe while speeding along the fucking cold high-way on the back of a motorcycle. (!!!) I did give him kudos for being chivalrous and insisting on carrying me into the condo build-ing—though the doorman's eyes bugged out, and I was sure Daniel was going to get an earful about this stranger sweeping his woman off her feet.

After showing him how to set Rhonda's ward, I crashed on the couch. I slept for several hours, and the sun was down when I woke up. He'd filled the tub for me and ordered me to soak after fix-ing me an egg and bacon sandwich. The bread was lightly toasted, buttered just right, and the eggs were good and soft, not dry. Even the bacon was crisp and not floppy. Mom tended to love floppy bacon.

He set the saucer on the side of the tub along with the pitcher of orange juice he'd found in the refrigerator, then sat on the toilet. I made sure my bubbles covered all the right places. "After watch-ing you drink that water, I figured getting you a glass was probably pretty moot."

I smiled at him and continued tearing away at the sandwich. When he got up I swallowed a large bit. *Where are you going?*

He stopped at the doorway. "Evidence. I figured I could get to whatever was there easier by myself."

You mean bribe your way. I put the sandwich back down on the saucer. There were bubbles along my arm. *They're going to know you helped me out of there. You think they'll come looking for me here?*

He shook his head. "No. You haven't committed any crime, Zoë. And I doubt Maddox would carry through with those threats—and that's what they were. Threats. That's illegal. You're a grown woman. And if Joseph's right, and Maddox is part of some wacky plan to hurt you—then you have every right to get the hell out of there."

So there wasn't any real reason to sneak out? I could have walked out?

"Hell no—the bastard might have drugged you if I stepped away. Which is why I wanted Dags there." He frowned. "He's a strange fella."

He's a nice guy. Don't mess with him.

"Stay put, relax. I'll go find this Eidolon—if that's what's there. I'll be back here this evening, and I promise to tell you why I was in that warehouse. Sleep."

And he was gone. I felt the ward engage, a slight buzzing in my ear. My sandwich was gone in a few more bites, and I finished off the orange juice a beat later. I smacked my lips. I wanted more.

More and a nap. But in a minute. I flipped the hot faucet and poured in a good bit more hot water, then relaxed back for a few minutes. I think I dozed 'cause abruptly I had bubbles up my nose, and I was coughing.

I reached over the side of the tub to the basket I'd set behind the toilet. Inside were a few candles, a lighter, and a paperback—wow—one that I totally forgot about.

I lit a few of the candles and relaxed back. Sigh—then wished I'd had Joe turn the light out. I stared at the switch by the door and thought about it flipping down.

The lights went out.

Wow! A new power.

No—I looked out at the hallway and realized *all* the lights were out.

Oh damn. This didn't bode well. Luckily, I had candlelight, and as I slipped out of the tub, my skin puckering with a thousand tiny goose bumps, I could hear my neighbors rustling about upstairs. There was a yell, then a thud.

Were they fighting? I didn't know the couple that had moved in above me. I dried off quickly and moved into my bedroom.

That's when I noticed something—I could *see* in physical form. Not astrally. But in the body.

I mean—I could see in the *dark*. Everything looked like a black-and-white movie, but I could see it all. I'd attributed my sight in the bathroom to the candles, but there weren't any candles in here. *Nada*.

Well, this was new. And scary. Were my Wraith powers slipping over into my physical self? Now that would be cool—if I didn't have to worry about my body anymore. The damned thing was becoming a real pain—not that I didn't want it, mind you.

I dressed in black jeans, a black pullover, and black socks. I looked down at myself and briefly wondered if Rhonda had been at my clothes. When did I amass this much black? I pulled on white sneakers, then pulled them off for my black Sketcher hightops. Well, they were more comfortable. And black.

Looking at myself in the mirror, the white streak seemed to glow. Hell, it stood out like a beacon against all my black. Whiter than my skin. But there wasn't much I could do. After braiding my hair, I moved through the condo to the ward controls by my front

door. Zero. Which meant my condo was as open to spectral entities as anyone else's.

A loud crash made me jump as I stood next to my door. It had
come from upstairs again. What were they doing? Having monkey
sex from the chandelier?

Sniff. No fair. That's what I wanted.

And then the icy cold was back. The same feeling I'd experienced
in the hospital. What the hey? I looked around the living area and
kitchen, but couldn't see anything. Even in physical form I could
always see ghosts, more so now that I had taken in a darker part to
myself. Mostly Abysmal creatures that lurked in shadows.

Nothing showed up on my radar, but I was sure I wasn't alone.
With no wards, I felt vulnerable, and the only place I could think
to go to was my mom's house.

Now that place had wards, but not just the electronic kind.
There was so much mojo on that house that I had to cut holes in it
sometimes just to breathe an astral breath.

I grabbed the coat from the couch and slipped it on, realizing as the sleeves moved two inches up my arm that I'd grabbed
Rhonda's coat. Something hard banged against both my thighs,
and I shoved my hands into the pockets and found items in each
pocket. Phones.

Rhonda's phone and the BlackBerry she'd given me.

Hrm—my mind turned down an evil road as I looked at
Rhonda's phone. Rhonda was always on the phone to her source—
and her source nearly got her killed today—I mean—back on
Saturday.

Phones carried call logs. The face didn't show any missed calls,
so I assumed the last call in the log would be from the source,
right?

Right.

I knew it was wrong. I knew it was deceitful. But damnit,

Rhonda's life was put on the line by this creep, and I wanted to know who they were so I could—

So I could—

Well—I'd go haunt them really bad.

I scrolled through the log and found the last received call. Didn't recognize the number in the illuminated face. I hit the little green phone icon to dial it and put the receiver to my ear.

One ring. Two rings. Three rings. "Hello, Knowles residence."

I almost dropped the phone. Instead, I held it out and stared at the face. Knowles?

"Hello? Is there someone there? Rhonda—is that you?"

I closed the phone, disconnecting. (Well, what else was I going to do? Show the phone my dry erase board?) Holy shit. Knowles? As in March Knowles?

Did Rhonda know this? And could the congressman be so stupid as to call her from his home phone? Unless...

Unless the two of them were friends. Oh. Damn.

What. The. Fuck.

I took her coat off and tossed it across the room. It landed against my fireplace and I sat down on the back of the couch.

Was this the same source she'd been using since she and I teamed up? An oogy United States congressman? How the hell did Rhonda know him—and—and—here I'd gone and listened in on his conversation with Rodriguez.

I felt the air leave my lungs as my heart raced. I'd thought the two of them acted and talked like they knew they were being watched—because they really did know I was there.

Shit.

If he was her source on things—then maybe she was his. And the she those two had been talking about—was it Rhonda?

No—somehow I knew it was me.

I felt like someone had gut-punched me.

I wanted nothing more than to march into the hospital, go Wraith, and scare the shit out of my best friend right now.

But—but she'd been shot. And I saved her. I remembered flashes of the dream, the one on the porch, and of Rhonda telling me I wouldn't want her in my life.

I stood, then sat back down. I needed to talk to someone. And usually that would be Rhonda. But I couldn't do that—not yet. Next would be Mom—but for some reason she'd become emotionally unavailable.

Mental note: *grab Mom by her boobs, and demand she talk to me about what the doctor said.*

So who do I talk to? Joe? I tossed Rhonda's phone on the couch and brought my new BlackBerry up to my face. I didn't have Joe's number!

Who—

Daniel?

I closed my eyes. Maybe everyone else was right, and it was time to trust Daniel—to let him know about me—before the relationship went too far.

Pulling up his number I text messaged him. NEED TO TALK. RHONDA'S SOURCE IS MARCH KNOWLES.

I paused. Should I type that in? It might get his attention, especially since I was sure they were still investigating the man. I mean, his business card had been found at the scene of a murder.

But then that'd bring Rhonda under fire from the police as well, having ties to Knowles.

No...maybe not yet. Not until I actually talk to Daniel and tell him I don't want it known. I deleted that last sentence, put a 911 in its place, and pressed SEND.

My mind wasn't wrapping around this new lead.

So—if he was the source she'd spoken with, why send Rhonda into an abandoned warehouse to be attacked by masked men? And had Knowles tipped off Heather as well? I sat on the edge of my couch for a few minutes, in the dark, and tried to gather my wits about me.

Mental note: *this is fucked up.*

And I needed to get out of here. To the hospital? No—if Maddox saw me, he'd come after me with a needle. I didn't dare go to Daniel's house—it was a crime scene now. Unless I wanted to find Heather's ghost. I hadn't liked her much in life, so I didn't dare want to see her in the astral.

I had no idea where Joe lived, and he was busy.

So—I guess it was to Mom's. There I could regroup in safety.

I grabbed my purse and left. There were neighbors moving through the hallways with candles, some with flashlights. I moved to the stairs. I was alone going down and was greeted by most of the tenants gathered in the lobby. I moved through them, unable to say, "excuse me," or "sorry," but doing my best to be polite. What was going on?

I soon found out what that was as I reached the glass front.

Snow.

Lots of snow.

Holy—

I hadn't really noticed the snow on Joe's bike. I'd been too freak'n cold and kept my eyes closed the whole time. Even coming inside I blew past it. But now, standing inside the glass in a semi-warm place, I saw it was snowing in Atlanta, and not just the usual flurry we were used to. This was serious snow, with flakes the size of small mice. I had my hands against the glass and could feel the cold radiating from it into my skin.

"You thinking of heading out, Zoë?" the doorman asked me. He was smart and had ducked inside as well. "Your friend already left in it—on a bike. I told him to be careful."

I nodded and made the motion for my mom to him too. He smiled and nodded. He was a middle-aged man, with a receding hairline and a crooked smile. His teeth were little more than yellow stubs from decay and smoking. But his eyes were kind, and I often enjoyed his company—if not his smell.

"Be careful. There are reports of power outages all over this area. Probably down Moreland too. We don't have much ice yet, but we will, so beware the black ice."

I smiled and, with a deep breath, stepped outside.

Mother guppy! It was freak'n cold. The snowflake mice hit my face so hard I had to turn away as I brought the collar of my coat up to cover my ears. I was going to have to let my hair down just to warm them back up. My car, a late champagne-painted model Mustang replacement (my old one had been silver) was nearby.

It cranked the first time, and I hit the heater. Within minutes it was toasty warm, and I carefully pulled out onto Monroe Drive and hung a left toward Ponce de Leon.

Most of the lights were out along the road, and I was careful. I switched the radio to WSB AM 750 and listened to them discuss the weather. Evidently we were having a blizzard—something this neck of the woods hadn't seen since March of 1993. It stretched from Boston all the way down the Eastern Seaboard to Jacksonville, Florida.

Wow. That was some cold front.

It was pretty, if not quiet. I guessed the flurry I'd seen when leaving the hospital was only a precursor. The world looked like it'd been washed with blue and gray as I drove down Ponce de Leon and turned right onto Moreland.

A few miles down it was obvious that Little Five Points, the local artist area of Atlanta, as well as home to some of the nicest restaurants, like Front Page News, as well as alternative cultures and lifestyles, was also under a blackout.

I eased through the light near the Vortex and turned right onto Euclid. Mom's house was just down on the right.

And damn if it didn't look like the spookiest place on the block.

Mom's car was home, and I didn't see any movements inside with candles, though I knew she had plenty of them. With a sigh I pulled up, turned the engine off, and fished on my key ring for my key.

The back porch was cluttered with local rags—the *Outpost* (a local pagan group), the *Aquarian* (a local Wiccan group), the *Marker* (a local happenings group), and the *Magical Majestic* (I had no idea what that was)—and I kicked at them as I unlocked the door and stepped inside.

It was as cold inside as out. And it looked as if the place hadn't been open in several days. Which was unlike Mom as she always opened the Botanica on Sundays and Mondays, which were her busiest days. I could always count on good eats left from the bakery deliveries for Tuesday afternoon.

The kitchen was empty. As was the front tea shop, as well as the Botanica. Nothing. Tim, I assumed, was still with Joe—though he'd been a no-show at my place. Which might explain why Joe didn't bother taking me along for the "heist" of evidence. He'd have a ghost with him.

So where was Steve? I rapped on a nearby wall with my knuckle and even called out to him with my thoughts. Not a sound. Was it possible he was downstairs in the basement?

Well, I was not going to go down there. No, no. Not where they died. Ew. Creepy.

I managed to light one of the oil lamps over the fireplace, then light the fireplace. Luckily, there was wood cut and placed nearby. Mom always did like a roaring fire. Though—the wood felt dusty. It'd been here awhile. Usually she was always after someone to restock her pile.

Mom kept a small cauldron propped over the fireplace sometimes to warm up potpourri. I cleaned it and warmed up some

milk instead and added honey. There was whipped cream in the
refrigerator as well and a few slices of cheese. I stood in the kitchen
looking up at the dried herbs hanging from the ceiling, then over
at the mail accumulating on the floor in front of the door, where it
had been shoved through the slot.

From the looks of things no one had been here in a few days—
at least not since Saturday.

I picked up the mail and brought it to the fireplace and lit a few
more of the thicker candles on the coffee table.

I grabbed up an afghan from the couch and settled down in
front of the fire. But I hadn't opened the first bill before tapping
started, and I looked around up at the dragon. It was bouncing
again—whatever it was they'd caught probably heard me. Sorry, I
wasn't in the mood to deal with some errant—thing.

I felt the house pop and creak, and I looked through the windows at the dark. I couldn't see the snow with no moonlight or
streetlight, but I knew it was there. It always amazed me that snow
made no noise. Nothing. Unlike rain. Or hail.

I noticed a glint from the couch. I moved on hands and knees
to the cushion and found the amulet Rhonda had removed Saturday in order for me to shadow her. I shrugged and shoved it
into my back jeans pocket and started looking through the mail.
Bills, bills, credit card ads, more letters. Ah, here was a letter from
Aunt Lucy. She lived in Portland, and I hadn't seen her in ages. Of
course, it was addressed to Mom and not me, and I hated it when
other people read my mail.

But it was postmarked a week ago.

I began to wonder if whatever news Rhonda said Mom had
gotten after her doctor's appointment had been so bad that she'd
felt the need to leave?

But no—she'd been at the funeral. She'd been at my house
Friday night before I left for the Westin, and Tim said she'd been
here.

The *Atlanta Journal-Constitution* lay rolled in a neat bundle to my right, and I picked it up and pulled the rubber band off of it. The front page blared out at me as it unfolded.

LOCAL OCCULT EXPERT JEROME ZELL DIES FROM SURPRISE HEART ATTACK.

I started reading as fast as I could. I didn't know who Jerome Zell was, but I caught "occult expert," and that was all I needed. The article told about the young man's abrupt slip into a coma and his heart attack Monday night. He was pronounced dead this morning.

At the age of thirty-seven. No history of any illness. Fit as a horse, so the paper said.

Mysterious coma.

Now what would cause a mysterious coma?

The clacking noise came back loud this time. No more timid clacking—this thing was trying to beat its way out of that dragon. I tossed the paper aside and looked up at the mantel.

I stood and stared at it. I didn't want to free whatever it was—maybe I should move it so it wouldn't fall off and go boom?

Just as I reached up to take the dragon down, I felt a slight vibration beneath my feet. I always knew when someone was walking in the house. Mom did too. It was how she knew where customers were in the Botanica while she was in the tea shop.

This particular vibration told me someone else was already in the house, as the movement wouldn't be so noticeable from the porch. Shit—my back was facing the house's two entrances.

Nuts.

Abruptly the scar on my left arm burned. I sucked in air and moved to my left just as that vibration banged against my shoes. Whoever they were, they were running.

At me.

"Careful!" someone said in a semi-whisper-yell.

I hadn't been to defense training in several months, but once the muscles were trained, there was little stopping instinct. And instinct kicked in big-time as I dropped just as something sailed over my head and hit the mantel. I looked up in the firelight to see a short cylinder sticking out of the wood. It had a cute little tail of red yarn.

Tranquilizer.

Double nuts.

I felt my attacker move behind me and dropped farther, bracing my aching left arm beneath me as I kicked out and swept the floor low, knocking hard into someone's ankles.

They fell back with a whomp noise. I heard someone curse as they flailed backward against a shelf, and the entire thing crashed down on top of them. With a roll to my right I moved back into the shadows of the Botanica, close to the alcove of books, and crouched low. Even without the added light of the lamps I could see three figures moving in the living area. One was on the floor unmoving amid the now-destroyed statues and pieces of art. Mom was gonna kill me.

The one stationed between the two stores held a camera in his hand and was pointing it around the room.

"Where is she?" said the one I'd knocked on the floor as he stood up.

"I don't see her." The one with the camera was definitely female. Or had just entered puberty and hadn't gotten the voice change yet.

Being in body was not going to get me out of this, especially if I got hit by a tranq. Lights out—and if I did that, there was no Wraith. Not till I woke. My first assumption was these were the guys from the warehouse come back to try and recapture me.

Was Joe among them again?

And if so—I hope I managed to wound him. Severely. Going to get the Eidolon my ass.

Time for some creative defense.

I placed my body into a ball at the base of the bookshelves and slipped out. A habitual glance at my watch showed me a full four hours. I could push it to five, but would rather not.

Making sure I stayed out of camera range, I eased around the back of the girl and got behind the third member. He had his back turned and was looking at some of Nona's pretties in the window. I went corporeal, grabbed up one of the goddess statues—the hippie one with the thin arms and legs—and nailed the guy in the back of the head.

As soon as he went down I went incorporeal, flipped back over the couch, and slid into the guy I'd knocked over earlier. He fought for a few seconds, and I felt an overwhelming fear come over me. There was little to no resistance in him—but there was an overwhelming need to pee.

What was with men and their bladders?

This guy was terrified. I pitched forward a bit and tossed the tranquilizer gun from my hand. It struck the girl with the camera, and she dropped it.

"Randall—what's wrong? Where's Herb?"

Randall.

Herb?

Oh hell. It was SPRITE. And if Herb was the guy I just KO'd, then... "I'm inside of Randall?"

Oh, juuuuust great. And now I'd talked out loud.

The girl—who, if memory served me right from my experience with these guys back in October, was called Boo—clapped both hands to her mouth. Her eyes became goose eggs over the tips of her fingers. She said something into her hand, and I shook my head.

"*No comprende,*" I said, and looked over at the mess where Herb lay. Yep, it was him, the same guy I'd seen in the poltergeist house before I met Daniel.

Before my life took a bizarre twist elsewhere.

"Please don't kill me."

I started and looked at her. "Kill you? Why would I kill *you*?" I pointed at the gun on the floor between her and me. "You tried to shoot me. If I'm reading things right here, you're *my* attacker."

She sort of bounced, and I feared she might wet herself. "You're really not Randall, are you?"

"No. I'm not. But you know who I am, obviously." I took a step closer and glared at her. "Do you know *what* I am?"

Careful, Zoë. Don't make her faint.

Blam. Too late. She hit the floor. Great. Now I had no one to get information from.

Wait—there was still Randall. Only I didn't want to relinquish my control over his body just yet. Randall was smart, and he had a vendetta. Either recapturing me on film or in person. I didn't want to hurt him—I could sense he was a good kid. But when this was over (and I really hoped that was soon), I didn't want him following me, or bothering me.

So maybe scaring the shit out of him was the best method of interrogation there was.

22

Sometime Tuesday night ... Where's my watch?

BOO moaned from where she'd fainted on the floor.

I concentrated on Randall, knowing he had to be somewhere inside that little room behind his eyes where I usually sat. A few deep breaths, making sure I didn't lose control of the man's physical body and—

You demonic motherfucker!

I whirled around to see Randall standing behind me. He had his arms out, his hands balled into fists and took a swing at me before I could blink.

Crack!

Ow! I stumbled back and nearly lost control of his physical body. It stumbled, and when I caught Randall coming at me again I dipped low, moved down on my hands, and swung my legs out, clipping him in the ankles. He fell backward and landed on his back as I jumped up and held up both my hands. "Whoa!"

I realized that I was talking from the outside, and Randall had spoken—or shouted—from the inside. It was the opposite of what I was used to.

Randall scrambled back up and was on his feet. *Get out of my body! You will not take my soul!* And then he spouted out something in Latin.

I lowered my own hands and looked at him. "Uh, Randall. I'm not a demon. And I'm not here to take your soul. But I am here to get some answers."

Luckily, the Latin stopped, and he narrowed his eyes at me. *Answers? But you're a ghost—you have all the answers of the afterlife.*

I held up my hand. "Uh—no. Sorry. I'm afraid I don't. Hate to disappoint you."

He stopped bouncing but didn't lower his hands. *You—you're not going to take my soul?*

"No, but I am going to blow your head off if you don't stop bouncing and start talking to me."

You wouldn't dare.

Sigh. I held the gun up to his head. Somehow he still maintained enough control of his body to realize what he was doing. His bouncing immediately stopped, but he unballed his fists and held them up at me in a gesture of supplication. *Okay—I give. Please. I have a daughter.*

Now that wasn't what I'd expected him to say. "That's nice, Randall. So why are you here breaking into someone's home and firing tranqs at them?"

Uh—I'm here to rescue Miss Zoë Martinique.

Hold the phone. "Say what? Rescue her from what?"

From—I made some things for our sponsor—a weapon. And I told them all about my ghost—the one I found back in October. They were very interested in capturing it, and somehow they discovered it sort of haunts Miss Martinique. And it's true! I've seen ghosts here.

My turn to hold up my hands. "Wait, wait, wait. You made a weapon—that shoots ghosts?" Could this be it? What I saw in

Randall's mind on Saturday? What the masked men used in the warehouse?

Yes. It works on an idea I got when we were filming the ghost in the North Georgia Mountains. Electricity. You see, ghosts emit some sort of field that—

I put up Randall's hand. "Yeah, yeah, yeah. I got it. I know. So you were afraid for Miss Martinique?"

They're coming here—for her so they can trap the ghost. And for something called an Eidolon.

"An Eidolon?"

Yes.

"They—these *they* don't dress in fatigues and wear ski masks, do they?"

Yeah, that's them. They call themselves L-6, and they're very powerful. They were looking for ghosts at the fund-raiser Friday, though I was sure they were looking for you in particular.

I watched him swallow.

I'm afraid of them and what they're doing. They threw a lot of money at us after the Web Ginn House mess-up.

"You should be afraid of them, Randall. They kill—did you know that?"

He swallowed. *Yeah. I did.* Randall was quiet for a second, then blurted out, *It's you, isn't it? You're the girl from the house, the one I had on my tape?*

Oh. Good. God. I knew that look. I'd had that look myself a few times. Christ. This guy had a crush.

On a ghost!

I realized then he wasn't after me to expose me. He was after me because he *liked* me.

Gah!

At first I'd considered SPRITE a threat—a force to be reckoned with if they'd teamed up with a more powerful group that believed in ghosts. But now I was seeing them as pawns.

"So you three came here on your own to save Miss Martinique?"

He nodded.

"And this L-6 wants Eidolons?"

He nodded again.

"What about body parts?"

He frowned. *Sorry—what?*

"Body parts. Is this L-6 group responsible for all these murders and dismemberments in the news?"

He blanched white. *Oh God—I hope not. I haven't heard any of them talking about them. I've been on several assignments— and we've never been ordered to cut off body parts before.*

What was neat about this was that from the inside I could sense Randall was telling the truth. At least as far as he knew. But I couldn't read his mind.

I pursed his lips. "Is this group responsible for the cop's murder at the warehouse on Gresham?"

He took a step forward, his hands at his side. *That wasn't L-6. That was the other group.*

"Who?"

He opened his mouth to speak—

I heard something a beat too late. Before I could turn something hit my back (Randall's back) and I was blinded by lights and some serious severe pain. I lost control of Randall's body and recognized the bite of a Taser weapon. Just like before, I felt myself catapulted out before the body fell in a heap, the tranquilizer gun in my hand clattering to the floor.

I felt sluggish as I stopped near Herb's inert form. I tried to go corporeal and was hit again by something familiar, something that drained the energy from every part of my astral form.

It was the same thing I'd been hit with in the warehouse. I lay on the floor, on my face, struggling to move.

Something vibrated the hardwood, and I knew that someone

with soft boots moved past me and close to my astral body. I managed to turn and watch as a man in dark clothing and a ski mask moved with grace to where my physical body lay by the shelves and held up a syringe before plunging it into my arm.

WTF?

"Don't worry—it's only a sedative. I understand it's the easiest way to contain you. You have two choices, Wraith," said the same metallic voice I'd heard in the warehouse. I pushed up on my elbows and managed to turn and look up. It was the same man from before—I recognized him by the sports brand on his ski mask—and he pulled the needle out. "You can return to your body voluntarily, or we can put you there by draining your resources down to nothing until you are forced back in." I could almost imagine him smiling behind the pause. "And I understand that sort of bodily return is less than enjoyable."

He pointed the funky-looking gun at me and glanced over at Randall. He lay a few inches from me, unconscious.

"Or, I can have one of my men shoot Mr. Kemp here with enough amps to cause significant heart damage. Your choice."

I lowered my head. I couldn't let him shoot Randall. Or Boo or Herb. They were in a sense bystanders (notice I didn't use the word innocent) and didn't deserve this.

With effort I pushed up onto my knees and hands. The old incorporeal me just wasn't working right—felt as if I were moving through sand. Or in a slow-motion dream where I'm naked and nobody's noticed but I can't get to the house to put on my panties—

"I don't have time for indecision." He fired again, directly at my astral body.

My chest rose in the air, and I opened my mouth to scream. Lightning bolted through every inch of me, and I saw flashes of pink and blue light. And a voice—

—a voice in my mind. My voice.

YOU CAN BE MORE. TAKE THE OPPORTUNITY.

Be more?

Right now the only thing I wanted to be more of was uncon-scious. Fire raged through every astral piece of me. But that wasn't all that had ignited.

So had my temper.

I was really tired of this. Ever since November I'd been chased, shot at, hit, kidnapped, trapped inside a stone statue, locked out of my body, and even had a dragon try and eat me!

And now there were testosterone-overloaded macho military freaks in my mom's house, threatening me and shooting my body full of GOD KNOWS WHAT?

Now, I don't remember getting up. Not a sliver of it. But abruptly I was up, off the floor, and nearly banging the ceiling. And all of these bad boys were backing up toward the door of the Botanica leading to the tea shop and the front door.

Even Mr. Sports-Mask was moving away from my body, hold-ing the funky gun up at me, his eyes goose eggs within the cutouts of his mask.

"JESUS CHRIST!"

"What the fuck is that? That the same bitch?"

"Paul—this isn't right. He didn't say nothing about no god-damned devil bitch!"

You know, I shoulda been questioning their reactions here. And the fact that they could all see me. Which should have triggered a, "Oh, new thing alert! What's happening here!" But it didn't. I just wanted to leap at each of them, punch through their weak, flimsy little bodies, and rip their souls right out of their backbones.

"Back off, bitch," Mr. Sports-Mask said.

Oh, little man? You think you can threaten me?

"Or I call my boss and he makes sure Miss Rhonda Orly never makes it out of the hospital."

But I moved closer to him. All of them backed up. All but

one—the one farthest away. The one that remained near the hanging beads separating the two stores. He was wide-eyed as well. But he was also very calm.

And as Mr. Sports-Mask opened his phone, a familiar voice resonated in my head. *Think of Rhonda! Don't do it, Zoë!*

That was—that was Joe.

Joe was here?

I hesitated—felt a definite loss of power. I was on the floor again, and my vision blurred.

"What's wrong with it?"

"The sedative's working," he said. "That intel from Hirokumi paid off. In a few seconds she'll be sucked back into her body and defenseless."

Who you call'n—whoa, dizzy—defenseless?

But he was right. I felt the pull as his shot coursed into my physical body, and no matter how powerful I might feel OOB, I was always reminded that I was physical first.

That I was alive.

I let myself be pulled back to my body, my conscious thoughts drifting into—

I bounced off, much like a raindrop would bounce off of a well-waxed car finish.

When I staggered back, Mr. Sports-Mask fired at me again, and I gave another silent scream. My cord tugged and tugged at me, but I couldn't get back into my body. What was wrong? There was something there, not allowing me to go back—

Oh shit—the amulet. Rhonda's necklace. It was in my jeans pocket.

Whatever charm was worked into that piece of jewelry had now stopped me in my tracks twice. I had to get the amulet out of my pocket. But I couldn't do that without becoming corporeal enough to do it. I didn't have strength to become physical.

I had to go somewhere. I had to disappear from his sight—

because it was obvious he could see me. The members of SPRITE were all out of commission, and I knew that once I disappeared, they had every intention of taking my body somewhere.

I had to hide. To wait. To recharge.

I looked over at Joe, standing masked behind the others. He was nodding to me. He knew what I was thinking.

YOU CAN BE MORE...

Sometimes being more is being less. I let myself dissolve and become little more than dust in the air, and I moved at a dizzying speed to the man that called to me, faster and faster.

Until I overtook him and disappeared inside.

Once again within the body of Joe Halloran.

23

I smell something fishy...

I don't know how long I rested inside of Joe. Time was little more than hands on a clock, and whatever it was they'd zapped me with had done a number on my battery. Not so much the tranq in my physical system but the laser against my astral self.

Not to mention my own body was off-limits until I could somehow either gain enough strength to control Joe so he could remove the amulet or I could do it myself.

When I did understand where I was, I was surprised to be looking at fried fish and french fries. Or that's what it smelled like. There were other smells as well—and sounds. The smells reminded me of a bar. The tang of beer, the bite of deep-fried foods all cooked with the same day-old grease. And the buzzing of conversation.

I could also hear what sounded like—football? No...yeah. That was football. Hadn't the Super Bowl already happened? Or was I that far behind on sports? Not that I really liked sports, other than watching cute men run around with cute butts.

"Stop thinking like that or you'll make me lose my appetite."

I sat up in the little dark theater I'd been in before, the one behind Joe's eyes. I felt like shit. And it took a lot of effort just to sit up.

And then everything that happened in my mom's Botanica came rushing back to me. *Let me guess—you were called in to capture the Wraith who had foolishly left her condo.*

I felt him smile. "Yeah. You could say that. I'd just managed to get a box with a necklace in it out of evidence. Damned thing had been packed down in a false bottom of one of the crates beneath another false bottom. Luckily, forensics hadn't gotten to it yet."

I put a hand to my head. *Where is it?*

"Safe. For now."

Where are we?

"We're at Fadó's waiting for Daniel. He called all pissed off at me, and I know he's going to want to know where you are."

I managed to stand up—stumble—and then right myself inside my little dark room. *Yeah. I'm sure. I text messaged him earlier—seems Rhonda's source? It's March Knowles.*

When he didn't say anything I felt my mouth drop open. *You knew she was friends with Knowles?*

"I just found out the other day. So did Daniel. Remember he's been investigating Congressman Knowles because of that card—and Daniel saw Rhonda leaving Knowles's house."

Mother. Guppy.

He chewed. Swallowed. "Now look—don't get all mad at Rhonda. I'm sure there's a logical explanation here. We just have to wait for Rhonda to tell us."

Bullshit.

"Suit yourself." He bit into another fish.

I can't believe you're eating when someone's made off with my body—again.

"Look, do you realize how much energy you drain when you sleep in there? I nearly passed out before I got back home. Food—rest—the best medical advice for a sickly soul."

Where is my body!

He shoved the pinky of his right hand into his right ear and wiggled. "Yeah, now see, if you'd calm down, I'd tell you all about what I've been doing."

I crossed my arms. I was feeling a little better. A little.

I tapped my foot.

And?

"I've been working undercover for a while, looking into a local group that's been spotted here and there. They've been pillaging small shops, mostly the hoodoo ones like your mom's, and Phoenix and Dragon. They take very little, and sometimes they leave things in place, and sometimes a mess. After working with them for two months I'm thinking the messes happen when they run into some pretty wicked spirits. We—as in me and my captain—call them the Commandoes, but they call themselves L-6, and their membership is strictly anonymous. It's an on-call job. Meaning I passed a few physical fitness tests, some background checks, they gave me a pager, and I go where they say when they call."

L-6. Randall's L-6?

He shrugged and took a deep drink of beer. Yum. I was getting hungry. I knew my body hadn't had much since the egg sandwich in my condo. That and a sip of hot chocolate and a snack at Mom's.

"Lately, since I joined, most of what *I've* been doing was staking out houses around the city. All of them were houses of important people. State senators, representatives, and businessmen."

Stake out for what?

"I didn't really know. Seriously, you think those people actually live in those houses? They're for show. I kept my captain informed of what I was doing—just not who I was doing it with. She's about as forgiving with this stuff as Cooper. I gave them a list of who I was watching. I only saw a few of the other team members twice. We worked as a unit—always watching. I'd been waiting for the day we actually hit a store—which now they've been doing recently—

only I haven't been put on those assignments. I wasn't there when Holmes was killed in the warehouse. But I heard about it."

So they have more than one team?

"Yep. I was staking out some old fart's house when a note on my pager appeared. It said to pick up a ticket to this fund-raiser at the Westin. No idea why, or what I was supposed to do. And then I saw you. Again." He sat forward and put his elbows on the table. Bad etiquette. "And I discovered what it was you really were—and what kind of dangers there really were out there."

And did you have to report what you saw?

"No. No one's ever asked me what happened. And I don't know why."

I sat back down and put my right hand to my chin. *You ever get the feeling you're being played?*

"Yeah. All the time. I thought that even more the night at the Westin, and I wasn't so sure at the warehouse. Mostly because a part of me didn't trust Rhonda. But once she was shot—the team went into retreat mode. All of them melted away in different directions. Don't look back. But I did, then came back to make sure she was okay." He cleared his throat. "I was so surprised to see her there, and you, then Heather Noir and my partner, Brian Davis."

Ah—the cameraman? Something made a shooshing sound to my right in the dark.

"Brian made sure Heather never saw me, and the second the police arrived with an ambulance, I ducked out the back. They never saw me either."

Smooth. I narrowed my eyes and started looking about. I had this overwhelming feeling I wasn't alone. Which was definitely in the creep-out section of not good feelings. I heard a noise to my left. *You ever get the feeling you're not alone in here?*

He straightened up in his chair. "What's that supposed to mean?"

I wasn't sure myself, but there was a familiar feeling associated with the noise. I'd sensed this before, only it'd been inside my own body.

Oh damn. This couldn't be good.

Joe—you know I don't know what happened to that Daimon, don't you? I mean—I know I sort of took the wino—but I've never been sure about that little thing.

"I'm not liking the way this conversation is going. I'm paying the bill and getting the hell out of here. Daniel can just wait."

I stood up and started looking at the darkness as Joe exited the pub. I'd been in Joe before, days ago, when I'd run inside for protection. When I'd discovered I could do this at all. I'd never stopped to wonder if there was anything else in here—*with* me.

"Zoë?"

I was abruptly cold and realized Joe was outside. In the snow. Walking to his truck with little or no jacket.

Shhhh. I'm looking around. I couldn't see much, and I wished I had a light—

Light abruptly filled the room like a hundred little tiny suns. Sometimes it's not so good to actually see the inside of someone else's head. I'm not talking about like brains or veins and such. I'm talking about other things—things that lurk in the darker parts of the insides of a man's mind.

It was there, hovering about two feet from the floor (now I don't really know if minds have floors, but this one did), looking like the other one did—the one I'd seen in Daniel's house. A fat, slimy—tadpole. Well, I knew it was the same one by its coloring, but it sure was a lot smaller.

Though it still had claws.

Joe—I'm not alone in here.

"What d'ya mean you're not alone in there? Who else is in there besides me?"

I got the impression Joe said that a little too loud. But I couldn't think about that right now—the thing in the corner started hissing. I stepped back, but it didn't fly forward. Instead, it moved to the edge of the circle of light surrounding me and waited.

"Joe? Is that you?"

Daniel!

My attention was split between two screens—my reality inside Joe's head with the oogy tadpole and the one I could see on the wall screen with Daniel approaching Joe. My baby looked cold, but good. He was bundled up in his brown trench coat and the Hufflepuff scarf I'd bought him for Christmas.

"Why are you out here in the cold?" Daniel's voice was both edged and tinged with concern. "Joe?"

The thing moved, then backed away, and my attention focused fully on it. So it either didn't want to come into the light with me, or it couldn't. I was hoping on the couldn't part. The *wouldn't* gave it more control than I liked.

"So this is where you've been hiding?"

Wow! I had an actual voice in here! Sah-weet.

"Yes," came the thing's voice.

It had a voice?

Was this good or bad?

It sounded more like someone with a bad cold. All nasal-like. "I'm here because you wounded me. You made me weak. Insignificant. I did not have the strength to return to my master."

Oooo-kay. "Who's your master? March Knowles? Francisco Rodriguez?"

The thing laughed. "You have no idea."

"*Who* is your master?"

It laughed. It sounded like someone strangling a moose. I put my hands to my ears.

"He that watches you now."

I was abruptly reminded of my little talk with Mitsuri on the way-back machine. And I was reminded that bad guys usually don't want to spill their guts if they think they can win.

"Daniel—look, maybe this isn't the best time—" Joe said from the outside. I was hearing it as if I were at a drive-in movie, only I was out of my car and facing down something ugly in front of the screen.

I looked back at the tadpole. "Do you know what I am?"

It nodded so fast and so hard I was afraid it would nod off its neck. It bared its teeth and I thought I saw drool pool over the side. Ew. "You are the Wraith. You are the abomination. A creature of living and Abysmal flesh. You are the Spectre of Death."

Well, it was kind of nice to know I had a reputation, though I wasn't happy about the abomination part. And I figured there was some Abysmal in there since I'd somehow switched parts with Trench-Coat. "Are you afraid of me?"

And once again it nodded. "We all fear you. All but one."

I didn't really need to know whom. I kinda got the 411 on that one as I glanced at my forearm. Trench-Coat's mark was as visible as ever in this astral, shadowy form. I had a moment of déjà vu, thinking back to when Rai had taken my body before and I was stuck inside a circle in my mom's living room.

I put up my hand so the glowing tattoo was visible. The tadpole backed up. "Yeah, I know. The Archer. We've met." I tilted my head to the side and moved toward him. He moved back into the shadows. Interesting. "Mind telling me who your master is? Who's behind all this?"

"My master waits, and watches for the day when we can all wear the flesh and rejoice in its glory!"

Oh great. This thing sounded like a religious fanatic. "So your master wants to be in the flesh. Was he watching me before you attacked me?"

It nodded. "He was looking for you." Then it did a little hop.

"And he will know *who* you are when I return to him—before I happened upon you while inside the flesh of the chosen horseman, he did not know if the rumors were true. Rumors of a living ghost. A Wraith! But now he will. I have seen you. I have touched your power. And he will know what I know."

This thing was really starting to sound more like a disciple than a servant. But a disciple of what? And who was the horseman? "So what exactly is your master's goal here?"

"...joking around, Joe. She needs to be in the hospital."

"Look, Romeo," Joe said, as his voice carried through the wall screen. "Looks to me like you should just take it easy..."

I looked back to the tadpole. Keep focused. "Does your master have my body?"

It was the tadpole's turn to squirm. "I do not know if my master has your body—how would he know who you were without me? He needs me to tell him the glorious news! Then he may seek you in physical form and destroy you!"

I shook my head. "I doubt that, asshole. But I'm getting the impression your master isn't the one that stole it."

"Your body is stolen?" The thing nearly leapt inside of the circle of light. But it stopped and howled at me. "Tell me who took it! Was it my master?"

"Hey, I don't know. I'm asking you. Someone took it. Someone who knows exactly what I am."

"I must flee to my master. Your body will not matter without the Wraith within." It then stopped and grinned at me. "I have this body...I can take it and lead you to him."

"Bullshit. You're nothing more than a lesser Daimon, created from Abysmal shadows and used as a listening device."

"You must go now and return to your body!"

I was ready to throw my hands in the air and let this thing have it with my bad Wraith self. This was not my element—figuring out the mumbo jumbo that had become my life. This was Mom and Rhonda's area.

And they were conveniently missing or out of commission. This thing's master had me right where he wanted me. But of all the things I could think of, I didn't know why.

I heard another door slam and a more authoritative voice speak. "Well, well, Halloran. Drinking on the job? At a pub?"

"Captain," Daniel and Joe said together.

I glanced at the screen. Captain Cooper looked angry as he looked at Joe. "You're supposed to be reporting your machinations to your captain. She knows you got a page tonight, but you haven't called her."

Uh-oh.

The tadpole was moving again. "If you won't go, then it's time to relieve you of this body's haven as well."

It disappeared.

Oh fuck.

Could be anywhere.

Joe? You feeling okay?

"Yeah, I'm just—" He stopped talking because he couldn't breathe. I felt his chest heave, his body thrust back against his truck. Captain Cooper was yelling at him.

What was happening?

I knew that little fucker was doing something to him. It couldn't actually control Joe's body, but it could really mess it up. Even stop his—

Heart!

Oh no, that little shit was not going to do this to Joe! I don't care how much he irritated me. But what exactly was I going to do? The light cavern I stood in was rocking back and forth, and I knew Joe was on the ground. If I looked through his eyes I could see faces, dimming in the light, and I could hear people screaming and shouting.

Screw this!

I dove into the darkness looking for the little creep. With my eyes closed I pushed myself forward, searching out through Joe's body for its presence. It was there, within Joe's heart, squeezing and tearing at it, causing the rhythm to falter, making it beat irregularly. It wanted to cause a heart attack.

And it was damned close to it.

Was this…was this how that thirty-seven-year-old had had his heart attack? From a Daimon?

I felt myself gliding closer to it, not allowing bone or flesh to stop me as I held my arms out at my side. I had this impression of wings branching out from my back, unfurling and giving me speed as I cleaved through time and space and reached out into Joe's heart to pluck the errant little piece of shit out.

And I was there with it in my hand. I could feel its fear radiating off of it, a familiar taste in my mouth, of power, and of life. It screamed at me and promised to be good, it promised to tell me everything I wanted to know, but it was too late.

Much too late. I brought it closer to me and it shrank smaller and smaller—and then I had it in both of my hands until it was the size of a small doll. It writhed and pleaded with a voice no louder than the buzz of a bee.

And like an insect I pulverized it between my hands.

My dark, taloned hands.

I watched as its remains sizzled and sparkled as it died away to nothing, and I felt the power again. A small boost given by such a small thing. Nothing really—but I was looking at my hands. Hands that didn't look human—but more like black metal. And the ends of my fingers had turned to long spikes.

I hung in the air—somewhere between Joe's life and death—and I looked at my body. A dark body, as curvaceous as I was in life, but black and cold. I felt those imaginary wings behind me, and heard their beating on the chaos winds as I fought the nightmare of realizing that I wasn't human.

My cord! Where was my cord?

There...a thin thread. Beaten and lifeless, no stronger than a spider's thread as it moved with the breeze my wings beat against it. I felt my anger cool, and as it did I felt myself float downward, back into the room inside of Joe, back to sanctuary with the tiny suns above and the darkness around me.

I watched my hands return to normal and the scar on my forearm fade but not disappear. I heard Joe talking, reassuring someone he was okay—that it was just indigestion. That he didn't need an ambulance. There were red-and-white lights, and men in dark blue jackets.

I looked up and saw lights moving overhead, then I saw the stars.

And I saw the snow. Flurries of snow as it fell over us.

I was no longer in Joe's body—and I couldn't remember leaving. I was amazed at how comfortable I felt like this, incorporeal. Invisible. Intangible.

"Zoë," Joe called out from where he lay on a gurney. I had a faint memory of Rhonda and me on a gurney together. Of faces and bright lights. "Don't—go."

I bent over him, an invisible being, an angel touching the cheek of the injured. *I can't stay here, Joe. I think it damaged your heart—and you're going to be sick for a little while. I know I was.*

"You can't survive out here—not without your body. Please..."

I couldn't survive long without my body. Returning to his would be wrong—he didn't need me draining his strength. He'd need time to sleep and recover from the poison the Daimon would leave behind.

"He's delirious—he's talking to himself."

I knew that voice. I turned.

Daniel.

He was dressed in a suit and long coat, his hands encased in leather gloves. He was glorious in his life that buzzed and burned around him with crackles of electric blue fire.

So beautiful. So—appetizing.

Hunger burned from inside. Images of lovemaking filled my mind, and I watched Daniel.

"Zoë," Joe said, and I looked down at him as Daniel came closer. "Stay with Daniel. Trust him. He's a good man. But don't kill him. Don't hurt him." He blinked at me as the EMT strapped him in. "God, Zoë...you have wings. Just like—"

An angel?

He shook his head. "A bat."

And then Daniel was there and he was moving through me. I was pulled in by his soul, his life, so sweet to the touch, and I feared I would take him there. That I would feed on his energy.

He stopped for a brief instant and put a hand to his head. "Wow—got dizzy there for a second."

Captain Cooper approached and put a hand on Daniel's shoulder. "You okay? You know, Daniel, when I agreed on you coming back to work on light duty—I meant *light* duty. When was the last time you rested in bed since you've been out?"

Daniel looked at his captain. I watched Cooper. He was an attractive man. With very large light blue eyes. He had a kind face—when he wasn't frowning. And right now he was honestly worried about his detective.

"I'm fine. But you're right. Look, I'm gonna head out. Get some sleep."

"Good. Just be careful on the roads. I know you're looking for that nutcase girlfriend of yours, but just think of you right now. She'll turn up. Girl's got more lives than a frak'n cat."

And with that he moved away into the snow.

Daniel watched as the ambulance headed out of the small

parking lot and turned out onto Peachtree North. I felt him sigh, and I wanted to tell him I was there.

But somehow I knew he couldn't hear me. Just like Rhonda couldn't hear me.

I was tired.

Very tired.

And I needed to sleep.

24

I think everyone goes through those moments of why. I think it's a regular event, and I think that if we didn't question life and our experiences, we'd all do nothing more than just passively go about our day. We always have to wonder if there is more out there, outside of our lives.

Or inside. I'd wondered that once, the day I'd been raped, then found myself outside of my body. And for the years after that when on occasion I'd be outside of it again, until I could one day actually do it myself when I wanted to. I'd needed concentration and quiet back then. And now?

Now I could do it at will. Maybe that was good. But somehow I thought it was more like wearing out a washer, and that one day my body wouldn't hold me in it anymore.

And then where would I be? In Heaven, if that was the Ethereal. Or part of the Abysmal that just seemed to like me so fucking much.

There. That was my philosophical spiel for the day.

Now—where was I?

Even I wasn't sure.

I did know it was cold outside. That the scene through my window was a blanket of white covering Piedmont Park. That the buildings in the city were little more than shadows against the snowy background. I knew that most of the city was frozen in place, and that businesses had shut down for the day. Driving was downright treacherous. And there were power outages all over the place. My condo wasn't one of them. My power had been restored twenty minutes after I'd left Tuesday on my way to Mom's.

The South was in a white wonderland, a month *after* Christmas. Yay. Go us.

Daniel was in my condo. I'd learned in a phone call that the members of SPRITE had been caught at my mom's place and charged with vandalizing the other New Age shops about town. Which wasn't fair—it wasn't them.

But those types of legal troubles would keep them out of the way, and out of trouble and danger for a while.

There were two messages on my machine from Jemmy Shultz. Daniel checked them. The messages said the same thing. "Zoetrope, you give me a call as soon as you get this, you hear me?"

And that was all.

He called Mrs. Shultz's number and got her answering machine. He left his name and his number and asked her to call him back.

Daniel tried my pager, but that yielded nothing. Then he text messaged my phone. But I had no idea where that was.

It was Thursday morning now, and my body was missing. Again. Talk about a rerun. Only this time I was inside my lover, my beautiful cop, instead of stuck inside a dragon statue. And somehow I'd sort of barked on Wednesday. It was kind of a hazy, feverish dream.

Now we stood in front of my sliding glass doors, looking out at the snow-covered patio furniture and my bike. He'd spent Tuesday night at my place, and Wednesday, hoping I'd call. Or come home. Or give him a sign of where I was.

Or where Nona was.

He'd made coffee. Really bad coffee too. And he was forcing himself to drink it. I reeeeally wanted him to put some creamer in it. Or maybe some sugar?

The doorbell rang, and he turned from the window in my living room. He was wearing a pair of my larger sweats—which were a bit baggy on him—and a tee shirt. One of my Halloween tees that said GHOULS GONE WILD.

He peeked through the peephole and felt the same surprise that I did. He opened the door to Joe and Rhonda. "Wait—aren't you two in the hospital?"

Rhonda looked pale, but then again she always looked pale. She was dressed in her usual black, only it was all fleece this time, and she had a black hat with floppy bunny ears on her head. She wasn't wearing any makeup, which is why I think I was a little surprised. No kohl around her eyes and no flat black lips.

Joe looked okay—he'd showered and was wearing a red plaid shirt, jeans, and a thick corduroy thigh-length coat.

The expressions they turned on Daniel were enough to make him look down at himself. "What?"

What? I echoed. I was giving Rhonda the hairy eyeball. I wanted to leap out of Daniel and scare her into telling me about her relationship with March Knowles.

Rhonda stepped into the condo and reached up to touch Daniel's forehead. "You okay? Shit, Dan—you have a temperature."

"I do?"

Hrm. That would explain the warmness I'd been feeling. And the hazy Wednesday?

Joe stepped in and shut the door. "Daniel—you look like hell. Go take a look at yourself in the mirror."

Even if Daniel wouldn't do it, Rhonda was going to make him.

She grabbed his arm and half dragged him into the spare bathroom next to the living room.

We both stared at Daniel's image in the mirror. And both of us had open mouths.

Dark half-moons hung beneath his eyes, which looked as if they'd sunk several inches into his skull. His skin was as pale as bleached bone. Even his usually radiant brown hair was dulled, and strawlike, as if something—me—had drained the life out of it.

And that's exactly what I'd been doing! Oh God. I'd been leaching off of him for over a day—

Shit!

Even Joe had said it himself when he'd been eating, that me being inside of him had taken a toll, and he'd needed to eat something, and that was with me inside of him for maybe an hour or two. Daniel hadn't eaten anything, except bad coffee.

"Wow."

Rhonda went through the drawers in the bathroom and found a thermometer. She checked it, hit the little reset button, and shoved it into Daniel's mouth. Then she and Joe led him into the living room and set him on the couch. Joe grabbed up a blanket and handed it to Daniel.

"I'm going to whip up a hot toddy. And maybe whatever is inside of you, sucking you dry, will come *out*." With a glare at Daniel—me—he turned to the kitchen.

Daniel leaned back into the cushions, and Rhonda removed the thermometer when it beeped. "Yeah—102. You're grounded, policeman. Rest."

"But I can't—I haven't heard from Zoë yet." He swallowed and sat up. Gathering the blanket around him, Daniel stood and shuffled into the kitchen. "I asked Matrice to run info on the prints we found at the warehouse and Rodriguez. So far zip." He shook his head. "Why would Zoë duck out like this? What the hell is going on? And where is Nona? Has anyone seen Nona?"

Rhonda frowned at Daniel. "Nona's missing too?"

"Dunno." Joe had found a clean mug in the cabinet over my microwave and poured himself a cup of coffee. I should have warned him it sucked, but I figured, let him suffer. Asshole. Make me feel bad. He'd *told* me to hide inside of Daniel. (He'd also told me not to kill him.) "Ever think that whoever it was that dragged her out of the Westin is after her?"

"Do you know something? Did she tell you something?" Daniel said. "I mean, Zoë said she only went into that bathroom and lay down because her sugar was acting flaky."

"True." Joe took a sip—and didn't make a face. Not even a grimace. Wow. "But what if they *think* she saw something?"

"So you think someone working for Rodriguez tipped him off that Zoë had seen them? God"—he ran his fingers through his hair—"this is the whole Reverend Rollins thing all over again. That girl just shows up on everyone's radar."

"You got that right." Joe smirked. It was kinda a cute look on him. Fit his smug face. I wondered if I could control Daniel's hand long enough to punch him. "Ever heard of a group calling themselves the Society of Ishmael?"

"Yeah, in passing. It popped up last week on something—along with some guy named Randall Kemp. A ghost-buster guy."

Joe kept a straight face as Daniel repeated things he already knew. I had to hand it to Joe—he could keep his outward emotions in check. Not sure I liked that quality. I wants to know when the man's eager. "Rhonda's got some interesting info on them. Go check out her iBook."

Daniel left the kitchen, and I stayed behind, slipping easily out of Daniel's body and glaring at Joe.

He made a horrible face at me with his tongue stuck out, then poured his coffee in the sink. "That stuff tastes like ass." He gestured to where Daniel had gone. "Did you see what you did to him? You made him sick, you dingy broad."

Dingy broad? Who died and made you Mickey Spillane? What the hell are you doing?

"My job, babe. I'm being a detective." He smiled. "And Rhonda really does have some fun stuff on her little lappy-top. Go look before you get yanked back into your body—and don't get back into Daniel. He needs to recuperate from you.

"I'm gonna make better coffee and get Daniel nice and drugged. He needs rest, then we can swap notes and get going."

Going where?

He beamed and looked way too smug for my tolerance. "Why, to bust the bad guys, babe, rescue your body." He beamed and danced his eyebrows up and down. "Now it's time to find out who's pulling the strings of what Rhonda's discovered is a group called the League of Six, otherwise known as L-6, and the sworn enemies of the Society of Ishmael."

What? You've got all that information? How long have you had it and not shared?

Joe was smiling at me. "You're starting to look a little Wraithy there, pumpkin. Reel it in. It's all a theory, but it hinges on what you said Knowles and Rodriguez talked about that night and an e-mail you got back from Maharba."

Maharba. Oh shit! I hadn't checked my e-mail since— Saturday? When I sent my report to them.

So did you ask Rhonda about Knowles?

"Yes. And she knows that you know now. Let her tell you—it's really quite an eye-opener."

Joe—what do you mean by Wraithy? Does that look different than what I normally look like?

He emptied the carafe into the sink, rinsed it, then refilled it before responding. His voice was low so he wouldn't draw attention to the fact he was in the kitchen talking to himself. "Zoë, right now, you look fine. To me and Rhonda you look like a transparent image of yourself. I know you're there. She does too. But you don't leave a shadow on the floor." He turned and emptied the water into the coffee-maker, set it under the basket, and turned it on.

And when I'm Wraith there's a difference?

I didn't really know this man—hell, he'd only seen me naked twice, which was twice more than Daniel. I didn't know his full background, whether he had a sister or brother, or living parents, or *where* he lived, either in a house, an apartment, or an alien pod. That was really lax of me because I usually had Rhonda do some checking on people I met in person.

Especially men.

But for some reason I felt myself trusting him. As much as I trusted Rhonda. He "felt" okay, he looked normal. And me being what I was didn't seem to upset him.

Or hadn't until I asked that question.

His usual cocky swagger disappeared, and his brows pinched over the bridge of his nose. He swallowed, and for a few seconds I was nervous. Really nervous.

"Zoë." He licked his lips. His voice quivered. "When we were in that alley near the Westin, and you burst out of me and hurled your-self at that creature when it tried to take the bum"—he glanced past me to the living room, where I could hear Rhonda and Dan-iel talking—"I was scared, Zoë. If I didn't already know you, or hadn't spoken to you, I probably would have curled into a fetal position and pissed myself. I was fucking scared off of my ass." He punctuated the last word by pointing his right index finger at the floor, then at his posterior.

He wasn't exaggerating. That much I could see in his eyes. In his expression. "And then you did it again in Daniel's house—only it was more intense. Stronger somehow. And I could feel you. For a brief moment you weren't the same. You were still you—you looked like Zoë—but you were something else."

Else?

"Hey, Joe—can you come in here?" Rhonda called out from the living room.

He seemed to relax, and I saw his shoulders lower. "Zoë Martinique, I like you. And I know you have a good, true heart. But if I were you, I'd start asking myself what exactly it was that I had become, because whatever it is"—he pinned me to the wall with green eyes—"it ain't right."

Luckily, he had the decency to walk around me and not through me. I didn't know what to say—he'd tapped a lurking fear of mine. A terror that I had indeed destroyed a part of myself to become—this.

I looked down at myself. At my hands.

Transparent. But human.

I turned and moved slowly to the kitchen door and watched Daniel. And Rhonda. And Joe. And I began to wonder—would there come a day when I wasn't human? When I wouldn't feel? And all that was important was the release of a spirit and the euphoria it brought me?

WHAT the two of them told Daniel was interesting—and they'd left out the oogy parts. They had found evidence of a small occult group operating in the Southeast—much like the Shriners or the Rosicrucians—groups that posed no apparent threat and gave back regularly to the community.

A group that called themselves the Society of Ishmael.

Daniel wasn't as enthused about this information as I was, but he listened—though I'm not sure if his lack of attention was from honest disinterest or the fact he was fading fast from exhaustion.

Induced by me.

Gulp.

For me it was cementing what I'd overheard in the room at the

Westin. Rhonda continued to show him what they'd found, along with several reports from the local occult shops of persons asking for Eidolon amulets. That's when she turned her iBook around and showed me what an Eidolon looked like.

I found myself staring at the same damned necklace I'd seen around Vanessa Stephens's neck. The same damned thing my mom wore all the time, the thing with the hideous green jewel.

I could see in Rhonda's expression she shared my surprise but was hiding it beneath a veneer of calm, at least until we could put Daniel to bed. Which wouldn't be long—he'd steadily sipped at the hot toddy Joe had made, and his eyelids were getting really droopy.

He was so precious.

We all needed to talk once he was asleep.

Much to my surprise I learned that Joe had taken down Mrs. Shultz's number, and Rhonda had also called her just as Daniel had. Rhonda got a response. Apparently Jemmy Shultz had lost contact with Nona Martinique over a week ago, which didn't jibe with what Daniel remembered about Nona saying she was going out with Mrs. Shultz on Saturday when he arrived at the shop to see me.

"I mean she looked at me and told me that's where she was going." Daniel shook his head.

Rhonda nodded. "The shop hasn't been open since her helper closed it down Saturday afternoon."

By her helper I knew she meant Steve with Tim's help. And we had left them in charge on Saturday when we'd gone to lunch. And—not one of us had gone back inside once we returned. Joe had taken off in his truck, and we had left for my place.

"Except for me," Joe piped up. "I went to check on her and found Tim and Steve. That's when I grabbed Tim's rock."

I looked around. *Where is Tim?*

"Tim's rock?" Daniel asked, his expression bordering on sleepy and bewildered.

Joe nodded at him with a serious face. "It's a type of herb. I use it in my coffee."

Rhonda suppressed a giggle.

Daniel mouthed an "oh" and closed his eyes.

After a few seconds Joe continued. "I put the rock back when I snuck in with L-6. I'm assuming he's back with Steve."

I had a really creepy feeling about this. *Steve didn't seem to be in the house when I was there. And we're sure Mom hasn't been back to the shop?*

Joe relayed the question, and Rhonda said, "Yep. 'Cause Jemmy's been watching. What creeps me out is that her car's still in the driveway. And Nona doesn't go anywhere without Elizabeth."

"Elizabeth?" Daniel opened his eyes and looked at Rhonda.

"Her Volvo." Rhonda winked at me. "Mrs. Shultz did report seeing Zoë at the house day before yesterday. She only lives a few houses behind her and keeps a telescope trained on the back door. Snoopy old broad."

"Well"—Daniel put his hand to his head—"snoopy or not, that's the first positive news I've heard about Zoë since yesterday." He ran his fingers through his hair again. Nervous habit. "It means she was okay. Did this woman happen to see Zoë leave?"

Rhonda shook her head. "No—Mrs. Shultz's stories came on, and she had to watch television."

Joe frowned. "Stories?"

"Soaps."

I thought of something at that moment.

My car.

Nobody mentioned seeing *my* car!

Joe heard my thought loud enough to give me a hairy eyeball. (A dirty look, according to Rhonda.) He cleared his throat. "Did she mention whether or not Zoë had her car?"

"Yeah, Mrs. Shultz said it was gone after the stories were over. And the place looked normal."

My car!

I groaned. My 'Stang was gone, again. Not again. Not fucking *again*.

"Well, if you two will excuse me." Daniel started to get up and nearly fell. Joe stood as well and helped the detective into a more stable standing position. "I think I'm gonna go lie down in Zoë's bed. I'm feeling a little woozy. If you hear from Zoë, will you promise to tell me?"

Both of them nodded. Both of them were lying.

The two culprits remained quiet until after Daniel left, stumbling to the back room, the blanket trailing behind him. Joe made himself a cup of coffee, and Rhonda joined him.

Apparently Joe made really good coffee. This was Rhonda's second cup.

I sat and stewed.

Once the door to my bedroom closed, they were back at the table and Rhonda was pulling up my e-mail on her iBook. "Joe filled me in on what happened yesterday. Man—I think I'd have given this asshole"—she nodded in Joe's direction—"a mental slap to find out he was one of the ass-hats in the house."

I was in front of her in an instant, my OOB self dangerously close to her precious iBook. *I wanna know what your connection is to Knowles.*

Never mind that she couldn't hear me. I wanted to know now!

Joe had tensed and stepped forward, watching me looming in front of Rhonda. "She wants to know—"

"I know," Rhonda said calmly. She straightened up her back and gave a long sigh before looking at me. "And she has the right to know. March Knowles is my uncle."

!!!

Of all the answers I expected, that wasn't one of them. I stepped back and just...stared.

Rhonda nodded. "I'm sorry I didn't say anything earlier.

But—I never expected Maharba to assign you to snoop on my own uncle. And I didn't know what he was up to either—meeting with Francisco Rodriguez. So"—she shrugged—"I was curious to learn what you found out as well."

They knew I was there.

Joe relayed my comment.

She nodded. "They knew something was there. And they knew that my uncle was being overshadowed—they just weren't sure by what. And apparently your presence did pull the Daimon out of him."

Bully for me. I glanced at Joe before looking back at her. *Were you planning on telling me any of this? Or was I just supposed to keep risking my life and yours on good times?*

After Joe relayed my words, Rhonda looked sincerely put out. "Zoë! I would never put you in any danger—that's not what I'm here for. I told you—I didn't know what Uncle March was up to. We hadn't spoken in several years. There was a family—" She pursed her lips and looked uncomfortable. "There was a family falling-out. But I confronted him about what happened, and he admitted he's spoken to Rodriguez. But he wouldn't tell me what it was about—or about the Eidolons."

"But he confirmed that's what was in the boxes?"

She looked at him. "Yes—there were supposed to be two. But they didn't find any."

I got Joe's attention. *You didn't tell her you got one of them.*

He shook his head. I figured I'd ask him why later. But maybe he didn't trust her as well as he had before either.

I asked about the warehouse.

"Uncle March called to tell me this other group—this L-6— had been seen at the warehouse after the shooting last Sunday." She took in a deep breath. "He didn't actually tell me to go out there. I sort of did that on my own. I figured if Charlie Holmes's ghost was still there, we get could a few more answers."

Oh.

I felt angry, but also deflated.

"Sorry, Zoë, but it looks like Joe and I both kept secrets from you."

"Hey." Joe managed to look honestly wounded. "Mine was harder. You should have been me playing it cool while they were firing that damned gun at her. When she sieved into her body and back out again, I realized she had to have put on your necklace."

Rhonda nodded. "Yeah, I left that damned triskelion on the couch, I think." She twisted in her chair and reached inside her backpack and pulled out that weird gun.

I backed up, remembering the stinging bite that thing had. I signed, "*Where—?*"

"I pilfered it out of his backpack while in his truck." She nodded at numb-nuts.

"Hey." Joe reached out for it. "That's classified."

Rhonda kept it away. "Uh-uh. I'm still not convinced you didn't know about the warehouse attack."

He looked hurt again. Man, he was good at that. "I didn't. I wasn't even sure those were the same ones I worked with on Saturday until I saw them fire that gun at Zoë."

I glared at him. *So you knew about this thing?*

Now he managed to look frustrated. "I knew it as a prototype. I was given the specs on it and told to study them in case I was ever called to use one to capture a spectral entity."

Wait. Hold the phone. In fact, let's smash it over Joe's head. I took a step toward him. *Here I am, pouring out what I'd seen in Randall's head, and you already knew about this?*

"Just a minute there." Rhonda frowned at him as she held the gun up. "You knew about this? And when Zoë told us what she'd learned, you didn't say a word?"

Mental note: *Yay for Rhonda! w00t!*

She couldn't hear me, but she sure as hell thought like me.

"Hey, you have no room to get defensive." He blinked. "I mean offensive. You knew who March Knowles was and still sent your best friend in there without all the info."

"My info wasn't life-threatening." She held up the weird gun. "This can hurt her."

Joe had his hands up, being attacked by two women. "Hey, look. I didn't know it was the same one. And it'd only been rumor, a prototype. I honestly didn't think it meant anything. Hell, it was a ghost hunter." He turned his hands palms up and shrugged. "Any kind of wacky thought can filter through that cranium."

I was so confused. I wanted my body back.

"But"—he held up his finger—"I was never assigned one of those. I don't think they ever really trusted me."

"Were there more prototypes that you know of? Other than guns? Do you think they've actually made a device to capture ghosts?" Rhonda looked intrigued where I looked scared shitless. "I'd love to look at it."

I shook my head. *What difference is there between that and the dragon in Mom's house?*

Joe frowned. "Good point." He related what I said to him.

"Hey, you're right, Zoë," Rhonda said. "Speaking of which— that thing's got a bogey in it at the moment—and I really need to get over there and banish it soon."

Good. Count me out.

"So we know L-6 was looking to import an Eidolon. There are five. We know three of them. The one Nona has, the one around Vanessa Stephens's neck, and the one that was supposed to be in the boxes at the warehouse," Joe said.

I frowned at Joe. *You know there are five?*

Joe looked at Rhonda. "Show her the e-mail."

"Zoë. What we didn't tell Daniel was that in the e-mail you got back from Maharba, dated on Sunday afternoon, was almost a warning for you to be particularly careful." She tapped a few keys, moved her fingers over the track pad, and placed the iBook in front of me.

Dear Miss Martinique,

Please do not feel guilt at your inability to keep the card we requested. The outcome of its loss has become a center of amusement, and we believe you were sincere in your attempt to acquire it.

The information you provided was most informative, and in return for your mending of bridges, we wish to impart to you a note of warning: There are two factions at work in this city that deal mostly with the occult. One is known as the Society of Ishmael, and the other is a most disreputable splinter group known as the League of Six, or L-6. Unfortunately, your recent actions—since the debacle with Koba Hirokumi and the more recent disturbance at the warehouse—have put your existence firmly on their radar.

Understand that these two groups are highly dangerous. The Society of Ishmael works above the law and directly within the light of society. L-6 prefers to work in the shadows and moves below the radar of most respectable establishments within the occult community.

Your next assignment is to retrieve three small amulets called Eidolons. These amulets will be very plain, but do not think their value is any less because they do not sparkle. Each possesses a dark power, one that cannot be allowed to fall into the hands of either faction. There were originally five in existence.

We know of three in the vicinity of Atlanta: Destruction, Possession, and Summoning. Find these stones and put them somewhere safe. We will make a deposit into your account once the job is complete.

Maharba

Rhonda nodded. "Their info on the Eidolon matches what I found with a little more detail about what they can do. I'm assuming the other two were Creation and Command. And we do know that someone was out looking for them and killed one of the owners."

I nodded. I looked at Joe. *So you're a member of League of Six?*

"It seems so, though I've not received any more pages since that last job at your mom's. And from the way this e-mail describes them—Maharba knows them pretty well."

"And to have weapons like these"—Rhonda held up the gun—"they've got backing. Could be from many sources, could be from one. They want you, Zoë, and they have your body."

And my car.

Joe gave me a smile. "I have your car. It's safe at my place."

I opened my mouth, then closed it. I was glad he had it, but I wished he'd tell me these things up front. I hate being blindsided. Really.

"So we have two occult factions that I'm assuming are working against one another." Rhonda shook her head. "I don't know what's worse. Fighting things from the Abysmal plane or human monsters in this one."

"Who said they were human?" Joe looked at me. "My first thought is that there's an influence at work here. And we don't have just two factions."

I nodded. *We have three.* I pointed at the screen for Rhonda and gave her a serious look.

She agreed. "Maharba. Yep—I'll agree on that one. We can assume from what you wrote down on the conversation you overheard and from other tidbits that Rodriguez and Hirokumi belonged to the Society of Ishmael. Rodriguez appears to be tied to them financially, and he's not afraid for people to know it."

"Of course not." Joe sipped his coffee. "They're by all rights no more harmful than the Shriners. Or the Masons."

"That's the same thing, Joe."

I giggled. Ha-ha. Doofus. Not that I knew that myself. I thought of the Shriners as the equivalent of the Royal Order of Water Buffalo. What did I know about this shit?

"Now, my thinking is this." Rhonda pulled the iBook back to her. "Robert Stephens had the clear Eidolon. My guess with occult color matching, that would make that one the Possession Eidolon."

Joe pursed his lips. "How do you figure that?"

"Long story. Look up colors and correspondences in magic class. Okay, Robert's dead, and the Eidolon is missing—according to Vanessa Stephens, who's now trying to collect on a million-dollar insurance policy, page 6 of the *AJC*."

I smiled.

"Charles Randolph, the first victim, had the purple one, which I assume is Command. We don't know which one is in the box. That leaves the green one, which Nona had, and I bet that was Creation. And then there's one more—so that means we're out yellow for Summoning and red for Destruction."

So are we thinking that Rodriguez is responsible for Stephens's death as well as Randolph's? And are we also thinking that he's the one behind collecting the Eidolons?

Joe relayed my question again. Rhonda looked at me and shook her head slowly. "I don't know. The problem here is that from all I've read about the Society—this really isn't their shtick. And Joe's already said he didn't get the oogy vibe from L-6, meaning they haven't really been going out and killing. Stealing yes. But not killing."

"No, we were given strict orders not to kill."

I looked at him. *What about Charlie Holmes?*

He pointed at me. "I'm beginning to believe that was an accident. He startled them."

Oh yeah, and that makes it all better. I glared at him. *So we're not really sure who took the Eidolons, are we?*

Joe relayed the question. Rhonda shook her head. "No. We aren't. We have bits and pieces of this but nothing really—whole. And I'm beginning to think the deaths and dismemberment aren't either one of these factions but something else entirely."

A pager went off, and Joe reached down to his belt. He removed it and checked the display. "Ah—wouldn't you know. L-6 is moving into action."

"Where?" Rhonda asked, just as a phone began to ring. Rhonda leaned over and pulled a new silver phone from her bag.

She smiled at the readout. "It's one of my sources."

I pointed at Joe to get his attention and started to speak when—

RETURN!—I slammed back into my physical form. Muscles spasmed from my neck to my fingers and down to my toes. I could feel the sinews snapping and tearing as my toes curled backward and spread apart in my shoes. My back arched up high as I clenched my teeth against the pain.

"She's back!"

I sucked in air and opened my eyes. I blinked rapidly, trying to fight the electric current threading its way through my body and could swear it was tearing the nails right off of my fingers. Muscles seized, and I slammed my head against something hard and unforgiving.

Something was shoved between my teeth. It tasted of rubber and oil, but I bit down hard as I could as the tremors continued. Why was it so painful his time? Why did it hurt so damned much?

And then I remembered the last time I'd been away so long. With Trench-Coat. And the convulsions I'd had then. I bit down hard and screamed and screamed and screamed.

Silent screams. No one could hear me.

Finally, the pain faded. Slowly. Much like waves moving back from the shore and thunder disappearing into the night. I breathed deep and someone removed the bit between my lips, and something plastic was placed over my mouth and nose. Whatever it was smelled like chemicals—antiseptic.

Wrong.

And it was cold.

I tried to push it away but couldn't lift my arms. I tried to lift my head but couldn't and felt a pain along my forehead. The smell grew stronger and I tried to make it stop.

"Sshhhhh...sleep, Zoë. Just sleep. Sleep is how you regain your strength. Sleep is how you become powerful."

I recognized the voice. I knew that voice. I just couldn't place it. So familiar. And when I turned my head to the right, I saw a man's face staring at me with dead white eyes and sewn lips.

25

January 31, time unknown

I was in a river—standing right in the middle of it. And I had on a white dress—which wasn't right because I don't like white, and I hate dresses. But it was more like a flowy dress, like the kind I saw in Renaissance fairs. On princesses.

Not on me.

And I had flowers in my arms. Lots of flowers. Flowers in my hair, and they were floating in the river all around me. Blues, reds, yellows, orange, purples—the rainbow in a floral mess. Wow, I'm Ophelia!

And it was snowing. Great. I'm going to freeze.

Daniel was across the river, and he was dueling swords with Joe. They both looked pretty good in their tight-fitting stockings, baggy shirts, and vests. Nice. Daniel was in white, and Joe was in gray.

Yep. It seemed, appropriate.

Rhonda was nearby. She was in black and lounging under a tree, reading a book as the boys hacked at one another. The snow gathered in her hair but never seemed to accumulate on the ground. Green grass. Flowers.

In fact, there were so many flowers, I sneezed.

"Bless you."

I turned to my left. Mom was there, on the shore, and she had her own bouquet of flowers. She was wearing red. Scarlet red. And it looked good on Debbie Reynolds. But so would white. I wanted the red dress. It spoke of wantonness. And lots of trysts in the closet.

Great—even in my dreams I was getting horny.

"Mom, where have you been?"

"Right here. Gathering flowers." She frowned. "Where have you been? You know we have a funeral to go to on Friday. Lieutenant Holmes was such a good man."

I frowned. "Uh—we already did that. You were there. Don't you remember?"

She shook her head. "No—it's only Wednesday, Zoë. And you've been a bad girl—not coming to see me all week."

"Because you nearly poisoned me with your tea on Sunday. Made me sick as a dog." I paused a minute, then said, "I have a voice."

"Of course you do, dear." She turned and stooped to pick up a bloodred rose. "You always have. Just like your father. Always doing what you're told not to do."

I dropped the bouquet. It was rare Mom ever brought up my dad. And she knew how much I wanted to know about him, the man I couldn't remember because he'd disappeared when I was young. I grabbed up my skirt and tried to get out of the water, but the rocks moved and piled around my ankles, making it impossible. My toes were cold. Icy. "Mom—what do you mean like Dad?"

"Oh." She straightened. "I told him to just forget about things. But he had to do it just one more time. And that one more time—" She stopped and looked at me. She looked so sad, and the snow clung to her blond curls and the flowers in her arms. "I can't talk about that, Zoë. We have to be careful here."

"Careful for what?"

"What're you two whispering about?" Rhonda was moving across the water. Her feet weren't getting wet either. "Are you talking about your dad?"

Mom answered for me. "No. We weren't. Zoë can't talk, remember?"

Something squeezed my throat, and I put my hands to it. I couldn't feel anything there, but it was getting harder to breathe. I opened my mouth and looked at Mom.

She shook her head, and I heard her voice inside of me. "You won't tell them anything! You will not speak!"

And I never spoke again.

"SHE'S coming around."

Loud. Very loud voice. My head ached, and I tried to pry my eyes open. They were stuck together. Careful—ah—there was the left one. And now the right. I tried to reach up and rub them but couldn't. I knew I had arms and hands, but weren't they full of flowers?

"Miss Martinique—can you hear me?"

Blink, blink. Oh yeah. I can hear you. It's like he was right in my ear. I moaned—silent, of course—and managed to focus on something dark, with brown lines striking through it in regular intervals. It looked like beams. A ceiling? I saw webbing here and there. Real spiderwebs that danced about in a light to my right. A single bulb that swayed just a little.

Yes, it was a ceiling. But it was a basement ceiling. Unfinished. Bare.

And there was a really bad smell from somewhere, like someone had left raw chicken out overnight. Ew.

"Zoë, you're going to feel a little woozy for a while, but it's the best way we know to keep you under control."

I tried to turn my head to the left, to the voice, but I couldn't move that either. Something was pressing down on my forehead. That was when I realized my entire body was pinned down, from my chest to my wrists, knees, and ankles.

Oh. Fuck.

I tried to slip out of my body for a better look.

Nothing happened.

I frowned—tried again. Nothing.

"You see? She can't become the Wraith, not while she's wearing this." A hand appeared from somewhere and moved something on my chest. I couldn't even lower my chin to see what it was.

But I suspected it was an Eidolon.

And whoever it was in the room was keeping well out of my line of sight.

"You sure?" came a familiar female voice.

Mom?

"I mean it seems so silly that a simple stone can contain a Wraith."

"Not just contain a Wraith, but *any* spectral entity."

I knew that male voice now. I'd heard it before I'd been drugged. But I didn't want to believe any of it.

Two faces peered down at me. Leaning over opposite sides of whatever I was strapped to.

Mom. And Dr. Maddox.

No, no, no, no, no, no—

"She's getting upset." Dr. Maddox smiled. "Zoë, please. Don't cry."

I cried out for Mom. The woman who made me biscuits, who cooked me bacon and eggs, and baked me cakes, who nagged me about the way I dressed and about my weight.

Mom!

The woman who looked like my mom put her hand on my

cheek. I tried to move away from her but couldn't. "You're upset, aren't you? You think I'm her?"

Yes, I'm upset, I—

Mom!

I blinked rapidly to clear away the tears that had pooled in the corners of my eyes. I wasn't understanding any of this.

"I'm not Nona, sweetheart." She smiled. It was sort of Mom's smile, only it didn't have her edge. "She's not here at the moment."

Where's my mom!

Her eyes grew wide. "Oh, Bertram, I heard her. That's wonderful!"

Maddox nodded. "Yes, I noticed it after I started treating her regularly and studying her blood work. I think it has something to do with death, you know?"

"Really? I haven't been dead that long though. Only twenty years." The Mom look-alike peered down at me again. "You know, she does look more like him than Nona."

Him? Him who?

"Your father, silly." She smiled sweetly. "He was such a handsome man too. All that olive skin and thick hair. Very handsome. And did you know when he came back he—"

"Charolette!" Dr. Maddox boomed. "Not now. We have to set the rules now." He waved her away, then disappeared.

The platform I was on moved abruptly and tilted forward, with my feet heading down. I was being tilted up into a standing position. I assumed it was so he wouldn't have to lean over me.

And I also realized in a gasp of horror that he wanted me to see the entire room.

It was a basement with the usual beamed walls decorated with household items. A broom. A mop. A water hose. And there was even a shelf to the right with a box of detergent on it, as well as fabric softener. Below that was a washer and dryer. Sears. Kenmore. Like my mom had.

To the left was a shelf strewn with tools. Drills, drimmel, soldering iron, and even a vise. Among those things I even saw a microscope, a rack of test tubes, and a crumpled bag from McDonald's.

Above the shelf was a window, the glass blocked out by black paint. I didn't know what time of day it was.

But it was what I saw in the corner that caught my gaze and held it. Tied to a simple wooden chair was a puppet. A large, oddly shaped puppet. Or so I thought at first, but a second later I realized it wasn't made of cloth or plastic.

But of flesh.

I knew I was staring at the head, torso, hands, and feet of the three victims. The head was sewn to the torso with leather, no neck to speak of. The hands were sewn directly to the shoulders, and the feet to the crotch.

Heather's hands and feet. Dainty bones, pale hands and feet.

The lips of the face were sewn shut, and the eyes were dead white. I had seen this face before, in the paper. This was Charles Randolph. And as I stared at it I heard something soft, like the muffled moan of a voice down a deep well.

The fingers moved.

I swore and tried to move away.

The head bobbed to the right, and I thought I saw the lips press out against the leather thread holding them together.

The thing was alive!

"Isn't it cute?" Charolette—Mom—said and actually put her hand on the shoulder. The thing started to bounce and would have fallen from the chair if it weren't strapped in. The muffled sounds from the sewn mouth grew louder. The woman gave the thing's shoulder a slight smack. "Now you hush, Nona. None of that now."

I blinked.

Nona.

NONA?

I started to breathe really fast. I looked from her to the thing and back to her. *YOU PUT MY MOTHER IN THERE?*

Charolette put her hands to her ears. "Really, Zoë. So loud? You want that we put *you* in there?"

I cringed. What kind of hell would it be—to find myself locked up in a body that couldn't see or move. I started to understand the torturous nature of giving the imprisoned spirit hands and feet, but no way to use them.

I couldn't take my eyes away from the *thing*—

I saw the necklace then. The clear stone. An Eidolon. Possession, wasn't it? Was that the one they had murdered for? Or was the one hanging from my neck the one? Did it matter? Somehow they were holding me hostage in my own body, and my mother hostage inside a monstrosity.

I swore at that moment if I ever got free of whatever magic or mayhem these two creatures had cast on me I would take their spirits, and I would devour them myself.

No matter what the consequence.

Maddox moved into my line of sight. "Frightening thing, isn't it?" He smiled, and I briefly wondered where Joseph had gone. Had he disappeared that morning in the hospital because this— whatever—had taken over his father's body?

Charolette frowned. "Honey—I'd seen his host's son hanging about, but we don't know where he went."

I glared at her. How was I going to think without them hearing me?

"I'm afraid not easily," Maddox said, and reached out for my chest and the pendant. I felt its weight on my breast. "Not with this around your neck. It took me a while to find the amulet you had stuffed in your pocket." He let the necklace bounce against my chest and wiggled a finger at me. "Very smart. Powerful magic too. Though I'm sure it made it hard to return to your body, which in the end, helped me delay your reentry long enough so that you would be weak, and pliable for your new life."

I felt my chest heave up and down as I breathed heavily. *What the hell is going on? Who—what—are you?*

Maddox smiled. "I'm sure this is where the bad guy tells the helpless heroine about his dastardly plan?" He shook his head. "Only I am not the bad guy, Zoë." With an intent stare he fixed me with his eyes. "You are."

I blinked, breaking the contact. *Me?* I wasn't a bad guy. Yeah, I cheated on my taxes sometimes, and I even lied about parking tickets—but I wasn't evil.

"You *are* evil." Charolette leaned forward and patted my shoulder. It was so hard for me to look into my mom's face and know she wasn't looking back out at me. The thing in the corner had become still and silent.

MOMMY!

"You just don't know it yet." Charolette smiled at me and looked at Maddox. "So what are you going to have her do first?"

Whoa—have me do? I don't plan on doing a damned thing for either of you.

"I'm afraid you will. For two reasons. One—because the Command Eidolon is around your neck. While your physical body wears it, I control your movements, your actions, your thoughts. You belong to me, which is why you can't slip out of your body now. Because *I* don't want you to."

Smug. I hate smug.

"And second, because if you try to fight me, or call for help, I will release your mother's spirit from the scarecrow."

I looked at the thing.

Scarecrow. This was what Dags had been talking about. This—abomination.

I don't see where that's a bad thing—I'm sure being anywhere but in there would be preferable.

Charolette clapped her hands together. "But that's just it, Zoë. If she's not in there, and I'm in here to stay"—she put her hands on her—my mother's—hips—"then there's nowhere for her to go. She'll be a wandering spirit. Stuck between the living plane and the mental. Not alive. But not dead either."

A walker.

No—they were lying. And then I knew they weren't. Spirits who lingered in the physical plane after their bodies died didn't move on immediately. They remained trapped between the two. Not like Tim and Steve, whose fetters were tied to Mom's house. These were creatures without ties.

Without a cord.

I looked down the bridge of my nose, still unable to move my head much. If I looked at the scarecrow's chest I could see a web-like thread. It moved out and still remained firmly connected to the body Charolette had stolen.

Mom was still anchored. If they cut that cord—

"Snip." Maddox made a scissor motion with his right hand. "So as long as you want your mother to survive, then you'll be *my* puppet, won't you?"

Damn. Shit. Damn. *Why? Why are you doing this? Did you murder those people just to make this horrific thing to keep my mother in? What are you?*

I struggled against the straps holding me in place. Obviously, the Eidolon had no power over my physical body, or there wouldn't be a need to keep me tied down. I was on the verge of tears again. I continued trying to slip out of my body, but nothing happened. It was like being trapped inside a fitted container, and I realized how much I had actually come to depend on being a Wraith.

Depend on the freedom it gave me.

"We didn't make the scarecrow originally for this purpose. And we have used it for what it was made to do." He tuned and picked up an *AJC* from the counter beside the microscope and showed me the front page I'd already seen.

The article about the occultist's mysterious death due to a heart attack. Too young.

You—you caused his heart attack?

Maddox nodded. "He was my first real test with the Possession Eidolon. He was also the man who told me who owned one of the Eidolons. I picked his brain, and when he came in for his physical last week, I took a sample of his hair and placed it on my scarecrow. Then I commanded his spirit inside." Maddox looked as if he'd just eaten the best chocolate in the world. His eyes closed slowly in ecstasy. "It was sooooo rewarding, hearing him scream inside and seeing him struggle to understand what was happening." He sighed. "I was at the funeral parlor and saw Knowles there. He didn't recognize me, of course. They never do. They all thought we died."

I caught his look at Charolette. She smiled back at him.

We died.

You're not Symbionts.

Charolette shuddered. "Oh. Please. Don't even think of those dreadful things. Parasites. They feed off the living and give little back."

Which wasn't really the truth. Most of them gave back health and the ability to achieve their dreams. Now, granted, their hosts were usually damned to the Phantasm's service later on, but that was such a small price—NOT!

But who was really worried about what would happen down the road when you were young, healthy, and wealthy?

If they weren't Symbionts, were they Daimons? Daimons could never be strong enough to control these bodies like this.

No...only one other entity that I had witnessed had been able to completely possess a body and shove out the host's spirit.

You're Rogues.

Maddox actually smiled at me. "Very good, Zoë! Brava!" He clapped. Weirdo. "Yes, Charolette and I were once Travelers as you were, in the beginning. Up until what—two months ago?"

I took a deep breath, feeling a little better now that I knew what they were. I just had to figure out now *who* they were. *You run the League of Six?*

Charolette nodded. "We do now. Bertram here came up with the idea of infiltrating them to our own ends, right, honey?"

Bertram—the rogue in Maddox's body—nodded. "Yes. Very clever. I knew the man who organized the watches, kept the archives of the Dioscuri, our mother group. It was easy to kick his spirit out, take the Eidolon, then order his little forces around to do our bidding." He looked at me. "And then I found Melvin Maddox, a little-known doctor, and he knew a woman named Nona Martinique." Bertram took a step closer to me. "Two things drew me to her. She possessed an Eidolon—which in itself was something rare, as only the Five originally owned the Eidolons, and how could this woman be involved with the Dioscuri?"

I watched him as he came closer, then traced a finger over my chin. "But the name Martinique. Ah—that is a very famous name among the societies. I only knew of one woman with that name—a woman who bore a single child. A miracle child. A child that shouldn't have lived. A child with a very interesting father."

Father. My eyes widened. *You knew my father?*

"Knew is right, little Martinique. He is long gone from this world. As your mother knows." He turned away, and I struggled again.

Come back! Tell me about my father!

"No, no—that's for another day. What you need to know is that I destroyed the leader's body and appropriated this one." He held out his hands. "And since L-6's work dogs don't ever see one another's faces, and I knew all the codes, I became the leader in this identity."

Somehow I knew the man he spoke of murdering was the first body, the head that sat atop the scarecrow. Charles Randolph.

Where is the spirit of Melvin Maddox?

He shrugged. "Gone. I kept him in the scarecrow for a while, then I needed it, and I released him. Clipped the cord."

You—you released *him.* I thought about Joseph's vanishing. *You released him on Tuesday?*

"Yes, sometime around then."

When Joseph had disappeared in my room. With his father gone, the fetter was gone as well. I would venture to assume he'd moved on. But I recalled the expression on Joseph's face. He'd seen something horrific. Something I hadn't seen. I hadn't been able to help him. I had always promised to be the one to release him, to see him move on.

And this asshole had robbed me of that.

"Bertram was so clever," Charolette said. "I needed a body, so I shoved Nona out of hers and she was sucked into that stone dragon she has over her mantel."

Mom? Mom was the one that was bouncing up and down in the dragon? Oh hell. She was there the whole time.

"Yes, so we grabbed it when the boys grabbed you, and I transferred her into the scarecrow," Bertram said. "I thought it made a much more powerful incentive for you." He took a deep breath. "Now—we have to get the evening started. There's much for you to do. You should be fully rested and ready to perform your first job." He leaned his head to the side. "As my servant."

Oh, this was insane! Pissed off didn't even cover the range of emotions that tumbled about in my head. All thought of rescue was useless. Joe and Rhonda could never find me. Even I didn't know where I was.

Bertram moved away from me and somewhere behind me. I heard rustling, and the clink of something like glasses. I couldn't help but look at the rotting, smelling scarecrow in the corner. Every other second or so the fingers moved, or the feet. Even the lids blinked. Blind eyes.

And there was a moan.

Mommy . . .

The table abruptly moved, and I was lowered backward. I gritted my teeth as it banged to a stop and I saw a hanging plastic bag. Tubes. Shit.

"Now, to make sure you don't dehydrate on me." Bertram moved my left arm and pulled up the sleeve of my sweatshirt. He whistled softly. "Charolette—come look. Here it is. The mark. The mark!"

He was talking about TC's mark. The handprint on my forearm. I felt their hands on my flesh and tried to strike out at them. But the strap holding my wrist was tight, and strong.

"Did it hurt?" Charolette asked me.

I looked at her. *Does it matter?*

She nodded. "Yes—to me. You don't understand, do you, Zoë?"

*Understand? Understand what? That I'm being held against my will, that you've locked my mom's soul inside a dead thing, and that you plan on using me to—*I felt the sting of a needle in the crook of my left elbow as it slid inside the soft flesh. *It doesn't matter what I understand—only that you'll both pay for what you're doing.*

"No," Charolette said. "No, we won't. There's nothing in this world or the next that can harm us, Zoë." She reached out and touched my cheek. "Except you. You are what we wanted to be. But we weren't given the opportunity."

I frowned at her. *What?*

"Enough." Bertram waved her away. I felt the cold of something entering my veins, then a warmth spreading all the way through.

What—there's something in that…

"Yes. I don't want anything to go wrong. Not tonight. So I've put in a little something to calm your body while you're out. Not to knock you out—that would defeat the purpose. This is insurance you see." He then stood back and said in a very commanding voice, "Wraith—come out and do my bidding."

The truth of the matter was he could have said, "Yo, get out," and it would have had the same effect. There was an overriding compulsion to slip away, to follow his words, and that's exactly what I did.

I stood beside myself, with my still body on my right and the shelf on the left. Bertram stood in front of me. I glanced at myself. I looked okay. A little pale. I noticed that the straps holding me down were all leather. Thick and well stitched. And fastened with small padlocks. There was one over my forehead as I thought. The IV dripped inside my veins. When would I stop seeing my body like this? Abandoned? Punished?

And then weight filled my spirit, raced through my astral body, until it coalesced in circling spirals around my wrists and ankles. It solidified and became shiny, silver shackles that locked themselves in place with an audible click.

Something grasped my neck, and I reached to pull the invisible fingers away—but too late I realized another circle had formed there as well, and within seconds I wore a collar of hard, cold, solid metal.

I bent over, falling to my knees as the weight pulled me down, robbed me of my strength. I had seen chains like this before.

Friendly the Clown had held them in his hands.

The Phantasm.

Bertram was beside me, kneeling beside me, his voice a whisper in my ear. "Yes, yes, yes..." He was nearly salivating at my imprisonment. "It worked—just like it worked on him!"

I struggled to move, to rise and wrap my hands around his neck and choke the life out of him. Melvin Maddox was dead. His soul gone. And this—this—monstrosity should pay.

But—I couldn't move. I was shackled. Controlled.

"Wraith," Bertram spoke into my ear, "it's come to our attention that we have been compromised. A former member of our group has turned traitor, and this cannot be tolerated. This person knows too much and they have seen too much. This person needs to be eliminated. And I thought that since you were close to the traitor, and you knew of the turncoat's affiliations with team members, this person's death would be a test of your power, and my control over you, before I set you on a bigger target."

My eyes widened. I only knew of one person who had infiltrated their ranks—who knew anything about L-6. That was Joe. He was going to command me to go after Joe.

How was I going to stop myself?

Chains appeared attached to the shackles.

"Rise."

And I did. The chains disappeared, but not before I saw Bertram holding them. But the shackles remained. Tight. Compelling me to listen and to obey.

He turned the picture around. I stepped back, but also felt myself compelled to study the image, though I knew the contours of the face almost as well as my own.

"Kill Rhonda Orly."

26

To kill . . .

NO!

"Obey me!"

The shackles tightened around my neck and wrists. I clenched my teeth against the pain and noticed my physical body shudder. My hair fell loose and long over my face, the white streak glowing as I watched the color spread down to the ends.

"You will obey me, Wraith. Kill Rhonda Orly. She sits even now within the house of the man responsible for your father's death. You kill her, and this cements your loyalty to me."

Bertram couldn't have grabbed my attention better than mentioning my father. Too bad I didn't believe him. *You never knew my father.*

"Oh, I knew your father. So did Knowles. It was he that ordered his murder, Zoë. Want to know the truth?"

I sneered at him and felt my astral body grow colder. The shackles eased their strength, but they were still there, reminding me I was bound.

"Go to them both, Wraith. Shadow him, take his memories,

and shred his heart in your hands as you drain the life from the woman who betrayed your friendship."

I...will...not...believe...you...

Bertram smiled at me. "Then see for yourself." He reached out and clasped the Eidolon around my body's neck in his left palm. "Go!"

And before I had any conscious thought of where I was or what I was doing, the world around me dissolved, and I felt light as air. I *was* air, and I was sailing up through the rafters, through the house, through the roof and into the snow-filled sky. I spiraled over the trees and stopped as I mingled with the clouds and looked out over the living world below me.

Kill Rhonda...

March Knowles...

My base thoughts shifted as I felt the pull of the shackles, the command of Bertram. Kill, kill, kill...

And there, miles away, in a house nestled back in the hills, I saw a golden light. I felt warmth beckon to me, and I'd not even realized I was cold. I was a creature of hatred, of darkness and cold, of fear and terror. The only thing that mattered to me at that moment was doing what I had been ordered to do.

I felt the wind move through me as I traveled toward that light, toward the house, toward my target. I saw the chimney with wild swirls of smoke, the angled rooftops, then I was inside the house, sieving through the wood, the insulation, and then I was solid, standing in the center of a high-ceilinged room before a five-foot-high fireplace, complete with roaring fire.

"Zoë?"

The shackles tightened, and I whirled around to see my prey. Rhonda sat in a soft mauve, high-backed chair, her computer in her lap. Her eyes widened as I took a step toward her, an inner part of me resisting the urge to—

Wait.

Mental note: *I just flew! I just fucking flew through the air! Booyah!*

"Hey, Zoë"—Joe moved from around the chair, a book open in his hand—"we were getting a little worried when you didn't— whoa! What the hell happened to you, and what is with the bracelets?"

"Never mind those." Rhonda stood and set her computer on the chair behind her. "Look at that necklace." She then put a hand to her face. "Joe—look at her. I mean really look at her—are those—wings?"

Wings?

Shit. I wished I could see myself, but the compulsion to carry out Bertram's wish was too strong. I could do one, and only one thing. I raised an arm and pointed a very sharp nail at her.

"Joe—she's actually Wraith."

"And she's being Commanded," came another voice, one I'd heard before, at the Westin, and on the phone. Rhonda's phone.

Knowles.

The congressman was dressed casually, in khakis and sweater. His feet were socked with brown wool. And he looked much calmer now than he had that night with Rodriguez.

Especially facing down a Wraith.

"Commanded?" Joe said. He too looked comfortable standing beside the man who killed my father.

"See the shackles?" He nodded at me. "They've sent her, like I knew they would. This is why I called you here."

I felt the collar around my neck tighten and took a step toward Rhonda.

Joe moved from his position and stood in front of her. "Okay— why does she keep looking at Rhonda like that? And why isn't she talking?"

"Because whoever is controlling her with the Eidolon isn't allowing her to talk. He or she is using her physical body like a voodoo doll, or a puppet if you would, and controlling her through it." Knowles moved out to the side of Joe and Rhonda. He had something in his hand. Something I could sense but couldn't see.

Joe moved out a few inches in front of Rhonda. "Zoë—can you hear me? Look—Knowles has been telling us about the league, and about what happened, twenty years ago. Look, we know what they're doing, Zoë. And Knowles is going to call in some help for you—"

But I wasn't listening. I couldn't. All I could hear in my head was Bertram's voice, over and over and over, commanding me to kill Rhonda, kill Rhonda, kill, kill, kill—

And then I was there, in front of Joe, and I was solid and grabbing him and tossing him away. He flew through the air and crashed into a second high-backed chair, and he and the chair fell away.

I went for Rhonda, my hands outstretched.

Knowles intercepted me, placing his own chest in front of me. My astral body was already obeying the command, shifting only my hands and arms into an incorporeal state, then taking his heart between my fingers. I felt my fingers become solid and he gasped as I ripped apart his insides and shredded his heart with my nails. I felt his spirit split from his body, and I grabbed it, pulled it to me, then pulled it *into* me.

Power. Raw. Feast. Charged.

And...

Innocent.

As I sifted through the memories of his soul, of his life, I saw flashes of children, of women with sweet smiles, and of sorrow standing beside a grave.

His wife's grave.

But I didn't see, nor did I feel, any part of my father.

March Knowles had never known him personally. He had known *of* him. He'd never spoken with him.

I had just killed an innocent man.

The shackles tightened again as the man's body fell to the floor in front of the chair. I reached up for them, tried to pry them loose. And again I was overtaken with the compulsion to kill Rhonda.

She was still there, her eyes so wide they looked as if they would pop from her skull. She was looking at the dead man at my feet. I stood inside of him, insubstantial. Incorporeal.

Joe was unmoving. I sensed several more life signs in the home, but they were all running into the snow away from the house. Little flickers of fire, of life.

I moved forward, through the dead man, toward Rhonda, my hands outstretched.

"Please, Zoë. Fight them...Please..." And she was crying. Backing up only to fall backward into the chair, on top of her machine.

I stopped in front of her, hissing with pain as the shackles dug into my wrists, ankles, and into my neck. I fought, kicked and screamed, to be free of Bertram's control.

But in the end, there was nothing I could do about the command, and I lurched forward at her, just as I had at Knowles. My arms went insubstantial, traveling through her rib cage and lungs, until I had her heart inside my fingers once again.

And I closed my eyes as I squeezed. I felt her kick and scream beneath me. I felt Joe beside me. He tried to pull me off, but his hands went through me. When he tried to pull Rhonda away, I wouldn't allow her to move.

I felt her spirit beat against me as I pulled her away. The heart beat very fast. Faster and faster. Until it just stopped.

Rhonda went limp, her head lolling to one side, her arms spread out to either side, her legs thrust out from the seat. I felt her spirit start to move away—

And nearly fell into her myself. A gasp escaped me as the pressure around my neck, my wrists and ankles vanished. I pulled my hand from Rhonda's body and put my fingers to my neck.

The collar was gone. The shackles were gone from my wrists and ankles as well!

I was free!

And then horror lodged in my throat as I looked down at the unseeing eyes of Rhonda as her body sprawled half-on and half-off of the chair.

Sonofabitch!

Something hard and very unforgiving struck me across the face. I wheeled backward, slamming hard into the floor, rolling a few inches from where Knowles's body lay.

"You stupid monster!" Joe was yelling as he followed me and started kicking. "You killed her! You fucking monster, you killed her!"

I let him kick me a few more times before I become incorporeal again. On hands and knees I crawled back to Rhonda and pulled myself up between her legs.

I drove my hands back into her chest and started massaging her heart, willing it to start beating. How long could someone be dead and not suffer brain damage? I didn't know.

I didn't know!

It wasn't working. I became completely insubstantial and slipped into her myself. Once there I thought of my own heart beating, and I moved my chest where hers was, thought of my life replacing hers.

Please don't die, please don't die, please don't die...

Over and over again I massaged the heart and imagined a rhythmic beat. Joe had grabbed Rhonda's body and set it on the floor. He was administering CPR, muttering the whole time. "You'd better help her, Zoë, you'd better damned well help her..."

Finally, she gasped, pulling in air. Her heart started again. Strained, weak, and erratic. The only thing I knew to do was what I'd done before. I sent happy thoughts. Thoughts of good times. Memories.

Feelings. My own feelings of sorrow.

Oh please forgive me.

"It wasn't your fault."

I looked up, realizing I was on the back porch again, and the sky was completely dark. A wind played havoc with a chime hanging near the back steps and blew the covers of the magazines back and forth. There were no houses around us, only empty wheat fields and a coming storm. I could see a twister on the horizon, but it never came any closer.

I stood on the porch, fully clothed in a black, shiny bodysuit. My bunny slippers grew fangs, and I felt something along my back touch the porch's roof.

Rhonda sat to the side, dressed the same as she had been when I'd see her here before, with the same sad smile. "Really. You were only doing what you were told to do."

I started to go to her, but she put up her hands. I stopped. "Please don't die!"

"I won't." She smiled up at me. "I can't. I have a lot of things to do yet. Things I have to tell you. Things you need to know."

I felt my body shift and change, and I was no longer a black image of death and destruction but just me, dressed in jeans and a tee shirt. I knelt beside her and took her in my arms.

"Please don't leave me."

I continued to hold her in my arms, not wanting to let her go.

"You have to, Zoë. I can't breathe when you're choking me."

I let her go and realized I was no longer on the back porch but in the living room of March Knowles's home. Rhonda was blinking and coughing, and Joe was rubbing her hands, cheering her on.

I stood up and pulled myself the rest of the way out of her. *I'm sorry, I'm so sorry, I didn't—I couldn't stop myself—*

Joe turned and glanced at me. "Tell me that later, when I'm not wanting to kick your ass."

I nodded to him. *Is she going to be okay?*

"I'll"—Rhonda coughed and then blinked quickly as she regained her focus—"be fine. Really. I'm just peachy."

I turned and looked at Knowles's body. *Oh, what have I done? What have I done?*

"You just killed a United States congressman," Rhonda said as she struggled to sit up. Joe was at her side, offering her his arm. "And I'm thinking we're going to need to get out of here soon before whoever it was that commanded you shows up and tries to reestablish command over you."

Reestablish? So—I'm no longer under the spell of the Eidolon?

Rhonda shook her head. "No—you carried out whatever it was you were commanded to do, but according to March, there was a fail-safe built in to each of the Eidolons that—" She blinked once, then looked at me.

I made the same connection and pointed to her. *You—you can hear me!*

Rhonda swallowed and put her hands to her chest. "Yeah, I can." She smiled. "Wow—that's pretty radical. I guess maybe it's a death experience?"

Joe held up his hands. "This is all nice, but have you forgotten that this"—he glanced at me—"this person nearly killed you?"

"No, she did kill me. And when the Eidolon released her, she brought me back. I told you, as did March, that if L-6 did have the Command Eidolon, as well as Zoë, then it made sense they'd try and harness her powers. It's what the thing was made for." She gestured for him to help her to a standing position. "The original group used the same Eidolon years ago—to control something they should never have messed with."

I moved forward to help as well, and Rhonda put up a hand. "No—not—I can't deal with what I just experienced yet."

I understood and stepped back. I was still on a slight buzz from Knowles's death.

Joe looked at me. "Where is your body?"

I blinked several times at him. *It's—I can find it. It seems I flew here. Imagine that.*

"So—who's calling the shots?"

Two Rogues called Bertram and Charolette.

Both Rhonda and Joe dropped their lower jaws.

"No way," Joe said.

And that's when I broke down and started crying as I told them what they'd done to my mother.

Joe moved to me then and held me. I didn't remember becoming corporeal. The act was second nature now. He held on tight, not a going-through-the-motions sort of thing. He really held me and patted my hair as I told them everything that had happened to me and everything I knew. From the Eidolons to the uncontrollable urge to kill.

I felt very tired when I was finished, but Joe didn't let go. And to be honest, I was afraid I'd fall if he did let go.

Rhonda moved beside Knowles and knelt. She reached into his clasped pocket and retrieved a red stone and silver chain.

The Eidolon of Destruction. She held it up and let it dangle from her hand. "He was going to protect me with this—this is the one Joe found in the box. He knew they'd send you after me."

He—he was going to destroy me?

She nodded. "But I didn't want him to. He didn't want to either. He thought of you as a distant niece."

I swallowed. *There's something else?*

Joe sighed and took his arms away from me. He moved over the body to stand by Rhonda, and I felt very cold in his absence. "Just tell her."

Rhonda said, "He knew your father, Zoë." She looked up at

me. "Not personally. But he was involved with the project. In his youth he worked for the Southern Controller for Astral Research and Examination, who managed an organization funded by a conglomerate of private businesses."

I blinked at her, knowing there had to be some significance to this.

Joe cocked his head to his right shoulder, and said, "The group called themselves Scarecrow."

"And your father was their best student."

And again Joe piped up. "He was an astral walker, Zoë. Just like you."

Rhonda gave a long, ragged sigh. "And they killed him."

27

Fear...

KILLED him.

My father was dead? I hadn't realized I'd been holding out hope that maybe he was still alive somewhere. Watching me. Mom had never actually said he was dead—she only said he was missing.

Knowles was lying...I stepped back, shaking my head slowly.

Joe moved to me. "Zoë, don't go la-la on me. I don't think he was lying because he knew a few things about Adiran—"

I started to breathe heavier and heavier. I wanted to run and hide, like when I was seven and broke Mom's only picture of Daddy. I'd been so mad he wasn't there, and I'd smashed it against the side of the house. Over and over again until there wasn't anything left. I'd killed the last thing to remind me he wasn't there.

And I'd destroyed the last thing that told my mom he'd ever existed. And now I'd done it again.

"Rhonda—she's going to freak."

Rhonda stood and put up her hands. "Zoë—don't. It wasn't your fault. You saved me."

But it was too late. The barrel was already over the falls, and I was plummeting along the downward spiral.

I thrust my head back and screamed. Silent.

Deadly.

The roof shook above me as parts of the plaster came loose. It crashed on the marbled floor around us as the floor beneath me shifted. I felt the foundation of the house move beneath me. The wood cracked. The nails came unhinged. The concrete foundation split along every fissure I could find as my conscious mind branched out and cried.

Arms enveloped me again and held me close. Joe was whispering in my ear. Rhonda's hands were on me as well, and they were telling me everything was going to be okay.

"Let's go get your mom back in her body, okay?" Joe said. "With the Destruction Eidolon, Rhonda thinks we can destroy the Summoning as well as the Command Eidolons—which should set you free."

"I don't think I'd like that," Charolette said from the doorway behind the overturned chair. She had put on a coat and had a purse with her as well.

And a gun.

"Please, everyone move away from the Wraith. Oh—I see you killed the wrong one, Zoë." She made little tsk-tsk noises. "I'm afraid Bertram's not going to like this at all. Now, you step over here so your friends don't get hurt."

Rhonda and Joe backed away, but I saw Rhonda palm the necklace to Joe, who put it out of sight. The green necklace Mom had worn so often almost glowed where it lay on Mom's ample breast. *I'm not going to be your slave.*

"I'm afraid you have no choice—though I do wish we'd known about the fail-safes before we started. Then this little excursion wouldn't have had to take place." She shivered as she leveled the gun at Joe and Rhonda. "It's so cold out there. Ah, traitor and witch. Seems fitting you two would end up working together alongside of the Wraith."

That was the second time I'd heard a reference to a witch and a traitor. Only the first instance had been in the warehouse, and Heather had been standing there.

Mental note: *what?*

Sprays of cracked plaster had continued to fall from the ceiling. Vibrations beneath our feet signaled imminent structural failure. I looked over at Rhonda and at Joe.

"Now, Wraith"—Charolette took a step forward—"time to get back to your body. Chop, chop. Bertram's waiting for you." She smiled sweetly. "Of course, we could just stand here and wait, and as time goes by you would grow weaker and weaker out of body, and eventually you'd have no choice but to return." With a sigh she shook her head. "But we all know how painful that can be."

All sorts of scenarios played in my head of how I could destroy the bitch inside of my mother's body. The one I enjoyed the most was going incorporeal and diving inside and choking the thing out. Only Charolette could see me no matter if I held a solid shape or not. And if I made a sudden move, she'd shoot Joe or Rhonda. Or worse, both.

I knew I had the ability to save maybe one—but not both of them. I was feeling very drained. The energy I'd stolen from Knowles had powered my saving of Rhonda's life. There wasn't much left inside of me, and Charolette was right—it wouldn't be long before I snapped back to my body, and my captivity started all over again.

"What exactly is it that—Bertram—wants her to do next?" Joe asked. He kept his voice even, nonthreatening. Mild curiosity.

And Charolette appeared happy to oblige him. "Oh—Bertram's got a very nice surprise next. He wants to go after the head of the Society. Yes, yes. And then it'll be time to discover who and what this Maharba is and destroy it as well."

The head of the Society? Was she talking about the Society of Ishmael? And how could I even think to destroy Maharba—I didn't even know who that was.

Charolette heard me. "You can't let that stop you, Wraith. And if you fail again, Bertram will have all sorts of torture in store for your mother—and you'll just have to watch! He didn't tell you that she can actually feel inside that scarecrow, did he? No, no he didn't. She knows she's rotting inside that body. And the pain? There's pain in there too. Poor Nona would feel so much terrible pain…"

I heard a growl start deep from somewhere. Low. Threatening. And I wondered where the dog was that was growling.

Until I realized it was me. And the sound was audible, not only to me, but to Joe, and to Rhonda. How dare she torture my mother—my mom who had done nothing wrong! An innocent, just as Knowles had been.

Their only crime had been knowing—knowing what I'd become.

I took a threatening step toward Charolette. She leveled the gun at Joe and fired. But I was lucky his cop senses kicked in and he dove at Rhonda, slamming both of them to the ground and then dragging her as they moved to shelter behind a shelf, which he overturned and turned on its side.

I lunged at Charolette, knowing that the two humans were no longer in her sights. But Charolette only reached inside of her jacket and pulled out another gun. Shit! It was one of the—

She fired it directly at me. I felt my incorporeal form nearly dissolve at the incredible pain that lanced outward from my chest. I fell backward and slid a few inches until I was beside Knowles.

"Tsk, tsk, Wraith," Charolette said. "Bertram has taken every precaution. We know how to bend you to our will." She moved until she was over me, hovering there with the odd-shaped gun trained on me. "This won't kill you, but it will hurt you. It might take a few days for your astral self to recover, but it'll put you back in your body like a good little girl, and we'll take care of you, until it's time for you to come out again."

"You know," I heard Joe say, then heard the rumblings of the ceiling again. More dust fell in tiny pockets around us. "As far as I can remember, Lincoln abolished slavery hundreds of years ago."

Charolette gave me a wink and turned around, and I knew she was certain Joe was bluffing in some way. I was on my back, fighting to keep myself from returning to my body, though I could feel my cord pulling. I turned onto my right side and searched for it. It was there, and it seemed—thinner than before. Almost as if it had lost strength.

"You really are a nice-looking young man—not quite as pretty as that other cop that keeps hanging around. Hrm, maybe I should have her kill him, just so he doesn't start getting suspicious when Zoë never comes home."

I pushed myself up onto my right hip. Strength was returning, slowly, and with agonizing pain. I'd been hit with that damned gun before—but I didn't remember its being this painful.

Joe nodded and rubbed his chin with one hand. "Well, as tempting as that is, and as much as Daniel and I dislike each other, I'm thinking"—he shook his head at her—"no. And besides"—he pulled out a small black gun from behind his back—"we also know what works with spirits."

He fired the Taser.

Two prongs shot out of the gun and buried themselves into my mother's breasts. Yow! But the electric charge had the same effect. She went down, dropping the gun, and her arms and legs flailed.

I saw Charolette fly out, kicked out the same way Taser attacks had kicked me out of the L-6 leader as well as Randall. She rolled like a giant dust bunny toward the fireplace, before lying still, her arms and legs out at her side.

Pushing myself up, I managed a wobbly stand and shuffled toward her. Out of Mom's visage, Charolette's own body wasn't much in the way of distinction. In fact—she was kind of smooth—with few angles or defining features. I could see she'd been beautiful in life, if my theory of retaining the shape of the physical plane was true. But it was like something had—erased parts of her.

She blinked up at me, and her eyes widened. *No, no—don't take me...*

Don't take you? Was that what my mom said before you kicked her out of her body? Did she scream? Plead for mercy? I felt my fists ball and my fingernails pierce my astral skin. *How would you like to spend all of eternity inside that damned scarecrow?*

Charolette screamed and held up her hands.

Rhonda was beside me. "Zoë no. Don't kill her. We can interrogate her. Through her we can find out more about L-6 and where she comes from."

But I didn't care where she came from. She had so callously taken my mother's place, trapped her inside of a statue, and then inside of—inside of—

No.

I reached out to take Charolette. To devour her completely so that she could never invade my mother's body again.

"Zoë, if you do, I'll have to shoot you," Rhonda said in a loud voice.

More dust fell, and I heard the groan of the beams above us.

I looked at her. She was holding the strange gun, leveling the barrel at me.

"Rhonda—what are you doing?" Joe moved beside her. "I'm with Zoë—get rid of this piece of shit."

"No, listen to me. We can learn from it. Study it. Find out why it's—"

NO!

And before she could fire, I bent down and reached out my

right hand. All I would need was a simple touch, a contact. And her life would be mine.

Rhonda fired the gun.

But it was too late.

Charolette and I were bound together, and I was consumed by pain as well as the euphoria as we twisted together, and I heard and felt and reveled in her screams.

Was this what you did to my mother?

Light filled me from the inside and I raised my hands up to the heavens as I let the energy that was once the memories of Charolette McGavin fill me up, strengthen me. I heard the voices of a choir, and somewhere in the distance, a laugh. Rich and strong. Then it all vanished. I was on my right knee when my head cleared, and the music disappeared.

The only noise was the groan of the house and the silence of the snow outside. I rose slowly, feeling the strength return to me. My cord fluttered before me, a ghostly spider's web. So thin.

So very thin.

"Jesus, Zoë," Joe said, and I could hear me swallow. "Remind me not to get on your bad side."

I was facing the fireplace, and the two of them were to my right. Rhonda still held the gun out in front of her, her knuckles white, and her face filled with something I'd never seen her look at me with before.

Fear.

"Zoë, your mom's not responding. Do you know where your body is? Where her soul is?"

I nodded slowly. I could allow my cord to guide me there, to the house in the woods miles from here. But I would only wake up to imprisonment. My body bound. And once again commanded.

Going corporeal, I turned and went to my mother. The gem gleamed in the light of the dimming fire. *This gem had protected my mother for a very long time. She must have taken it off when Charolette took her, and then the rogue placed it back on so that nothing could harm her, or drive her from her new body.*

Joe sneezed as more dust fell. "I'm guessing those things really can't protect an astral spirit through a Taser blast, huh?"

No.

"Well, that's great. So—will it protect her now until we can get her spirit back?"

I nodded. *Rhonda will call for an ambulance and see that my mother is taken care of.* I turned my head to look at her then. She nodded, though her eyes remained wide, and she still clutched the gun in her hands. I knew she was both angry and afraid of me. Angry that I'd destroyed such a prize as Charolette. And afraid that her new little toy had not stopped me.

Joe nodded and held up the jewel. "I've got the Destruction Eidolon. Come on. Let's go."

And with a single motion I stood, and ran at him. He held up his hands as I slipped inside. There was little interference from him, and I knew he couldn't stop me now. My entire being was singing with the power I'd taken from Charolette.

Nothing could stop me.

I allowed Joe control as he winked at Rhonda, turned to a nearby drawer, and pulled out two more fully charged Tasers. Huh—apparently Knowles had been prepared.

Rhonda was looking at Joe with a surprised expression. "Joe, your eyes."

He moved back to the chest with the drawer and looked at himself in the mirror hanging on the wall. The pupils of his eyes glowed red. Pinpoints of me.

With a shake of his head, Joe moved to Rhonda and took the special gun from her. She took a step back, then, after grabbing a jacket, he stepped outside into the sparkling snow.

* * *

THE outside of the house that held my body was dark. Only a single light came from around the edges of the black-painted window of the basement where I and my mother were being held.

I charged Joe's muscles with adrenaline as we burst in through the front door and down into the basement. He held a loaded Glock in his right hand, the Taser in the other. The ghost-zapping gun was tucked into the back of his jeans.

Everything was as I'd left it. My body lay on a board, still bound by leather straps. And the scarecrow sat in the corner, bouncing and moaning as the spirit inside tried to break free.

"Holy shit, shit, shit," Joe continued to say under his breath. And though I knew he was looking around at the room to see where danger would be, his gaze continued to be pulled back to the scarecrow.

Joe moved forward and checked my body's pulse. Steady. I was healthy. I slipped out of him then and went corporeal enough to hold the Taser while he cut the straps off and carefully pulled the needle out of my arm.

"I don't know what it was he stuck in you," Joe said quietly, as if he were afraid to wake me. With a glance around the room he took the Command Eidolon from around my body's neck and turned to the scarecrow. "Holy shit," he said again.

You need to remove the Summoning Eidolon from her neck.

Joe nodded, but before he could get to her, something dropped out of the ceiling and toppled Joe to the ground. I moved away and leveled the Taser at them both. Bertram was trying his best to wrench a gun from Joe, but he wasn't strong enough.

Joe pushed the doctor off of him and scrambled back from the corner where the scarecrow was as Bertram moved closer to his creation. He stood up, his forehead and cheeks sweating, and looked at my body. "Ohhhh...you took the Eidolon. Now I won't be able to control you."

I shook my head. I stood on the other side of my body and held the Taser at him. *No. You won't. Charolette is dead.*

He nodded. "I knew it the moment you took her. We'd been together for so long, a part of the astral plane." Bertram's eyebrows rose on his forehead. "Did you see it though, before you took her? The way that time and lack of a body had molded her into something without a form?"

I nodded.

"It's doing the same to me. Without a physical body—the astral reclaims itself. Did you know that?"

I shook my head.

"But with the Eidolons..." He took a step closer to the scarecrow and the Summoning Eidolon still resting around its neck. Joe and I both held up weapons and pointed them at him. He stopped his movement. "The Eidolons can change that. That's what they were built for."

I glanced at the scarecrow. I needed to get her out of there, and the best way I knew how was to remove the necklace and guide her to her cord. I could still see it. Strong. Thick like kite string. Unlike the thinness of my own.

But there was something else—something I now regretted not asking Charolette. *You knew my father.*

Bertram nodded. "Yes. Yes a good man."

What happened to him?

He hesitated. "I can't say—I really can't say."

You can't say because you don't know or because you're afraid?

There was a serious pause, and Bertram put his finger to his lips. "I'm afraid. Fear is enough to survive on the other side, Zoë. But it was as Domas said, you know. That life as Pollux was filled with as much danger as life as Castor."

I didn't know what he meant, nor did I care. *What happened to my father?*

Bertram backed away, reaching out to the shelf with his hands, knocking over the microscope. Was he looking for a weapon?

I dropped the gun and moved to Joe. I took the Command and Destruction Eidolons from him and moved past the scarecrow to the small area where Bertram had lodged himself, between my physical body and the shelf. I held up both of the Eidolons so that he could see them.

Bertram's eyes grew as wide as golf balls and he pointed to the swinging stones. "Never touch that one to any of the others! You'll destroy them."

That was my plan. You tell me what happened to my father, and I won't destroy them.

Bertram was almost in tears. He started shaking and looking around the room. "I can't—I can't tell you!"

You started to before. Charolette was so ready to tell me.

"And you killed her. You killed her!"

I knew that was going to come back and bite my ass.

Joe moved behind me. "Look, why don't we save this till later? Put the Command Eidolon on him and make him tell you the truth?"

I felt a smile creep over my lips, the first I'd had all day.

But as I approached him, holding the necklace with the Command Eidolon out to him with my left hand, the scar on my forearm burned as if someone had smothered it in gas and lit the flame.

I yelled out and dropped both Eidolons, clutching my forearm close to my body. I could feel the flesh pulling away, the muscles cooking beneath and the bone charring.

A wind swirled in the room and the debris on the shelf was taken up and tossed about. I held up my hand and turned toward Joe. But it wasn't Joe that caught my attention.

Shadows had formed along the wall behind where the scarecrow sat. They crept out along the wood and insulation like black ink, spreading and filling out the cracks as it grew. The blackness became deeper and deeper, and I moved from where Bertram cowered to where Joe now stood, too close to the encroaching darkness.

The Vice cop had his gun out and was swearing softly under his breath. No—he was saying a few Hail Marys under his breath. Was he Catholic as well?

"Holeee shit!"

That wasn't Catholic. But I had the same sentiment as I watched a male hand poke through the consuming darkness, followed by a large, black-booted foot. A body came next, and the shine and polish of a bald head—

I knew who it was. I felt him inside of me as he manifested in front of me.

He smiled at me and touched his shades.

Trench-Coat.

"Mother of all—" Joe pointed at him. "Is that—"

I nodded.

The Archer.

"So nice of you to call me by my title, doll," Archer said in my voice. He turned and looked at Bertram, who had become a sniveling mass on the floor. "Oh, Bertram—you are in so much trouble."

Before TC could focus his attention back to me, Bertram scrambled out from where he was and grabbed at the red Eidolon that lay on the floor between him and the Symbiont. He held it close, and I yelled out at him not to—

But it was too late.

Melvin Maddox's body began to stretch and ooze, as if someone had run it through a meat grinder, only we couldn't see the grinder. It twisted and turned inside out, and in the middle of all the blood and gore, I could see Bertram's spirit. It had the unformed look that Charolette's had, and it looked like a sponge left out in the sun.

And the screams—the screams that resonated inside of my

head. They traveled in waves over the astral plane, the mental, as well as the Ethereal and the Abysmal, and I understood then that the Eidolon was doing its job, destroying Bertram on every level of existence possible. On every plane he had touched, his fingerprint was erased.

Until there was nothing left.

I stood with my hands to my ears, Joe's hand on my elbow. I couldn't believe what I'd just seen—to choose that sort of death over life—just so he wouldn't have to tell me about my father?

Trench-Coat gave a low chuckle. "Bertram never really was the brighter of the two." He shook his head and looked at us. He was behind the scarecrow and reached out to put a hand on its shoulder. "Time to come home, Mommy."

And like that, he was gone. The darkness was gone.

And the scarecrow—

The scarecrow was little more than decaying meat on the floor, coating the chair.

Mom!

I went onto my knees then and shoved my hands into the putrid flesh. Maggots squirmed over and in the oozing mess. *Where is my mother?*

WHERE IS MY MOTHER!

"Zoë!" Joe hovering over me, pulling at my shoulder. "Get out of that. She's not there. Look, will you? She's not there! No cord!"

No cord.

No cord? I sat back, and though my astral hands were clean, I still felt the unclean aura of death over me. Surrounding me. I sat back on my butt and wrapped my arms around my chest. *I want my mommy...*

"Shhh..." Joe said as he knelt beside me. "She's not here, Zoë. She's not here."

I turned and looked at him. *Where is she, Joe? Where did TC take her?*

He shook his head. "I don't know. But we can find her. Are you listening to me? Do we still have the Summoning Eidolon?"

I didn't know. I didn't care. I was crying, but I didn't remember when I'd started. Maybe I'd never stopped before. I shook my head and felt Joe's arms encircle me. *Why? Why did he take my mother? Why, Joe? She'll die if she stays out of her body* . . .

But he didn't have any answers for me. He was so warm, where I was cold. Corporeal like this, I could feel temperature. I could smell the foul rot of meat permeating the air. And in the middle of the death I felt his life beside me.

Folding me in his arms, Joe Halloran held me tight, and said softly, "Cry, Zoë. Please cry. Show me you're still human. Show me you're still alive. I—I have to know."

His words made sense to me. Today he'd seen me take life, not only that of a rogue but of an innocent man who didn't deserve to die, but had while protecting a young woman. But through all of it I was human. I hurt, and I felt guilt. So much guilt it was almost too overwhelming to bear. I wanted to disappear . . . to curl up inside a hole and never wake again.

He was looking at me as we sat side by side in that basement, the scarecrow's body slowly melting behind us. I looked up at him, into his eyes, and he touched my cheek. Timid at first, then with more confidence.

"Are you still human, Zoë?" His voice was deep, and husky.

I nodded to him, and I opened my mouth—

He kissed me. Deep. Hard. And with passion—a passion so full and complete that I felt it inside of my Ethereal toes. I was almost lost in the kiss—

Until I thought of Daniel. I saw his face. He'd looked so drawn. So weak. And I'd done that to him. Taken from him and then I'd left him. Abandoned him.

Here. Kissing—Joe!

I pushed away and moved to the foot of the table, where I lay so still, almost in death.

Joe was blinking, his expression confused. "Zoë? What is it? What's wrong?"

Too many thoughts crowded in on me, drowning me alive. My mom was missing—was her body dead as well? I had made Daniel ill, draining him like some freakish psychic vampire. I killed the only other man that knew how my dad died—and that was the hardest. I'd always believed my father was still alive. I'd known he was alive. I had felt it inside.

Guilt upon guilt, upon guilt...

"What's that tapping noise?"

I hadn't heard the noise—not through my own suffocating guilt. But Joe was right—it was there. Softly. Not the sound of a mouse. Rhythmic.

"Is that Morse code?" Joe stood and started looking about the room. I watched him look up to the shelf over the washer and dryer. There he reached up and brought down the stone dragon.

The stone dragon! The Soul Cage was still intact. They had said they'd kept Mom's spirit inside of it until now. Was it possible she'd escaped back into it?

I charged upward, half-visible, half-tangible, as Joe held it out. Without thinking, without really knowing what I was doing, I took the thing from him and smashed it into the floor.

Two figures whirled out, twisting like small tornados, dust devils, churning up the debris and dust on the floor. I knew their forms even before they took them on.

Tim and Steve. They too had been forced inside the dragon. Looking around, the two ghosts became completely tangible and fired questions off at me and Joe. Joe tried to answer them, and I was aware of his eyes on me. I knelt beside the pieces and touched them, hoping to find even a trace of my mom's spirit.

There was nothing.

She was gone.

And the worst part of it all was that I didn't know if she was dead, set free, or if she was still bound, held as a prisoner. In a prison I couldn't find.

"Zoë—what's wrong?" Steve was beside me.

I ignored him and turned away as I stood. Tim moved in front of me, his dark gaze focused on me. "Don't do it, Zoë. We'll find her. We have to find her."

I didn't know what it was he thought I'd do, and didn't want me to. I just knew life had become too unbearable. Too complicated. Too painful.

I turned to my body and touched my ankle. I felt the tug of my cord, lightly now, as I allowed it to draw me back inside. There was no pain—I had only been away a few hours, and my taking of two lives had given me strength. But I didn't want to face those I'd upset, and so I found the darkest, deepest shadow of myself and curled up there.

And cried myself to sleep.

28

THE snow melted the next day. And the sun broke through the monochromatic skies. A warming trend fooled the cherry trees, and they started to bloom early. February 2 came and the groundhog saw his shadow.

Six more weeks of winter. And it came with a vengeance.

Mom remained in a vegetative state at Grady Memorial. The hospital was pushing to have her transferred to a long-term-care facility because they needed the bed. Daniel solved the case of the murdered and mutilated victims. Melvin Maddox was accused, and though he was little more than goo in a test tube at the GBI, it was enough to appease the paparazzi. He was also blamed for Congressman Knowles's death.

Joe? I don't know where Joe went. No one did. He'd vanished that night from the hospital, when they'd brought me in, once again. And me? I lay in my own self-induced vegetative state for several days. Tim and Steve came by, helped along by Rhonda, who brought the key and brick they'd attached themselves to. Daniel came every day and brought flowers. I never looked at him. Instead, I stared at the wall through my own eyes but kept myself away from it all.

February 6, I woke, and got up, dressed, and left the hospital. I went to my condo and arranged for everything to go into storage. My computer and clothing I carried to Mom's shop. A black wreath decorated the door. I stood in front of it for a long time, only vaguely aware of the drizzling rain and the biting cold.

A footfall on the wood. "Gonna take a lot to get her back up and running," came the voice of Jemmy Shultz. "Gonna need some help, at least till Nona comes to her senses and walks out of that hospital."

I nodded, but didn't turn around. I reached up and took the wreath down, then Jemmy and I went inside.

IT was Tuesday, February 12. Jemmy was busy baking. There were customers in the Botanica, where Tim was busy helping. The new free Wi-Fi was up and several of the local kids were inside drinking tea, eating cake, and surfing the net.

The cold was still around, the temperature reported not to climb much higher than forty-two. It was windy, and I had on my gloves as I swept the porch. Daniel had been in for a quick drink and slice of Jemmy's orange spice cake before checking out a few new condos over off of Monroe. He'd sold the house, though he hadn't gotten a fair market price—what with it being a former crime scene and all.

He wanted something smaller. And he wanted me to go with him today to look for them. But I'd said no. I had things to do here. And I had my afternoon visit over at Crestview, to sit with my mom and drown in my despair.

Rhonda had been gone for several days—getting business taken care of for her deceased uncle.

I missed her. She'd been so good to me since Mom—and I felt naked without her.

I'd not been online or answered e-mail for weeks. I'd put the green Eidolon over the door to the shop and made sure the nurses never removed the triskelion amulet from around my mother's neck.

As for the other Eidolons? I didn't know where they were, and I didn't care.

I was straightening up the Botanica when the front door jingled again. Absently I heard Jemmy's voice, muffled and upset. Scuffed footsteps on the floor and I turned to look through the beaded curtain separating the two shops. I couldn't see the kids in the tea shop anymore.

The house had gone quiet.

I moved through the curtain, a folded copy of the *Aquarius* in my hand.

"Ah, Miss Martinique."

I recognized the voice. I saw the two men in black suits at the front door too late. To the left, at the counter, looking rather dapper in his black trench coat and black gloves and carrying a walking stick, stood Francisco Rodriguez.

I signed to him calmly, though my heart thundered against my rib cage. *"You're not supposed to be here."*

He nodded. "Yes, I received the notice of the restraining order. But in some instances, my work supercedes conventional law." He gestured with a gloved hand to the curtain behind me. "Please. You and I need to talk."

I took a quick look around the shop. The kids were gone, but their computers and backpacks were still nestled at their seats. Where were they? Where was Jemmy?

I glanced at the two brutes guarding the door and moved back through the curtain. Rodriguez took a seat on the couch as I sat on the papasan. The fireplace crackled and popped with warmth.

"I'm here for two reasons." Rodriguez set his cane on the floor and looked relaxed. "First I'm here to help you understand your past. I know you want more information on your father, Zoë. But the truth of that injustice is, that we simply do not know what happened to him."

He noticed my sudden start and nodded. "Adiran was a friend of mine, Zoë. As was your mother. Many, many years ago. We were all part of a think-tank organization run by a man named Ishmael Domas."

I nodded. That much Bertram had told me, though until this second I hadn't really given anything he'd said to me much credence.

"Ishmael was more than just a scientist. He was also, among other things, a practitioner of some very dark arts. Ceremonial Magick was his love, and his hobby. And through the combination of his love of magic and his love of science, he discovered a way to contact the different planes of existence. Albeit crudely through tested subjects who showed a slight ability to astrally project their consciousness."

Okay—this was interesting.

One of the suited men stepped through the curtain, a teacup and saucer in each hand. He set them on the coffee table and moved back through the curtain.

"Ah." Rodriguez smiled. "Gerome is an excellent brewer of tea. And Nona has such a delightful assortment." He picked up his cup and sipped his tea.

I ignored the one placed in front of me.

"There were maybe five subjects who eventually learned to slip out of their body after strict meditation. Your father was one of those subjects."

This much Rhonda had told me. I seemed to have inherited the same ability.

"They were able to return and describe their adventures in what we now understand as the mental and astral planes. But Domas wouldn't accept that this was the end—he wanted to prove there were more planes, more worlds, but worlds we have no access to."

Ah...the Ethereal and Abysmal planes.

"Domas created experiments that pushed the boundaries of the subjects' abilities. And slowly—one of those gifted people showed an aptitude for adapting to the other planes, and broke through the astral into the Abysmal."

I closed my eyes. I knew he meant my father.

Setting his tea down, Rodriguez leaned forward. "Now you just pay attention to me here, Zoë. It was during this time that Adiran met your mother. She was Domas's secretary, and she was—most importantly—his youngest niece."

I put my hands out beside me and grabbed the woven wooden base of the papasan. I hadn't seen that coming.

"It was a romance that was doomed, Zoë. I never even thought it would bloom the way it did. Your mom was, and is, a rebel." He sighed. "And Domas was blind. Very blind—to what his niece was doing with one of his test subjects—as well as to what his experiments were doing to the delicate balance between the planes." Rodriguez lowered his gaze and reached out to his teacup. He ran his finger along the rim. "And to what he was doing to Adiran and the others."

I reached into my jacket and pulled out the notepad Daniel had given me the other day (just to keep it handy since he had a hard time reading my ASL) as well as a pen. I scribbled quickly, WAS MY FATHER LIKE ME? WRAITH?

He read the note when I held it up and then, to my surprise, shook his head. "No—no. Though I'm sure Bertram and Charolette told you different. They were two of the subjects and never really moved on past astral walking. It isn't so much what happened to them as it is what followed them back, Zoë." And with that he swallowed. Hard. "We never knew it was there—hiding inside of Domas as it did—and it had even more twisted ideas than the human it joined with."

I flipped the book over and scribbled, SYMBIONT?

He shook his head. "No—something even more powerful than a Symbiont, Zoë. A greater power—one that had never traveled the physical world before. At the time, we called it simply a ghost. But later it would be known as a Phantasm."

I put my hand to my mouth and thought of Friendly again. I flipped the page and scribbled, AND YOU USED THE EIDO-LONS ON IT?

But at that he frowned and shook his head. "Not in the beginning because we didn't know it was there. It had its own ideas of what to do with the subjects, and it spoke to Domas's more powerful side. And there it created the Eidolon necklaces, each reflecting the powers of the elements, which are also present in the other planes."

Wait—what? The Phantasm created the Eidolons? I flipped the page again. I really needed to write smaller. BUT YOU USE THEM ON IT?

He nodded. "March Knowles and Charles Randolph, two of Domas's right-hand men, suspected something was wrong with Domas just as a fire started in the middle of one of the more lengthy out-of-body experiments. Bertram and Charolette were trapped in that fire, their bodies destroyed."

That explained their anger and the loss of their physical forms.

"The project was shut down, and, for a while, Domas disappeared, slipping our control. Adiran and Nona were married, and led very normal lives. Until you were born."

Me? I put my hand on my chest.

"That's when the phone calls started, threats against your life unless Adiran did what they said. He contacted the only other surviving member of the team to see if they too had been threatened, but they were gone. Disappeared. They had vanished from their house weeks before Adiran's call. He left Nona and you that night to find them, and he was never seen again."

And that was where my mother had told me the truth. That Dad had left one night and never come home. I scribbled again. WAS HE KILLED?

"When I told you that we didn't know I was telling the truth, Miss Martinique. After the group was disbanded, the knowledge we'd learned could not be buried. And we needed to find Domas. We scattered the Eidolons in order to protect them—the thing inside of Domas would want them destroyed. While your family went on about their lives, another war was raged between those of us who were left."

I wrote, OVER WHAT TO DO WITH THE KNOWLEDGE?

"Yes. You're very bright, Zoë. We eventually found Domas, completely possessed by this Phantasm. He had a small group of followers, gifted people whom he taught to astral travel as well. He'd also found the Command Eidolon and was using it to manipulate them.

"Some of those followers were previous members of the research team—the ones who didn't understand that Domas was possessed. Eventually there were two factions made from the same whole. Those who followed Domas and those who feared he would succeed, gain control of the Abysmal and Ethereal planes, and unleash all manner of terrible things on the world."

I nodded. Took a deep breath.

"Domas was eventually destroyed, by the very thing he created. And his memory carried with it a lesson that has been passed down since his death over twenty years ago. The planes are not for us to meddle with, Zoë. The Society of Ishmael, of which I am a member, as was Knowles and Koba Hirokumi, was formed in order to remember that lesson, and to prevent anyone from making the same mistakes."

I moved the page over. L-6?

"Ah—those that followed Domas and gained a little power. Run by a man named Robert Stephens. Robert was a backer of Domas's work, and wanted power. Believed in it. Without him, or Charles Randolph, we can all but believe his League of Six is gone. Disbanded." Rodriguez put his hands on his knees. "He'd followed Adiran's lineage after your father disappeared. You left Oregon and vanished into the bowels of the South. Nona had money for the taking—but she knew if she touched it, that would alert everybody to where she was."

He held up his hand and gestured. One of the men came through the curtain and stood just inside. "Adiran became sort of an icon for those who know about Ishmael and his work. Adiran fought back, Zoë. He refused to be enslaved in Domas's work."

The story made sense—and I couldn't help but wonder if he was just telling me what I wanted to hear. I'd wanted answers for so long—and though my father wasn't Antonio Banderas, he was a hero of sorts.

I abruptly felt a vibration on the floor. There were more people here, and I heard the back door open. How many men had Rodriguez brought? My heart beat faster—I wasn't liking the fact I was alone with this man.

"But all that leads us to why I'm here." He picked up his tea again and drank a good bit before continuing. "Your appearance, and the reports of your abilities. You being what you are—has caused a slight problem within the Society of Ishmael."

Uh-oh.

"Through the years, the running of our Society has been left up to the last of the project members, who have spent their lives documenting what happened. They used the Greek term Dioscuri to refer to the research. Are you familiar with it?"

I had heard the name spoken a few times but never gave it much thought.

"In Greek mythology, the Dioscuri were twin sons of Zeus. Castor and Pollux. Castor was mortal, or human, and Pollux was immortal. Domas had used the same terms to describe the physical state, Castor, and the astral state, that which lives on even after the physical body dies, Pollux. What most don't remember is that the twins shared the immortality, living half in one world and half in the other." He fixed me with a look. "You, Zoë Martinique. You are the birth of Castor and Pollux, and some of the members of SOI see you as the fruit of Domas's life's work."

I was not liking the way this conversation was going. But something came to me then, and I scribbled it down. YOU WERE ONE OF THE FIVE—ONE OF THE TEST SUBJECTS.

He shook his head. "No—not one of the five. I had been in the original group for first-round tests, but I could never actually leave my body. I understand the mechanics, but I no longer believe it's something we should be doing. We were given this flesh by God, and we should never leave it until the day of our death."

I felt danger surround me. I started projecting how fast I could slip out of my body and whale on this man and his henchmen. And I had lost too much in the past few weeks to really care about my own physical state. I was Wraith after all.

Boo. Fear me.

"I'm sorry, Zoë. But I can't let you destroy all I've worked for. We cannot allow what you are to spread. Others within our group now seek to be what you are, believing that you bear some hidden fountain of youth. With your mother's soul gone, it only stands to reason you would agree with me."

I scribbled, AGREE ABOUT WHAT?

"That you cannot be allowed to live unrestrained." He reached inside of his coat and pulled out the Command Eidolon. I felt my heart leap into my throat and stood.

He remained seated, but his henchman moved, pulling a gun from inside his coat and pointing it at me.

"Please, Zoë. Understand that I can't allow my agent to split the Society apart with her ideological beliefs. I put her in place to watch you, and to study you, to see what you could do. But for her to protect you now and raise my own Society against me? Preposterous."

I sat back in my chair and took up the pad. WHAT ARE YOU TALKING ABOUT?

He leaned forward and held out the necklace. "My agent, Zoë. The one I planted in your life to report every new power to me in her daily reports." He held the necklace out. "It would be so much better if you'd just put this on with no fuss. If you obey me, I can promise that no harm will come to Daniel Frasier or your mother."

You better not touch my mother, you fucker. The henchman moved across the room to me and held out a pair of handcuffs. I stared at them. This was not happening to me. What—this idiot just expected I'd do as he said and become a meek captive?

Oh, I don't think so.

Rodriguez sighed and reached inside his coat pocket. He took out a syringe. "I'd hoped this would go easier, Zoë. But you leave me no choice. Lars, please secure her."

The big guy stepped forward and pressed the gun to my head. "Put these on."

I felt footsteps again on the floor. Lots of them.

"I suggest *you* put those on, asswipe."

Wait—wha? I didn't move. (Well, of course not—there was a gun to my head.)

"Step away from Miss Martinique. NOW."

I knew that voice, and it wasn't one I'd expected to hear.

Lars moved back, his face expressionless. And as he moved back I saw Captain Cooper standing just inside the curtain of beads, flanked by two uniformed officers. All three of them had guns trained on the two men.

"Well, well." Rodriguez took up his tea again. "Captain Kenneth Cooper. How are the wife and kids?"

I glared at the businessman and recognized the greeting as a veiled threat. A way to show Daniel's captain that he knew Cooper had a wife and kids.

"Shove it, Rodriguez."

Lars continued to step back, his hands up, the cuffs in one and the gun in the other. One of the uniforms stepped forward and took both, then cuffed the man and took him out of the room.

"Put him with the other three," Cooper said, and lowered his gun. "Okay, Miss Orly. It's clear."

I could hear Jemmy in the background then, fussing at someone.

Rhonda came barreling through the curtain then. She stopped short and glared at Rodriguez. "You fool."

But the businessman only shrugged. "You're the fool. You think you can trust her? Trust the thing that lives inside of her?"

"It's not like that—"

Rodriguez stood up at that moment. Cooper raised his gun. "Sit down."

But Rodriguez ignored him. "It's *exactly* like that. She has to be controlled. She cannot be allowed to roam free."

"You just want to control her, just like you did Domas. I'm not stupid, Francisco. I was for a very long time—but my eyes are open now. What you want to do with the Society goes against the dogma we set into action twenty years ago. You're wanting to take us back into the madness Dr. Domas suffered from. We can't let you do that."

"You disappoint me, Rhonda. As my agent, you held so much promise."

I hadn't been really paying attention—not to all of it—but as I looked at Rhonda, openmouthed, I knew he'd already told me the truth.

He'd mentioned his agent before. His agent. Sent to watch me. And this—this explained so much.

Of where Rhonda came from. How she knew so much about what was happening to me. How she always seemed to have the ready answers. Her knowledge of the Ethereal and the Abysmal planes. It all made sense.

Rhonda was Society of Ishmael.

And she had never really truly been my friend. I was an assignment.

Rhonda looked at me, now able to hear me in her mind. "No, Zoë. Maybe at first—but we grew to be friends. And that was the turning point for me. Francisco wanted me to somehow destroy you before you grew powerful. But we never counted on a Symbiont tipping the balance. I *am* your friend, Zoë."

But I was already standing and backing away from both of them. Captain Cooper reached his hand out to me and pulled me close to him, away from the two crazy-talking people.

Captain Cooper gestured toward Rodriguez. "Cuff 'im."

The other officer stepped forward. Rodriguez sighed and turned his back to them. "You know this won't stick, Captain."

"Oh, I think it will this time, Mr. Rodriguez. Miss Orly called and said you were here—against a restraining order—and I walk in on a possible kidnapping? Well"—he smiled—"I think with Zoë's testimony I can make this one stick."

I liked the smile. He needed to do it more often.

"I was not kidnapping Miss Martinique."

"Well, I'm not sure cordialness includes guns and handcuffs, Mr. Rodriguez. It doesn't in my book."

The officer finished cuffing Rodriguez, and he was led out of the room through the curtain. Cooper reholstered his gun and turned to me, putting his hands on my shoulders. "You okay?"

I nodded to him—forget the welling tears in my eyes.

He looked over at Rhonda. "Miss Orly, I need to speak with Miss Martinique in private."

Rhonda tried to get my attention, but I wouldn't look at her. She finally moved back through the curtain.

Cooper gestured for me to sit. I did. Back in the papasan again.

He sat where Rodriguez had sat. "The truth is, Zoë, that I was on my way here already." He reached inside his suit jacket and pulled out a plastic bag. He held it up. It was the bloody business card of March Knowles, the one I'd taken from the arranged meeting. "Just got this back from the Georgia Bureau of Investigation's Crime Lab."

I nodded, unsure of where this was going.

"They found fingerprints on it."

Uh-huh.

"Yours."

!!!

"Now"—he leaned forward, his elbows on his knees—"I saw the card picked up off the floor, and the lab tells me the prints were under the blood. Made before it was bloody. My investigation tells me Rodriguez gave Knowles these cards in a meeting—the meeting we'd learned about and the reason I sent Detective Frasier into the Westin to begin with. I didn't think it was odd that you'd received an invitation until I got this intel." He nodded at the card and set it on the coffee table, next to the tea I never drank. "I'd like to know if you were in that meeting between the two of them. It's the only way you could have gotten your fingerprints on these cards."

Fingerprints.

But—I'd never touched the cards with my physical body. So did that mean when I became corporeal I could leave trace clues to where I'd been?

Oh, this could be bad.

I wanted to answer him truthfully, but I couldn't. If I did, then he'd be asking all sorts of questions as to what was said in the meeting. As far as I knew, they didn't know Joe had taken anything from those boxes. They did know about the two groups, and blamed the dismemberment deaths on the now-defunct League of Six.

I shook my head and shrugged.

Cooper watched me for a few seconds and nodded. "You really can't talk, can you?"

I shook my head again. I grabbed up my notepad and scribbled on it. IT SUCKS. BUT I FOUND CARD IN BATHROOM BEFORE I LAY DOWN.

Ouch. Another lie. And a bad one.

"Oh?" Cooper nodded slowly. "So one of the men had been in that lounge earlier."

Uh, no. Not really. Damnit all.

I shrugged. I scribbled, WAS ON COFFEE TABLE.

Another one. Ding, ding, ding! You win the outright lie-to-the-cops award for the year.

Wouldn't Mom be proud?

Cooper took the card and returned it to his suit jacket pocket. "Why—why would Rodriguez try and kidnap you, Zoë? For what purpose?"

Oh, because I'm a Wraith, and he wants to control me?

I shrugged again. That wasn't a full lie. I honestly didn't know what he was afraid of—well—besides the fact that now that I knew what I knew, I was going to kick his rich ass someday.

"Did you see something? Did you see either one of them in that lounge?"

I shook my head. Truth! Justice!

And the Wraith way.

He pursed his lips and rubbed at his chin. "Maybe he thought you did, and wanted you out of the way. If he thinks you saw him, I can use that as leverage. Okay. Thanks, Zoë. Too bad Knowles is dead. But I have Rodriguez." He stood. "Sorry about the mess. Just text if you need me."

And he moved to the curtain and paused before turning back to me. "And please...try to stay out of trouble?"

He left.

"Zoë—" Rhonda came through the curtain toward me.

I put up a hand. *Stay right there. You're no longer welcome here.*

"Zoë, don't do this. Please. I was going to tell you—I'd already told your mom. She forgave me. She believed me."

Oh, that's convenient, seeing as she's not here to back you up. I took a step back. And I'd saved her life. Twice! *You gave him the Eidolons, Rhonda. Why?*

"I didn't know this would happen, Zoë." She held her arms out to her sides. "I trusted Rodriguez. So did my uncle."

And I trusted you. Just leave, Rhonda.

"We have to find your mom, Zoë."

No, I have to find my mom. You need to get the fuck off of my mom's property. And don't you ever, ever, show your face here again.

It was a perfect little fit. I just wished I'd actually had a voice to scream with. I wanted the world to know how she'd betrayed my trust. How she'd betrayed me.

Rhonda took in a deep breath, turned, and moved through the curtain and out the door.

But it was done, and she'd heard me. It was all I needed before I moved to one of the shelves to look up a spell to banish traders in lies.

EPILOGUE

DANIEL accepted the fact that Rhonda and I had gone our separate ways. I knew he wanted to ask me questions—but he didn't. He was a good man like that. And though I was still a bit unsure of his opinions about ghosts, I really didn't want to talk about them myself.

Francisco Rodriguez was charged with disobeying a restraining order as well as attempted kidnapping. His lawyers waved around a lot of money, and Rodriguez was released on bond. And when Daniel went to his Buckhead home to speak with him, he'd vacated. The house was up for sale.

Empty.

A few days had passed since the big reveal to me, and I was feeling a bit alone. Daniel sensed it, and only offered help now and then. But something nagged at me in the back of my mind. On Thursday, after cutting myself a piece of Jemmy's lemon ice cake, I realized what it was—Charlie Holmes.

Was his ghost still there, in the warehouse?

It was a little past ten in the morning. I wrapped my cake in a napkin, grabbed my shoes and coat, and stepped out the door.

Rose petals had been spread all over the back deck, and a card was left on the hood of my Mustang, tucked beneath the windshield.

It was from Daniel.

I'd forgotten it was Valentine's Day.

"Where are you going?"

I didn't jump, though his voice surprised me. I looked to the end of the porch. Daniel stood there, dressed in his casual clothes and peacoat. He looked—beautiful.

I signed to him, *"To see Mom."*

"Can I come with you?"

I hesitated.

He noticed.

Daniel took several steps toward me. "Zoë—you can't shut me out. Please. I love you. I need you—and right now—I think you need someone. I'm not going to say it has to be me." He smiled. "But I'd like it to be."

I returned his smile, and for the first time in weeks it felt honest. He closed the gap between us and took me in his arms. I returned the squeeze and reached up to him, took his face in my hands, and kissed him as deep, and hard, and passionately as I could.

It was wonderful—probably almost the perfect kiss.

Almost.

The memory of another kiss lingered in my mind, and I brushed it irritably away.

He smiled down at me. "So can I come with you?"

I pulled back and signed, *"Have one errand first."*

"I'll come on that too."

I agreed. What could it hurt?

The sun was high and warm to the touch, though in the shadows it was still very cold.

Picking up a white mocha from Starbucks (Daniel had a dopio), I drove out to the warehouse. It didn't look as spooky in the daytime, and I waited for Daniel to say something. But he sat in the passenger side of my Mustang and kept quiet.

Parking the car, I reached inside my purse and pulled out my notepad. I scribbled on it. I HAVE TO GO IN FOR A FEW MIN-UTES. YOU STAY HERE?

He frowned at me. "Zoë, it's taken all of me not to ask you what the hell it is we're doing here. I can't just let you walk into that place alone—it's a crime scene. The scene of *two* crimes."

I flipped the page. THEN I TAKE YOU HOME.

He reached out as I started to turn the key in the ignition. "Wait. Stop. Even if you take me home, you'll come back out here, right?"

I nodded.

"Why, Zoë? Why are you here? What the hell is going on with your family? What happened to your mom? Where are Tim and Steve? Did you know that Joe's vanished? He's reported missing. The only person that hasn't vanished is Dags—but he's not talking. So"—he held out his hands—"please—be honest with me."

Be honest. Be honest to the man who doesn't believe in ghosts. Be honest to the man who thinks my mother is a swindler.

I put my hands on the wheel. Why is it I loved this man?

Ah, that's easy. Because he loves you for you, and not for what you've become.

Yeah, but what if he discovers what you've become?
What then?

I took up the pad and flipped a page. LET ME GO IN THERE, PLEASE. I HAVE TO. YOU STAY HERE. THEN WE SPEND DAY TOGETHER.

This was quite a monumental thing. He and I hadn't spent more than an hour together since my mom's spirit disappeared.

He appeared to think it over. "Okay. But here." And he removed his gun and held it out to me. "If there is any trouble, fire this, and I'll be there."

"No," I signed. *"I'll be okay."* He didn't look happy, but with a lingering kiss, I got out of my car, leaving the keys in the ignition.

I slipped through a hole in the fence. The side door was open, and I stepped inside.

I was in the center of the room, and a wind whistled through the collapsing ceiling. Sun filtered through, and in between two of those shafts of light Charlie Holmes appeared. Just as he had that night in January.

"Hello, Zoë."

Hi, Charlie. It's done. And I'm here to tell you why you died.

And I did. I told him everything. I used those few minutes to purge my own demons. I laughed. And I cried. Until finally I was done. And my coffee was cold. And my fingers were ice.

He removed his hat and came closer to me, looking directly into my eyes. "Thank you, Zoë. I feel better. Though the man who actually shot me wasn't brought to justice, at least the group never got their treasure. They're gone, right?"

Yes. I'm alone, Charlie. Really alone. Joe's disappeared. I've banished Rhonda from my life—I can't trust her. Tim and Steve seem quieter without Mom around, like she gave them energy or something. Daniel—I can't talk to him about any of this. He'd never understand. Rodriguez is gone, for now. I've gotten a few e-mail queries from a group calling themselves Pollux, but I've ignored them.

"And your mom?"

No change. Coma. Vegetative state. Pick one. She's in a long-term-care facility. And the money's draining as quickly out of my accounts as I can make it, with the store or with my small jobs on eBay. Rhonda always arranged my work—and now I wonder how much of it I did for the Society, you know? I kicked at a stiff piece of cloth. *And if she isn't Maharba herself. I haven't heard from them either. So . . . I* shrugged. *Go figure. I've reached the bottom, Charlie. I just don't think I can go down any further.*

"You're never alone, Zoë. And you're wrong about Daniel. He's a good boy. I think you should give him a chance. He deserves that opportunity to make up his own mind about you and what you can do. You can't keep him in the dark forever."

And I knew Charlie was right.

He glanced up at the sun. "There is one favor I'd like to ask of you."

I know. But—Charlie—I'm not sure if I release you, you'll go where you're supposed to.

"What do you mean?"

I mean—how do I know if I release your fetter, you'll go to Heaven? How do I know something terrible won't happen?

And he smiled at me. "I guess you don't. But, Zoë, you're a good girl. A good person. You can't possibly do anything evil."

Somehow I didn't feel so confident about that. Bertram and Charolette had called me the bad guy. The villain. Joe said what had happened to me—what I became as a Wraith—wasn't right. And I'd killed an innocent man. Easily. With only my hands.

Rodriguez feared me so much he wanted me caged and controlled. And that in itself had me stumped and worried. What was it about me that scared him?

And should I be scared of it too?

Going OOB didn't occur to me at that second. Didn't even think of it. So I didn't know why I did what I did next. Or how.

I touched him with my left hand. He flared once in a bright glow of gold and smiled at me. I heard his thank-you in my head and smiled at his release of joy inside of me.

Seconds after he disappeared I stared at my hand. I'd—I'd just released a spirit with my hand. With my *physical* hand. And it tingled. I pulled back my sleeve and looked at the scar there.

It no longer looked dark red, but now glowed silver, then dimmed until it wasn't there at all. And there hadn't been any of the previous feeling of euphoria for me. I'd felt—nothing.

There was a noise behind me. I turned.

Daniel stood in the door—his eyes wide. He had his gun out, lowered, his feet spread wide apart. He was pale.

And he was perfectly quiet. Until—

"I heard you. Just now. Talking. You were talking to Holmes, Zoë. I saw Holmes standing beside you. You can't talk. You told me you couldn't talk!"

Mental note: *what the*—